SACRIFICE

CINDY PON

Month9Books

SACRIFICE by Cindy Pon
All rights reserved. Published in the United States of America by Month9Books, LLC.
No part of this book may be used or reproduced in any manner whatsoever without written permission of the publisher, except in the case of brief quotations embodied in critical articles and reviews.

EPub ISBN: 978-1-945107-20-7 Mobi ISBN: 978-1-945107-21-4
Paperback ISBN: 978-1-944816-92-6
Hardback ISBN: 978-1-944816-52-0

Published by Month9Books, Raleigh, NC 27609
Cover design by Najla Qamber Design
Cover illustration by Zachary Schoenbaum
Interior illustration by Grace Fong at www.gracepfong.com

33614057810292

Month9Books

SACRIFICE

CHAPTER ONE

Skybright

Daybreak unfurled across the gray horizon, tendrils of light illuminating magnificent jade peaks, their sloping and jagged points dissolving into mist. Skybright had seen these famous Xia mountains painted by artists on vertical scrolls—the masterpieces hung in the main hall of the Yuan manor. She remembered being mesmerized by the paintings in ink, touched with the subtlest hints of stone green or accents of red. But as evocative as the paintings were, they were nothing compared to the actuality—her mind couldn't have imagined this landscape if she had tried.

The sunlight was distant, and the chill from the night lingered on this mountain ledge. Warmth emanated from Stone, a constant, as was his rich, earthen scent that had become familiar to her. Dressed in full armor—silver and gold etched in crimson—the sole piece missing was his helmet. His black hair was pulled back in a topknot. Stone had brought her here through a portal with no explanation.

Skybright stepped toward the edge and peered down; it was impossibly high. A giant lake glinted like obsidian far below. Two

1

fishing rafts drifted on the dark water, more minute than a child's toy, although even from this distance, she could sense the humans' presence. The fresh scent of pine needles drifted to her always, *always* reminding her of Kai Sen. Clenching her jaw, she willed the ache in her chest to disperse.

It had been nine days, she believed, since Stone had forced her to give up everything she had ever known and had ripped her from her mortal life so Zhen Ni and Kai Sen would live theirs. Skybright's sacrifice had been enough to satisfy an age-old covenant between the gods and mortals; it closed the breach from the underworld, putting a stop to demons escaping into the mortal realm. But when she was with Stone, time felt amorphous, stretching onward, languid and never-ending—the days melded together, difficult to track.

She hummed to herself, not realizing until Stone asked, "What is that tune?"

Abruptly, she stopped. "I don't know … I think it was 'The Hermit's Climb,'" she replied after a pause.

"Your mother used to do that," Stone said. "Opal was always singing or humming a song under her breath."

"Tell me more about her," Skybright said. She had never given a second thought to her lineage before, not until she woke one night with a serpent's tail, and Nanny Bai told her she had found Skybright as a newborn, abandoned in the forest.

He turned and regarded her. "She was beautiful," he said, "and a powerful serpent demon."

She jerked her chin up, challenging him with a stare. "Was there nothing *human* about her at all? Or did she merely seduce and kill men for pleasure?" She craved to know more about her mother. There was no denying her serpent half; that she was Opal's daughter. But how alike were they?

"I always thought her pleasure in song was her most human trait," Stone said. "It softened her."

His perceptive observation surprised Skybright. Stone was often hopeless when it came to understanding mortals. Skybright had been a handmaid all her life and had learned to read people, to pick up on their moods and anticipate their needs. She had thought she was very good at it, until she met Stone. He simply didn't think or react the same way she expected a person to, but then again, he was immortal. "She must have had a beautiful voice," she said.

"A *beautiful* voice? No. It was *glorious*. It was part of her natural charm. Men fell in love with her simply for her voice." He smiled, his chiseled jawline cut so perfectly, it mimicked the statues hewn of gods. Stone had always been cold and aloof with others but seemed to allow himself to open up in her presence, as if he'd known her even before their first meeting.

"Oh." Skybright tried hard to imagine her mother, her face lifted in song. What did she look like? "Thank you," she murmured.

"I have finally said the right thing?" he asked.

"Yes," she replied and almost smiled back. He sounded so proud, like a boy who had caught a fish in the river for the first time. But she could never confuse his seductive charisma and the scraps of information he divulged for kindness. She was Stone's captive, a prisoner of his will.

"I have never heard you sing," he said.

"I usually sing when I'm alone ... and feeling content." The barb was probably too subtle for him.

"Will you sing for me?" Stone asked.

Skybright colored, and a burst of annoyance shot through her. "Is that a command?"

"I do not command you."

"You force me away from the people I love forever in exchange for their lives. And you have the nerve to say that you don't command me?"

He raised his shoulders in a gesture of indifference. "That was a necessity. The mortals you love will be dead before you even realize. Your life is endless, and theirs are guttering flames."

Stone knew exactly what to say to wound her, although she was never certain if it was his true intent. His manner was always direct, yet he remained an enigma. She hated that he was right, that he was always so removed and logical, uncomplicated by emotions like love and grief. "Tell me more about who *you* are, and I shall sing for you." She didn't have much to negotiate with in this game they played, and knowing more about the immortal would be to her advantage. "What exactly are you?"

His dark brows drew together for a moment, so brief she might have missed it if she were not observing him so intently. "I was mortal once, long ago. I do not remember anything from that time. But I was made immortal when I was eighteen."

"Why?"

"I caught the eye of a god and was chosen by chance. The gods in both the heavens and underworld work together to keep the mortal realm in careful balance, but there was very little interchange between the Immortals who ruled above and those who tended to punishment and reincarnation below. When I was granted my magical powers, I became the intermediary." Stone spoke in a soft voice as sound carried far on this tranquil peak.

"So they stole you from your mortal life to do this … job?" she asked. "What of your family?"

"I severed my ties with them the day I was chosen." When he tilted his face to the sky, Skybright guessed this was something difficult for Stone to share. "There was no reason for them to learn the truth. I could never again be their son."

"But did the god give you a choice?" she asked. "Did you want to give up your mortal life?"

He met her eyes with his own, so dark it was impossible to distinguish his pupils. "There is no choice once an Immortal has selected you for her purpose, Skybright. I have fulfilled this role with diligence ever since the responsibility was bestowed upon me."

A chill breeze lifted the hair from Skybright's face, and she suppressed a shudder. Pine needles rustled, the softest whisper, and Skybright imagined she could hear the water lap against the lake's shore far beneath them. "So you would force upon me exactly what a god did to you?"

Surprise registered on his smooth face in the slight lift of his dark brows. "This is different. You are demonic. I am showing you what your mother would have wanted you to know."

"You don't remember it, the pain of being taken away, but deep down, deep down the loss and grief remains in you. I can feel it." Skybright touched her hand to her chest, then threw her shoulders back, drew a deep breath, and began to sing. She didn't know many songs—only the childhood ones Nanny Bai used to croon to her and the more popular ones sung during holidays and festivals. Closing her eyes, she let sorrow wash over her, let the feeling of loss swell in her voice.

She sang of the fragility of love and the brevity of life, her throat closing over the last lines:

> *Long have I stood here waiting*
> *The pale moon distant*
> *And yet you never return to me*

She held the final note, and the word seemed to spiral upward, rising into the mist-filled sky. Foolishly, she had been thinking of Kai Sen as she sang, and Skybright lowered her head, smoothing her features, even as her heart continued to race. She blindly stared at her embroidered slippers until Stone broke the silence.

"Beautifully done, Skybright. You sing with such emotion."

She risked a glance upward, and Stone's face was as revealing as a blank wall. She had only ever sung for Zhen Ni when she requested it. And that one time, for Kai Sen, after they had made love. The act had felt uncomfortably intimate, as if she were exposing her soul, rendering herself even more vulnerable to Stone.

"It was worth the exchange," Stone said, scrutinizing her with a tilt of his head.

She flushed and brought a cool hand to her cheek. "Why have you brought me here?" Skybright glanced again over the ledge to the lake below, its placid surface mirrored the sweeping vista of mountains surrounding them.

He followed her gaze across the expansive scenery. Sunlight

had broken through the dense fog, swathing the skyline in a deep fiery orange. "I visit this particular province for the beauty of these mountains and the serenity. It is also where I often enter the underworld."

Perplexed, Skybright turned around, expecting to glimpse the mouth of a cave or a crater in the earth, but only majestic pines towered behind them. "I don't understand."

Stone pulled her into his arms then. Surprised, she resisted, before submitting to his embrace. He had never overstepped boundaries since taking her captive, and she knew when he did touch her on rare occasion, it was for a reason. His armor made no noise when he moved, and when she pressed both hands to his chest, she felt a tunic beneath her fingers. Soft and worn.

The immortal was truly never as he appeared.

"You will see," Stone said as he tightened his arms around Skybright's waist, clasping her close like a lover.

It was unexpected, both thrilling and terrifying; his usual warmth felt uncomfortably hot against her skin.

Then Stone leaped off the cliff edge.

A strangled scream tore from Skybright's throat, but the sudden rush of air snatched it away in an instant, and she couldn't draw enough breath to even gasp as they plummeted toward the lake far below.

Skybright plunged at a stomach-wrenching speed through the air, her arms wound tightly around Stone's neck. The immortal couldn't die, but she probably would, smashed like a melon against the water's surface the same as if it were rock.

"Trust me," Stone's calm voice somehow said within her ear, and she would have bitten him hard on the shoulder if she hadn't been so frightened.

They slipped under the frigid lake moments later, as seamless as an arrow. The change from rushing air to the oppressive weight of the dark waters was shocking, and Skybright threw her head back, seeing the glimmer from the lake's surface grow faint. Water filled her nose and her ears. Instinctively, she opened her lips to scream, and it whorled into her mouth, pressing against her throat. She closed it too late; she would die like this.

Drowned.

Skybright squeezed her eyes shut in panic.

Then she felt Stone's mouth on hers, gently parting her lips with his own. With an intake of his breath, the water rushed from her; then he breathed out, and sweet air filled her mouth, easing the tightness of her throat, the ache in her lungs. She opened her eyes. His shoulders were edged in a faint silver light, making his form the one thing she could see in the darkness they were now floating in. Stone always glowed.

She pressed closer to him, hysteria threatening to rise. She had never learned to swim and had an irrational fear of drowning she had shared with no one but Zhen Ni. Her throat hitched, and she moaned inside, a sob suppressed by Stone's mouth. His eyes flickered open at the small noise. She was certain he could taste her horror.

Then his lips began moving against hers, warm and insistent. She gasped, breathing in the precious air he gave, even as she felt his tongue against hers. He was kissing her, and there was nothing she could do but cling to him desperately because to let go was to die. Even in the frigid water, his flesh was hot, and she began to feel lightheaded, like the first time he had kissed her in the forest.

If kissing Kai Sen was like grounding Skybright in her own body, heightening all of her senses until her soul was drawn taut, kissing Stone was like falling away from herself, as if he was literally pulling her spirit out by a thin thread into oblivion. She could no longer feel her own flesh, the wet, or the cold but instead drifted in a sea of starlight, not knowing at all which way she was reeling.

Skybright jarred against something, the motion flinging her neck back, and her head lolled. She didn't want to open her eyes, feeling as if she'd drunk too much rice wine; her temples throbbed, and her lips tingled. Someone set her on her feet, and her knees shook, causing the arms that had clasped her waist to tighten again.

"Hmm," Stone said to himself.

Hearing his voice snapped Skybright back into consciousness, and she pushed herself away from him with both hands, so hard she almost fell backward. She looked down and saw that her tunic and trousers were sopping wet, clinging to her body, revealing curves she'd always kept hidden within their loose folds. Furious, her vision blackened for a moment. She lifted her eyes to see Stone standing before her, as dry as a sheet that had been hung on a line in the sunshine for a day, immaculate.

She slapped him hard across the face. He didn't even blink. "I could have drowned!" she shouted, her voice quivering. She fisted her hand, ignoring the sting of her palm. It had been like hitting a statue. She had left no mark on his cheek.

"Of course not," he replied. "I would not have let that happen. You are safe in my care, Skybright."

His care. She bit down on her lip. She didn't want to be in *his* care. "And ... and you kissed me! Without asking!" Her shoulders jerked, as if she were going to hit him again, and he had the sense to lower his head. Not from fear, she knew. She hadn't hurt him. She couldn't hurt him. He was too powerful.

"I know you do not like to be kissed," he said.

She almost laughed aloud; he was so far from the mark, missing her point entirely. She felt hysteria rising again, the weight of the endless waters pressing against her, trying to invade every pore of her being, and shivered violently.

"The kiss was the only way I could think of to help you forget where you were." He raised his hand, and a dress with pink and lavender silk panels shimmered into existence. "The journey with you in the lake took longer than when I travel through it on my own. You are frozen and wet. I apologize, Skybright."

She snatched the dress from him, even as her teeth clacked together, and swept the wet strands of hair from her face. The kiss *had* made her forget where she was—drawn her soul away from herself. But what did he feel when they kissed? *It is how I learn more about you*, he had told her once. Likely, he felt nothing. Stone raised his other hand, and a thick, white towel manifested, which he handed to her. Snuffling, Skybright glared at Stone for good measure. She refused to thank him, so they simply stared at each other for a long moment.

"Turn around," she demanded.

Stone opened his mouth, then clamped it shut without speaking before turning his back to her. He folded his arms, his shining armor making no noise, and stilled, as immoveable as his name.

Skybright rubbed her hair furiously with the plush towel before peeling the clothes from her body. Her gaze never left Stone's broad back. It wasn't as if he hadn't seen her naked before—in both serpent form and as a girl—but it was the last transgression she could endure after that terrible descent into the dark waters. She then took in her surroundings as she dried herself. They were in a magnificent foyer. The long chamber was built of rectangular white brick, but the crevices between them glowed a deep orange-red. The light from behind those walls pulsed, like a living entity, casting the entire room in its angry hue. The high ceiling was pitched into a triangular peak, and the one exit in the chamber was a gaping square hole flanked by two demon statues.

There was no sound within the chamber except for the rustle of silk as Skybright pulled on her dress, but the stone floor seemed to throb beneath her bare feet, and she could sense with her serpentine powers that she was surrounded by thousands of beings—none of them mortal. She finally slipped on her cloth shoes, preferring to suffer with cold, wet feet than ask Stone to conjure up a new pair for her. Her wet clothes had magically disappeared. Winding her damp hair into tight buns, she walked to stand beside Stone. "Where are we?" she asked.

Skybright's feet squelched against the ground, but she kept pace. Stone was more than a head taller than she was, and his stride was long. "We are at one of the doors into the underworld," he replied in a low voice.

A rumble reverberated through the chamber the closer they drew to the dark, square hole; the identical demon statues guarding the entrance stirred to life, shedding their dull gray color. They towered over them, at least twice the height of Skybright, with bulging muscles that made Stone look like a boy. The demons wore nothing except a loincloth, and their arms were thicker than her legs. Despite her frustration with Stone, she kept close to him.

Stone halted in front of the exit between the demons. Conquering her own fear, she tilted her head back to gaze at them. The demons' skin was a dusky blue, and although they had physiques modeled after mortal men, their heads were a different matter. Their hair was leaping orange flames, and the same fire seemed to fill their large bulging eyes so that they glowed red. Thick tusks jutted over their lower lips; their expression was a furious grimace. Both wielded giant axes, their silver blades so long and sharp she was certain they could split her in half with a single stroke.

The demons shook their heads so the flames jumped higher and thudded their axe handles against the ground at the same time. "Master Stone," they ground out in grating voices simultaneously, and the chamber shook when they spoke. "Welcome back," the demons said, and each fell onto one knee in unison, their heads lowered. Even in this subservient position, they were still taller than Skybright.

This close, the demons tasted like ancient magma against her tongue, filling her nose and mouth with the overwhelming stench of sulfur. She fought the urge to shift to serpent form, to slither away from the demons as fast as she could. Skybright realized that she had her hand pressed against Stone's back, feeling his shoulder blade beneath the soft material of his tunic.

Stone bowed, his armor clanging, crisp enough to be heard above the rumble. She knew now that his armor was often an illusion. "Stay close," he murmured without so much as a glance behind, his voice magically within her ear. She dug her fingertips into his back in response and followed him through the gaping entrance.

Skybright tumbled headlong into a black void, empty of everything except for the agonized screams of thousands that tore through her entire being. Her soul shuddered. She wanted to cover her ears to drown them out but had no hands. She tried hard to regain her sense of physical self, but there was only the reeling sensation of erratic freefall and that desperate howling, so intense, it seemed to buffet her spirit.

A red glow suffused her vision, bringing Skybright back into her own body again. Stone was grasping her hand in his; she recognized the heat of his touch. She forced her eyelids open, and it felt as if they had been stuck together with rice glue.

"Are you all right?" he asked.

The screaming had subsided to a din that echoed from farther off. She and Stone stood in the middle of a deep cavern that seemed to stretch endlessly before them. Its dark rock walls and ceiling were irregular, bulbous, and pulsated an eerie red—a bloodier hue than the color in the grand foyer. The floor was dirt and grit beneath her sodden shoes.

She swallowed, then nodded. "I'm thirsty." Her voice croaked.

Stone conjured a flask and passed it to her. She drank the cold water greedily, angry that she needed to rely on him for something as simple as this. She wiped her mouth with her fingers after she finished, feeling more steady.

He had never been deliberately cruel since sealing their pact; actually, Stone often seemed to try to be considerate. But it was difficult to reconcile her attraction for him with the terrifying situation she found herself in: being his prisoner for however long his whim desired.

"I was not certain how you would travel through the entrance to the underworld, being half-mortal. Most demons are spawned in hell, but you were not. And mortals are not allowed here at all— not while they are alive."

"It felt as if I had been torn from my own body." She forced her voice even.

Stone peered down at her, curious. "I am glad you were allowed to enter. Your demonic nature was recognized."

She stepped back from him and turned a small circle, taking in the giant cavern. She could see the ceiling but not an end to its length, the walls curving away from her into eternity. The entire cavern thrummed, like a beehive, calling to her. She wanted to respond, wanted to shift into her serpent shape and slither deeper into the abyss, to lose herself in its hypnotic song. It was liberating to *choose* to change rather than be forced, as Abbot Wu had made her do with a spell. The healed scars from the characters he had carved into the tender inside of her forearm could still be easily read: *Show yourself true.*

Skybright resisted that visceral urge to shift, rising like a flood and expanding in her chest. She didn't know what to expect down here or who she might encounter. "What is this place?" she whispered.

"Are you afraid?" Stone asked, his black eyes following her every motion.

Skybright turned her back to him and did not reply. Two could play at this game.

She walked toward the wall and pressed her hand against the

protruding rock. It was smooth and pulsated red beneath her fingertips. "What—" She looked toward Stone, and he tilted his head, quiet. "Is there something *alive* within the rock?" she asked.

The glowing cavern wall had looked opaque, but she began to examine it more carefully, running her hand along the stone. It seemed to respond to her, growing brighter where she touched. Skybright saw now that the wall wasn't entirely impenetrable, that some areas were translucent, emitting strong light. Leaning closer, she thought she glimpsed something within—a snout jammed near the rock's surface, and a snarling mouth with a dark tongue lolling out.

She jumped, biting back a scream.

"We are in the depths of the underworld," Stone said. "The demons are spawned here."

Skybright spun from the wall, arching her neck to take in the endless cavern again, finally understanding. Each bulge in the rock was like a pod, encasing a demon within. She flinched to see the face of a goat demon, dull eyes open but unseeing, visible beneath the translucent rock. Running down one length of the cavern revealed curved horns and giant hooves, the outline of a black wing cradling a beast within.

Skybright ran until it felt as if her lungs would burst, sharp pebbles digging into the soles of her feet. The acrid scent of smoke filled her lungs, and she tasted the hard grit of ancient stone upon her tongue. She finally skidded to a stop, forced to press both hands against her knees.

She had run so far that she had lost sight of Stone. The red glow of the cavern thrummed on, spanning forever.

Stone manifested beside her, but his earthen scent had given her a heartbeat's warning, as if heralding his arrival. For an instant, she was comforted by his familiar smell in this fathomless place. He wielded power in the underworld. It had been obvious from the way the giant demons had treated him with reverence in the grand foyer. No harm would befall her here. She might be his captive, but he would keep her safe.

"Is this where serpent demons are born as well?" she asked, out of breath. "Where my mother came from?"

Were these her brethren?

"No. I do not know how serpent demons are created. I have ever only known Opal, and now you. These demons are spawned with the essence of hell and are used for the Great Battle in the mortal world as well as for grunt work in the underworld. They are obedient but violent creatures. What they lack in intellect, they make up for in brute strength." Stone tapped his knuckles against the glowing rocks. "These warrens protect the demons as they grow."

The hypnotic thrumming and reddish glow in the vast cavern was beginning to drive Skybright mad. It seeped into her, as the water had during her descent into the underworld. She suddenly felt exhausted and overwhelmed. Then her stomach growled, reminding her that she hadn't eaten since the previous night. She was working on smothering her pride and irritation to ask for food when Stone whipped around, casting his gaze into the deep cavern behind them. Her eyes followed, senses on alert. Skybright smelled the demon before she heard him.

A demon with yellow wolf eyes and a wide muzzle emerged from the shadows. Although his face reminded Skybright of a wolf's, giant horns jutted from his brow, and the floor echoed with the sound of his two hooves as he approached. He was taller than Stone by a head and wielded a pike twice her size, ending in three lethal points.

"Master Stone." The demon inclined his head. "I was not expecting your visit … and accompanied by a woman." His voice was rough.

Skybright tried not to twitch as those unsettling yellow eyes met hers, and the demon's wide mouth pulled back in a grimace, revealing a row of sharp teeth and long fangs. He smelled as ancient as the rocks that surrounded them, perhaps older even than Stone.

"Ye Guai." Stone gave a terse nod after speaking the demon's name, his stance indicating that although he knew the demon, they were not friends. "I wanted to visit the caverns after our last Great Battle—to make certain the next generations are breeding well."

"Yes. They are growing within the rocks, becoming stronger." The demon made a guttural sound in the back of his throat, before saying, "Many of my brothers died in these last months, slaughtered by the monks. They fought courageously." He pressed a fist to his heart, and Skybright saw that his nails were yellow talons, his thick knuckles covered with coarse black hair.

Ye Guai lowered his massive head, horns forward, waiting for Stone's reply—as if he had posed a question.

Stone turned his back on the demon, a move that made the hairs on Skybright's neck prickle. *Don't look away from him*, she wanted to say. *He's dangerous.* Instead, Ye Guai remained with his head bowed in subservience as Stone walked a length of the cavern, peering in on the monsters flourishing within. "They fought the same as they ever did," Stone finally replied. "You know their role as well as I do. They are born to obey. Most are born to die."

A long pause followed, in which Skybright could only hear and feel the soft vibrations emanating from the uneven walls.

"It is a hard life," Ye Guai said. "Cut short."

Stone strolled toward the demon, his hands clasped behind his back, a picture of ease. "You speak as if they owned their lives. As if you did not know exactly what they were bred to do."

Ye Guai's giant muscles bulged, even the cords of his thick neck stood taut.

"Look at me," Stone commanded.

The demon lifted his head, and Skybright swore she saw hatred there before the demon blinked his yellow eyes and his powerful jaw softened a fraction.

"You have done a fine job providing the demons we have needed to rule the underworld as well as the mortal realm. Have the Immortals not rewarded you enough?" Stone demanded. "Are you dissatisfied with this honored role?"

Ye Guai sank to one knee, his fist still held against his chest. "Apologies, Master Stone. I am but a humble servant to the gods."

His voice was docile, but his scent was not.

Skybright almost leaned in, to catch a better trace of the demon's true temperament, but Stone stepped forward, blocking her way. "As am I. We both serve the gods," Stone said and touched the demon's muscular shoulder. "All is well here, as I knew it would be. The demons are thriving. Come, rise."

Ye Guai stood, his hooves clacking against the ground. "Thank you, Master Stone." His gaze flickered in her direction. "How can the lady visit the underworld? She is not dead. Is she one of us?"

The observation was so unexpected that Skybright was unable to keep the shock from her face. What could this wolf demon know of her? She smoothed her expression but not before the demon leered. Stone's hand shot out, his arm a blur of motion, and cuffed the demon on the side of his head hard enough that Ye Guai let out a hideous howl.

"She is not like one of you," Stone said, and she would have sworn that the temperature dropped around them. "We are done here. Do not forget your place."

When Stone wrapped an arm around her shoulder and conjured them from that seething abyss, the demon was still whimpering.

Skybright was better prepared when Stone pulled her through the frigid lake this time. She remained still when he placed his mouth over hers once more, giving her the precious air that she needed, keeping calm by thinking of the morning rituals she used to perform with Zhen Ni: arranging her thick black hair into elaborate loops, threading jade and rubies into them. She *had* to stay calm, lest Stone judge that she was too panicked and felt obliged to make her literally forget where she was by kissing her again.

To her dismay, her thoughts ran to Kai Sen, and she remembered how it felt when his arms were wound about her waist, the way his dark brown eyes seemed brighter whenever he leaned over to seek a kiss, as if the anticipation of it lit him from within.

The hot sting of tears threatened beneath her closed lids, and Skybright willed her mind to be a blank void, blaming the tightness in her chest on the cold water that swirled against them.

They emerged on the muddied banks of the tranquil lake, the same one they had been peering down upon before they leaped into its depths. She quickly untangled herself from Stone's hold, and he released her without a word. Incredibly, she was dry down to the hair on her head. Stone had some foresight this time.

"Thank you," she muttered with reluctance.

"I am better prepared now that I know what to expect when traveling with you. What was your impression of the underworld?"

"I don't believe that Ye Guai likes you." she replied, not answering his question. She needed time to mull over what she had witnessed—mull over where she had been.

"He does not need to like me," Stone said. "He simply needs to obey."

"Like you obey?" she asked. "I had thought you were immortal—all powerful. Why must you listen to the gods?"

He raised an eyebrow. "Because I am not a god. My powers were granted by them, as was my immortality."

Skybright wrapped her arms around herself but couldn't suppress the tremor that ran through her. Even though she was not wet, the iciness of the lake seemed to linger, having burrowed its way to her bones. "Am I immortal too now, as part serpent demon?"

"I believe you are, Skybright," Stone replied. "As your mother had been."

"But you think she is dead."

"Only the gods can never die," he said. "We may live long, but we can still suffer an accident or be slain."

Had her mother been murdered then, decapitated, or set on fire, like Skybright had seen the monks do to countless other demons? "Even you can be killed?" she asked.

He paused, then threw his head back and laughed. "Anyone who had ever been foolish enough to try never lived to tell the tale."

Stone manifested a coat with a flick of his fingers and proffered it. Zhen Ni would love this trick of his; Skybright could imagine her mistress demanding that Stone conjure all sorts of ridiculous and extravagant things. Her merriment quickly withered. No, Zhen Ni was no longer *her mistress*. That was another life—her mortal life. She pulled the richly brocaded jacket over her shoulders and buttoned the front with stiff fingers. The collar was lined in ermine, warming her neck.

"I forget that your body requires sustenance. Half the day is gone and you have not eaten." Stone spoke words under his breath and made a slashing motion with his arm. "Come. Let us dine somewhere nice." He reached for her hand, and she allowed him to grasp it, not knowing what to expect when she stepped through the portal.

CHAPTER TWO

Kai Sen

"Again," Abbot Wu commanded.

He stood before Kai Sen, swathed in a crimson robe, gripping his tall walnut staff in one hand. The sun had barely risen over Tian Kuan Mountain, and the abbot was training him in a small courtyard located behind his private study. It was near the end of the twelfth moon, but despite the chill, Kai Sen wore a sleeveless tunic tied at the waist over loose trousers; the bite in the morning air helped him to focus.

He chanted the spell Abbot Wu had taught him, centering himself as he did so, gathering the fire element that suffused this mortal world, radiating from the underworld and heavens, then back again. These elements resonated all around them, unfelt by the majority of people. Kai Sen had to be taught to sense these energies, trained to harness them. He drew a deep breath and pulled, tugging threads of fire element to him, and a small blue flame flickered within his curved palms.

"Well done," Abbot Wu murmured. "Hellfire cannot harm mortals but can kill creatures of the underworld and the undead—

everything we have warred against."

Kai Sen felt no heat, only a slickness against his skin as the ball of flame jittered in his hands. After three months of intense training, the abbot had finally taught him the most powerful weapon he could wield against the creatures of hell.

"Pull more threads," Abbot Wu said. "Make it grow."

Kai Sen concentrated, casting his senses wide, drawing more strongly on the fire element spiraling in the air around him, pouring its power into his palms. The flame vibrated and grew, pulsing from apple-sized to that of a large watermelon.

"Impressive," the abbot said. "You're a quick learner, and your gift of clairvoyance makes you an especially strong magic user."

But Kai Sen barely heard Abbot Wu, his voice like a mosquito buzzing in the distance. Sweat slid down the back of his neck, and his hairline dampened as he opened himself more, tugging greedily. The hellfire he held undulated, expanding to the size of a giant gourd, so large that it obscured the abbot's face.

Grinning with triumph, he extended his arms, admiring his work, suffused in the power of the element rushing through him until Abbot Wu smacked his shoulder hard with his staff. Kai Sen lost hold of everything, and the blue flame winked out of existence.

"Humph," Abbot Wu said. "It doesn't matter how powerful you are if your focus can be so easily broken."

The man spoke in an even tone, almost casually, but Kai Sen caught something else in his words. There was an edge to them; was it surprise or … wariness? His mentor had not expected Kai Sen to meet his challenge.

He bowed his head. "Yes, Abbot Wu."

"That's enough for today," the abbot said. "You are learning more quickly than I thought possible. When I was taught, it took me well over half a year to conjure a small flame."

The abbot had chosen Kai Sen as his successor—the next in line to rule the monastery and uphold the covenant. It was an agreement between the mortals and the gods, offering countless monks' lives up in a vicious battle with the underworld, sealed with an innocent life given as sacrifice to close hell's breach. Kai Sen had agreed, blatantly lying to Abbot Wu, the closest thing he ever had to a father figure, so that he could learn all of his secrets and break the covenant.

Morning light filtered through the tall cypress tree in the intimate courtyard, and an image of Skybright by the creek, sunlight dappling her cheek and caressing her bare arms filled his mind. *She* had been the sacrifice this time. This twisted covenant would end with her.

His mentor was already sliding the study's paneled door back when Kai Sen stopped him with a question, "We've discussed the five core elements that can grant us magic in this world, Abbot Wu. But which one allows us to create portals?"

Standing beneath the shade of the eaves, the older man's eyes were hooded.

Kai Sen went on, undeterred. "I would guess the earth element?" He needed to know. If he couldn't create portals, he could never find Skybright.

"Portals utilize earth, wood, metal, and water, as you must bend all these elements to your will to form a rent," the abbot replied in his rich voice. "To allow you to step from one place into another."

"Four elements at once?" Kai Sen asked.

"Many of the more advanced magic require the use of multiple elements," the abbot explained, easing the door panel back fully. "You won't be learning how to create a portal for some time. It is much too advanced. I couldn't conjure them until after over three years of training."

Kai Sen inclined his head once more, hiding his face. The longer he couldn't create portals, the longer the abbot could keep him leashed.

"I'm meeting with a visiting scholar in the main library," Abbot Wu said. "Will you walk with me?"

"I'd like to stay a while longer to practice, if I may?" Kai Sen asked. "It is tranquil here."

"You are doing well, Kai Sen. A true prodigy." The abbot waved his hand with a flourish, the wide sleeve of his robe billowing. "Stay as long as you need."

Kai Sen remained in the empty courtyard, listening for the abbot's retreating footsteps. Birds sang overhead, chattering excitedly in morning greeting. Beyond the curved rooftops, his brother monks were emerging in the main courtyard; Kai Sen could hear their low voices and an occasional whoop of laughter before they settled down to practice their forms. After he was certain Abbot Wu had gone, he too entered the private study with quick, silent steps.

A long blackwood table was set near the paneled doors so the abbot could enjoy the courtyard view on a pleasant day. The rectangular chamber was lined with shelves against three walls, stacked full of books above with scrolls stored in wide drawers and cubbies beneath. Kai Sen had taken tomes and scrolls from the abbot's library before without permission, to study text and spells on his own, in subjects the abbot would have considered too advanced or powerful for Kai Sen so early in his training.

But the magic came easily to him, like quenching thirst with a long drink of water. Once Abbot Wu helped his inner eye to see, Kai Sen always felt nature's elements around him, perceived the tug of their power. This connection and awareness had become a natural part of his being. He glanced over the crowded shelves, organized by subject, letting his instincts guide him. Wandering over to the far corner of the study, his fingers grazed over thick texts. Dust particles swirled in the dim morning light, and his senses were filled with the musty scent of ancient pages.

Kai Sen's fingertips tingled when they ran across a thin book bound in red leather. Deftly, he popped it from the shelf. Its cover was worn, with a simple title that might have been gilded in gold once but had long since lost its luster: *Transitions*. He slipped it into the leather pouch at his waist without bothering to glance at the pages inside.

He knew this book was what he had been looking for. As soon as he could master how to create portals, he could begin his search for Skybright.

Zhen Ni

Rose, Zhen Ni's head handmaid, arrived even earlier than her usual time in the morning.

"It's barely past dawn!" Zhen Ni moaned into a brocaded cushion as the young handmaid drew open the large lattice windows in her bedchamber. "Even the birds are still asleep!"

As if to be contrary, a bird trilled a long song in the courtyard beyond her quarters. Zhen Ni moaned again. "Wretched bird," she said in a muffled voice.

"I apologize, mistress, but your mother asked that I prepare you early today." Rose extended a hand, offering to help Zhen Ni from the tall platform bed. The girl was a few years younger—sweet and earnest, a hard worker—but not someone Zhen Ni could tell secrets to or have adventures with, not someone she considered as close as a sister.

Rose was not Skybright.

Over four months had passed since that horrible day in the cave at hell's breach, when Skybright had inexplicably disappeared before her eyes, taken by the frightening immortal called Stone. Zhen Ni never even got the chance to say good-bye. It was a regret she lived with every day.

She slipped out of bed reluctantly, shivering as her bare feet touched the stone floor. It had been a mild winter but still too cold for her tastes. Faint morning light cast random patterns against her bedchamber walls, papered in the palest green. She let the handmaid wipe her face and hands with a rose-scented towel, then Zhen Ni rubbed her own teeth with coarse salt before rinsing her mouth out over the ceramic basin. Rose then helped her into a turquoise tunic and skirt, embroidered with dragonflies and lotus.

Finally sitting down in front of her vanity, Zhen Ni covered a wide yawn with the back of her hand as Rose began to brush her long hair, then braid and twist it into elaborate loops. Zhen Ni fiddled with the various bottles and jars on the vanity, choosing a sweet honeysuckle perfume to dab onto her wrists and throat. "That's fancy," Zhen Ni said, observing the handmaid's deft fingers in the polished mirror.

"Lady Yuan said it's a special day," Rose replied, smiling shyly at her mistress. "She requested for the rubies and jade to be threaded in your hair." The girl's dark brown eyes shone with excitement.

Zhen Ni's chest constricted, as if she could already feel the breast binder she would have to wear as a married woman. These days, there was nothing her mother would mark as a special occasion for Zhen Ni—except for a betrothal.

Zhen Ni took her time on her way to the main hall, meandering through the courtyards of the Yuan manor. The gardens lacked color except for the deep green of the pruned pine and cypress trees, their gnarled branches reaching toward a pale winter sky. Plum blossoms were beginning to grow on barren sprigs, their pale pink buds like an unexpected sweet after a bland meal.

Rose had draped a fur-lined cape over Zhen Ni's shoulders before she set off to see her mother, and Zhen Ni tugged it closer, the collar's ermine fur tickling her earlobes and offering warmth. Her breath plumed like mist, and she quickened her steps. There was no use in dragging this out. The news would be the same no matter how long she took to meet her mother.

She entered the main courtyard, passing the tall rock formation trickling water into a deep pond, its rippling surface reflecting the twisting branches of a plum tree above. Zhen Ni paused before the main hall, the grandest structure in the Yuan manor. Polished white stone steps led to a wide deck enclosed by a low jade railing, elaborately carved in a cloud motif. Red pillars flanked the wide paneled doors, closed to the cold morning air. But she could see the lanterns blazing within the hall, their bright light gleaming through the intricately carved panels.

Drawing a deep breath, she squared her shoulders, climbed the steps, and pushed the door panels aside. A gust of warmth greeted her.

"Zhen Ni," her mother said. "Your father and I have been waiting for you."

"Ba!" Zhen Ni uttered in delight. She ran over to where he sat and kissed him on the cheek, his beard scratching her nose. "When did you return?" Her father was a merchant and traveled throughout the kingdom much of the year on business.

He laughed; his eyes turned into half-moons. "Late last night. The journey took longer than I had expected." He squeezed Zhen Ni's hand in his rough palm. "And how is my favorite daughter?"

She laughed in turn, the sound big and bold, like her father's. "I am your *only* daughter left in the house," she teased, and slid into a curved back chair across from her parents.

Her father chuckled in that jovial way of his, but she saw the touch of sadness in his eyes. Zhen Ni's gaze flicked to her mother, who sat with her back as straight as a bamboo stalk, her hands folded neatly in her lap. "Detailed cards have been exchanged, dear daughter," her mother said, a small smile lingering on the corners of her mouth. "And a match has been made. You will be wed in a few months."

Zhen Ni felt the blood drain from her face. "So soon?" she whispered.

"We've consulted a seer for the most fortuitous date. The wedding will take place in early spring, in the third moon."

Zhen Ni tried to swallow the knot down her throat, but her mouth was dry, as if she were an effigy made of straw. "I see," she managed to say.

"It is a good match, my little lotus."

Her heart clenched to hear her father use the pet name he had given her as a little girl. But little girls grew up, and society dictated that they were given away when the time came, familial bonds made so tenuous, it was sometimes less painful to simply sever all ties.

"Who is he?" she asked.

"Master Bei," her mother replied. "He is very wealthy but without family, all lost tragically in a fire. He was wed before—"

Nightingale, her mother's head handmaid, entered the hall with her head bowed, trailed by two servants. They quickly placed enameled trays on the table in front of Zhen Ni and her parents filled with covered dishes and bowls. Another handmaid, Oriole, poured tea for each of them, before they disappeared with light steps.

"An outcast then," Zhen Ni said, as if they hadn't been interrupted.

"He is a well-to-do man from a good family, Daughter," her mother said. "It has not been easy for us to find a proper husband for you …" She trailed off meaningfully.

Yes. Zhen Ni was said to be willful and a runaway with a tainted reputation that was well-known to every prosperous family who mattered when it came to arranging a good match for her.

"A widower," Zhen Ni said.

"Looking for a new start," her father replied.

"He seeks another chance at love," her mother added. "You would have the status of first wife."

If she should be so lucky that Master Bei would take on more wives and leave her alone.

"The best news is Master Bei has built his manor here in town." Her mother's mouth widened into a true smile. "We'll be neighbors and can visit each other."

Zhen Ni tried to return her mother's smile, but it wavered. "That is a comfort at least."

"The betrothal gifts have been delivered," her father said, "and they are as resplendent as my favorite daughter deserves." He waved a hand, and Zhen Ni noticed the gifts stacked behind him.

She went to examine them, feeling like a woman meeting her fate head-on, a woman who could not change her own path. Eight jars of betrothal wine were set near their ancestor altar. The gold-colored bottles reached above her knees, etched with chrysanthemums and swathed in crimson silks embroidered with butterflies.

There were three massive gilded chests, laden with mutton, pheasant, exotic dried fruit and nuts, candies, cake, and fragrant orange blossom tea. Bolts of bright silks and brocades—twenty in all—were placed beside the chests. Her mother had risen and joined Zhen Ni, her round face beaming with pleasure.

"These will make wonderful newly-wed tunics and dresses to take with you to the Bei manor, Zhen Ni. We will have the seamstress come tomorrow." She lifted her head from a bolt of emerald silk and smiled.

Zhen Ni nodded, unable to feign enthusiasm.

"Master Bei requested that you open this present personally." Her mother handed her a wooden box.

It was carved with peaches and bats, symbols of fertility and good fortune. Zhen Ni carefully lifted the lid revealing a beautiful jade hairpin engraved with the double love knot. Three emeralds dangled from delicate gold chains. She passed the piece to her mother, as something else nestled in the red satin caught her eye. Pushing the cloth aside, she lifted a pair of earrings, the rubies were larger than she had ever seen, set in finely etched gold.

Her mother drew in a breath when she saw them.

The Yuans were wealthy, but it was obvious that Master Bei had coin to match. More than enough to buy Zhen Ni from her own family.

Skybright

Thank the goddess traveling through the portal didn't seem to take much time. It was like stepping into a deep indigo, and immersed in a crackling noise that pinged against Skybright's skin, then stepping out to a different locale. She was glad that she could feel Stone's fingers gripping hers as the experience was disorienting, even if brief.

They emerged onto an arched stone bridge overlooking a tranquil canal. Two-storied teahouses and restaurants lined either side of it, interspersed with private residences. Skybright could tell which were the eating establishments as their lattice windows were flung wide open and pearl-shaped red lanterns were strung beyond them as decoration. A boat drifted away in the distance, steered by a man dressed in bright yellow, gripping a single paddle.

Skybright pressed herself against the railing, peering over, delighted by the scene despite herself. Beautiful yet so *normal*. The waters below were a deep, clear green, and she caught the impressions of silver fish darting within its gentle ripples. It was midday; the sun was warm against her neck. She shrugged out of her coat. The oppressive heat of late summer seemed to have given way to the crisp coolness of spring. It smelled of new blooms— the faint scent of peach blossoms, the more pungent fragrance of wisteria. She knew she could rely on her serpentine senses, but the impression that the seasons had changed confused her.

"Are we in southern Xia?" she asked. "It feels and smells like springtime."

"That is because it is spring. I took the liberty of shifting us forward in time."

Skybright could only gape at him.

"I thought it would be nice to enjoy the weather here in Qing Chun," Stone said. "And to move temporally away from the Great Battle, put some distance—"

"You can do that?" She tried to speak without choking on her words. She didn't even understand what *temporally* meant, but she thought she got the gist. "Move us in time?" The notion was horrifying somehow. Paralyzing.

"I cannot veer far into the future. We've shifted a few months forward." He said it all so offhandedly, as if he were discussing the scenery.

"And the past?" she whispered.

He gave a shake of his head. "Never the past. Even I cannot go back."

She clutched the balustrade, carved, she saw, into a lion's head. Stone could move between time and distance and whittle away months as if it meant nothing. But then, Skybright supposed it really did mean nothing when you were immortal. She couldn't stop measuring time as people did—as she had done her entire life—in its steady cadences, marked by the faraway gongs from Kai Sen's monastery back on Tian Kuan Mountain, by festivals and observances. If it was truly spring already, then Zhen Ni would be turning seventeen years soon, as would Skybright. But what did birth dates matter now for her?

Suddenly, she was filled with such homesickness that her chest felt hollow. What were Zhen Ni and Kai Sen doing, two seasons into the future? Did they still think of her, or had they moved on with their lives?

"You are weak with hunger." Stone touched her sleeve briefly, and she noticed that her clothing had changed, become opulent enough to befit an imperial concubine. She now wore a silk dress in the subtlest blush of pink, the collar and sleeves banded in lavender. The silk was the softest she had ever touched and reflected a sheen in the sunlight. Delicate sprays of plum blossom were embroidered on the dress, and it hugged the curves of her body, revealing more than she was used to. The fur-lined coat magically disappeared from her hands.

Stone had changed his attire as well. Instead of his usual armor, he wore a tunic and trousers in a deep blue, decorated with silver geometric shapes along the collar and sleeves. Skybright had seen Zhen Ni's father, a wealthy merchant, dress in a similar fashion.

Stone's warrior topknot was loosened and pulled lower, as civilian men would wear it.

"This is the best teahouse in the province." Stone crossed the small bridge, and Skybright followed him into the cool interior of a two-story establishment.

The teahouse appeared to be filled almost to capacity, and they stood at the edge of the main floor. Dark columns supported the large building, and Skybright saw similar beams lining the ceiling. The banisters along the stairs and second floor balcony were carved elaborately, gilded in gold, conveying an understated opulence. Sunlight filtered through the space; bright and airy. The patrons seated at the square wooden tables were mostly men, and the few women who were present appeared to be consorts. They wore their hair unbound, something no respectable woman of virtue would do in public. Virtuous women, in fact, would have never been seen in such a place.

The roar of the patrons dimmed slowly, as one head turned, then another, to appraise Skybright and Stone near the entrance. The men considered Stone, disguised as a rich merchant, but none had the gall to let their eyes linger, much less hold Stone's gaze, as if they could somehow sense his power. But they were not so shy in examining Skybright. They stared blatantly, eyes roving from her face, then down her body before returning to her face once more. The drunk ones actually gawked at her.

She had never felt more on display. Self-consciously, she raised a hand to her cheek. "They are staring at my scar," Skybright whispered to Stone.

"They are staring because you are stunning."

"They think I am a consort."

"No. They wish you were a consort," he replied with a tinge of amusement.

A stout man, his fingers laden with gold and jade rings, hustled over and led them upstairs to a quiet corner table with a lovely view of the canal and glimpses of the rest of the famous town. A server immediately set a ceramic jug of rice wine and two cups before them.

"Bring us your most popular dishes," Stone said.

The young man nodded before rushing off without a word.

Stone poured into both cerulean cups and passed one to her. "Have you visited Qing Chun before?"

"I've heard of it." She took a cautious sip of the wine; it burned her throat yet seemed to steady her insides. "But I have never traveled so far south within the kingdom." Her gaze wandered above the slate blue tiles of the curved rooflines, catching peeks of peach trees in blossom and the sweeping leaves of weeping willows along the banks of the canal. "It is as beautiful as they say."

Stone smiled. She noticed he had not touched his wine.

The same server from before returned holding a round, lacquered tray. He placed a plate of chopped roast duck, a bowl of beef stew with carrots, and a platter of mushrooms and young bamboo before them. Then he set down a bamboo basket filled with steamed dumplings. Skybright plucked one out with her eating sticks, unable to resist. The filling was a mixture of shrimp, pork, and chives. She ate three more without speaking before taking another sip of rice wine. Her cheeks felt too warm, and she draped a hand outside the lattice window, enjoying the soft breeze that brushed against her palm.

Two rowboats floated along the canal beneath them. One man sang in a hearty voice a song Skybright wasn't familiar with, about the flow of the river giving life even as the days slipped by. He moved his oar to the rhythm of his song, and she listened, humming the refrain under her breath as he drifted around a bend and out of sight.

"You should eat some more." Stone's voice jarred Skybright from her reverie. He sat across from her, unmoving, and still unnervingly handsome. Stone had kissed her three times already but never in passion or desire. Each time she had literally been taken away from herself, stripped physically, as if flung into the heavens. It was unimaginable that she desired this remote immortal, so lacking in emotion and condescending to humans, ludicrous that he had somehow worked a sexual charm on her.

"Eat with me," she replied. "I feel strange eating alone."

Stone picked up his eating sticks, and she reached for two more dumplings before filling her plate with beef, mushrooms, and bamboo. The food was cooked and flavored as well as any dish served in the Yuan manor. She ate until she was satisfied, feeling the contentedness of a full stomach. Skybright couldn't remember the last time she had a nicely cooked hot meal—not since she left the Yuan manor in search of Zhen Ni so long ago, it seemed. All the meals she had eaten had been conjured by Stone before this. He had mostly kept her away from towns and other people until now.

They dined in silence, and she felt Stone's dark eyes studying her as the server came and removed their dishes, leaving them with a pot of tea and a platter of lychees. "What?" she finally asked, uncomfortable beneath his gaze.

"You make quite the vision of a lady."

"I wasn't born to be a lady."

"No," Stone said, and she heard the weighted emphasis behind that one word. "You are a serpent demon." He leaned an arm across the top of the carved redwood banister that displayed a scene of the Immortals in a heavenly garden in perfect detail. "Look at the patrons below."

She obeyed, filled with an unease that tasted sour at the back of her throat.

"What do you see?"

The teahouse had become even more crowded since they had entered. A few consorts had moved into the laps of their various patrons, and most of the men below were red-faced and becoming increasingly boisterous. All the tables were cluttered with half-empty dishes and multiple jugs of rice wine.

"Nothing out of the ordinary," she said.

"Look closer."

She opened her mouth to retort, but the seriousness of Stone's expression stopped her. Skybright narrowed her eyes and observed the faces of the patrons below: the drunk man in his fourth decade with a long beard, tapping an erratic beat against the table with his fan; the beautiful woman reclined on the lap of a man who looked like he could be her grandfather, his hand gripping her hip so tightly, her dress fabric creased. There was a profound sadness in the woman's eyes that contrasted harshly with her pretty features. Then something strange happened—a soft glow of light seemed to emanate from the woman's face, creating a fuzzy halo around her features.

Gasping, Skybright lurched away from the railing. "That woman, her face seemed to be unnaturally lit."

"Interesting." Stone paused, as if considering this. "And what else?"

Curious, she leaned over the railing again, concentrating on the faces she could see. Her gaze settled on a brooding man sitting at a table with others but silent as if he were all alone. The golden cap he wore had caught her attention. He couldn't have been more than thirty years, but a deep furrow already marked the place between his thick eyebrows. The man lifted his wine cup and tipped his head back, emptying its contents. He pounded a fist against the table, and a server scrambled up, filling his cup before dashing out of the way, as if afraid he'd get hit.

A bleary haze began to obscure the man's features, and Skybright could hear a distant buzzing in the back of her mind as she gazed at him. Frightened, she looked away, scanning the other patrons who appeared normal before she let her eyes rest on the man with the golden cap again. Now she could no longer make out his face; it appeared as if an angry swarm crackled over his countenance. The effect was aberrant and frightening, like some faceless monster sat among the other patrons in the body of a normal man. Then an image began to fill her mind: the brooding man staring in horror at a bloody knife he clutched in his hand as his victim writhed in agony at his feet, blood spilling from his abdomen onto the cobblestones.

Skybright shook violently until Stone gripped her wrist, releasing her from the vision. "You can see then," he said, "as your mother used to."

She snatched her hand away, her heartbeat thundering in her ears. With trembling fingers, she took her teacup and drank deep, welcoming the feeling of the hot liquid scalding her tongue. After she emptied the cup, she wiped her mouth with a handkerchief placed on the table—her upper lip damp with perspiration. "What is the meaning of this?" she demanded, her tone not as strong as she would have liked.

Stone refilled her cup before replying. "Your mother was able to see the true essence of people; gauge their sins. I was not certain if you had inherited this ability. It seemed unique to Opal. She used it to choose her victims."

Skybright began to feel lightheaded. "Do you mean that Opal was some sort of ... vigilante?"

"I never thought of it like that, but I suppose she was." Stone took in the raucous scene below them, his expression unreadable. "She killed men she thought deserved to be killed—bad men."

"But who is she to judge? She was not a god or a hell lord—"

"She seduced and killed, Skybright. The fact that she singled out the cruel men: murderers, thieves, and rapists, that was her own sport. I have told you she took much pleasure in it."

Skybright gazed downward again, unable to believe what she had seen. All the faces were blurred: some haloed dimly, some with a fiercer light from within. Then there were those men whose features were obscured, buzzing with dissonance. For some, she could still see their eyes, catch the tip of a nose, or an angular cheekbone, but other men's faces were completely clouded over, as the brooding man with the golden cap had been.

She shoved back from the banister, feeling as if she'd throw up all she had eaten. Stone seemed not to notice.

"I was hoping her gift was passed on to you," Stone said. "You can continue with Opal's legacy—be a judge of sinners and give punishment. You will select your first victim today."

"You want me to murder a man?" Skybright whispered.

Stone's emotionless expression was answer enough.

"No," she said, so loudly that the lone patron sitting near them gave her a sidelong glance. Ignoring him, she leaned toward Stone. "I will not do this."

"If you refuse to use your gift," Stone replied, "I will choose an innocent bystander instead." His dark gaze swept over the noisy crowd, settling on a quiet man sitting in the far corner—a young scholar by the looks of his simple robe.

Skybright saw that his face shone with light. But then the young man's eyes widened, and he clasped his throat, mouth opening and closing like a fish flung out of water. She jumped to her feet, gripping the railing.

Stone watched the young man with detached interest, as if observing a slow game of Go.

The man had scrambled to his own feet, eyes bulging with panic, his face gone white, both hands encircling his neck, as if he were strangling himself as he struggled to take a breath. Two other patrons sitting near him had risen, gaping at the helpless man in alarm.

"It seems such a foolish way to die, does it not?" Stone asked. "Choking on a piece of meat."

The young man crashed into a table, knocking plates and cups to the floor in a loud clatter. Patrons shouted in alarm. A large man with a thick beard slapped the scholar on his back, trying to dislodge the food from his throat. But it didn't help. Skybright could see the light in the young man's face slowly dimming, like a flickering candle at wick's end.

"Stop." She lunged across the table and grabbed Stone's arm—the first time she had ever willingly touched him. "You've made your point."

"We are agreed then?" he asked.

"Yes," she said. "I will choose."

Another thwack brought something large and dark from the young scholar's mouth, and he collapsed against a table, chest heaving as he gulped down air. The teahouse owner ran up, then helped the man onto a stool pushed to the wall. A few patrons banged on the tables with their fists in approval, then returned to their food and drink.

"Good," Stone replied, his mouth curving into the ghost of a smile. "Who will it be then?"

CHAPTER THREE

Kai Sen

The night was so deep that it was impossible to see in the forest. Kai Sen relied on his senses as he trod carefully between the trees and walked for a fair time before stopping somewhere within its depths. He cocked his head and listened to the night noises that surrounded him: the soft rustle of leaves, the steady hum and chirping of insects, and the stirring of nocturnal animals.

Kai Sen cupped his hands and looked down, but his vision remained black, too dark to discern anything. He chanted the spell Abbot Wu had taught him and opened his senses to the night. The elements enveloping him felt eternal—endless—twining tight around his own spirit and unraveling into the stars, then reaching down again as deep as the world's core. Sifting in his mind's eye, he tugged at the intense fire element, bypassing the wavering water strands and the solidity of earth, which tasted like grit against his tongue when he called its magic. The wood element was overpowering here, supple and surprisingly light, as it commanded the air and wind and sound as well. He tasted a sharp tang every time he touched metal magic but focused on pulling threads of fire to him. The slickness of hellfire settled into his curved palms.

Gazing at the tiny blue flame, Kai Sen smiled and willed it to grow. It vibrated as it did so, like a living thing, until it was as large as an apple. He was in a part of the ancient cypress forest that was familiar to him, less than half a league from the creek that wound its way down Tian Kuan Mountain. That creek always brought to mind Skybright, and his chest felt weighted, remembering the handmaid, the girl serpent demon he had fallen in love with, whom he hadn't seen or sensed in over six months since she had been taken hostage by Stone.

The fireball guttered, then dimmed, and Kai Sen focused again, weaving the intense energy around it tightly, relinquishing the memories of the brown-eyed girl who sang so beautifully, who smelled of the forest so he could never enter it without always being reminded of her. The hellfire was as large as a pumpkin now, barely contained in his hands, when he heard a familiar shuffle, and all the hairs on his arms stood on end. An undead creature emerged between the trees, jumping toward Kai Sen, its arms held stiff in front. It was an old corpse, its face long rotted away, and its funeral clothes faded and tattered.

Kai Sen cursed. He had left the monastery with no weapon except for the dagger at his waist, not wanting to be encumbered during his nightly wanderings. The undead thing hopped a few more steps, closing the distance between them as another crashed through from behind it. This creature was a fresher corpse, bloated with greenish skin pulled tight around its decomposed face. Kai Sen almost gagged, but the reflex fled when five more undead appeared. Seven now. How many were hidden in the depths of night?

He backed away even as he raised his arms, speaking a spell that Abbot Wu had never taught him, but he had studied secretly on his own. He'd practiced on boulders and dead tree trunks until now. His voice deepened as he said the last archaic words and thrust his arms out at the closest undead creature. A wall of blue flames shot forth from between his curved palms, igniting the corpse. The fire didn't feel hot to his touch but like liquid, something more malleable than water. Kai Sen willed his arms steady and began chanting the spell anew, tugging hard on the fire threads around him. They seared his core, wound around his heart and lungs, binding him tightly before he flung them forward again, blasting five more undead with hellfire.

The last undead creature continued to jump his way, intent on turning its prey. One bite or scratch and Kai Sen would become a living corpse as well. He unsheathed his dagger, wanting the danger of closeness, the thrill of thrusting his blade. There was no other noise now within the forest except for the crackling blue flames that wreathed the six undead as they shambled in their last death throes, illuminating the scene as bright as midday, and the heavy-footed thumping of the last remaining corpse. It had been a large man in life, its dark blue tunic in rags now, revealing the fetid body beneath.

Kai Sen knew little fear after fighting hell's creatures for weeks when the underworld had opened into theirs; days and nights had melded into each other in an endless nightmare. He had trained every day relentlessly after his return to the monastery in an attempt to forget those horrifying weeks. Forget the final confrontation that had resulted in losing Skybright forever. Rage and anger had helped to ease the loss, to help erase the horror.

He gripped his dagger tighter as he leaned down to seize a large branch from the forest floor, his eyes never leaving the undead creature. The other six had long since crumpled to the ground, filling the forest with the harsh stench of burned clothes and hair. When the last corpse was near enough, Kai Sen stabbed the long branch into the corpse's throat, and it halted, skewered like a beetle, yet it still fought to stagger toward him, scrabbling its skeletal fingers in the air. It was strong, but so was Kai Sen. He had the advantage of training and muscle, and this thing was mere rotten flesh.

Forcing the thick branch even deeper, he shoved the corpse back until with a final thrust, the thing toppled onto its back.

He was on the creature before it could rise again, stomping on its extended arms with furious kicks, breaking them, before driving the branch into the earth and pinning the corpse. It struggled still, thudding its feet as Kai Sen crouched above it, one hand clutching the branch tight as he hacked at its neck with his dagger. It was exhausting and gruesome work, but the undead could only be killed with fire or decapitation. He needed to train and fight in every capacity, by magic or weapon or with his own hands. As a warrior, he knew it was crucial to his survival.

He would never leave the monastery again without his saber, Kai Sen vowed.

His senses filled with the decay and must of the corpse, its head finally detached even as its legs continued to jerk for some time after. Kai Sen stood and kicked the head away, watching as it rolled into the other undead, now not much more than ashes. The hellfire flickered low, a ghostly blue, clinging to the last remnants of flesh and bone. He retreated from the forest, feeling a rush from the battle, but not foolish enough to linger there.

How were undead still roaming these forests? They could only be summoned from the earth by demons, and the breach to the underworld had closed more than half a year ago. Hadn't it?

If you were to believe that immortal, Stone.

Kai Sen touched his throat for a brief moment, where his birthmark had been, wiped away by the arrogant god. He trusted Stone as much as he trusted a nest of starving rats. He ran past the rushing creek, weaving his way back toward the monastery, letting the wind blow away the cloying, rotten fetor of the undead.

He'd get to the truth of this.

Zhen Ni
Five days later.

Rose had doused the lantern more than an hour ago, yet Zhen Ni lay in her massive bed, staring into the dark. Insomnia was a constant bedmate now, plaguing her since she had returned home from seeing Lan. They had exchanged a few letters, unknown to her mother. Zhen Ni had used her own coin to bribe a handmaid who could find someone to carry them. But in the last letter, Lan had explained that she had married, to the second son of a cobbler not far from her hometown of Hong Yu. *Perhaps it is better that we stop corresponding*, Lan had written. Some of the simple characters in the women's language had blotted on the page, where Lan's tears had fallen.

Zhen Ni never replied.

Soon, it would be her turn to wed—in three day's time.

She shifted onto her side and drew her knees into her chest, holding herself. The fountain outside pattered softly, a soothing sound; it had been a gift from her father. Zhen Ni had never felt so alone in these last months, surrounded by dozens of servants and tended to by several handmaids each day. Within the span of a few days last summer, she had lost her first love and Skybright, who had been her companion and friend her entire life, her sister. Six months had passed, and already, Zhen Ni was finding it hard to picture Skybright's face in her mind.

How faulty human memory was. How fickle!

She had asked her mother to have a portrait commissioned of Skybright, so she would never forget how she looked, and Lady Yuan had refused, saying that it would merely draw out Zhen Ni's melancholy. She did it anyway behind her mother's back and had a small portrait painted of Lan as well. She kept both in a drawer by her bed and pulled them out to study before sleeping each night. The artist had captured Skybright's eyes perfectly but not the shape of her mouth. Zhen Ni hadn't asked the artist to include the long scar that ran down the left side of Skybright's face. That was the other Skybright, the one she didn't truly know. The one who had lied to her.

A soft scrape came from outside her bedchamber.

Zhen Ni sat up noiselessly and held her breath. The panel of her reception hall was being pushed aside, slowly, the sound too surreptitious to be a handmaid or her mother. Besides, no one ever visited her so late at night. In one swift motion, she grasped the dagger she always kept now beneath her cushion. Rolling off the platform bed, she bounded in a few steps to crouch in the corner of her dark bedchamber.

Someone opened the panel of her room quietly. "Zhen Ni?" a male voice whispered.

She smothered a scream. No man had ever been within her bedchamber, except for the doctor on rare occasions, and even then, she had been hidden behind silk drapes on her bed, offering her arm so the man could examine her pulse. No common man had ever been allowed within the inner quarters, unchaperoned much less, and in the dead of night. Blood pounded in her ears, and Zhen Ni gripped her dagger tighter, prepared to use it if she had to.

"It's me. Kai Sen."

Recognition dawned. She had thought the voice sounded familiar, but she hadn't seen Kai Sen since they parted ways over half a year ago, after he had escorted her home from visiting Lan one last time. What in the goddess's name was he doing here, breaking all rules of decorum? Her reputation could be compromised if he were caught.

Zhen Ni smiled in the dark then. It was a wonder anyone would take her as a wife at all. She was notoriously known as a stubborn runaway and truly didn't give a donkey's ass about decorum now, but she had behaved perfectly to please her parents since returning home. She held still in her dark corner, waiting to see what Kai Sen would do.

A bright flame ignited within the bedchamber. She squinted,

thinking he had lit a lantern, but it appeared as if he cradled a ball of blue fire in his very palm. Astounded, Zhen Ni stared as Kai Sen drew to her empty bedside, peering down at the rumpled coverlet, then turned to survey the room.

Dressed in a black sleeveless tunic, he seemed taller than she remembered and definitely bigger. Kai Sen had been all wiry muscle when they had traveled together but thin, still boyish in some ways. His time in the monastery since had filled his frame, as if he'd finally grown into his adult physique. He had looked strong before; now he looked *powerful*. She watched while the flickering flame danced across his face. Kai Sen's dark eyebrows were knitted together as his alert eyes swept the large bedchamber. Zhen Ni could see why Skybright had been drawn to him—he was handsome. He exuded masculinity. Assuming a girl appreciated that sort of thing: rough hands and deep voice, the odd metallic tang of sweat. She knew from their travels together that he even *smelled* different.

Zhen Ni wasn't attracted to these things.

For a brief moment, she remembered the soft curve of Lan's neck bent over her embroidery, smelled the rose perfume she used to dab at the hollow of Lan's throat, the scent sweet and mellow when she would kiss the same spot hours later ... Zhen Ni blinked the memories away and whispered, "What are you doing here?"

The sole indication of Kai Sen's surprise was the waver in the blue flame within his hand. It dimmed for an instant, then flared, brighter than before. He lifted his arm and saw her crouched in her hiding place. Zhen Ni straightened, holding the dagger in front of her; its long blade gleamed, even in the dim chamber.

"You sleep with a knife now?" he asked, sounding amused.

"And you break into young women's bedchambers in the middle of the night?" she countered.

Kai Sen laughed softly, and for the first time, truly appeared like the young man she remembered. "I apologize. But I could think of no other way to speak with you directly."

Zhen Ni set the dagger down and pulled on a silk robe before picking up the weapon again and returning to her bed. She slipped the knife under her cushion once more. Kai Sen retreated and stood back at a respectable distance. They scrutinized each other for a long moment before she asked, "What is that?" Zhen Ni nodded at the ball of fire glowing in his hand.

"I think it would be simplest to call it magic," Kai Sen replied.

"You are a conjurer now? I'm impressed." Zhen Ni smoothed her embroidered robe. "I would say that I didn't think such a thing possible, calling fire from thin air, but then I had never believed in demons or the undead until recently either."

Kai Sen's features hardened. He lifted the top from the glass lantern beside her bed and dropped the round flame within it. "Yes, I've been studying under Abbot Wu since returning to the monastery. There is much that most people don't know exists within our world—it makes for easier living."

She believed him after all that she'd been through. "You wanted to talk?"

"Actually, I was supposed to come and kill you." There was no humor in his voice.

"What?" Zhen Ni slid her hand closer to her dagger. She could never believe that of Kai Sen, but the world had gone mad before her very eyes a few months back. And how well did she truly know him?

He gave a slight shake of his head, his dark eyes missing nothing. "Don't," he said. "Of course I wouldn't."

"Sit down." She swallowed. "You're making me nervous towering over me like that. Explain yourself!"

Kai Sen pulled a stool closer to the bed and ran a hand through his black hair, cropped close now to his ears but still not shorn like the other monks. "It was the first thing Abbot Wu said to me when I returned. 'That Mistress Yuan needs to be silenced.' Only the heir to the covenant is supposed to witness what takes place when the breach is closed. You're a loose end."

"I see." She let out a small breath. Instead of becoming the chosen sacrifice, Skybright had given up her mortal life to save Zhen Ni's. And yet, Zhen Ni still couldn't find it in her heart to forgive her friend.

"It was what decided it for me." Kai Sen clasped his hands in front of him, bowing his head. He looked too large for the carved stool. "I had no intention of accepting the role as Abbot Wu's heir—but it became clear to me that he needed to be stopped. That this twisted covenant had to end. So I agreed to be his successor."

"With the secret purpose of overturning the covenant? Of going against the gods?" she asked, incredulous.

"Well, when you put it like that." The corners of his mouth quirked. "Don't make it sound so hopeless."

She stared at him. "You're dreaming."

He stretched his arms overhead, reminding her of a lithe panther, clothed as he was in black. "I had to say yes or both of us would be dead now, Zhen Ni. And some other chosen fool would have taken my place."

"So you convinced the abbot not to murder me somehow?"

"I said you would keep your mouth shut. It appeased him for some time, but he brought it up again this week. The need to be rid of you. I convinced him I'd work a memory spell on you instead. So here I am tonight, supposedly making you forget everything."

"This conversation isn't improving. Perhaps I should have stabbed you in the dark when I had the chance."

Kai Sen gave a low chuckle. "Of course I wasn't really going to take your memories." His expression softened. "It'd be wrong, but you're the one person who cared for Skybright as much as I did. The only one who was as close to her."

She observed him as he stared at his feet, hands clasped so tight the knuckles were white. The faint scent of sandalwood incense lingered in his clothes, and she wondered if he had been praying earlier in the evening before this visit.

"I miss her," he said and raised his head. "Don't you?"

Zhen Ni sighed. "Of course I do. But she knew what she was doing when she agreed to save us, Kai Sen. We have to make peace with the fact that we will never see her again. Besides—"

She stopped when she saw his eyes narrow.

"Besides what?" he asked in a gruff voice.

"She's a *demon*. She isn't the same girl we knew."

Kai Sen leaped off the stool and began pacing in front of her, his frustration barely contained. She noticed that the ball of fire trapped in the lantern had grown, touched at its core now in a bright, pale white. It filled the glass lantern, tremoring, as if it wanted to escape its confines.

"She gave up everything she knew and loved to save us, and you would judge her so harshly?"

A twinge of guilt threaded through Zhen Ni's chest. "It isn't that I no longer love her. I simply don't know if I know her anymore. She's not *my* Skybright. My Skybright would never have lied to me so well and for so long."

Kai Sen finally paused before her, and she noticed the saber, curved and lethal, strapped to his waist for the first time. "I think I'm close to finding her," he said.

"What?"

"Abbot Wu was reluctant to teach me how to create portals—they allow you to travel anywhere within our world—but I learned on my own. I can sense Skybright's presence when she's near, and I've been using the portals to travel through the provinces looking for her."

"All twenty-three provinces, Kai Sen?"

He shifted on his feet, saying nothing, looking as if he were ready to make a portal right then and leap through it.

"The Kingdom of Xia is massive!" she exclaimed.

"Not extensive enough to deter me." He smiled. "I couldn't sense her anywhere in all this time I had searched. It was as if she had disappeared from our earthly realm. But today, I felt the faintest trace of her presence in the south."

Zhen Ni shook her head. His devotion to Skybright was obvious. "But aren't you going against the agreement? Skybright isn't ours to track down—"

"That bastard Stone lied. The breach isn't fully closed." Kai Sen fingered the silver hilt of his saber, shoulders set in a tense line. "I was attacked by the undead five nights ago, and both demon and undead sightings have been reported since then. Nothing like what we were battling last year—but I've warned Abbot Wu."

"Goddess," she whispered, then shivered, remembering the undead creature that Skybright had so bravely killed with a cleaver. Recalling again being abducted by that monstrous bull demon, its rough hands clutching her thighs as she dangled over its shoulder; feeling once more the coarse hair of its skin stabbing into her own flesh.

"So the agreement is off as far as I'm concerned. I can rescue Skybright and find a way to break this covenant once and for all."

"I'm coming with you," Zhen Ni said.

"No. It's too dangerous."

"Does anyone else know about your plans?"

His eyes narrowed a touch. "No one else can know. Abbot Wu doesn't even realize that I can successfully create portals."

"Well, if you don't let me accompany you, I shall tell on you."

Kai Sen's mouth dropped. "You wouldn't."

"I would. I could go to the monastery this very moment and knock on that grand door." She lifted her chin. "It's my right to see her again too."

He flexed his fingers into tight fists. "You're the only one I can trust in this, Zhen Ni. The only one who can know. Please don't put yourself in danger—"

"I'm to wed, Kai Sen."

His dark eyes widened, then he cursed. "When?"

"In three days." She twisted her face away and blinked back her tears. "This might be my last chance to see her. Even if Skybright returned with you, my mother would never allow her again to be my handmaid. As far as she knows, Skybright has abandoned our family."

He touched her sleeve, and she forced herself to meet his eyes. His handsome features had softened. "We'll do this soon then," he said. "I know I'm close. I can feel it."

And as mad as he sounded and as far-fetched his plan seemed,

Zhen Ni had to go with him. The thought of seeing Skybright again, to be able to speak with her, eased the weight she had carried in her chest all these months. The confusion and betrayal she had felt over Skybright keeping the secret of her true self from Zhen Ni was nothing compared to how much she'd missed her every day.

"I'll come for you as soon as I'm certain," Kai Sen said. The blue flame grew brighter in the glass lantern by her bedside.

"I will wait for you," she replied. "I'll be ready." And on impulse, she offered her hand; Kai Sen clasped it as if they were sealing an oath.

Kai Sen returned two days later in the early afternoon, scaring Zhen Ni half to death when he tapped softly on her lattice window. All her handmaids were in the adjacent reception hall, preparing the multiple trunks she would take with her to the Bei manor as a new bride. Zhen Ni lifted a hand, indicating that he should wait for her, and he disappeared from view like a ghost.

She sent all her handmaids away, asking them to leave her alone for the rest of the day and used the stresses of the impending wedding as an excuse. It was the perfect ruse to gain some precious privacy—almost impossible to have when she had servants tending to her every need from sunrise until bedtime.

She made herself even more sharp-tongued than usual, so that they left her alone gladly. Zhen Ni smiled at herself in the bronzed mirror, looking like the neighbor's dog that had made off with a stolen sausage. She'd been a good daughter ever since she'd returned home, following all the rules of decorum, even agreeing to marry some wealthy man she had never laid eyes on. She could allow herself this—one last escapade to see Skybright again.

And if Kai Sen did manage to save Skybright from that horrible man called Stone, would Zhen Ni be able to continue to have a relationship with Skybright? Would she come with Zhen Ni to serve her in her new husband's manor—despite her mother's objections? Zhen Ni gave a sharp shake of her head to dispel such notions. How could they ever return to how things used to be?

A soft *tap* at the reception hall door leading into the courtyard broke Zhen Ni from her reverie.

"Enter," she said softly.

Kai Sen slid the panel open and peered inside, before coming in and closing the door behind him. "I saw everyone clear out like a fire had been lit under their feet."

She chortled. "I can make myself very disagreeable."

"I believe you," Kai Sen said, grinning. "I don't think I've ever seen you wearing trousers before."

"I stole them from one of the taller handmaids. She'll get a nice pouch of coins at the end of the week." She tugged at the waist of her pale peach trousers nervously, then touched the dagger she had strapped to her side. The feel of its elaborately carved hilt calmed her. "You don't look as menacing in the daylight," she said.

Kai Sen laughed. "I didn't think it would be wise to be dressed entirely in black while skulking around town in bright sunshine." His hand grazed the hilt of his saber too, as if for reassurance.

"Am I to assume from your good humor that you've found Skybright?" she asked.

His dark eyes became serious. "Yes. Her presence had seemed faded all these months. But today I felt it like a kick in the chest." He touched a hand to his solar plexus. "She's in Qing Chun. But we have to hurry. Stone has the ability to travel through portals too, and I have no inkling how long Skybright will stay put."

Zhen Ni nodded, feeling solemn. They were going to do this. Try and save Skybright. But how could Kai Sen ever best an immortal who could draw snow from thin air and call lightning to strike down on them? "Do you have a plan?"

"The plan is to bring Skybright home safe," Kai Sen said with more confidence than she felt. "Stone has broken his agreement in closing the breach to hell. He no longer has a hold over her."

"You hope to reason with an immortal?"

He gripped his saber's hilt once more—a weapon that would be of no use to him were he to face Stone in a fight. "I can summon hellfire against him. It can kill any creature from the underworld."

"You think Stone is from the underworld?" She didn't know much about the immortal, but she knew he was powerful, cold, and inhumanly handsome. One glance at Kai Sen and she realized he knew as little about Stone as she did.

No true plan then. Zhen Ni should never have asked.

They slipped out the side servant entrance near her quarters and ran toward the forest, Kai Sen having to slow his long-legged lope so she could keep up. Zhen Ni was grateful she wore trousers, even if the feel of the fabric against her legs as she ran was odd.

Kai Sen halted in a small clearing. She and Skybright used to sneak out and explore these same grounds when they were together, but ever since Skybright had gone, Zhen Ni had chosen not to step within these trees again. Her short forays were into town to buy sweets, a new trinket, or favorite fruit in season, always chaperoned by Rose and Oriole, and always at the prodding of her mother.

When they went, they were trailed by a muscular guard from the manor as well. Her mother believed that she didn't know, but Zhen Ni did and said nothing.

Kai Sen was pacing in front of her, more nervous than she had ever seen him.

"I've never brought another person through the portal with me," he said. "But I know it works from Abbot Wu's books and teachings. Be sure to keep hold of my hand the entire time."

He cleared his throat and began chanting an intonation under his breath. Zhen Ni's mouth went dry, realizing they were truly going to try and travel to a town leagues away from Tian Kuan Mountain through some magical rent in the air. She had traveled through a portal when she had been kidnapped by a bull demon but remembered nothing of the experience, as she had been so terrified.

Kai Sen swept his arm in a half arc, and the air before them appeared to split. Zhen Ni caught a glimpse of water with the light green leaves of weeping willow hanging over it. "Don't let go." He extended a hand, and Zhen Ni grasped it. Kai Sen grinned and winked at her in reassurance, but it didn't ease her sudden panic.

"I'm afraid," she whispered.

"Don't be." He squeezed her palm. "I've done this many times before. It's quick, and no harm will befall you. I promise."

Zhen Ni nodded. "For Skybright."

"For Skybright," Kai Sen repeated and led her through the portal.

They emerged on a narrow path along the canal, shadowed by the eaves of the building beside them. An acrid odor of burned hair and sulfur suffused the air, and Zhen Ni wrinkled her nose at the unpleasant scent. Kai Sen released her hand and scanned her quickly. "You're all right." It was more a statement than a question. The relief was plain on his face.

"It was quick, as you said. But strange." She rubbed her arms. "It felt as if I had ants crawling on my skin."

"You get used to it. And as long as you are in contact with the person who created the portal, you can travel through unharmed." He let out a quick breath, then lifted his chin. "Skybright is still here in Qing Chun. She had spent some time in there."

Zhen Ni followed his gaze to the magnificent teahouse perched on the opposite side of the canal. A rowboat had docked near its entrance, and two men stepped from the rocking boat and entered the establishment for a late midday meal. The sounds of patrons enjoying their food and wine within drifted to her through the gilded lattice windows.

"Follow me," Kai Sen murmured.

They walked along the cobbled path edging the canal, passing other restaurants and teahouses doing brisk business. The enticing scent of steamed buns, roasted chicken, and grilled sausages wafted to them from the establishments, and Zhen Ni's mouth watered, even though she had already taken a meal before Kai Sen arrived. A low stone balustrade wound its way along the canal. Many restaurants built an extension out onto the waterway, setting tables and stools there so the diners could enjoy their meals and wine right on the water.

It was a lovely, picturesque town, and Zhen Ni was struck with missing Lan, an ache that made it hurt to breathe. She followed Kai Sen's straight back. His gait was long and loose, but his fists were clenched. He stopped at the corner of an alleyway and peered into its shadows. Drawing back, he said in a low voice, "Skybright is down this alley somewhere. Stay near me, but don't do anything. Let me see what's going on first."

Zhen Ni's eyes widened, and she nodded. It felt like a diversion almost. Similar to many treasure hunts and hide-and-seek games Skybright and she had played. But now Skybright's life was at stake.

Kai Sen turned the corner and crept with stealth down the shadowed alley. She slipped in behind, mimicking him, and pressed herself close to the wall. The passage was dank and cold, and she could hear the slow drip of water pinging somewhere in the distance. It was as if they had stepped through another portal to a different place, the contrast was so great. The delicious smells of food had been replaced by damp and mildew. Her cloth slipper slid on slick stone, and she thrust a hand out and grabbed Kai Sen's arm to steady herself, muffling a cry of alarm. He half turned to gauge her, eyes hooded in the gloom, and she realized how used to this he was—sneaking around in the dark like some kind of assassin.

They had walked far enough down the narrow alley that the din of the restaurants and people along the canal had quieted to a distant hum before he paused again. Another passage veered to their right and she thought she caught low voices. Kai Sen glanced around the corner before leaning back, almost bumping her nose. Even as he pressed a finger to his lips and mouthed "Skybright," Zhen Ni heard rising tones reverberating against the stone walls. She recognized Skybright's voice as if it were her own. The other voice was a man's, deep and rough, and it was becoming louder, more passionate.

Zhen Ni kneeled onto the cold stones, wedging herself beneath Kai Sen, and looked around the corner as well. Kai Sen made a low hissing noise but did not push her back. The next alley was better lit, being surrounded by lower buildings, but dead-ended beyond where Skybright stood with a man Zhen Ni had never seen before. The stranger was broad and wore a gold cap. He towered over Skybright's petite frame, gripping her by the wrist, and she was speaking to him in a hushed tone.

Her scalp crawled at the sight. What was this? A lovers' tryst or was Skybright in danger? Her handmaid would never be the type to meet strange men in deserted alleys. But Skybright was no longer her handmaid, was she? Zhen Ni rose a fraction on her knees and felt Kai Sen clasp her firmly on the shoulder. She looked up, and he gave a slight shake of his head, warning with his eyes for her to stay put.

The man wrapped his arms around Skybright, trapping her against him. He leaned in, trying to force a kiss. Skybright didn't struggle, but neither did she allow their lips to meet, so that the man's mouth planted on her cheek, then her forehead instead. Zhen Ni felt Kai Sen stiffen, then almost jerk forward before pulling himself back against the wall, for the man's laughter had turned into a scream.

Instead of the exquisite dress Skybright had had on, she was now completely bare, a serpent coil winding its way around the man's legs and up his torso. Skybright had risen higher using her serpent length so that she towered over him now. Zhen Ni trembled violently; it was so horrifying to watch. Every instinct within her shouted for her to run. The alley was so narrow that Skybright's monstrous coils scraped against the stone walls, undulating, making a smooth rasping sound.

The man's eyes bulged in his purple face. Skybright's forked tongue darted out as if to taste him.

Kai Sen's fingertips dug into Zhen Ni's shoulder, but she welcomed the touch because it kept her still. The man's wretched screaming never relented, filled with a raw terror that made her stomach cramp. It reverberated down the narrow passage toward them.

"Aren't you going to stop her?" Zhen Ni asked, knowing she couldn't be heard by anyone but Kai Sen.

"I sense someone else near—Stone."

"She'll kill the man!" she said in a loud whisper.

"No. And if so, only in self-defense."

"Or perhaps she lured him out here. I know you love her, but she is a serpent demon, Kai—"

Zhen Ni broke off mid-sentence at the sound of retching. It was eerily quiet now that the man had stopped screaming. He lay motionless on the cobblestones, dead. Murdered.

Skybright was on her hands and knees, naked and returned to human form, head bowed as she continued to throw up the contents of her stomach. She looked small now, frail compared to the monstrosity she was mere moments before. Zhen Ni stared at Skybright's curves, her full breasts, the soft roundness of her hips, with a detached sense of fascination mingled with revulsion.

The immortal called Stone appeared from nowhere, his back to them, standing over the dead man. He made no move to help Skybright, and she did not acknowledge his presence. "Well done," Stone said in that rich voice Zhen Ni would never forget even though she had only met him once.

Kai Sen spoke beneath his breath, and a flicker of flame shot forth like a blue star and hit Stone on the back of his neck. The immortal, speaking intently to Skybright, didn't react.

Feeling hopeless and sick to her own stomach, Zhen Ni wrenched herself away from Kai Sen's grip on her shoulder, stumbling noiselessly backward onto her rump, before rising and running down the dark alley back toward the canal. She couldn't bear to watch anymore, to have to acknowledge Skybright as a murderous demon, the seductress that the old wives' tales warned everyone about. She couldn't stand to witness more between Skybright and Stone—to see them talk and behave completely unlike ordinary people.

Her lungs burned by the time she reached the canal and emerged back into the daylight. The sun felt so good on her skin. She ignored the curious glances cast her way and leaned against the stone railing, peering down into the swirling water. Zhen Ni knew she must have looked like some runaway handmaid, but she didn't care. Kai Sen was beside her after a few moments, not even out of breath.

"She's not the same girl we knew, Kai Sen." She swept at the tears on her cheeks in an angry motion. "I know you love her. I love her too, but you can't be so foolish to be blind to what we saw. How can we know how many other men she's killed?"

"No. This was the first time, I'm certain—"

"How can you be certain?"

"She was upset after." Kai Sen's jaw flexed. "You saw. She didn't enjoy it."

"What does it matter if she enjoys it?" she cried out. "She's still a murderer!"

An old woman carrying a basket of eggplants paused mid-shamble and stared at them. Zhen Ni glared at her until she moved on, too riled to be polite, and twisted back toward the water. "I'm not convinced Skybright wants to be saved," she said in a low voice.

Kai Sen made a strangled noise beside her. "You would give up on her so easily?"

"I don't know." Zhen Ni's shoulders sagged.

"Have you considered that you might be resentful, that she's not yours to command any longer?"

"I love Skybright not because I could command her!" she exclaimed, feeling her face grow hot from anger.

"But she catered to you your entire life," Kai Sen said in a quiet voice. "You *were* her mistress, even if you loved each other like sisters. She was always *your* Skybright. And now ..."

Zhen Ni felt the tears gathering behind her eyes. Kai Sen was right. No matter what, her relationship with Skybright had always been defined by their status in society. Now nothing defined them. Everything was now unknown, uncomfortable. Unfathomable. Zhen Ni had believed she'd never see her again. "I don't know how to help her," she finally said. "I am to wed tomorrow. I have no control over my own life. How can I hope to help Skybright regain hers?"

He let out a long breath. "Would you like to sit and take tea somewhere?"

"What about saving Skybright?"

"You were right. I need a plan. Stone is powerful, and I have to think of a way to get Skybright away from him long enough so we can rescue her. I can't assume a god will keep his word."

"Your hellfire had no effect on him."

Zhen Ni could almost feel Kai Sen's shoulders sag.

"No," he said. "Whatever Stone is, he is not of the underworld."

They began walking along the canal, and Zhen Ni took deep, slow breaths to try and calm her nerves. Peach blossoms were in full bloom, and the branches were laden with them. The trees dotted the canal path, many seeming to lean over the water, as if gazing into it. The sight of the familiar burst of delicate pink blossoms soothed her. Spring had always been her favorite season, and Qing Chun truly was a charming town.

They were silent for a long time, each lost in thought. She had spent a short amount of time with Kai Sen but enough to see that he was impulsive and a dreamer. Was his judgment clouded because of his feelings for Skybright? Zhen Ni watched the green waters of the canal swirl past, remembering her friend—the one who had taken her place for a severe beating from her mother, Lady Yuan; the one who had snuck away from the manor to find her when Zhen Ni had run away ... the one who had given up her mortal life so Zhen Ni could keep her own.

Kai Sen was right; there was little certainty in this world they lived in, but Zhen Ni was certain of Skybright's goodness, was certain of the kinship and love they shared all their lives. This epiphany, the surety of it, brought tears to her eyes. She lifted her face, feeling the warmth of sunlight on her cheeks, and blinked the tears away.

But it had been over half a year since she last saw her friend. Could Skybright have changed and given in to her demonic side? Had she turned into someone Zhen Ni didn't know any longer?

Finally, Kai Sen led her into a small teahouse, empty except for one other patron. The proprietor nodded at them, indicating they could sit wherever they pleased. Zhen Ni chose a table overlooking the water. "What if they see us?" she finally asked, not having to refer to whom.

Kai Sen shook his head. He looked weary, his dark brows drawn together into a line. Seeing Skybright again had affected him as well. "I felt her presence fade. They've left the town already through a portal."

"We've lost her again then."

The server, a girl no older than Zhen Ni's sixteen years, set down a pot, two cups, and a small plate of peanuts and red bean rice cakes. She poured the tea for them and left. The fragrant scent of jasmine tea filled the air.

"I know I will find her again. And next time, I'll be better prepared. It's just—" His voice hitched, and he took a long sip of tea, wincing at how hot it was. "I wasn't ready," he repeated. He scrubbed a hand through his hair before pounding a fist onto the table, causing the plates to clatter.

"You don't just mean ready with a plan." Zhen Ni swallowed. "It was easier for me to believe she was dead. This—It was hard for you to see her again too."

"I was so excited by the prospect of actually finding her after all these months, I didn't think." He gave a sad smile. "I've always been too spontaneous."

She took a small sip of tea and nibbled on a rice cake, savoring its subtle sweetness. "Skybright has always been the very opposite of spontaneous. Unless she had to save me from trouble. Then she was a quick thinker and acted fast."

Kai Sen laughed. A soft but genuine one.

"This ability you have to sense her, is it magic as well? Like the fireball you conjured in your palm? Can you track anyone?"

"No. It was faint at first but has since grown much stronger. I felt it before I ever began studying magic under Abbot Wu."

"Then how?"

He lifted his head. "I think ... I think it's because I love her."

She recognized the yearning in his eyes. She'd seen it too many times in the sallow-skinned girl reflected back within the bronzed mirror after visiting Lan for the last time. And just as she couldn't hold that girl's gaze in the reflection, she couldn't acknowledge the pain she saw in his.

The feelings were too close again. Too raw.

Zhen Ni simply nodded.

It would have to be enough.

CHAPTER FOUR

Skybright

Skybright began to wipe her mouth with the back of her hand, but Stone crouched in one blurred motion and gave her a damp handkerchief, scented with mint. She snatched it from him without a thank-you. The smell of the mint helped to settle her a little. He offered her a hand but she refused to take it, instead pushing herself unsteadily off the cold cobblestones.

"I will never do that again," she choked out. "I don't care how much you threaten to harm others if I don't obey. If you take such pleasure in killing mortals, do as you please."

"But Opal—"

"How many times do I have to tell you I'm not my mother?" She put on the soft tunic that he gave her, hating that she couldn't even choose her own clothing. Stone dressed her as if she were an expensive doll. "Why are you so thickheaded?" she snapped as she pulled on the silk paneled dress. He seemed to be able to alter her attire if she were already clothed but could not simply manifest clothes onto her body if she were naked. For that simple thing, she was grateful. If she chose to, she could remain nude—a ridiculous

58

notion—but it offered a sense of control, no matter how slim.

"He is not dead."

"What?" Skybright whipped toward the inert man at their feet. She had been so sickened and horrified by what she had done, her keen senses hadn't registered that the man was still breathing.

Stone nudged her victim with his boot. "So badly frightened that he fainted. Lack of air from the powerful squeeze of your serpent coils helped, but you did not hold on long enough to kill him."

The man twitched even as Stone was speaking, and she almost fell onto her knees in the narrow alley again from relief.

"You know he does not deserve to live, Skybright. What sins did you see weighing on his soul?"

Murder. Theft. Envy. He coveted. But he also felt despair and regret.

"Perhaps not," she whispered. "But it is not for me to decide who lives and dies."

"Then your gift is wasted," Stone said.

"I did not choose my gift. And people can change. They can redeem themselves."

Stone straightened, drawing to his full height. She always felt dwarfed beside him when she was in mortal form. He still smelled of rich earth and ancient forest, and she welcomed it over the dank, stagnant odor that surrounded them. The walls seemed to press in, looming.

"Redemption isn't for every mortal," Stone said. "Some souls become so twisted there is no unraveling it. They are compelled to do wrong, to hurt and kill over and over again without remorse. There is no way to change them. They do not want changing. Their spirits cannot be cleansed." His dark gaze flicked over to the crumpled man at their feet. "You've been attached to the mortal world for too long—mired with their mores and sensibilities. You have to understand the valuelessness of human lives. They are replaceable. Life chews them up, they get spat in the underworld to pay their dues, then they come back again. Not always wiser."

"You think the worst of mortals. But for every shadowed soul I saw, there was one that glowed brightly. The human spirit is resilient. It's strong." Skybright felt a fervor at her core, a hotness that expanded as she spoke on, careless of what Stone thought. "You say you took me under your wing because of Opal, that you are drawn to me because I am her daughter—but the qualities you admire most in me are *human*. You think so little of mortals, say how controlled they are by their emotions, how short sighted and meaningless their lives are, yet you are drawn to me for those reasons. Mortals may not live as long as the gods, but they feel deeply. They *care*."

Stone's smile was faint but unmistakable. "Perhaps you are right. You are observant."

"I've had to be all my life." She drew a shaky breath, aware how quickly her heart was thumping. "I will never do that again, Stone. You can kill me if you have to, but I refuse to be a murderer." Stone could take her life at any moment, but she would not let fear stay her words any longer. He had wanted a prisoner—a plaything to keep him company. Instead, he would have one who expressed her opinions.

Stone's dark eyebrows lifted for an instant. "I would never hurt you, Skybright. I did not agree to this pact to deliberately cause you pain. It is important that you learn about your demonic half—about the world beyond the mortal realm. If you wish not to kill bad men, I will not force you to do so again."

She stared at him, shocked. He had said something similar immediately after kidnapping her. But now, she almost believed him.

"Let us leave this place." He paused and answered her question before she asked it, "He will be all right. He will suffer a headache and will never follow beautiful women down dark alleys again."

He reached for her hand first, then created another portal for them to step through. "I have been summoned."

Skybright wondered who could summon Stone's presence but stepped through the rent before she could ask. She was only too glad to leave this damp, claustrophobic place and the unconscious man behind.

Zhen Ni

Zhen Ni's bridegroom, Master Bei, was a large man.

Head bowed, she had been sneaking glances through the red haze of her silk veil for what felt like an eternity. But she could gauge nothing except that he towered over her (and she was tall for a woman), and that his feet appeared extraordinarily small— almost misshapen—for a man his size. Rose had wrapped the breast binder around Zhen Ni tightly before she had dressed her in her bridal clothes, a ritual that would be repeated each morning after her wedding. Zhen Ni couldn't seem to draw a full breath, and feeling faint, she resisted the urge to rip the heavy, oppressive layers off and run home to Yuan manor. She took a step back when Master Bei raised her veil, so she finally had a clear view of him.

He smiled, a closed-mouthed smile that was awkward and strange, as if it was something he had never done before. Her groom was not a handsome man. His features were coarse, too blunt: his broad nose was crooked at the bridge, his large eyes set too far apart and protruding, the eyebrows thick and unkempt. He had two large lumps on either side of his high forehead, as if he had run into the corner of a pillar, twice. Had he, she wondered?

Dear goddess, what would their children look like?

And what, Zhen Ni couldn't help thinking, was in store for her on her wedding night?

As it was, after the enthusiastic and drunken crowds had sung their lewd songs, recited their couplets, and shared their bawdy innuendos at the end of the banquet, Master Bei, her new husband, had left her alone in their grand marriage bed without speaking a word. She lay with the coverlet clutched to her chest, still clothed, as it was his right to undress her on their wedding night. Her hairpins dug into her scalp, and her jade earrings felt too heavy in her lobes.

Two lotus-shaped lanterns burned on either side of the bed, emitting a soft glow in the giant bedchamber. The marriage bed was draped in gold and red silks, casting the room in warm tones. She knew the effect was meant to be romantic, but it was all wasted on her. She felt no stirrings of love or desire—only anxiety overlaying a gnawing fear. She felt completely alone in the newly built Bei manor in her hometown of Chang He. For that, she was grateful and fortunate. Most daughters married and were sent away to the groom's family to live in their estates, often several provinces away. The likelihood of visiting your own family was once a year—at best.

But Master Bei was an orphan. A very wealthy orphan who had no ties elsewhere. The sprawling estate now bested her family's Yuan manor as the most opulent in town. It took three months to build, and it wasn't until the main hall within the largest courtyard was constructed that Master Bei introduced himself to the Yuan family, and much to Lady Yuan's delight, asked to be betrothed to Zhen Ni.

Her new home still smelled of fresh wood and lacquer. The smallest noise echoed loudly without the usual sounds and rituals of a large family and their servants readying for bed or preparing to run a full household for the next day. Zhen Ni had brought Rose and Oriole to tend to her. They were sequestered away in some other corner of the manor and would not come for her until late the next morning most likely. Her mother had also given Cook's assistant, Pei, to her as a wedding gift, but the rest of the staff Zhen Ni would have to begin hiring on her own.

If Skybright had been here, she would have known how to ease Zhen Ni's distress. She would have noted when Master Bei left her mistress alone on her wedding night and would have sneaked in with Zhen Ni's favorite treats and games to comfort and keep her company. But Skybright was not here—was gone forever. Instead of the capable, quiet girl she remembered, the one she had grown up with, an image of Skybright dressed like a rich courtesan flashed in Zhen Ni's mind, followed by the thick ruby coils of Skybright's serpent body, squeezing the life from her victim with slow deliberation. Her scalp tingled to remember that awful, terrifying scene.

She was utterly alone in this world now. No one could save her from this. Her first love, Lan, had been forced to marry, to obey and give as a dutiful daughter.

Now it was her turn.

She breathed quietly, trying to make no sound. This must be what it felt like for a hare to burrow deep into its nest, knowing that a fox waited quietly at its entrance to devour it. Her husband was fetching wine for them. Or perhaps he was guzzling a virility elixir like the kind that Nanny Bai used to concoct for her own father. Her hands were damp, and she rubbed her palms against the cool brocade of the coverlet, straining her ears at the same time to anticipate her husband's return. Her mind stuttered over the word *husband*. The waiting felt almost worse than the doing. She just wanted to get it over with.

Zhen Ni knew what men looked like down there. *The Book of Making* was quite explicit in its illustrations. She couldn't help wrinkling her nose with distaste every time she had pored over those drawings in their various states and angles. So different from the soft curves of a woman's body. She remembered gliding her palm across Lan's inner thigh, her skin smooth and scented, the swell of Lan's breasts under her mouth. So unlike the hard shapes of a man's body. And the notion that Master Bei—she didn't even know his given name—might have an organ that matched his blunt looks and burly physique made her ill.

"Wife."

She jerked so hard in fright that she literally jumped in the bed. How had she not heard him return to the bedchamber? Had she been so lost in thought?

"I wanted to bid you a good evening." He had a gruff, low

voice, much like his looks.

The gilded lanterns had burned low while she waited for his return, so he was merely a hulking shadow in the doorway, but she thought she saw the gleam of his eyes. Sitting up and pressing the brocade coverlet against her, as if for protection, she asked, "You will not be … joining me tonight, Husband?" Her words sounded small in the vast bedchamber. Every bridal ritual she had endured was in preparation for this moment. Besides the breast binder, she had been bathed, scented, and dusted with gold powder, all in an effort to please her groom. She was a gift to be unwrapped. Her stomach cramped at the thought, and Zhen Ni swallowed the sour taste in her mouth.

Master Bei loped toward the bed in a manner that was utterly predatory. She twisted the coverlet in her fingers, wondering why she had asked. Wondered if she had it in her to shame her family again and run away from her duties as a daughter—her duties as a new wife.

He stood at the side of the bed, studying her, as if the chamber were brightly lit instead of cast in flickering shadows. She had to tilt her head back to look into his face. He had changed out of his elaborate groom outfit into a tunic and trousers. The belt had been tied haphazardly, so that the tunic wasn't pulled close and exposed part of his muscular chest, thick with wiry hair.

She swallowed hard and tried not to cower from him.

"No. You will forgive me if I do not join you?"

She nodded, uncertain if it was a question or a statement.

"You are tired. And I have much business to attend to."

She thrust her head up and down again, mute with relief. Then suspicion. Did he find her undesirable? Lacking in some way? Or goddess forbid, did he know that she preferred women?

He bent down and gave her a perfunctory kiss on the cheek. His skin was rough and his lips hard, like he was hitting his mouth against her face. It was almost as if he had never kissed anyone before. He was a man of thirty years—that wasn't possible. But perhaps his previous liaisons hadn't required gentle kissing. Master

Bei straightened, silent. He smelled of fire burning. Had he made one in another bedchamber within their large, empty manor?

"Yes, Husband," she whispered.

Then he was gone, disappearing into the darkness of the reception hall beyond, as noiselessly as he had entered.

Zhen Ni rose shortly after dawn the next morning. She had not slept well and pulled on a robe and slippers to wander the manor. Her manor, now that she was Lady Bei. Tian Kuan Mountain was thick with morning fog, and she meandered down unfamiliar garden paths as buildings and halls loomed over her, emerging from the mist. The place seemed even more enormous when she had no notion of where she was or where she was headed. Master Bei had spared no expense in the construction of their new home. She saw it in the details, from the gilded calligraphy of *Bei* worked into the carved lattice doors of the main hall to the jade animals that perched in the corners of every building's eaves. There were lions and frightening dogs with their fangs bared, horses and bulls and goats with unusually long and sharp horns.

She spent so much time looking upward, squinting at the elaborate animal carvings that she began to get an ache in her neck. The sun had risen to the usual time that Skybright—no, Rose—would come and prepare her for the day, but Zhen Ni doubted that her handmaids would bother to come to her until late morning, if not until midday. Had her husband already risen? Was he taking his morning meal alone? She knew that he had inherited his family's wealth—they had all died in a terrible fire, the details of which were scant, so what business was it that he tended to?

Zhen Ni climbed up the steps to quarters that stood empty. She had heard no other person during her explorations this morning, even the birds seemed muted in their song. Sliding the door aside, she peered within. The spacious reception hall was empty except for a pair of guardian dog statues set on stone pedestals. She drew the lattice windows open so she could examine them better. Gray morning light spilled in, and the new stone floors actually gleamed. She padded over to one of the dogs—the pair appeared to be identical.

The guard dog was exactly like all the others she'd seen set outside a manor or hall's entrance as a symbol of protection, but these dogs had giant rubies set in their sockets for eyes, and the facets were cut so there seemed to be depth there. It created the illusion that the hound's eyes could see her, track her every motion. The effect was so realistic that she shivered in her thin silk robe, pulling it tighter across her chest. It was when she broke her gaze from the ruby eyes that she saw the tiny horns protruding from its head; no longer than the length of her index finger, they were thick and carved from jade.

She touched the blunt end of one of the horns and snatched her hand back, before gliding her fingertips over the beast's giant paw. The stone was warm as if it had sat under the hot sun for hours instead of being stashed away in this cold, deserted hall. Zhen Ni turned to examine a side door off the reception chamber, perhaps a bedchamber or a study? Unable to shake the feeling that she was being watched, she whipped her head around, only to see the dog statues, still as ever, their ruby eyes shining too brightly in the dim morning light.

She threw the door carved with a hunting scene open and ran in without looking first. The chamber looked as if it were built to be a study, with one single wall lined with dark redwood shelves. But nothing sat on the shelves, and they were so newly built not even a layer of dust touched their surface. A strange scent lingered in the air. It tugged at her memory, yet she couldn't place it. She was shuffling in her slippers back toward the door, preparing to run past the eerie looking hounds, when her toes tripped over something on the smooth stone floor.

Stooping, Zhen Ni gazed at the culprit. What looked to be

a silver ring lay on the ground, too big for her to wear it on her finger. She reached for it. The metal was cool and smooth, but could not be lifted from the ground. It had been attached to the floor somehow. *How strange.* Zhen Ni tugged harder at the ring and felt the floor lift a fraction, heard the sound of stone scraping against stone. Stunned, she pulled her arm back, as if the ring had burned her. Running her hands along the cold floor, she felt the faint lines that formed a square. What was it? A hidden compartment to hide Master Bei's most precious items? Whatever it was, her husband hadn't had the chance to hide it yet. Would he have thrown a rug over it after furnishing the study?

This was something she never should have discovered. Zhen Ni was certain of it.

A rooster crowed loudly, and she jumped to her feet, feeling the sweat that had collected at her hairline. It was well past dawn now; she needed to return to her bedchamber in case Master Bei chose to visit this morning. How could she be so foolish? She'd been gone for too long.

She quietly slid the empty study chamber's door closed as she had found it and tiptoed past the seeing dog statues before peeking outside into the courtyard. Deserted. She slipped out and closed the reception hall's door too, then hurried down the cobbled path from where she came. But she had not taken notice of her exact route and went from one grand courtyard to the next. One had a man-made mountain built from rough rock that stood more than twice her own height. A gentle waterfall cascaded from it into a large, clear pond below. Another courtyard had a lovely garden pavilion with a jade green tiled roof. The pillars appeared to be hewn from jade and carved with dragons intertwined with clouds. But Zhen Ni didn't have time to stop and admire the view; she so desperately wanted to return to her own quarters.

She was in such a rush that she rounded the corner of a corridor and nearly slammed into the broad chest of her husband. Throwing her hands up, she let out a frightened cry before she could stop herself.

"I was looking for you, Wife," Master Bei said. "Have you been admiring the grounds?"

She pressed a hand to her chest, feeling the wild gallop of her heart. "Yes. It is beautiful. You've done an admirable job, Husband."

"I am glad it pleases you."

He grimaced in a grotesque imitation of a smile. She forced herself to smile back, her cheeks feeling too stiff. Master Bei was dressed in a simple dark blue tunic and trousers today, with no embellishment at all. Even the button at his collar was a simple black. He dressed plainly for all his wealth.

"I had the fruit trees hauled from the south. All the exotic kinds that are more difficult to find in these mountains. They brought soil as well, so they could be planted in the best earth to help them thrive."

It took him a long time to speak those few sentences, and Zhen Ni waited, a tight grin plastered on her face. She nodded and turned toward the courtyard beside the covered corridor they stood beneath. The trees and flowers truly were flourishing, looking full and lush instead of newly planted. "You have done well, Husband," she said.

His brutish face relaxed. "I have always wanted a garden."

She opened her mouth, then snapped it shut. How could he never have had a garden, being from such a wealthy family as his? Master Bei stared at her with those umber eyes that almost seemed to glow. "Well, you have more than a few gardens now."

He looked beyond her, and the soft scent of fire drifted to her again. "Yes. I am pleased." Then as if remembering his original task, he asked, "Could I speak with you in your quarters?" He glanced at the thin silk robe Zhen Ni wore, and she crossed her arms over her chest. "You have not taken your morning meal yet?"

"No. I went out for a morning walk and fear that I've gotten a little lost." She hoped that her tone sounded natural.

"Look for the lotuses."

"Pardon?"

"Your mother said it was your favorite flower. I had the

craftsman carve a lotus on the corner of every building, with an arrow pointing to the direction of your quarters."

"Ah. That was very … thoughtful." And a little disturbing—the notion that anyone could find her at any time within these large, empty grounds if they knew how to look. She couldn't shake the feeling that she was prey in her own home.

He began leading her down the covered pathway, then stopped and pointed at the corner of a building. "See?"

A beautifully carved lotus rested on a leaf with a stem that served to point Zhen Ni to her quarters.

"Your mother said that you aren't very good with directions. But you will become used to the layout of the manor in time."

She was certain that her hapless new husband had misunderstood her mother when Lady Yuan had divulged that her daughter wasn't so good with directions. A laugh bubbled up inside of her, and she had to feign a cough to disperse it. "You are too kind, Husband."

He reached out and patted her awkwardly on her arm, hard enough she could have winced. But she kept her face smooth, and he didn't seem to notice.

"Here we are," he said, and she could detect the pride in his gruff voice. "The Lotus Pavilion."

Master Bei had led her to her new quarters in the dark the previous evening, and although the path had been lit by red lanterns, she had not been able to see the full magnificence of her new quarters. The curved roofline had been tiled in a deep red, edged in gold, *real* gold, she had little doubt. And fierce jade tigers perched at the corners of the eaves, ready to pounce. Zhen Ni had been born in the Year of the Tiger. The two pillars that stood on either side of the grand entrance to her reception hall were painted with lotus from faint to dark shades of pink in various stages of bloom and surrounded by the deep green fan of lotus leaves. The geometric pattern that edged her doorway was carved from jade and also accented with gold. "It is too much," she whispered.

It was then that she glimpsed the large rectangular lotus pond, nestled among trees and flowers in the courtyard beyond her quarters. The flowers had not yet begun to bloom, but she had a feeling the display would be gorgeous come summertime.

They stepped into her reception hall together. The walls had been papered in pale green and the room decorated with accents of pink and gold; the entire effect was romantic and feminine. "You have exquisite taste, Husband." She couldn't keep the surprise from her voice. Zhen Ni couldn't have decorated much better herself.

Master Bei laughed, brief and emphatic. "I know nothing about architecture or beauty. I hired all the best craftsmen." He pivoted to take in the entire space. "There is nothing money cannot buy."

Zhen Ni flinched, for hadn't she been purchased in a fashion? Master Bei had showered her and the Yuan family with extravagant gifts that impressed even her discerning mother and well-traveled father. As a merchant, Master Yuan had seen the best there was to offer in Xia. She frowned, but her husband made no note of her displeasure. Instead, he sat down in one of the curved backed seats with a deep turquoise cushion and nodded to the one beside him.

Rose had set a tray of tea, fruit, and rice porridge with various pickled dishes and vegetables for Zhen Ni's morning meal. Her stomach grumbled at the sight. She was starving.

She sat down and poured a cup of tea for her husband and for herself, but he waved a large hand. "I have dined. You eat."

She breathed in the fragrance of the tea leaves before taking a long sip. Lukewarm but still delicious. Selecting her favorites from the small dishes, she ate the rice porridge ravenously as Master Bei watched on in silence.

"You are pleased by your new manor, Wife?" he finally asked when she set her bowl and eating sticks down.

Zhen Ni took another sip of tea before dabbing her mouth with a silk handkerchief. "I believe it would be beyond any new bride's expectations, Husband. I am more than pleased."

"It is a large manor that will require a big staff to manage it. You will see to the hiring of them?"

"Certainly, Husband."

"Good." He nodded to a large chest set against the wall. "I

believe that will be enough coin for you to work with."

"Thank you. I will start on it immediately."

His unkempt eyebrows drew together, and his large eyes seemed to bulge out even more than usual. "And there is the matter of the marriage bed."

Zhen Ni's face flushed hot despite herself. She clutched her hands tightly in her lap. "Yes, Husband."

"I have my own quarters and will not be visiting you … for that purpose."

"Do I not please you?" She spoke the words before thinking, parroting her obligations as a new wife. Anxious or not about copulation, this was a very strange and unexpected turn of events. Zhen Ni was curious and suspicious by nature. This entire scenario smelled like rotten cabbage to her.

"You please me very well. I am simply otherwise occupied right now." He jumped to his feet, and she leaned back in surprise. "It is a bad time. For me." Master Bei inclined his head a little before leaving her staring after him as he stalked away on those strange and small feet.

What had she gotten herself into? It was too good to be true. A rich, indulging husband who didn't expect her to give herself in the marriage bed. Did he not want children? Surely this was important to him after losing his entire family?

A lover then. He already had a lover. One that wasn't an appropriate match in station, so Zhen Ni could have her respite for now.

She rose and bent over the large cedar wood chest, incredibly plain compared to the rest of the furnishings in the reception hall. She lifted the lid and let out a long breath. The chest was filled with gold and silver coins—more money than she had ever laid eyes on. She ran her fingers through the coins, to be certain they were real. They clinked and thunked heavily against each other. Plucking an individual gold coin from the rest, Zhen Ni studied it. It was unlike any other coin she'd ever seen. She squinted at the marking—it was nearly five hundred years old.

Sifting through the chest, she saw more old silver and gold coins ranging from a few hundred years old to almost eight hundred. Zhen Ni chewed on her lower lip and sunk down to the cold stone floor, not caring she was in her robe and behaving in the most unladylike manner.

Who exactly was this man she had married?

And what did he hide in that secret compartment in the empty study?

Skybright

The rent in the air revealed brilliant blue skies and a glimpse of lush gardens, a scene entirely different from the shadowed alleyway they had huddled in. After Stone led her through the portal, the crackling noise and pinging against Skybright's skin seemed to last longer than the previous times. Her world was so suffused in rich indigo that her eyes seemed to pulse with it. *One, two, three ...* She counted slowly until panic began to surge in her chest. Stone squeezed her fingers, and she was reluctant to admit that it reassured her. He knew what he was doing. It wasn't until she reached twenty-three and her skin was tingling as if bees crawled all over her body that they stepped through to the other side.

The deep perfume of roses, sweetness of orange blossoms, and the sharpness of mint filled her first. Beneath the earthy richness of the soil, there was a subtle fragrance—ethereal—her serpentine senses had never encountered before, as fresh morning dew would smell, mingled with spring sunshine. They had stepped out onto a broad cobblestone path made of a clear, green jade, more extravagant than anything she had ever seen. "What is this place?" she whispered in awe.

"I have been summoned to The Mountain of Heavenly Peace by the Goddess of Accord," Stone said.

"We are ... I am where the gods dwell?" She gaped at him, disbelieving. But where else except in the heavens would the fragrances be so crisp, the colors so true and intense? "Do you visit here often?" She had to ask. Stone had taken her into the depths of hell; she had no inkling he could bring her into the heavens as well. Truly, how powerful was he?

Stone smiled, though it did not reach his eyes. "Unlike the underworld, I must be invited in order to enter Heavenly Peace. It is not a place that is usually open to me."

"But why were you summoned?"

"I believe the goddess wants to speak with me about the Great Battle that just ended. I was granted permission to bring you with me."

She almost reached out to clutch his arm. "Am I to meet the goddess too?" Skybright had become accustomed to the grotesque visions and monstrosities that emerged from hell. But this, this was something else entirely. She drew a hand to her breast and pressed it against the soft fabric of her silk dress. "How should I address her? How do I behave?"

"There is no need to feel anxious. I will introduce you to the Goddess of Accord. You can pay your respect by bowing to her." Stone smiled again, this time more genuinely. He seemed pleased by her awe.

They continued down the curved path, walking side by side. She caught glimpses of green meadows tucked behind peach trees, filled with wildflowers in vibrant oranges and fuchsias, so bright they dazzled her eyes. A soft lapping of water caught her attention, and she craned her neck, seeing the clear green of a pond in the distance, hidden behind ornamental pine trees.

She stopped, her hands gripped at her sides, as if she were playing some childhood game of stop and go. "Is that a dragon?" she whispered.

Stone paused and followed her gaze.

A beast with shimmering light blue scales had its head dipped in the water, drinking from the pond. Small red horns protruded from the top of its head, and long whiskers in dark blue, gray, and white curled from its pointed snout. It was the length of a grown man, with a pair of short, sturdy legs near the front and back of its body.

"Ah," Stone said. "A *fei long*. A very young one. The flying dragons often whelp here under the gods' protection."

"It's a baby?" she asked, then incredulously, "It can fly?"

Stone nodded, studying the amazing creature. "Many of the dragons can fly. But the *fei long* dwell in the skies, among the clouds. That one will grow to more than twenty times its current length."

The young flying dragon stopped drinking and shook itself as a dog would. Its whiskers splattered droplets all around, and its sinuous body undulated up and down like waves upon the sea. It wiggled, obviously taking pleasure in it.

Skybright clasped her hands in front of her to stop herself from clapping. "It is beautiful." She shook her head in disbelief. "It's wondrous."

"Many more fantastic creatures from Xian lore dwell upon this peak. But not all are as benign as the *fei long*. Let us not disturb him," he said. "They are shy creatures unused to human contact."

They walked on. Skybright simply turned her head this way and that, even tilting it toward the sky, trying to take in all the colors, sights, and smells. Leaves rustled overhead as a gentle wind stirred the loose strands of her hair from her face.

Finally, Stone stopped before a pavilion with golden walls supported by jade pillars. Its curved roof was tiled in red, and grand jade steps led up to an expanse of gold wall where the entrance should have been. She examined the intricate carvings on the jade columns with strange beasts of lore: dragons and winged birds with human heads gliding among the clouds. She and Stone walked up the pristine steps. When they stood in front of the wall, it was quite clear to her that the pavilion was hewn from solid gold.

She swallowed hard, the enormity of the situation settling in—

she would be face to face with a true goddess. Skybright tucked errant strands of hair behind her ears, and smoothed damp palms over her paneled dress.

Stone pressed his fingertips against the wall and it disappeared, revealing an empty, rectangular hall supported by more jade columns. He stepped inside and Skybright quickly followed. Within a breath, the gold wall shimmered back into existence, blocking them from the lush garden beyond.

She couldn't see for a long moment as her eyes adjusted to the cool, dim interior. When her sight returned fully, she was amazed by the vastness of the space. Surely, this was a palace of some kind. The roof was much taller than it appeared from the outside. It reached so high the walls turned from gold to azure blue that softened and slowly faded into white, giving the illusion that the ceiling opened into the skies.

A stream wound its way through the palace. The clear water trickled over rocks and pebbles in every color imaginable. The melodic trill of a songbird caught her attention. The chamber was empty of furniture except for the bird's golden cage, large enough that she could stand within. She had never seen a bird such as this. It regarded her with emerald eyes that flashed exactly like the jewels set in Zhen Ni's hairpins. Its body was covered in lavender plumage while its wing feathers were a brilliant turquoise. The bird wasn't bigger than the palm of her hand but had tail feathers the length of her forearm in a deep, shimmering gold, tipped in emerald. She leaned in and squinted at the bird's gorgeous tail. Small emerald stones actually dangled at the ends of some of its golden tail feathers.

Cocking its head, the bird looked Skybright in the eye and burst into another melody so full of yearning her chest ached.

"She sings what she sees in your heart," Stone said.

Skybright turned toward him. He had changed wardrobe again, dressed in his armor of silver and gold, etched in crimson. He was walking along the length of the stream, hands clasped behind him. Relaxed. As if this incredible chamber was one he visited every day.

"It would appear that you are forlorn, Skybright."

Wrenched from the only life she ever knew, never again to see her mistress and first love. Forced to travel through all the realms with an enigmatic immortal until he tired of her … the bird truly was singing the song of her heart.

"How do you know it isn't a song of your heart?" she asked quietly.

"I do not feel deeply enough for the bird to sing with such fervor." He came and stood near her. "I am sorry that you are sad."

"But not enough to give me my freedom."

Stone slanted a glance toward her, and her heart jumped when their eyes met. She hated that she was still so drawn to him. "And where would you go? Back to your mistress as a humble handmaid?" He caught her arm and pulled lightly so that they faced each other. As always, she felt the heat of his touch, even though he grasped her silk sleeve. "Who would you be?'

Her lips parted, but she had no inkling what she would say. Without warning, the gold walls began to tremble, then shudder violently. She had felt earthquakes before—minor ones which left her unsteady on her feet and a strong one that had jolted all the jars from Zhen Ni's vanity—but she had never experienced anything like this. The walls vibrated and rippled in turn, knocking her from her feet. She gawked at the walls in horror, as the gold seemed to have liquefied, streaking in shimmering ropes.

The songbird sang in strident tones, more like screams of distress than a melody. It hopped from one dark branch to the next, the lavender feathers around its throat ruffled so that it appeared bigger. Then it spread its wings, beating them in time to its fearful cries. Somehow, this was the most terrifying thing of all, as if its song could worm its way into her heart.

Stone stood firm on his feet, towering over her. The water in the river was bubbling until large drops leaped into the air, as if its temperature had been brought to a boil.

Skybright cowered with her hands covering her head, the thudding of walls seizing her own heartbeat, so strong she could feel it in her teeth. She feared the ceiling would cave and bury her beneath. "What is happening?" she shouted at Stone.

He didn't spare her a glance but instead stared straight ahead toward the far end of the long hall.

A goddess shimmered into view. There was no mistaking her divinity. First appearing to be twice as tall as any mortal, the goddess's form wavered as if she stood behind a waterfall, then became the same height as Stone—still taller than any mortal woman Skybright had ever encountered. She couldn't help but stare at the goddess's face in rapture: flawless and beautiful, her features emanated serenity. Yet there was a cold aloofness there, the feeling that although the goddess might seem mortal in her appearance, she was as human as an ancient pine or immoveable boulder, as human as the moon.

She had thought that she wanted to throw herself at Stone's feet when she first met him, to revere him. How little she knew then. Without any control or thought, Skybright knocked her forehead against the cold floor thrice, overtaken by uncontrollable shaking. Still, after, she could not cast her eyes away from the goddess's face. She knew her mouth hung open, but she didn't have the mind to close it.

The goddess was attired in a dress that flowed over her like water, the colors subtle and ever changing, as varied as the stones that rested in the stream nearby. Her ebony hair was pinned to her head with two thick loops woven with rubies and emeralds. The stones winked like eyes in the goddess's thick locks. She inclined her head toward Stone.

He dropped to his knees, bowing his head in acquiescence. "Greetings, Goddess of Accord," he murmured. Skybright almost gasped aloud. She had never seen Stone make himself servile to anyone.

"You are late," the goddess said. Her voice was clear and crisp, reminding Skybright of cool autumn mornings. It rang clearly through the entire hall. The bird ceased its shrill cries the moment the Immortal spoke.

"I came as soon as—"

The goddess raised a hand, and Skybright saw that her long nails were the color of iridescent pearl. Stone clamped his mouth shut, and his jaw flexed. Fear radiated from him—a sour odor so unlike his usual scent. And confusion. He was not expecting such a violent reception.

"You have done poorly. The breach between the underworld and mortal remains open." Her hand was still raised, as if ready to make a divine declaration—or to strike.

Stone's eyes widened in surprise, and he rose in one motion to his feet. "No. It is not possible, lady. I had made certain—"

"Do not argue with me." The Goddess of Accord's voice had dropped—softer, yet somehow, more threatening. The goddess gave no scent that Skybright could detect with her heightened senses, but tension wavered in the air around the Immortal. Wrath manifested in a way she had never felt before.

Skybright resisted the urge to shift into serpent form. She felt safer—stronger—as her demonic self, but she was too frightened over how her monstrosity would be received by the goddess. What would happen if the Goddess of Accord hurt Stone? Or even killed him? What then, would be her fate? She held very still, not wanting to draw the attention of the angry goddess. She didn't want to die here in the heavens.

Stone's dark gaze flickered toward where Skybright crouched, and she saw him give the smallest twitch of his finger. Then he continued to speak, and the goddess answered him, but Skybright couldn't hear the conversation. It was as if Stone had robbed her of her hearing. But she caught the rustle of bird feathers behind her, and Skybright knew that Stone had used sorcery to make the conversation between himself and the goddess private.

Fascinated despite herself, she watched as the goddess and Stone continued to argue, if one could call it that, as both their faces were impassive as statues. But finally, Stone curled his fingers ever so slightly, the equivalent of fists clenching for any mortal man, and dropped his chin in submission to the goddess. The goddess let her hand fall, and Skybright heard a whoosh like wind and rain.

"Do not presume to work your small magic in my own palace, Stone," she said. "The half-demon child can hear what I have to say; she will bear witness to your punishment."

Stone's hands did clench then.

"Your sole job is to manage the covenant between the mortals and the underworld—to be certain that when hell breaches, the monks are ready to fight the demons, then to close that breach with a sacrifice. Yet it remains open after the last Great Battle. You have failed in this simple task." The Goddess of Accord glided closer to Stone so they stood but a hand's width apart. "For your disobedience and overstepping your station, I am stripping you of your status."

Stone's head snapped up, and he stared at the goddess in disbelief. "Please. I will amend this, lady."

"If so, it will not be with any aid from the gods. You have ten days to close the breach, or you die." She swept both arms up in a dramatic arc. "I will leave you with enough magic to help you in your tasks—and remind you of all that you have lost." The goddess's words thundered powerfully against the walls of the palace, and Skybright cowered further, even as the goddess pressed her fingers to Stone's temples.

He stood frozen, stunned, as he gazed helplessly into the goddess's eyes.

Brilliant white light began to flow from her fingertips, suffusing Stone's face in bright beams. He gasped, and his body began to shudder, first rocking gently, then as if invisible hands had seized him by the shoulders and were shaking him like a boneless puppet.

The light was so searing it burned her eyes, but Skybright couldn't turn away from the vision. The goddess tilted her head and said, "Look away, child." If Stone could speak in Skybright's inner ear from afar, the goddess seemed to speak from *within* Skybright herself. Then, as if in afterthought, the goddess said, "You will lose your sight permanently if you continue to gaze upon him."

Terrified, Skybright snapped her eyes shut, hearing nothing

but her own ragged breathing as the room pulsed with immortal power. When the vibrations ebbed within the hall and the whiteness slowly disappeared from behind her tightly closed lids, she mustered enough courage to slit one eye open.

The goddess and Stone stood exactly as they were, except Stone was clothed in a frayed tunic and trousers in a muddied tan color like the peasants wore.

"You are no longer powerful as you were, Stone." The goddess said it as if it were a sentencing, and Skybright realized that it was. "Perhaps this will teach you not to overstep your bounds, *farm boy*." The goddess turned toward Skybright in one fluid motion, her liquid gown rippling with her movement. Skybright scrambled back on her hands and knees, away from the Immortal. "He is vulnerable to your venom now, little one. Do with him what you will." And with that, she evaporated from view, as a dew drop on a leaf in the sunlight.

Stone had held still until the goddess disappeared, then began swaying on his feet. In a heartbeat, Skybright morphed into her serpentine form. He crumpled to the ground a moment after, gracelessly, and she lashed her serpent coil out to cushion his head from striking the hard ground.

She slithered to him. His eyelids fluttered; then he focused on her face. His eyes were a lighter shade than they had been—rich brown like camphor wood.

"Goddess," he whispered.

Skybright didn't know if it was an invocation, or if Stone was actually calling for the Goddess of Accord.

"She has abandoned you," Skybright rasped as his eyes rolled toward the back of his head and he fell unconscious.

CHAPTER FIVE

Skybright

Skybright sat with Stone for hours. No one else magically entered the palace hall. The song bird began its trilling again after the goddess left, singing its song of loss. Of betrayal. She knew it was the song of Stone's heart. She studied his face to her contentment, curious over his transformation. Was he something in between now, as she was, not immortal but not fully mortal?

The planes of his face had softened, his jawline and cheekbones less chiseled. A sprinkling of freckles dabbled across his cheeks, and there were faint lines near the edges of his eyes that had never been there before. She picked up his hand, feeling the rough calluses near the top of his palm. The nails were cut short with a hint of dirt beneath. His skin was tanned golden, dark against her own pale complexion. Stone had been attiring himself as a regal warrior from the past, when he was instead a farm boy who had been plucked from the fields by some god on a whim. Why had he been chosen? Because he was handsome? Or simply because he was there?

He let out a low moan, and she leaned in close. His breathing was steady, as was the thrumming of his heart. She could gauge it all with her heightened serpentine senses. He still smelled of forest and earth, but it was muted, like fragrance that had been worn on the skin an entire day. She drew nearer, breathing him in, enjoying this freedom while he was knocked out. Stone had always been the one in control, who had the upper hand in all their interactions. How would it be now?

"What are you doing?" Stone croaked.

She had had her face pressed near his neck and jerked back in surprise. "Nothing. I was making sure you hadn't died." She winced at the monstrous grating sound of her voice.

He let out a small breath that might have been a laugh, then grimaced. "Have you finally sunk your fangs into me, then?"

"The goddess did say my venom can kill you now," she ground out.

"Is that why my head hurts so much?" He winced in pain, then closed his eyes again.

"I did not use my venom on you—"

"Why not?" He opened one eye to peer at her, looking so boyish she was taken aback. "You can be rid of me once and for all."

"I cushioned your head when you fell. It'd probably be split open like a melon otherwise." Skybright arched her back and hissed deep. "I do not kill people for sport."

"Thank you, Skybright, for saving my skull." He shifted his head and seemed to realize that he was resting against her thick serpentine body. Stone then lifted his gaze, his eyes following the curve of her hip covered in crimson scales, then lingered at her bare breasts. He blushed a deep red, something she had never seen him do, as he scrambled to rise. Her nudity had never elicited any reaction from him before. "Ah!" Stone touched his temple with a hand. "My head. It certainly feels like a split melon."

"I'm surprised you aren't suffering more."

He doubled over, his hands pressed against his thighs, and swayed like a drunkard.

She gathered her coils. "Perhaps you need more rest."

"Water," he replied.

"There is the creek behind you." The waters had calmed since the goddess's dramatic entrance, and the creek flowed smoothly now, its surface glimmering.

He gave a shake of his head and muttered under his breath. A ceramic jug of water appeared at his feet. Stone drank deep from it before drying his mouth with the swipe of a hand. "I have not thirsted in over two thousand years." He gazed into the empty jug, then held his arm out in front of him, before glancing down at himself. "I look like a peasant."

"I think you were one."

Stone ran his hands over the dusty tunic in disbelief. "Goddess," he said again, then considered her. "Why are you still here?"

"Where am I to go? There's no exit, and I have no notion as to how to get off this Immortals' peak. Besides, I couldn't leave without you."

"You couldn't?" He half smiled, his eyes crinkling at the corners. It made him look entirely different than the Stone she had known a few hours before.

Skybright snorted. "Don't be foolish. I don't know the way back."

"You're magnificent in serpent form, you realize?"

She didn't respond. Only Stone could ever think her demonic representation was *magnificent*.

He said another incantation in a low voice and slashed his arm to open a portal. Nothing happened. He tried again, then a third time. He cursed, loud enough that the jeweled bird shrilled in complaint. "I cannot summon the portal any longer." But despite the statement, he kept trying, uttering the ancient spell loudly now, making the motion of his arm more emphatic, his dark brows drawn together in frustration. "Damn the gods," he finally muttered beneath his breath.

"Stop, Stone," she said. His feelings of anger and impotence tasted like bitter medicine against her tongue. "We're trapped here then?"

"No. Not unless the goddess willed it. And I don't think she intended for us to remain here." He bowed his head. "You place your fingertips on the wall and command it to open for you."

"Let's go then," she rasped.

But instead, Stone slouched to the floor. His sense of desolation was so acute, it felt like something physical was shrouded over him.

"I thought you told the goddess you would fix this," Skybright said.

His broad shoulders shook, and for one terrible moment, she thought he was sobbing. But he lifted his face and she realized he had actually been laughing. "How? I can't even make portals any longer." He continued to laugh, verging on hysteria.

She crossed her arms, human skin brushing against the smooth scales of her torso, and tried to reconcile this young man so full of angst with the powerful and assured one she'd been forced to accompany. It was almost as startling as seeing a goddess with her own eyes. "You begin by returning to the mortal realm. You cannot close the breach from the heavens."

His mouth twisted, and he wiped his eyes. "That seems practical." He rose unsteadily to his feet. "Have you always been so practical, Skybright?"

"Yes," she replied and touched her fingers against the gold wall, which again appeared to be normal and solid after the goddess's departure. "Come. There's no time for this."

The wall undulated like water, as the goddess's flowing dress had; then all four walls disappeared. The grand jade columns remained, holding up the arched roof, but spectacular views of The Mountain of Heavenly Peace spanned before them. From this higher vantage point, they appeared to be floating in the sky. Cloud wisps drifted by, so near it felt as if she could rise on her serpent coil and touch them. The small stream that had curved its way through the palace continued on, growing wider into the lush gardens beyond.

A grand six-story pagoda glinted in the distance, its roof tiles golden in the sunlight. Several pavilions dotted the expansive garden; the closest had an eruption of wisteria hanging from its eaves. Its peppery fragrance carried to her on a gentle breeze, potent even from a distance.

She slithered down the steps and cast a backward glance. Stone remained at the top, taking in the unearthly views, his expression uncertain. She could read him as easily now as she had Zhen Ni. "Do I need to drag you from this place?" she asked, then shifted back into a girl.

He ran down the steps, speaking a spell. "At least I can still clothe you." His tone was sarcastic as he thrust out his hand to offer her the beautiful pale peach paneled dress he had conjured, head turned so he could not look at her.

Stone's new discomfort with her naked body made Skybright feel modest, and she quickly pulled her clothes on.

"I had not seen you change into serpent form," he said.

"No," she replied. "You were already falling to the ground by then." She had an alarming thought. "Am I safe here in my demonic form?"

"You are safe." He glanced at her; then his eyes flicked away, as if unable to hold her gaze. "You are a creation of the gods, after all." Stone gave her a sardonic smile, one that conflicted with his tangible grief. She felt it strongly even in her mortal form. "We all are," he said in a low voice. "They give, and they can take away."

She almost felt sorry for him. "Do you know how to fix this—close the breach?"

"I will fix it. I have no choice." He walked past her, giving wide berth as if afraid over the notion that their sleeves might touch. "I want to live."

Skybright walked beside him but with much more space between them. She sensed that she made Stone uncomfortable in a way he had never felt before. It was puzzling, but she didn't dwell on it, as she concentrated on keeping up with his long strides.

As they walked, Stone kept conjuring various objects: apples, a wine jug, tunics, a dagger, and inexplicably a duck. The duck stared at Stone for a moment before flapping from his hands and waddling off. Skybright burst into laughter.

"Just testing my magic—what's left of it," Stone said, looking sheepish.

"Your conjuring ability is impressive."

He shook his head in frustration. "It's mostly useless to me in a fight." He manifested a painted silk fan and a ruby necklace, then let those drop along the path. *Zhen Ni would have loved both items*, Skybright thought with a faint smile.

He paused and seemed to be staring at a large rock beneath a cherry tree in the distance. It tumbled a few times toward them, as if light enough to be stirred by the wind. Stone let out a low whistle. "Earth," he said.

She gave him a questioning look.

"My ability was always strongest with the earth element; Stone was the name given to me by the Immortals. I still feel it, the earth magic, all around me. Not as potent as before, but—" He narrowed his eyes, and the large rock rolled several rotations before actually jumping straight into the air, then crashing to the dirt again.

"Do you think the Goddess of Accord intended it—for you to have kept your earth magic?"

Stone chuckled, his wry amusement a sharp scent in the Immortals' fragrant garden. "It's impossible to try and guess a goddess's intentions. She does want me to close the breach. I'd be useless without some magic to aid me."

They walked on, and he continued to gauge his power, so a rubble of rocks in various sizes trailed them, like strange pets. Finally, they reached the wall of the garden. A nondescript wooden door was set in its side, no taller than Stone himself. He pulled the dull brass circle in the middle, and the door creaked open.

They stepped through, and the door thudded shut behind them. Skybright stopped short, letting out a cry. They were on a narrow ledge high in the sky; pale blue stone steps led down into a blanket of white clouds below. She wrapped her arms around herself, deathly afraid of plunging over the edge. "We are not jumping like we did into the lake," she said. "I'll knock you unconscious first."

Stone smiled. "No jumping this time." He paused, his face becoming thoughtful. "Besides, I'm not certain I'd survive that any longer. We simply need to walk down the steps."

"Where do they lead? We are in the heavens!" The steps had no railing on either side and were just wide enough for one person to descend at a time. She really would plunge to her death.

"They lead to where you'd like to go," he replied. "Trust me."

She laughed, and it was harsh in her ears. "I have no choice but to believe what you say, Stone. But I will never trust you."

He spun around so they faced each other. She almost jerked her hands forward to steady him. Quickly, she clasped them in front of her, hoping he hadn't noticed. Because she stood one step above him, they were almost eye level. Still, Stone was taller.

"Have I ever lied to you?"

He spoke in earnest, lacking the detached arrogance that had become so familiar. And in truth, she had never known him to tell her a lie. Until today. "You said you would take me as the sacrifice to close the breach to the underworld. You deceived all of us."

He turned to go down the steps but not before she saw him blanch, so obvious now in his tanned face and very human tells. "I did not lie. The breach closed. We both saw it with our eyes. Something else is going on—and I'll find the cause behind it." Stone continued down the steps, assured in his stride, and she trailed behind him with care into the opaque clouds below.

Zhen Ni

Rose finally returned to Zhen Ni's quarters as she was finishing off her orange slices. She had eaten everything on the lacquered tray, having had very little at the wedding banquet the night before. She'd been too anxious and felt ill the entire evening. *Ah, the glamorous banquet night of a new bride,* she thought, and snorted beneath her breath.

"Lady," Rose said, interrupting her thoughts. "I came earlier this morning but your quarters were empty."

She smiled at her handmaid, fifteen years and very kind and devoted. But not at all fun as Skybright had been, willing to conspire with her and break rules. "I was out for an early morning walk and became lost. But Master Bei found me and led me back."

Rose actually blushed. Zhen Ni knew what the girl was thinking and how far off from the truth she was. "Can you dress me? I'd like to begin interviewing and hiring for new staff today." As Lady Bei, it was up to Zhen Ni to see to the smooth running of an entire household, as her mother had done all these years at Yuan manor.

"Of course, lady. The notices have been posted around town, but everyone already knows that the new Lady Bei is hiring for the most opulent manor in Chang He!" Rose led her back into her bedchamber, throwing a glance at the barely rumpled marriage bed. "Shall it be the deep pink dress today, lady? It complements your complexion so."

Zhen Ni waved her hand, not really caring. Then as an afterthought, "Do we have guards securing the manor, Rose? The estate is so large."

"Yes. I have seen some guards on the grounds, lady," Rose said as she undressed Zhen Ni. The handmaid carefully bound Zhen Ni's breasts with a white silk binder, and Zhen Ni had to resist fidgeting before Rose slipped the tunic over her head. The silk whispered over Zhen Ni's skin, cool as a spring morning. "Oafish looking men." Rose shivered as she helped Zhen Ni into her skirt. "I came across one lurking in the outer garden. He said that Master Bei had asked them to make certain you are safe in the manor as he is away for business."

"Thank you, Rose," Zhen Ni said. "It is good to know that we are protected. It wouldn't do if there were just a cook, two handmaids, and me, would it?"

Her husband had not bothered to tell her that he would be away, only that he would not be coming to the marriage bed. Bless the goddess for brutish guards who loved to divulge household gossip to pretty handmaids in an attempt to impress them.

Rose began drawing her hair up in elaborate loops, as befitting a wealthy lady of the manor instead of the more modest hairstyles for an unmarried maiden.

"No," Zhen Ni said. "Plait my hair and pin it close to my head. There is much to accomplish today, better to keep it more practical."

"Of course, lady."

It was only an excuse. Zhen Ni was glad she had kept the gray tunic and trousers she had stolen from one of the handmaids for her excursion with Kai Sen. It would be perfect for exploring what was beneath the secret door in her husband's unfurnished study before his return. Was it simply a place for him to hide things, or did it actually lead somewhere beneath the manor?

Rose had just rubbed gardenia perfume into Zhen Ni's wrists and at the hollow of her throat when Oriole tapped on the lattice door before peering into the bedchamber. "A Master Jin is here to see you, Lady Bei."

She lifted her eyebrows. "I know no Master Jin."

"He says he is the master carpenter of the manor and wished to speak with you privately. He said it was of matters most urgent."

Zhen Ni gave her reflection one last quick inspection in the bronzed mirror. "Very well, Oriole. Please show him into the main hall and bring some tea and sliced fruit. I'll be there shortly."

Oriole inclined her head. "Yes, lady."

"Rose, the jade and ruby hairpin, please. I was not expecting a guest today."

Her handmaid stuck the expensive pin into her locks, making it look like a light green bird nestled among winterberries. Zhen Ni pinched her cheeks and nodded. "I believe I am ready to receive my first guest as the lady of the manor."

Rose led her from one courtyard to the next until they reached the main hall. The lattice doors carved with fish for good fortune had been drawn open, letting in the fresh air and sunshine of a beautiful spring morning. The main hall had been furnished in impeccable style, with six carved chairs placed in pairs of twos—one set facing the open courtyard, and the other two sets facing each other to create an intimate space for conversation.

The master carpenter sat in a chair facing the courtyard, and he twisted a cap in his large hands, obviously nervous. A long ancestor table was pushed against the back wall and was curiously empty. No paintings of ancestors adorned it; no offerings of fruit—not even a stick of incense to light for her husband's loved ones who had died.

Zhen Ni glided into the room, holding up the panels of her dark pink skirt, before sitting down in the chair beside Master Jin. Oriole had already brought and poured the tea. A plate of sliced oranges and a large bowl of peeled lychees were set on the square inlaid table between them. "Master Jin, it is a pleasure to meet the man who helped to construct such a beautiful manor. I am indebted to you."

The man jumped to his feet, gaping at her. He was probably near forty years, with a thick head of hair and a bushy beard peppered with gray to match. Not as broad as her husband, yet Zhen Ni could tell he was muscular beneath his dark tan tunic. "The honor and pleasure are mine, Lady Bei." He looked as if he were ready to drop to his knees, and Zhen Ni suppressed a smile, gesturing toward the chair.

"Please do sit, Master Jin." She took a sip of her tea. This was the first time in her life she'd ever met a man so publically in the main hall before. But she was the lady of the house now, and it was her duty to receive guests when necessary. "Would you like anything besides fruit? We are not operating as a full kitchen yet, but I'm certain that our cook could make you something if you desired it."

"Ah, no. Thank you for your generosity, lady. I couldn't eat." He clamped his mouth shut, wrenching the cap in his hands even more. It would be ruined. "I heard that Master Bei would be out of town and came to speak with you alone today. I know it's forward but—"

Curiosity piqued, Zhen Ni smiled into her teacup and demurely lowered her lashes in the hopes that she was the picture of femininity. "You may speak to me openly, Master Jin. What is troubling you?"

"The manor, your husband will not allow us to bless it," he blurted, then drew out a handkerchief, dabbing it against his forehead, before tucking it away again. "It is unseemly. I don't want to appear ungrateful, lady, this is the most expansive project I have ever led. The manor is magnificent, and it has been a pleasure to help build it. But you have to understand—" He held up his large hands, as if beseeching her. "When we break ground to build a new home, it is a great disturbance to nature, to the environment where the home is built. It's essential that we placate the gods and discourage … unwanted spirits."

Zhen Ni knew that rituals and ceremony were involved with building a new home, as with any major event, be it birth, death, or wedding. "And my husband didn't allow you to bless Bei manor?"

The master carpenter shook his head emphatically. "He was quite adamant against it. We weren't allowed to set off fireworks or use chicken blood to ward off evil spirits, nor offer fruit and burn incense to the Earth God. A ridgepole wasn't even raised for the manor!" Master Jin's lower lip actually quivered. "I didn't want to go against Master Bei's wishes, but I had to do something to bless this home." The large man reached into a hidden pocket in his tunic and drew out two coins. "I buried these coins in the location where the main door of the manor was to be positioned, as tradition dictated. They were above ground again the next day, as if spat out."

Zhen Ni stared at the two silver coins in the man's hand, their carvings edged in dirt.

"So I buried them again. Deeper this time. And the next morning …" He drew a long breath.

"I see, Master Jin," she whispered.

"I'd never seen the like. So I tried again. I used calligraphic charms, the best kind, mind, written on peach wood slips and stuck them in a bowl with a handful of earth from where we would break ground." He gulped, then wiped at his forehead again with the plain handkerchief from his pocket.

Zhen Ni nodded and placed her hand on his armrest to encourage him to speak on.

"They erupted into flames, lady. The moment I planted the charms into the earth, they burned."

She straightened and stared out into the courtyard. Her husband had filled it with orange trees, the scent of their sweet blossoms drifted into the main hall, and she breathed deep. *Cursed then.* This home was cursed somehow, and her husband knew it. Perhaps welcomed it. "I understand, Master Jin. Thank you for informing me."

He reached out, almost as if to grab her hand, then jerked his arm back. "You are the new lady of the manor. Certainly, you can talk to your husband on my behalf, yes? Bring in a monk to bless the house? It is not too late to complete the rituals, lady."

He rose, jittery. He had not touched his tea or the fruit.

"I did my best, lady. I took into account the lay of the land and the small stream that wends through the manor. The buildings are constructed to welcome good fortune and avert disaster. I built a small shrine amid the grove of banyan trees near the back of the manor, lady. And found the best rocks to place around the estate. Your quarters, I set the tigers on the eaves as protection."

"You did that? I thought my husband had thought of it."

"He wanted something. And I asked what sign you were, and when he told me, I suggested we use it. Tiger couldn't have been a better symbol, lady."

Zhen Ni stood as well and smiled up at the master carpenter, then inclined her head. "I am truly grateful for your attention to such details, Master Jin. My husband did say that he hires the best."

He grinned, and his cheeks were red above his rough beard.

"Be assured that I will speak to my husband on the matter."

Master Jin bobbed his head and retreated from the main hall walking backward, as if she were an empress he could not turn his back on. Amazingly, he navigated the steps without a hitch. He had built them, she supposed, watching him lope off toward the main entrance.

Zhen Ni sat back down and drooped against the curved back chair, feeling as if all strength had been sapped from her. She had wondered if this marriage was too good to be true; now she wondered how bad it could become. Was her new husband one who dabbled in the dark arts, who consorted with demons?

The flesh of her arms pimpled as if a cold wind had swept through the main hall. She had wanted to explore her husband's study due to her usual curious nature, but now she knew she had no choice.

It might be a matter of survival.

Zhen Ni postponed further interviews for the day, feigning a headache. She had Oriole tell everyone who was waiting outside the manor in hopes of securing a job to come back early the next morning. "We had a late start today, and I'm still weary from the wedding banquet."

Oriole grinned. She was eighteen and much better versed in what happens between a man and a woman on their wedding night. Zhen Ni had glimpsed the handmaid once on her day off at the town market, lips locked with some boy in the shadows of an alleyway. Let Oriole make her presumptions—it was the safest way for now.

She dismissed both handmaids, giving them the day off, saying that they would be very busy beginning tomorrow when they started to select the new staff for the manor. The two girls ambled away, each clutching a gold coin Zhen Ni had given them, looking as pleased as newly groomed kittens. She waited awhile to be certain they had left the manor before changing into her stolen tunic and trousers. It took a long time of rummaging through the rosewood cupboards to find a smaller lantern to take with her, as the lotus ones set on either side of her bed were too cumbersome. She made certain that it was filled with oil and lit it, hoping she wouldn't come across any of the guards Rose had mentioned. Zhen Ni had glimpsed two loitering in the main courtyard after her meeting with the master builder.

The guards were not normally allowed within the women's inner quarters where her building was located, but her husband's study and its surroundings were not off limits to them. She would say she was exploring her new home if she ran across a guard, and that she knew not all the quarters had been furnished yet and some were quite dark. The ruse would have to suffice, and she prayed to the Goddess of Mercy she wouldn't have to use it.

Zhen Ni slid her reception hall door open and peered into the lush courtyard. Her husband had filled it with crabapple and persimmon trees. The deep pinks of the crabapple blossoms mingled against the crisp green leaves of the persimmon trees. It truly was a gorgeous estate, and she could almost imagine herself leading a normal, fulfilled life here, but the prickling at the back of her mind prevented it. She only had to remember the fear in Master Jin's broad face, and the hundreds of centuries-old gold and silver coins her strange, awkward husband had given her. Coins so old they should have shown their age but instead looked almost brand-new.

She hurried along the covered path. Afternoon sunlight slanted through the geometric lattice framing the top of the walkway and the low railings below, casting odd shadows upon her slippered feet. Although her stolen outfit was worn and modest, her shoes were befitting a lady of her rank: they were made of silk in the lightest green and embroidered with lavender and gold butterflies. Zhen Ni wasn't certain of the way back to the study and turned around at various corners, trying to recollect landmarks such as ponds, benches, and pavilions. The grounds were completely void of the sounds of human occupants. It was like living somewhere abandoned. She was actually grateful when she heard the distant *thunk* of cleaver against board as the cook prepared her dinner in the kitchen Zhen Ni hadn't visited yet, but she soon passed out of earshot.

She was terrified of running across an oafish guard each time she turned a corner but never did. When she glimpsed a stone bridge arched over the small rushing stream that meandered throughout the estate, she at last had her bearings. She ran up the steps of the study and closed the door behind her. Dust motes swirled in the dim sunlight, and the demon hounds (for she was certain that was what they were now) stared at her with glittering ruby eyes.

Zhen Ni skittered past the stone beasts, breath held, until she was in the empty study, shutting the door as to not feel the hounds' gazes. The chamber was quite dim without the lattice windows drawn, and the air smelled of an unfamiliar musk and fresh-cut wood. Setting down her lantern, she then dropped to her knees and tugged at the small ring on the floor. The stone grated and groaned but barely budged. She hooked both index fingers and clasped her hands so she could use both arms. This time, the ledge lifted, and she pushed it aside. The stone piece matching the floor was a facade, set against a square wooden door beneath, and it hinged open all the way, revealing a dark hole below.

She lowered the small lantern. A rope ladder swung into the darkness—she couldn't see the bottom. Goddess, she thought. Could she do this? If not now, she might never have another chance. Zhen Ni touched her waist, grateful for the dagger stolen from Nanny Bai that she had strapped there, then lowered herself down, clinging to the bronze lantern handle even as she clutched at the swinging ropes of the ladder.

Wobbling precariously, she lowered one foot down to the next rung. It was farther than she had expected, probably accommodating a much larger frame, like her husband's. She squeezed her eyes shut and drew a deep breath, whispering a mantra and gathering courage before she lowered the other foot and shifted her hands down one rung. Her arms already felt sore, but she kept going, one foot then the next, one rung at a time. The more frightened she was, the more the ladder shuddered, writhing like a snake in the air. She had no choice but to keep as calm as she could, minimizing the rhythmic swinging as she crept lower and lower into the darkness.

When her foot finally hit hard ground, she let out a soft sob, wiping the dust from her eyes and mouth. The square opening above her was so dim it might have been a figment of her imagination. *Goddess, help me to survive this.* If Skybright had been here, she would have told Zhen Ni to leave it alone, that her husband obviously kept secrets that were never meant to be found out. But Zhen Ni was certain that in the end, the old Skybright would have accompanied her into this tunnel—leading the way to ensure her mistress's safety. She half smiled, remembering all their misadventures together.

Would Skybright help her now, knowing that her former mistress was in trouble? Her chest felt tight as she held the lantern before her, pretending her old handmaid, her beloved childhood friend and companion, was walking the tunnel beside her, whispering assurances and admonitions, both comforting in their own ways. Not the new Skybright, the one she didn't truly know, the demonic one with the frightening voice, long serpent coil instead of legs, and forked tongue.

She shivered to remember it.

The tunnel she walked was long and deep, high enough for Master Bei to traverse without having to stoop. It curved downward, as if leading her into the mouth of the underworld itself. Did it? The lantern's small cone of light offered her little comfort, and her arm wobbled from tiredness and fear, causing shadows to jump along the walls. This was a stupid, dangerous thing she was doing. But how could she not investigate and learn the truth about her new husband?

The air was dry and stale and grew colder the farther she went. She heard no sound except for her own hitched breathing and the scraping of her slippers as she plodded on. After walking for what felt like an eternity, the tunnel opened into a large cavern, too massive for her light to show her the entirety of it.

She stopped at the opening when the smell hit her. It reminded her of the butchered animals Cook would chop and slice with expertise in their family kitchen. But beneath the scent of blood and flesh was rot and decay. Like the undead smelled when they weren't so fresh from their graves. Had she stumbled upon dead bodies? Some lost cemetery? Heartbeat hammering hard in her throat, she shuffled forward.

She heard a squelching noise.

Followed then by wet suckling.

She unsheathed her long dagger, clenching it so hard the carved hilt bit into her skin. Her lantern wavered in her hand, as if she were drunk, and she tried to will her arm steady. A few more steps. She had to see.

A slippered foot. The shoe was not as richly decorated as her own but still pretty. The owner of the shoe had a thick, white ankle.

Zhen Ni suppressed a moan.

The dead woman had probably been five years older than Zhen Ni. She lay on the stone floor with her arms flung out, legs splayed wide. She wore a plain peach dress that had been slit open down the middle, revealing her naked chest. It seemed to bulge unnaturally. Zhen Ni bit her lip hard to keep from crying out as she crept closer, letting the dim lantern light reveal more. The dead woman's chest had been split open, the flesh peeled back. Her chest cavity and torso were empty of organs. The stench of rancid flesh overwhelmed Zhen Ni's senses, and she swallowed hard against the strong impulse to retch.

Zhen Ni stumbled back, her lantern swinging wildly. She caught glimpses of other dark bodies lying close. Sobbing silently now, she forced herself to walk farther into the cavern, to see how many corpses there were. Six, she counted, as she pressed her knuckle into her mouth, her hand still clutching her dagger. The dead people were both men and women, of different ages and stations. She didn't know which was worse, the visual of what was taking place in front of her, or the stomach turning smells. Had Master Bei done this? Had she married some sadistic, ritualistic murderer?

Then she saw something even more unbelievable and horrifying. A baby of about one year sat near the head of one of the corpses. It leaned over the body, making soft suckling noises with its mouth. Zhen Ni walked toward the baby, a sense of dread rising within her—darker than the discoveries of the massacred.

She stopped when she was close enough to see the details of the child. It was a girl. Naked and plump. Beautiful. Perfect. The baby had a chubby fist thrust into the socket of the corpse, gouging an eyeball out with a wet sound. Contentedly, it lifted it to its mouth and began eating.

The thing had a full set of sharp, little teeth.

Zhen Ni stuttered incoherent gibberish, horror smothering her.

The baby noticed her and stopped mid-chew. It cooed. Its wide set eyes were dark brown and expressive. It smiled at Zhen Ni, revealing a dimple in its left cheek. Its arms and legs were so chubby they were ringed with folds of pudgy baby fat. This thing had grown plump from feeding off corpses. Zhen Ni jabbed her dagger at it, her skin crawling with terror, so much so her scalp itched. The thing blinked, looking exactly as a sweet infant would, except for the remnants of an eyeball clutched between dimpled fingers.

She should kill it.

She didn't know if she had it in her to slash its throat with her dagger or plunge it into its tiny chest—but surely she could set fire to the thing. She couldn't be certain if it would work, if the monster could be killed, but it was obvious it was evil and could not be allowed to grow. Allowed to be let loose into their world. Zhen Ni shook violently.

But she couldn't do anything without her husband finding out. If Master Bei knew that she knew, Zhen Ni was certain he would kill her. If she ran to her family, he would kill them too.

The baby had finished eating the eyeball and had two fingers shoved into its mouth, suckling them. It tilted its head, then began crawling toward her, babbling baby talk all the while. Zhen Ni thrust her dagger forward again, crying out. The thing stopped, then raised both chubby arms toward her, fingers opening and closing in supplication. As if it only wanted to be picked up and held. Only wanted to be cuddled.

Scrambling past the dead bodies, Zhen Ni ran back toward the tunnel entrance. She had wanted to know the secret that her husband kept, and now she did. And she could do nothing to help herself, to help protect her town from what was breeding deep beneath her beautiful new manor.

She raced up the tunnel, losing her breath, but not caring, desperate to be above ground, away from that perverted creature. Her mind ran as wildly as her feet did, but it spun in circles, unable to come up with any solution. When she reached the rope ladder, she collapsed against the hard stone wall, tears streaking down her face, her limbs weak with terror.

Zhen Ni had never felt so impotent or so utterly alone.

CHAPTER SIX

Kai Sen

Midday, and the sunlight overhead pierced through the branches and thick foliage of the trees in thin slivers from above. Kai Sen had escaped the confines of the monastery to be alone to think. But no matter how many ways he approached the problem of saving Skybright from Stone, he couldn't conceive a solution. Kai Sen broke through the forest and walked along the stream. He always seemed to return to the place he first met Skybright without ever planning to, like a reflex. The water swept over the rocks, creating a soothing sound, unlike the noise that filled his mind. Stone had shown how powerful he was that day within the cavern, at hell's breach into their world.

Kai Sen had pored over dozens of ancient texts from Abbot Wu's personal library, hoping to find something that could be used against the immortal. But while there were thousands of pages devoted to banishing or destroying demons and monsters, not one word was said about tricking a god—much less defeating him. There was no chance he could take Skybright away unless Stone agreed to it. But could Stone be reasoned with? Did he feel any obligation to keep his word?

It had been two days since he had gone to Qing Chun and tracked down Skybright with Zhen Ni. Two long days as Kai Sen re-imagined what he had witnessed over and over in his mind. Zhen Ni had said that Skybright had changed, that she was demonic, and they weren't capable of knowing what Skybright could do now. Would do. He saw again her powerful serpent's body winding its way around her victim, the man's choked cries of terror. Could she have turned into a murderer? Was he too blinded by love to see the truth?

But Kai Sen had always relied on his instincts—born with the gift of clairvoyance, as Abbot Wu called it. Gift or curse, he was able to see hungry ghosts trapped in this realm when no one else could. His gift was what had tied him irrevocably to Skybright, so he could sense her presence if she were near enough. That coupled with his love for her.

He knew he could trust Skybright in the same way that he was unable to trust Abbot Wu since that terrible day at hell's breach. He didn't like lying to the abbot, but he was good at it. He'd told half-truths and outright lies his entire life—pretending he didn't see the spirits who wandered in this earthly realm. Grunting in frustration, he ran full speed toward the creek before taking a flying leap across the water to land on both feet with a satisfactory *thump* on the other side.

Pacing the water's edge, he had a sudden urge to see Zhen Ni again. She was the only one he could talk to about this. Perhaps she could see a solution where he could not. Or talk some sense into him, although he could never imagine giving up on Skybright, no matter how dire the odds. Kai Sen knew Zhen Ni had just married and moved into the new Bei manor—an estate so magnificent even he had heard about it within the monastery. He uttered the incantation to create a portal into the Bei manor and drew his arm in an arc, but instead of the usual rent that would appear for him to step through, the tear opened, then snapped closed with a fizzling noise. Puzzled, he tried again, and a third time, with the same results.

He'd never had a portal snap shut on him like that before, and it felt as if his magic was being thwarted.

The familiar scent of sulfur, thicker than he'd ever smelled, lingered in the air from the failed portal. It had been that strong at the breach to the underworld. What could this mean? Was there some darker magic at work here—or was Kai Sen's ability failing him? But his natural skill wielding the elements had never failed him before, not once he mastered a spell.

Tilting his head, he perceived the eerie silence that had fallen over the mountainside. Pinpricks danced across his scalp; Kai Sen realized the gong to announce the midday meal at the monastery had never sounded, when it was always rung throughout the day precisely on time. *Something was wrong at the monastery.* Not caring if any monks saw him appear from thin air, not caring if Abbot Wu discovered he had been practicing magic forbidden to him, Kai Sen worked to create another portal right into the heart of the monastery—the massive square where the monks converged each day. To his immense relief, it worked this time.

The portal opened for him, and Kai Sen stepped into chaos.

Cypress trees along the edges of the giant square were burning; dark plumes of smoke bellowed into the sky. Monks swarmed around Kai Sen, setting fire to the undead that lurched, thick as locusts. Corpses littered the stone floor, undead and brother monks alike, even as some of the dead monks began to rise unsteadily to their feet—reanimated after being tainted. His closest friend Han ran up to Kai Sen, muscled arms covered in gore and soot. He gripped a saber in his hand that matched the one Kai Sen held.

"What happened?" Kai Sen asked, decapitating two undead creatures that had jumped too close to them.

"They seemed to appear out of nowhere before our midday meal." Han grunted as he lopped off the head of another undead corpse. "The monastery is overrun."

"Any demons?"

"We've managed to kill five of medium size."

The medium-sized demons towered over the tallest monks.

"But—" Han seemed to choke on his own breath. "Some of the demons are unlike anything we've ever seen before."

And they had seen and fought all sorts of monstrosities from the underworld. His friend stabbed the air with his saber, ready to return to fighting. But Kai Sen knew him well enough and caught the fear that had flashed across his friend's tanned face and the involuntary gritting of his teeth. Whatever Han had seen scared him.

"The one big one got away," Han said. "We weren't armed—"

"Where?"

"Toward the private library—"

"Abbot Wu," Kai Sen said.

"No one's seen him—"

Kai Sen ran toward the grand building that housed Abbot Wu's quarters, vaulting over bodies as he did so.

"If the enemy ever broke into our monastery," Abbot Wu had said to him once, "protect our library first. These texts are knowledge—containing history, wisdom, and power that is irreplaceable. They cannot be lost, Kai Sen."

He burst through the paneled door of the abbot's study in time to hear the demon's roar, so loud it rattled within his ears. The long blackwood table where Abbot Wu studied had been thrown onto its side, and the two chairs in the room smashed to pieces against the far wall. Shelves had been knocked over, and ancient tomes littered the stone floor. The room stank of the demon's thick, rancid musk and the abbot's sour fear. Abbot Wu was pushed into a corner, holding his staff up as the giant vulture demon thrust its talons at him. The abbot struck out with his staff, glowing a fierce blue, and the vulture jerked its arm back but not before a talon punctured the abbot's side. Abbot Wu crumpled against the wall, barely standing, breathing hard.

Kai Sen shouted a war cry, a guttural noise from deep within, and slashed his saber across the back of the demon's knees. Dark brown feathers that covered the demon's legs flew as Kai Sen struck again. The vulture demon squawked. It pivoted to face Kai Sen, then stabbed its sharp talons at him. Spreading its wings, the monster seemed to fill the entire chamber as it launched itself toward Kai Sen. He twisted and rolled out of the way before leaping to his feet and jumping to plunge his saber between the demon's shoulder blades where its wings were rooted. He dangled off the ground because the vulture demon was nearly twice his height.

It writhed and shook, trying to dislodge Kai Sen from its back, but he shoved the saber in deeper. He muttered an incantation under his breath, drawing the strands of fire from the air, focusing its power into his blade. It began to glow, dimly at first, then in a blue so bright it hurt his eyes to look at it. The vulture demon's flesh began to sizzle, the feathers of its wings curling as it burned. Acrid smoke filled Kai Sen's senses, and his eyes watered.

The demon bucked now, shrieking an unearthly cry that shook the study's walls. But Kai Sen hung on, pulling more from the fire element around him, feeling his chest tighten with its power, his breath catching as the thing pivoted and slammed Kai Sen into the wall, pinning him there.

Dark spots scattered across his vision, but Kai Sen shook his head and used the wall as leverage as he wrapped his legs around the demon's thick torso and shoved the blade burning with hellfire in to its hilt. The demon shuddered, jerking so erratically Kai Sen almost lost grip of his saber, before it thumped to its knees, then collapsed facedown onto the stone floor. Its sharp beak cracked with an audible *snap*.

Kai Sen kneeled on the dead demon's back, hands gripping his hilt so hard it didn't feel as if he could loosen his fingers. Sweat slid from his brow, dripping like tears onto the vulture demon's massive wings. It had been a difficult kill, but this demon had been no different than those he had fought during the breach in the underworld.

A whisper of fabric came from behind him.

He caught the sly shuffling of cloth shoes against stone between the abbot's ragged breathing from the corner.

Kai Sen's skin crawled; he jumped to his feet and spun toward the study's door. A woman clothed in white glided toward him, but everything about her was *off*. She undulated, her long limbs moving in smooth and assured motions in one instant, then jerking into impossible angles the next, knees and elbows bending backward like a broken puppet. Black hair obscured her face, and as she writhed closer, a strange clacking noise filled the air.

He realized it was the sound of teeth knocking against each other, too fast and too loud to be humanly possible.

Kai Sen stiffened both of his arms so they didn't tremble while he gripped his saber, raising it to meet this new enemy.

"So delicious," the thing cooed in a husky voice. "So delightful."

None of the demons he'd slaughtered had ever spoken before, and Kai Sen shuddered despite himself to hear this grotesque voice speak mortal words.

"Your master's dead." She paused an arm's length away from him.

Kai Sen stood his ground, lifting his saber; ready.

The creature's thick black hair lifted, although no air stirred within the chamber, revealing two faces wedged together on a misshapen head. Its four eyes were sunken holes, filling a third of its pale face, the lower part dominated by two yawning slashes for mouths, jammed with overlarge, perfect human teeth. "Now," one mouth uttered. "*You* die," the other mouth finished.

The thing was on top of Kai Sen before he could blink, the rabid clacking of teeth so loud it seemed to beat against his skull. Putrid saliva fell in thick ropes onto his arm and his throat, burning like fire. He tried to shove the demon off, but it had wound its limbs around him, tight as a lover, and he realized every part where it touched him was immobilized.

Losing control in his arms, his saber clattered to the stone floor. Still standing, he snapped his head back and slammed it into the demon, where its two faces joined in a lumpy seam. Her arms loosened a fraction, and Kai Sen took the advantage to barrel himself forward, as he still had control over his legs. But though the demon was the same height as him, it was strong—stronger than any he'd ever fought. The thing shuffled back a half-step, leering at him with both mouths, all teeth and no lips. Its arms tightened; then it hooked one long leg over his hip, trapping him, so his groin pressed against the thing, and they stood thigh to thigh.

Kai Sen felt all his will sucked from his limbs until his head was too heavy to hold up. He swayed on the one leg he could still feel and resisted the urge to lean into the demon, to rest his cheek on her shoulder. His vision bleared along the edges, as did his mind.

"Kai Sen." Abbot Wu's firm, low voice cut through the haze. The abbot—he was still alive.

Shaking his head, Kai Sen tried to ground himself into reality, even as the demon squeezed him tighter, robbing him of breath.

"Hellfire," the abbot said and fell silent.

Hellfire. Kai Sen didn't know if he had enough strength left in him. But he clenched his jaw and drew on the magical strands of fire that floated in the air all around, stubbornly pulling on them. The element gathered and coalesced, until he felt like a wick dipped in oil, ready to be ignited.

The study exploded with blue flames so bright that Kai Sen was blinded. The demon reeled backward, shrieking—a sound so terrifying and inhuman that he forgot where he was for a long moment. When his vision returned, he saw that he was enveloped in hellfire. It didn't harm him, as he wasn't a creature of the underworld, but he felt a tingling across his skin, and the air wavered. He tasted it on his tongue, sharp and potent, like the air after a lightning strike.

The demon cowered now against a knocked-over shelf, its robe and hair lit in blue flames. Kai Sen raised his arms and directed the energy through his entire being, feeling the rush of it vibrate hot at his core, until a burst of fire shot from his palms, enveloping the demon. She clawed at her double face, continuing her unearthly shrieking, rending her flesh into bloodied strips. Kai Sen looked away, the sight too grotesque and the flames beginning to burn too bright, until the chamber filled with sudden silence, and the hellfire disappeared like a wink. The only thing that remained of the demon was a silhouette of her form in ash, smudged into the stone where she had been struck down.

He staggered toward Abbot Wu on trembling legs. The older man had fallen in the corner, one hand pressed to his abdomen. The front of his gold robe was soaked crimson, and blood ran between his fingers.

"No." Kai Sen fell to his knees beside the abbot. He pulled his tunic off, bundling the fabric, and pressed it to the man's wound. He had conspired against the abbot for months, despised him even, and yet part of him never stopped caring for the older man. Kai Sen could never forget his six-year-old self, cast off, shunned, and unwanted. And the one person to open his door and take him in had been Abbot Wu.

The abbot gave a weak shake of his head. "My spirit is barely tethered. Listen, Kai Sen." Abbot Wu swallowed, throat working. "Everything is off balance. There's a new breach into our world. The dark magic has grown stronger these past few days, allowing demons through. I tried—" he coughed, splattering blood "—to pinpoint where. You are powerful, Kai Sen. I've never seen one draw so strongly on the elements of magic. Use your gift to find the new location—"

"How, abbot?"

"The divining stone on my desk. Detects evil. I could never—" The abbot drew a rasping breath. "Get it to glow bright enough. You can."

"I'll try, Abbot Wu."

"Be wary ... not to draw too deeply on nature's magic. It ... will cost you." With tremendous effort, the abbot moved his hand to grip Kai Sen's arm. "You must make things right again. You are my chosen, the one to keep our secret and pass it on. To uphold the covenant."

Kai Sen repressed a shudder, fought not to snatch his arm back from the man he had respected until half a year ago. Maybe the abbot had taken him in only to groom him for this role. But Abbot Wu saw it as an honor, a legacy. Kai Sen saw it for what it truly was: a corrupt contract between the mortals and gods. And the mortals lost every time.

"Abbot—"

"Promise me, Kai Sen. Take your vows. Devote yourself to a monk's life."

Kai Sen bowed his head, eyes blurring with both sweat and tears. "I promise, Abbot Wu," he lied. "I'll take your place and fix this."

I'll do everything to break what you have upheld for so long, Kai Sen thought.

The abbot sighed, and his head lolled back. His hand slackened, releasing Kai Sen's arm.

He was gone.

Kai Sen buried his face into the crook of his elbow and sobbed once, body tremoring from grief and exhaustion, from the lies he uttered to his mentor as his soul slipped into the afterlife. It had been no place for accusations and hard truths. Kai Sen would take those with him to his own grave. He tried to rise, hearing the screaming and chaos from beyond the study's walls, but it felt as if all his bones had dissolved. Even his thoughts seemed liquefied.

The sickening scent of sulfur, blood, and sweat hung heavy in the air. His vision darkened, and he blinked, shaking his head, trying to clear it. There was no time to take care of Abbot Wu's body now. Scanning the chamber, Kai Sen grabbed a tan robe hanging on a hook and gently laid it over the man's body, covering his face.

He needed to join his brothers outside where there were more demons to slay.

Zhen Ni

It took twice as long to climb up the rope ladder as it had to come down it, Zhen Ni was shaking so badly. She would pause between rungs and bite her knuckles hard, the sharp pain helped to calm her nerves, to ground her. Skybright, whom she'd never seen cry in the last ten years, had always told her that tears were a silly thing. They made one's eyes swell and snot run from the nose. They ruined the powder she had applied to Zhen Ni's cheeks and the rouge on her lips. Tears were a nuisance and a waste of time. Zhen Ni smiled grimly as she struggled up another rung. Skybright had always been so practical—she always acted with sense. What would Skybright do in this instance?

Get out of there.

And survive.

When she finally dragged herself from the trap door, she doused her lantern and didn't even allow herself a moment to rest, before rising on trembling legs and dragging a sleeve across her wet face. She had no inkling how long she had been down below or what time of day it was. Guards might be searching for her. Master Bei might have returned early from business.

The thought chilled her heart as she shoved the secret door closed and pushed the stone slab over it, then crept back out into the courtyard. By the slant of the sun, it was dusk, not yet time to take her evening meal. She forced herself to walk at a brisk pace and not run as fast and wildly as her heart was beating. It wouldn't do to have one of the guards reporting to her husband that the lady was racing around the manor as if she'd lost her head. Zhen Ni swallowed. Poor choice of imagery.

She stopped at each corner and searched for the lotus flower pointing to her quarters, until she knew the way herself, recognizing some of the gardens and covered corridors leading back to her reception hall. She desperately wanted a bath but had no handmaids to help draw one for her. Instead, she took a short detour to the kitchen and asked for the cook to bring a large basin of hot water to her bedchamber. Zhen Ni had known the woman, Pei, almost all her life, and trusted her. Pei was twenty-five, of middle height but muscular, with a no-nonsense attitude even more brusque than Skybright's had been.

She looked at Zhen Ni askance. "Been wrestling a hog?"

Zhen Ni glanced down at herself and saw how covered in dirt and dust she was. There was dirt even beneath her nails. "I fell," she said in a weak voice. "Twice."

Pei shook her head. She didn't need to wear her hair in buns; she opted to have it cropped short to her ears. "I'll bring the water as soon as it's heated. And a pot of tea. Or would you prefer wine?"

Zhen Ni swallowed. "I think I would like the wine."

"I'll ask Rose to take some to you straightaway."

Zhen Ni shook her head. "I gave both girls the day off."

Pei grunted. "I'll make two trips then. That means it's just you and me and those lurking guards in the manor tonight, Lady Bei. And I trust those men as much as I'd trust a two-headed rat. They watch me too hungrily as I butcher the meat."

Zhen Ni wrapped her arms around herself, and the cook's face softened. "Go. Return to your quarters. I'll come soon."

She stumbled into her reception hall as the sun was setting. But instead of collapsing into the chair like she desperately wanted to, she kneeled on the cold floor and began rummaging through one of the many chests she had brought with her from home. Finally, she drew out a small chime that Skybright had given her as a gift. They were pieces of round opalescent shells threaded through silver wire. It used to hang right outside her reception hall at home and would chime delicately whenever there was a small breeze. She grabbed a green ribbon and tied it to the chime, then knotted it to the inside handle of her reception hall door.

Now, the chime would warn her when anyone was sliding the door open.

Even those few moments could count for something.

Zhen Ni had taken dinner alone, although Pei had kept her company, not saying much. But the woman's presence was reassurance enough. She felt as if she had been cast aside and abandoned on her own small island with no friends or familiar faces to comfort her. Without her handmaids to help draw a full bath, she had wiped herself clean as best she could with the water Pei had heated for her, then changed into her sleep clothes by herself before crawling into bed, weighted down by exhaustion.

She kept all the lanterns burning, as she used to after she'd had a nightmare as a child. If only matters were so simple. Skybright would often climb into bed with her on those nights, and they'd hold hands until Zhen Ni fell asleep again.

Hours passed, yet still, she could not fall asleep, unable to put aside the atrocities she had seen deep beneath the manor. Was that baby sleeping now, contented after gorging upon human bodies?

The soft scraping sound of her bedchamber door opening made her entire being grow cold. She forced herself to lie still, keeping her breathing even, as if she were asleep. She felt the dark shape of her husband standing in the doorway, eyes upon her, could smell the scent of fire burning that seemed to linger on him.

Her ears were sharp, and she hadn't heard the clink of shells from the main door in her reception hall. Master Bei had bypassed it somehow. Did he come through a secret door he had built to access her bedroom, or from a hole in the ground like the one in his unfurnished study? She began to tremble and drew her knees into her chest to try and quell it.

Had he finally come to consummate the marriage? Or to use her as the next meal for the demonic baby he kept?

Zhen Ni bit her lower lip hard, then heard the door slide closed again, making the pungent odor of smoke and fire less potent in her bedchamber. There were soft sounds of movement in her reception hall—nothing that would have woken her if she had been asleep. But her keen sense of hearing and heightened awareness from fear made it so it seemed as if someone was skulking about in this very bedchamber.

Easing her hand beneath her pillow, she reached for Nanny Bai's sharp dagger, then slipped out of bed like a phantom. She had stabbed a demon before, and it had been hurt and bled like any mortal. There was no chance Zhen Ni could best Master Bei physically, but she could get at least one thrust of the knife in; if she were to die, she would die fighting.

She stood behind the lattice door carved with pairs of mandarin ducks and round peaches, signs of marital bliss and fertility. The entire grand manor seemed a mockery to her now—an elaborate prison and false facade. It was a sliver moon this evening, casting little light through the carvings of the lattice windows.

Her husband was like a hulking shadow in the middle of the hall, kneeling on the ground. A ball of bloodred fire floated before him as he crouched over the floor, mumbling in a low voice. Not the blue hellfire that Kai Sen had conjured. Master Bei began gesturing his arm wildly across the floor, and she realized that he must be writing. Red characters glowed on the ground with the movement of his fingertip, then dimmed. She couldn't read the words and wished for the first time that she had been taught the Xian language fully, as her brothers had been.

Master Bei lifted his head, and she smothered her small gasp with a hand. His eyes glowed like the embers of hell, and sharp curved horns jutted from his brow, where those strange knots had been. The dim ball of fire didn't provide enough light to see his features clearly, but she got the impression of a muzzle and razor-sharp teeth. He lifted his nose as a wolf might do, to sniff the air, and she saw how thick and powerful his neck was. He then picked up something that had been hidden behind a chair: a young lamb, fat and heavy. He held it as if it was as light as parchment.

Although its legs and muzzle were bound with rope, she could see the lamb lived by its heaving stomach and flicking ears. The thing was terrified. With a sudden wrench, Master Bei twisted its head off in his bare hands, and she saw that his fingers ended in sharp talons. The lamb's body made a snapping sound of sinews and bones, and her husband proceeded to dribble its blood on to the floor, still muttering low words.

He was casting some spell or enchantment. What evils was he inviting into her quarters, forcing upon her?

Glimpsing the lamb's slack body, she wanted to retch. Zhen Ni scurried from the doorway, breath hitching in her chest. She hid in the far corner of the bedchamber, behind a large curved back chair, not caring if her husband looked in on her again and found her bed empty. She couldn't return to it, like some unknowing creature about to be sacrificed. Zhen Ni gripped the dagger in her hand and pressed its sharp tip into the ground, ready to strike if Master Bei were to return.

Instead, the evening passed without further incident, and she almost cried with relief when the gray morning began to peek through her lattice windows. She finally crawled into the cold bed, hand thrust beneath her cushion, never letting go of the dagger, and fell into a fitful slumber.

CHAPTER SEVEN

Skybright

Skybright walked behind Stone, keeping in the middle of the stairs as best she could. The color of the steps blended with the blue skies and drifting clouds around them, so it felt as if she walked on air. She was scared of missing a step, the camouflage worked so well. If it weren't for Stone's straight back leading the way, she wouldn't have had the nerve to descend into the empty skies by herself.

They wound their way down, neither speaking, and she could see nothing until the distant glint of the sea emerged below, its surface deep blue and appearing flat. She looked too long and became dizzy, squeezing her eyes shut, then stopping dead in her tracks.

"Skybright?" Stone asked with concern.

"I'm feeling woozy," she whispered, shame creeping hot from her neck into her cheeks.

"It's not that much farther. I promise," he said. "Put your hand on my shoulder if it would help."

She opened her eyes, and Stone was standing on the step below, facing her, and for a brief instant, it felt as if she were gazing into the face of a stranger. After being held captive with him as her sole companion, she knew Stone's features better than her own. She had spent so much time scrutinizing his expressions, trying to gauge his moods, next thought, or impulse. Getting to know him better was her best chance of survival, her best chance for escape. But the young man who stood before her appeared barely a few months out of boyhood, tall and muscular, not like a warrior, but like a farmer. Someone who was used to physical labor day in and day out. Stone tilted his head, his expression open and guileless.

But she knew better than to fall for it. Mortal or not, Stone had lived more than two thousand years and was smarter than anyone she knew, if not skewed in his perceptions.

"Thank you, Stone," she said.

He turned around, and she clasped her hand on his shoulder. The material of his tan tunic was not only threadbare; it felt coated in a layer of dust. But she was reassured as they continued down the stairway, sensing his muscles and bones glide beneath her fingers.

She would rather die before she would ever admit that he could be a comfort to her.

They entered a bank of rolling clouds after a few moments, cool and smelling of the sea. It became so opaque that she lost sight of Stone entirely, her arm stretched out into white wisps. The next step felt different, like earth instead of the unyielding blue stone stairs, and she took another step downward but tripped as the ground had leveled.

Stone caught her, and she stayed within his embrace for a moment, disoriented, breathing in his new scent: tilled soil mingled with lemon. He was the one to step away from her, saying in a strange voice, "We're here."

Skybright shook herself mentally, trying to be more alert after all the impossibilities she had witnessed. She glanced toward him first to gauge the change in his voice. Stone's tanned face wasn't impassive as before; instead, he appeared uncomfortable. Perhaps a little stunned.

Her eyes swept their surroundings. The clouds had magically lifted, and they were standing in a narrow alleyway, tall mud-colored walls rising on both sides. "Where are we?" she asked.

"Not where I expected." He cleared his throat. "This isn't the location I had focused in my mind when we were descending from The Mountain of Heavenly Peace."

Understanding dawned. So this was why he appeared so discomfited. She turned in a full circle, grinning. "I know where we are."

"What?"

"We're in Chang He." She easily recognized the narrow alleyway now. "Right by the Yuan manor."

"Impossible—"

"It was the destination *I* had in mind. You said—"

"The magic defers to the most powerful ..." Stone paused, turning pale. "Goddess." He rubbed his face with his hands. "It really is true then. She's stripped me of everything."

"You did conjure water and other things," she said. Skybright remembered the duck flapping indignantly away from them but thought it better not to mention it.

Stone's laugh was abrupt and bitter. "True. I'm like a roadside magician, manifesting random and useless objects for passersby's entertainment. I should carry a cup to collect coin." He let out a string of archaic curses, fast and furious, something about a mule and a sack of rocks in the mud, then clamped his mouth shut. "I hadn't realized I had fallen so low. Skybright ..."

She had been craning her neck, trying to see if she could hear anything from within Yuan manor but turned at the quiet urgency of Stone's voice.

"You have to help me close the breach." He paused. "Please?"

"That's your task and problem, Stone. I'm no longer bound to you. And I certainly don't owe you anything." She picked up her skirt and began walking away from the town toward the woods. Being surrounded by trees always cleared her mind, calmed her. She didn't know if she had enough nerve to face Zhen Ni so soon.

She knew her old mistress had felt betrayed by her secret, but what of Kai Sen? Could he be by the creek now, jumping across rocks, as he had shown her once? Remembering him brought a tightness to her chest. She'd heard enough tales of star-crossed lovers but was never fortunate enough to indulge in the notion of happy endings.

Stone followed easily with his long stride, interrupting her thoughts. "I know. But I'm begging you. This breach poses a threat to all mortals."

She knew he spoke truth. But she didn't want to accompany him any longer—constantly fighting her attraction, annoyed with herself that she was so drawn to him, angry that he had snatched her away from her life. "You still have some magical ability," she said. "Take care of it yourself."

He wasn't giving up so soon, still beside her when she caught a glimpse of the tree line and ran toward it, her heart feeling full. The tang of pine needles filled her senses. She stopped abruptly near the forest edge. She hadn't been ready to face Zhen Ni, too afraid her former mistress would reject her after all these months apart or reject her for hiding the fact that she was half-demonic. But she couldn't bring herself to run to Kai Sen, either. For what? She had only ever been a distraction, a forbidden romance.

She turned on her heel to walk toward the town center. Stone changed direction with her, as stubborn as a goat. "Please, Skybright. You can go and do whatever you'd like after we close the breach. I know I have no hold over you. But I wouldn't ask if I didn't need your help."

"I'm going to find something to eat," she replied. "How long do you plan on following me like a lost dog?"

"Until you change your mind?" He grinned, his uncertainty more charming than he realized. Thank the goddess. "Here," he said gallantly and whisked an apple out of thin air.

She laughed despite herself and took it. "I'll need more than an apple."

Stone nodded and in the next instant held a spade in his hand. She gave him a questioning look. "It was the first thing that came to mind when I wanted to conjure a weapon." He let out an incredulous laugh. "I guess I'm a farm boy after all." Setting the spade down on the side of the empty dirt road, his expression became pensive. Stone uttered another short incantation, and a saber manifested in his hand, its sharp edge gleaming in the sunlight. He sheathed the weapon at his waist, after conjuring a scabbard and sword belt. "I'd probably do better with the spade," he said with sarcastic amusement.

She imagined that Stone was realizing all that he had lost just as she had at hell's breach, when he had taken her away from everything she knew.

Skybright didn't know how she'd feel if she ever returned to Chang He. She had been abandoned in the forest as an orphan, left to die. But although she had no true family, the Yuans had taken her in and cared for her, treated her better than any other servant. Zhen Ni had loved her like a sister. Skybright thought she'd feel joy or relief, but as she walked through the familiar town of her childhood, her throat constricted. There was only the sense of loss. Of never belonging again or leading a normal life. As much as she missed Zhen Ni, her mischievous smile and warm laugh, the way she'd clasp Skybright's hands in excitement as she planned their next big adventure, Skybright knew that there was no returning to it. She had been through too much since she discovered her demonic side—seen too much—to ever go back to simply being a handmaid. She was more than that. Stone had been right. The sudden realization made her lightheaded for a moment, and she swayed on her feet, until Stone reached for her arm to steady her. Embarrassed, she shook him off, walking faster.

People stared at her as they hustled past. For once, it wasn't

Stone, looking majestic, drawing all the attention. Her fingertips flew to her cheek, then traced the raised scar that ran its way from her temple to the corner of her mouth. Skybright stiffened and lifted her chin as young boys and handmaids scurried out of her way on the dusty main street. As if the gods were anticipating where her thoughts ran, she heard the distant gong of the monastery. Where was Kai Sen now? Had he forgotten about her after all these months? And no matter how much it hurt, part of her hoped that he had—that he'd moved on. It was for the best.

Skybright led Stone to a restaurant tucked near the edge of their small town. It was more a shack, popular among the workers because the food was tasty and also priced low. One wouldn't find any ladies or masters from fine houses dining in this questionable establishment.

It was well after the midday meal, and the place was empty. The owner, an older man with a long beard, gawked at her, then waved a hand vaguely indicating they could sit where they pleased. Another advantage to this place—people didn't ask questions.

They chose the table in the very back of the small room and sat down beside each other. The table was next to a wooden door that opened onto a grove of cypresses, and her heart eased to see their gnarled branches, to taste their fresh scent against her tongue.

"A jug of wine, please. And whatever food is hot, double portions," Stone said to the lanky boy who came to take their order. He bobbed his head and ran off to the kitchen. "You wasted no time asserting your power, Skybright, to come home again." Stone drummed his fingers against the coarse, unpainted wood of their square table.

She stared at her own hands, folded in her lap. It was all that she had wished for. But why was it that when you were given that wish, so often it wasn't as you'd imagined. She didn't reply.

"It was cruel, I know, to force you away from everything you knew. But it was the only way I knew to help you realize who you truly are. To show you that you're not merely a mortal girl."

"And have you been successful?" she asked in an impassive voice.

"If I had had more time, I know I would have been."

"To make me like my mother."

His fingers stopped, and he pressed his palm against the table. "No. I was shortsighted there. When I said you were unique, Skybright, I never realized how much so."

The boy returned and poured them each a cup of wine, then set down a large bowl of beef stew with carrots, two tea stewed eggs, stir-fried cabbage, and eggplant with ground pork. He loped away, then returned with a large bowl of steaming rice. Skybright's stomach growled, and she helped herself to everything, eating slowly and savoring all the flavors of the dishes.

Stone drank two cups of wine before he started to eat. His cheeks had flushed pink from the alcohol, and Skybright marveled again at how boyish he looked. They ate without speaking, and it was when the server delivered two bowls of sweet peanut soup with rice balls when Stone finally broke the silence. "Your mistress will be pleased to see you."

Skybright nodded, not meeting his eyes. Stone didn't need to know that she couldn't return to her former life, didn't need to know that he had been right all along—that she didn't belong. He leaned back in his stool, head against the wall, and surveyed the ramshackle restaurant. "I've never visited this type of establishment as the goddess' intermediary, but somehow, the feeling of it is familiar. I think it is similar to places I had been when I was mortal."

In the short time since Stone had his status stripped, she'd noticed his speech patterns had become erratic, falling from his previous formal way of speaking to a more lax language and accent that hinted at his former life. The effect was disconcerting. She wondered if Stone himself noticed.

"Skybright." He fidgeted, long fingers flexing, one knee bouncing with nervous energy. "I would ask another favor of you. I know you owe me none—far from it, but this is personal."

Her eyes widened for a moment before she smoothed her features. What could she possibly do for him now? Is this how quickly the situation had turned on its head? "What would you ask of me?"

"Could you look at me?" He drew a deep breath and stilled, sitting straight on his stool. "I mean *truly* look at me, with the gift that you've been given?"

She suddenly understood and shook her head. "It's intrusive. And strange." Skybright didn't want to be reminded of seeing those souls weighed down with sins, the men's faces blotted out by angry swarms. She didn't want to remember what happened in the alleyway—that she had almost killed a man. "What if I see something that you don't want to know? Something awful?"

"It's a risk I am willing to take. Please, Skybright. You see the truth. I want to remember who I am—who I was before my mortal life was taken from me by the gods. I think you could help me."

"Why should I? After what you've done?"

He clasped his hands together in a tight fist. His dark brown eyes flickered to her face, pleading, before his chin dropped and he stared at the floor.

"All right. Look at me then." She would never admit it to him, but she was curious as well. Who was Stone as a young man barely out of his youth?

His face brightened with hope, and he met her eyes, held her gaze. Steady and intense, as he had been before. Skybright steeled herself mentally, preparing for what she might see. She tried to ignore his handsome features—the high cheekbones and hard lines of his jaw, still strong even after his face had softened in mortality.

His full mouth.

She couldn't believe of all the tricks the goddess let Stone keep, having this seductive pull was one of them. Skybright gritted her teeth and narrowed her eyes. Stone's dark eyebrows drew together a fraction, his old expression of amused aloofness replaced by very human uncertainty.

Then his features began to glow.

Brighter and brighter.

Skybright gasped.

She wanted to shield her eyes but instead held his gaze.

A brilliant sunset, in hues of stunning golds and deep oranges. The sun hung over the terraced rice fields so that the water within reflected the colors back. It was one of those views that made his chest expand, seemed to fill him with the wonder of life, lifting the ache from his shoulders and lower back, taking the pain of the brutal work day from his body.

Until he woke the next morning and felt all the strains on his muscles once more.

He was in a cramped shack, lying on a bedroll placed on the dirt floor. A soft hand was petting his cheek, and he opened his eyes with reluctance. Round black eyes peered down at him, gleaming. "Da Ge," she whispered. "It's your day off. Let's play!"

Big brother, she had called him and grinned so widely with adoration that her eyes disappeared into those round cheeks. She was four years old, his youngest sister among the five siblings. And she was not shy about letting the family and everyone else know that he was her favorite. He reached over and tugged at one of her braided pigtails; she squealed in delight, butting her head into his bare chest. He laughed and held her and said, "Mei Er, you were supposed to let me sleep in."

"I did," she exclaimed. "The rooster has already crowed. Then I counted to a hundred, just like you taught me!"

He knew how Mei Er "counted" to one hundred. So it was barely daybreak then. But how could he be peeved with her? She was his favorite as well.

"Should we go fishing today?" he asked, pulling a tunic on. "Or catch frogs and race them?" Despite their thirteen-year age difference, they never failed to have fun adventures together.

His family lay on their own bedrolls, dark lumps in the spare room. Lao San grumbled in his sleep, and Xiao Di kicked his legs as he was prone to doing while dreaming. Even his mother hadn't risen yet.

The incense from their small ancestor altar had burned out, but its subtle sandalwood fragrance still permeated the air.

He grabbed her little hand and pressed a finger to his lips. "You ready?" he whispered.

She nodded so enthusiastically he felt dizzy watching her. "Don't forget the bucket!"

Skybright's eyes fluttered, and the vision dissipated in her mind. It was as if she had been there herself—she could sense the chill in the morning air, smell the incense, and feel Mei Er's small fingers squeeze Stone's own.

She teetered on her stool, and Stone's arm shot out, clasping her shoulder gently.

"Did it work?" He swallowed. "What did you see?"

"Your family farm, Stone. And your home. It was modest. You had four siblings, and the youngest one was a girl. She adored you, and you loved her."

"A little sister." He blinked.

"She called you Da Ge."

His eyes widened. "And I called her Mei Er."

Skybright nodded.

"I wish I could remember my given name. All of my memories feel as if they're trapped behind a dam." His fingers tightened against her shoulder. She didn't think he realized he still held it.

"I did see a character by the ancestor altar, written onto a red slip of paper," she said, remembering, and snapped her fingers. "Give me a brush with ink, and I'll draw the character for you."

Without even bothering to check if anyone was observing them, he magically summoned a calligraphy brush, its tip so laden with ink it dripped onto the rice paper conjured on the table beneath it. He passed it over with an unsteady hand. Hopeful. Nervous. She could taste it. He held the corner of the paper down, seemingly holding his breath.

Skybright couldn't recall ever grasping a calligraphy brush in her hand. There had never been a reason for her to learn, although Zhen Ni had taken lessons in the more simplified women's language. Fortunately, this word was easy to replicate, straight lines and boxes, stacked almost like windows in a building. "It looked something like this," she murmured.

"Gao!" Stone exclaimed. Then he squeezed his eyes shut, as if seeing something beneath his lids, and said, "Gao Yong Ming. That was my name."

"Tall as your family name. Courageous and bright as your given name? Your parents had high hopes for you."

He opened his eyes, and they shone with unshed tears. He blinked them away. "They did. I was the eldest son. They hoped that I would become more than a farmer. That I would become educated ..." He smiled a small smile. "They never knew how high I actually climbed."

He grabbed for her hand, startling her. They had held hands many times before, whenever he led her through the portals like an obedient lamb. But this time, it felt different. Stone stroked her palm with his rough fingertips, sending warmth through her, igniting all her senses, until her ears felt as if they were on fire. "We share the same character in our names," he murmured.

Ming.

Bright.

She didn't even know who had given her her name. Certainly not her own mother. Most likely Lady Yuan when she had accepted the bundled baby as a present and servant to her unborn child. Or perhaps Nanny Bai did, believing Skybright might have fallen from the sky on a clear day. Skybright didn't know. She probably would never know.

"Thank you, Skybright. For doing this for me." He leaned closer. "I knew you were kind."

Something strong resonated between them. His touch against her wrist, where he had moved his rough fingers, was all she felt; her senses leaped to that point. But then she smelled something unfamiliar, something she'd never smelled from Stone before: desire. The unmistakable scent rendered her lightheaded for a moment, and her entire body reacted, flushing. He was watching her with those warm brown eyes, hesitant.

Uncertain.

She wound her other hand behind his neck and guided him to her until their lips met. She drew in a small breath from shock, but then was falling into all the sensations of having his full mouth upon hers. Oh, so different from the few kisses they had shared before, where his magic would actually tear her sense of self away from the physical pleasure. This, this she felt to the essence of her being, as he kissed her deeper, tasting sweet like the dessert he had eaten. She breathed him in, laying a hand on his cheek rough with stubble, desire pooling hot at her core. Her serpent self hissed deep inside, writhing to be unleashed, but she quelled it. This was no time to turn.

She had wanted Stone from the start but had fought the desire. It was so much easier when he was immortal, removed, something above herself. But this young man who had kissed a hot path from her throat to nibble on her lobe, with one hand gliding from her waist to her hip, squeezing her there, pulling her closer so that the stool actually tilted—he was much harder to resist. Stone made a low sound, seeking her mouth again, and all she could think about was dragging him by the sleeve into the copse of trees behind them and stripping him free of his dusty clothes. Of feeling his bare skin against hers, of being closer than she ever thought was possible.

Like when she had been with Kai Sen.

Kai Sen.

Feeling guilty and confused, she pulled away from Stone. His cheeks were even more flushed than after his two cups of wine, and he appeared to be in some sort of daze.

"Stop trying to seduce me," she said vehemently.

He was rubbing the back of his head, then gawped at her. "Me? Seduce *you*?" He began laughing uproariously. "But *you* kissed me," he managed to choke out.

"Don't deny it. You had some sort of sexual charm. I can't believe that magic's lingered."

Stone adjusted the obvious bulge between his legs, grimacing. "I have no magical charm, Skybright. Even you, as a seductress type demon, do not. You were blessed with good looks, a beautiful singing voice—it doesn't take much to convince a man if you were to try."

"But Kai Sen ..."

Stone's face hardened. "The false monk boy. He loved you for you. Is that so hard to believe?"

Kai Sen had said the very same thing to her. She slumped over the table, her head in her hands. "And you bedded my mother. For you to want me as well is … vile."

Stone gave another incredulous laugh. Skybright saw the servant boy hovering on the other side of the small shack, trying very hard not to stare. "Whatever gave you that notion?"

"You're always talking about her. Opal this, Opal that. She was beautiful. She enjoyed seducing men. She was such a fantastic murderess. You loved her so well you wanted to make me *into* her. I can't imagine that she wouldn't have wanted—that you didn't—"

"Opal and I were cohorts. It's true I admired her, but she had no interest in having a sexual liaison with me. Nor I with her. I was too busy handling important Immortal tasks." He shifted on the stool. "Goddess, I need to be thrown into an ice-cold river. And I thought hunger for food was an annoyance …"

Head still lowered, Skybright couldn't suppress a smile.

Stone cleared his throat. "As I said, I was wrong in trying to make you into your mother, Skybright. You are your own person and every bit as formidable as your mother ever was." He leaned back, taking a gulp from his wine cup before saying, "Do you regret it then?"

His directness unsettled her. Did she?

In truth, she had missed Kai Sen, but she was never able to imagine how they could be together longer than the stolen moments they had shared. She had given up the hope of ever seeing him again, after Stone had forced her away from her mortal life. Now that she was free, she didn't know what to think—*what* she wanted. Marriage, keeping house, a domestic life seemed impossible and ludicrous the more comfortable she became with her serpent half. And Stone, he galled her as much as he charmed her.

"It was only a kiss," she finally replied. A kiss that she had desperately wanted. A kiss that she had initiated. If Stone was speaking the truth, then her attraction for him had always simply been that. She had to come to terms with this.

He considered her with those dark eyes, taking in every part, setting fire to where his gaze touched, until she had to force herself still so she didn't leap from the stool and run out the back door. "Agreed," he said. "But what a kiss."

She stood calmly, then took slow deliberate steps toward the restaurant's front door. Even the brushing of her thighs as she walked made her weak with desire. If she had stayed a breath longer, she would have hauled him out by the collar and given in to her passion.

Damn Stone to the underworld, she thought, then burst out laughing.

The servant boy, reeking of fear and excitement, scrambled away from her to settle the bill with Stone.

The boy had gotten quite a show.

Skybright leaned against the wall of the restaurant; the bricks were cool, and its rough surface dug into her back, calming her senses. Stone appeared some time later, rounding the corner from the rear of the building. He had conjured and changed into a gray tunic and trousers—nothing elaborate but more presentable than the peasant clothing he had worn before. He lifted his dark eyebrows when he saw her. She didn't think she looked as refreshed as he did after their shared kisses.

"I'll help you," she said. "I know the way to the breach at the base of the mountain. It'll be at least five days of travel by foot." Stone was right. Even if this place no longer felt like home, even if she might not be able to return to Zhen Ni or the Yuan manor again, she could not let more innocent lives be lost to demon attacks. She felt like an outsider looking in when it came to ordinary mortals' lives, but it didn't mean she cared for them any less. If anything, she saw human lives as shorter and more fragile now—precious—after her brief time in Stone's captivity.

His relief was plain. "I need to investigate the goddess's claim first hand. It doesn't make sense the breach could still be open." They turned from the narrow alleyway and continued down the main street. Most of the vendors were napping in their bamboo chairs by their stands in the late afternoon sun, still keen for a sale but not so much that they kept awake. "Five days," Stone said after a long silence. "That's half the days I've been given to live." He punched a fist into an open palm in frustration, a gesture she'd never seen from him before.

They were walking side by side but careful not to graze each other. Her lips felt sensitive and swollen from their prolonged kissing. She was exceedingly annoyed with herself that she wanted Stone so much.

"I've always relied on magic to travel," he said, interrupting her mental flagellation. "I'm fortunate to have you as a guide."

"I'm helping you because I don't want any more people to get hurt," she said. "Not as another favor to you." And definitely not because of that kiss they had shared.

"Of course," he replied. "Understood."

Skybright was walking back to the Yuan manor from habit, even after having been gone for what felt like a lifetime. She stopped and stood beneath a peach tree, its elegant branches laden with scented blossoms. She needed a moment to collect herself, to say good-bye again to this place that was home but no longer felt like home. Leaning a shoulder against the trunk, Stone folded his arms across his chest and considered her. His skin was not as hot as before when he was immortal, but warmth still emanated from him. He didn't say anything—did not rush her. He seemed more perceptive now to her moods, which alarmed her. Stone was already shrewd, this would give him even more of an advantage in their dealings with each other.

"You smell different now." She said whatever came to mind, hoping to throw him off.

"Do I?"

"It used to be of rich earth and ancient trees. Now it's looser, newer earth, tilled perhaps, mingled with lemon."

"Better than an old buffalo, I suppose. We kept a few of those as well."

She laughed despite herself, then quieted. "You were good, Stone. I didn't tell you before, but your face glowed. It wasn't obscured like those men who had sins weighing against their hearts. I don't know if it accounted for all your deeds as an immortal, but you were good when you were Gao Yong Ming."

He was gazing into the distance, a pensive look on his face, as if seeing something from the past, before his focus sharpened again, and returned to her. "Thank you, Skybright, for telling me."

The leaves rustled overhead; it was cool and comfortable in the shade of the tree.

"Why lemon?" she asked.

"What?"

"I understand you smelling like tilled earth. You grew up on a farm. But I saw terraced rice fields, not lemon groves."

"Ah." He gave a small smile. "Some memories are returning to me now, thanks to your help. I kept a lemon tree with my little sister. We planted it ourselves behind our house and watered it. I had bartered for the tree, and it was beginning to bear fruit for the first time that summer—when I was taken away." He slanted his head, so she saw the sharp profile of his face. "Strange what stays with you. I am sorry I wasn't there to harvest our first lemons together with Mei Er."

She only had a few people she cared about in this world, but at least they were still alive. Stone's family died thousands of years ago, their lives obliterated by the passing of time, until no one alive could possibly have known of their existence. Except Stone. But he had nothing to return to, even if he desired it. The earth had long shifted, hills eroded flat, the sea flooding lands or drying to desert since he had been a boy tending a lemon tree with his little sister.

He turned toward her. "Your mother did not see the light in people."

Skybright shook her head, not understanding him.

"I mean that she could only read the sinful, the wicked. She did not have the ability to see the good in people as you do. As you saw in me. That is your gift alone." He straightened and touched her hand, so lightly she barely felt it. "I thought you should know, given our previous discussions of Opal."

A large crowd of a dozen people trampled past them, speaking excitedly. Skybright spotted one of Lady Yuan's handmaids among them, Pearl, who looked taller than when she saw her last. The handmaid saw Skybright at the same time, and her face lit up with surprise and curiosity. Pearl rushed over, hands outstretched toward Skybright, but eyes roving toward Stone. Her cheeks were pink from taking her fill of him by the time she reached them.

"Skybright!" she exclaimed, grabbing for her hand. "They said that you had run away, and the mistress, I mean, the lady was heartbroken over it. We all asked and asked where you went, but she seemed convinced that you wouldn't return and that we would never see you again." The words came out rushed enough that they seemed to collide with each another.

"I didn't want to leave, Pearl." She squeezed the handmaid's fingers. Pearl had always been excitable and a terrible gossip. "Is Mistress Yuan all right?"

"She is Lady Bei now." The girl pursed her lips in pleasure that she was the one to deliver the big news. "Newly wedded this week to the richest man in town!"

Wedded.

Skybright reeled backward, and Stone caught her by the waist. Pearl looked from him to Skybright, then back at Stone. She batted her eyes at him. "You're dressed so beautifully, Skybright. I mean, Lady Bei always treated you well. You were her favorite. But this ..." The girl waved an arm up and down. "This is exquisite!" She hopped closer. "Did you run away to marry?" She leaned in even nearer until Skybright could smell the gingered candy on her breath. "Or to deliver a secret babe?" She arched her brow.

Skybright disentangled herself from Stone, resisting the urge to swat at the girl. "No, Pearl. I left ... I left to meet my birth mother for the first time. She had taken ill, and I cared for her. Until her passing." She winced inwardly, even though the lie came easily enough. "Yong Ming here is a ... long-lost cousin I never knew I had."

"And what a handsome cousin." Pearl peered up at Stone coquettishly beneath lowered lashes.

Skybright almost snorted aloud.

Stone smiled but took a noticeable step back from the girl.

"We're all going over to the new Bei manor now to try and gain a position in Lady Bei's household. Today is the first day she is interviewing for new staff. Lady Yuan said that she would allow me to go and work with our old mistress if she hires me." Pearl clasped her hands together and rolled her eyes heavenward. "I am *aching* to see the new estate. It is meant to be grander than even the Yuan manor!"

Skybright felt faint again at the thought of her former mistress now wed, living in her own estate without her. Who had Zhen Ni taken to look after her? Only Rose? "Good luck then, Pearl." She clasped the girl by her arm.

"Thank you, Skybright! I take it as a good sign that I saw you before my interview." The girl waved and sauntered off but not before looking back one last time and giving Stone a suggestive wink.

Stone scrubbed a hand over one pink cheek, as if he could rub away his embarrassment. "Are all the girls so forward these days?"

Skybright laughed. She still wasn't used to his very human reactions. "I think that Pearl has recently discovered her interest in boys. There aren't many to look at within the Yuan manor." And Stone was very nice to look at. He still towered over everyone— one couldn't help but notice him. She had assumed his height was a part of his immortal status, but he must have been this tall as a young man.

She watched the crowd of hopeful servants round the corner, filled with a myriad of emotions she couldn't identify and didn't want to face. "I have to go to her, Stone. See Zhen Ni."

Stone touched her sleeve. "But the breach—"

"The breach can wait." Her words sounded sharper than she had intended. "You don't understand. She had loved this girl Lan with all her heart, had grieved so much when they were forced to part. Zhen Ni had never wanted to marry, and now she has. Coerced to, I'm certain of it. No one else would understand how devastated and afraid she'd be right now. I must see her." Skybright fisted her hands. "She *needs* me."

He stared after Pearl's retreating back. The girl sashayed as if she hoped he were looking.

"If you want my help," Skybright said, "the breach can wait until after I see Zhen Ni." But then she remembered, Stone only had ten days. "I won't delay."

Stone lifted his shoulders in resignation. "I'll go with you. It is as Pearl said, a sign that you ran into her."

"I just want to see her—tell her I'll return to her if she needs me." Skybright paused. "I'm afraid to meet her again. I know I hurt her." It was a confession. She needed to say it out loud, and Stone was the one there to listen.

He cupped her cheek, surprising her; she resisted the urge to close her eyes. "For the first time since I can remember, I am afraid too, Skybright. And I feel a rush of so many other emotions." He dropped his hand and smiled wryly. "I guess this is what it means to feel more human."

He turned from her and began down the path the others took. Skybright drew a deep breath, then followed him.

CHAPTER EIGHT

Skybright

The Bei manor was indeed impressive, even from the exterior. The outer walls seemed to stretch on endlessly, encompassing the large estate. Lush pomegranate trees, more than she could count, were planted along the length of the front wall with stone benches beneath some of the tall trees. The crowd that had passed stood in a tight knot in front of the grand double wooden doors. Two fierce jade lion statues sat on either side of the entrance. As she drew closer, Skybright saw that large rubies formed the statues' eyes, and she marveled that Master Bei was rich enough that he wasn't concerned some passerby would gouge out the precious jewels. She had no doubt the stones were real gems. Two magnificent door pulls made of brass were set into the doors, each with a large bat holding the rings in its mouth—a symbolism for fortune.

She glimpsed Pearl in the throng of people. The girl clutched a rolled message in her hand—probably a letter of introduction from Lady Yuan herself. Stone stood apart from the crowd, chin in one hand, staring at one of the lion statues. A few servants threw curious glances at him. He wasn't dressed as a rich master but carried himself with natural authority after becoming used to being obeyed over thousands of years. Noticing Skybright observing him, he gestured her over. "Do these lions seem … strange to you?" he asked in a low voice.

She leaned over to peer into the lion's face, and its jeweled eyes glittered, seeming to follow her movement, causing the hairs on her arms to stand on end. "They barely have a mane, and their fangs look sharper than normal. The eyes have the effect of seeing you." She hugged herself, chilled, even beneath the afternoon sun's warmth. "I'm sure it's a trick of the imagination. But what is that on top of its head?" She pointed, reluctant to touch the statue.

Two rounded points were set in the curved etchings of its mane. Stone drew closer to examine where she pointed, then let out a string of curses about a hag and fallen teeth and warts on the backside—he spoke too fast for her to catch it all. In an instant, he had grabbed her by the arm and was pushing their way to the front of the crowd, pounding so loudly on the brass knocker her ears rang. The servants didn't resist as he shoved past them, but their animated chatter hushed to low whispers.

One of the grand doors swung open, and a brutish guard stood before them. He had beady black eyes and a nose that flipped up so much at the end it almost appeared to be a snout. She glimpsed a massive spirit wall behind the guard, more than twice Stone's height.

"What do you want?" the guard growled, hefting the giant axe he clutched for emphasis.

The smell hit her then. This guard was not human; he was demonic. She glided closer to Stone, touching his elbow in warning.

"We are here to see Lady Bei," Stone said.

"She is occupied interviewing others. Wait your turn."

"We're not here to gain positions," Skybright replied, keeping her words even. Did Zhen Ni know her guard was demonic? Was she trapped inside? "I'm a friend."

"And him?" The demon bared sharp yellow teeth at Stone.

"He's my cousin, escorting me."

Stone and the guard stared at each other; then the guard tilted his head back and sniffed, like a dog would, his nostrils quivering. "Lady Bei's not taking visitors. Not your kind." He thrust his sharp axe blade at Stone. Stone didn't move a fraction but instead glared at the guard. "If I see you again, I'll bash your skull in," the guard said and slammed the door in their faces.

Stone raised a fist as if to pound on the door again, then twisted around and drew her aside, walking until they were a fair distance from the entrance. His anger and frustration were palpable.

"He's demonic," she said beneath her breath after they had cleared the crowd.

"I suspected," Stone replied. "You are certain?"

"I smelled it. His poor disguise didn't fool me." Skybright paused midstride and clutched his arm so hard her nails bit into his skin. "We have to get Zhen Ni out!"

"The house is tainted. If I were still as powerful, I would have sensed it the moment I stepped within this town. I would have been able to rid the demons just as easily as well." He scanned the high walls of the estate, as if searching for a different way in. "But I've lost most of my magic. I don't know how it is that they are disguising themselves as human—demons shouldn't have the ability, but this one does. Are there more within the manor?"

She cast her senses wide, afraid of what the answer might be. "Six total. Zhen Ni is in there with three other humans. But I feel something more evil than the guards. Can't you?"

Stone gave a humorless laugh. "Not anymore. This is a new breed of demons I've never encountered before. Our underworld demons do not appear human, they are also unable to communicate except in the most primitive terms. This one held an actual conversation with us. I don't know how it's possible."

She turned back toward the manor, feeling her body grow tense with fear. "We must find another way in!"

He glanced back toward the main entrance to be certain the guard hadn't reemerged. "Even if we could scale these walls, it's too much of a risk. We don't know what form of opponent we're dealing with. Not only could we put our lives at risk, we could get Zhen Ni in trouble if we were discovered."

"Oh dear goddess," Skybright whispered. How could this have happened? Did her former mistress know that she was in danger? "A note!" she exclaimed. "We can smuggle a note to her, warn Zhen Ni. And hope that she can make a reply. Pearl is still waiting outside—she can do it."

"Your mistress can read?" Stone asked.

"She was taught the women's language." Her heart dropped. "But I don't know it. I never learned."

He turned his back to the crowd in the distance and conjured a small piece of rice paper and calligraphy brush. "I know it. Tell me what you want to say."

It is near time for our game of Go. I await outside. The guard is a brute and would not let me enter. Be wary. Please let me see you. Sky

Skybright dabbed a sleeve against the corner of her eye. "We always played Go this time of day. She will know it's truly me."

Stone blew on the short message, testing to be certain the ink had dried, then rolled up the rice paper. "Let's hope this works."

She took the note and hurried back toward the group of people milling outside the grand doors. The hopeful workers smelled restless, eager. Pulling Pearl aside, the girl's eyes widened with interest, and Skybright gestured for her to keep quiet. She drew the handmaid to a stone bench far from the others. Bats were carved along its arms, interwoven with a square geometric design. "I need a favor," Skybright said in a low voice.

Pearl clasped her hands together, her excitement barely contained. "Of course. What am I to do?"

"I need you to pass this note to Lady Bei when you see her. Roll it with the letter of referral from Lady Yuan so that it's hidden." There was no risk of Pearl reading the message as she had never been taught either.

"Who's the letter from?" Pearl whispered. "A lover?"

Skybright was almost tempted to say yes to end the conversation. But the handmaid was such a gossip, it'd be all over town within a day. "No. It's from me. Lady Bei has refused to see me—the letter is a plea."

"Ah," Pearl said, nodding sympathetically. But there was no mistaking her disappointment.

"No one else may see the note. This is a secret between us, understand?"

The girl tilted her head, a glint catching in those dark eyes. Skybright knew Pearl was conniving and no fool. "If you deliver the letter successfully and are able to carry a message back in return, this hairpin is yours." Skybright touched the enameled lotus hairpin Stone had conjured for her, studded with small emeralds to form the flower's leaves.

Pearl pressed both hands against her mouth, drawing a sharp intake of breath. "Truly?"

Skybright nodded. "As long as you do exactly as I say."

Pearl took the small note and rolled it within Lady Yuan's larger letter. "I will, Skybright. You can depend on me."

The handmaid strolled back toward the front door and was waved in a few moments later by the unseen guard. She cast a quick glance back toward Skybright, her pink lips forming a small, secretive smile, before disappearing into the manor.

Zhen Ni

That fool girl Pearl flitted into the main hall wreathed in a too bright smile. Her eyes took in Zhen Ni's dress, her gaze lingering on her jade and gold bracelets and rubies dangling from her earlobes. Once the handmaid had calculated their worth, she swung her neck this way and that, like a hungry crane searching for fish in the water, taking in every detail of the hall, from the sumptuous brocade chairs and exquisite ceramic vases, to the full wall length scrolls of the "four gentlemen" paintings: orchid, bamboo, chrysanthemum, and plum blossom. Zhen Ni had no doubt they were painted by a master as each piece had a long-dead emperor's multiple red seals on them, as if to say "I approve, and these are mine." She had no inkling how her husband came to possess them.

Pearl took her time between bowing to Zhen Ni and taking a seat across from her, actually turning two full circles before Zhen Ni cleared her throat and rapped impatiently on her carved armrest with her closed fan. The handmaid covered her mouth with a hand in feigned embarrassment and sashayed over, proffering a rolled rice paper tied with a gold ribbon.

"From my mother?" Zhen Ni asked, taking it.

The handmaid nodded, but Zhen Ni didn't miss the faint curl of her lips, like she kept a secret. Zhen Ni unfurled the roll and immediately recognized the clean sweep of her mother's calligraphy written in the simpler woman's language. Even this brought the sting of tears to the back of her eyes, and Zhen Ni blinked, then stiffened her spine. She wouldn't give Pearl the satisfaction of knowing how homesick she was or how afraid and alone she felt.

Or the danger she faced.

Her husband was a demon. Zhen Ni was certain of it after what she witnessed the night before, and even her shrewd, resourceful mother couldn't save her from that. If she ran home crying for help, she'd bring trouble right to her family manor's doorstep. Then she caught sight of the smaller note tucked at the bottom of the rolled paper. Zhen Ni raised her head to meet Pearl's eyes, and the handmaid fiddled with a copper ring on her finger, lifting her chin. "We all at the Yuan manor miss you, lady, and wish you well."

She had sent Rose to fetch a midday meal for her before Pearl had entered. They were alone, although she knew her husband's repulsive guards were always lurking. Unrolling the paper further, she read the small note written by an unfamiliar hand, then felt the blood rush to her face when she saw the signed name at the bottom: *Sky*.

Skybright was here. Waiting outside for her. She didn't know how it could be possible, but it was. "Did my sister visit alone?" Zhen Ni asked casually.

"No, there was a cousin with her." Pearl gave a knowing grin. "He was very handsome."

Stone? But Stone would never have let Skybright return here. "Was he dressed well? Like a wealthy merchant?"

"No, lady. Quite plain." She giggled. "But I wasn't looking much at his clothes."

Kai Sen then. Had he succeeded in freeing Skybright from Stone?

A dark shadow fell across the main hall just after Zhen Ni had tucked Skybright's note into her sleeve. Her husband, dressed in gray, filled the doorway. He entered, and Pearl stared, mouth wide open. Zhen Ni didn't know how she could ever have mistaken him for human, noting now his strange gait to the too long limbs and lumps on his brow, where his horns protruded when he revealed his true self.

Zhen Ni stood gracefully, composing her face. She gave her husband a small, polite smile, revealing nothing. "Husband, this is an unexpected surprise."

She heard a childish burble, and Zhen Ni was gripped with terror. She knew that soft cooing. A girl of about two years peeped from behind Master Bei's loose trousers. She smiled sweetly at Zhen Ni, then Pearl, revealing small, perfect teeth—not the sharp little knives that had bit into a human eyeball. This was the same girl Zhen Ni had stumbled upon in the vast cavern beneath the manor yesterday, even though she was a full year older and walking now, when she could only crawl before. There was no mistaking the dark, expressive eyes, the perfect features. The girl's cheeks were rounded with a faint blush of pink, reminding Zhen Ni of a perfect peach.

"What a beautiful little darling!" Pearl leaned down and extended a hand.

Zhen Ni almost swatted at the handmaid, envisioning the demon child ripping her arm off to gnaw on it.

The girl darted behind Master Bei, clutching the fabric of his trousers, and giggled, a delightful, joyous sound. It would have lightened Zhen Ni's heart, had she not known the truth of what the girl really was.

Her husband's mouth stretched into what Zhen Ni imagined he thought a smile was but instead was a strained sneer. "Blossom can be shy," he said. Pearl nodded and straightened, blanching when she looked Master Bei full in the face. She shuffled back from him, bowing her head.

His black eyes captured Zhen Ni's, and she felt sweat gather at the nape of her neck, but she held his gaze, damp palms clasped in front of her. "Blossom is my daughter from my first marriage." His voice was like gravel. "You will treat her like your own."

"Of course, Husband." She wondered what became of his first wife—did she die of natural causes? She must have been beautiful, for Blossom looked nothing like her father. But the child, Zhen Ni had no doubt, was part demon—and that was every bit like Master Bei.

She plucked a dried mango slice covered in sugar from a lacquered tray and offered it to the girl. "Hello, Blossom." To Zhen Ni's astonishment, the girl dashed out from behind Master Bei and leaped into her arms. Blossom was attired in something coarse and baggy. It might as well have been a rice sack, and her black hair was knotted and disheveled. The little girl twined her chubby arms around Zhen Ni's neck and rested a plump cheek against her shoulder. She smelled sweet, reminding Zhen Ni of the delicious aroma of walnuts cooking in sugar; something she'd steal in large handfuls from the kitchen.

"Mama," the girl murmured.

Zhen Ni pulled back, enveloped in a blissful haze, dimly aware of Pearl gawping at her like a toad. Faint red smudges ringed

Blossom's bow-shaped mouth, like dried berry juice. But from far away, a thought reached the soft tendrils on the edges of her mind. *Not juice*, she thought. *Blood.* Human blood. Her little daughter had been dining and growing these last hours since she'd seen her, and Zhen Ni had been too cowardly to stab the child in the throat with Nanny Bai's dagger.

A part of her wanted to throw the girl aside, jerk her head away so her face wouldn't be eaten by the little monster. But she had to pretend she liked Blossom to fool her demon husband. And even more frightening, Zhen Ni realized she enjoyed holding the girl in her arms, feeling the soft chubbiness of her, breathing in her honeyed scent.

She'd never liked children before. *What was happening?*

"Mama," Blossom whispered again, sighing contentedly, and Zhen Ni's heart filled with love for her.

She was being charmed. The demon girl was weaving some magic spell over her. Dread tugged at the edge of Zhen Ni's consciousness like dull pinpricks. She tried to set Blossom down, but the girl clung to her like moss to stone.

"How could you let her run around dressed like this?" Zhen Ni reprimanded, speaking more boldly than she ever had before to Master Bei. She discreetly tugged at Blossom's round arms, trying to disentangle herself from the girl's grip. "And her hair is like a crow's nest!" The demon child was strong, already stronger than Zhen Ni.

Her husband folded his massive arms, obviously expecting Zhen Ni to take care of such feminine matters. "What is the letter?"

She felt faint alarm, and in that moment, Blossom dug sharp nails into her back, as if in warning. "From my mother," Zhen Ni said and tilted her chin toward Pearl. "News from home and a letter of recommendation for her."

Home was a few streets away, in the same town she had grown up in, but behind these massive walls, trapped with a demon husband and child, it might as well be worlds away.

"You will write and say all is well," Master Bei said. It wasn't a question or request. "We don't want to cause worry … or trouble."

For the briefest moment, she thought she glimpsed red flames in the depths of her husband's eyes. "No, no trouble. All is well, Husband. Of course I'll write and tell her." The implied threat to her loved ones was clear enough, even in her fogged mind. Zhen Ni would suffer alone to keep everyone she loved safe. "I'll write a letter to my mother and send it back with Pearl—tell her how perfect everything is."

Perfect. Like this girl she held in her arms. Zhen Ni's fear of Blossom was being swallowed by happy feelings. Feelings of love, comfort, and peace. She strained to hold on to her terror, that knife-edge of anxiety, but she'd been frightened and distressed for so long, her mind was unwilling to cling to the fear. Why not feel love instead? She hadn't felt truly loved since she had said farewell to Lan months ago, since she had lost Skybright …

Master Bei nodded and left without so much as a word or glance back at his new bride.

Pearl watched his hulking back, her brown eyes as round as teacups. "Master Bei … Master Bei is a formidable man."

Even in her blissful, loving haze for the child, the handmaid irritated Zhen Ni.

"Mama, down now." Blossom's strong grip eased around Zhen Ni's neck. "Please."

The girl had some manners at least. Already more polite than Pearl—which wasn't saying much. Who had taught the little girl to talk? Certainly not Master Bei, whose speech was halting at best. But then, Blossom had grown a full year in less than a day's time. There were no logical explanations here. Zhen Ni's sole task was to survive.

She put Blossom down gently as Rose swept into the main hall bearing a tray laden with dishes. Casting a curious glance at the little girl, Rose set the food on the oval rosewood table where Zhen Ni took her meals. The aroma of garlic, scallions, and black bean sauce drifted to her, but she had no appetite. Still, she would force herself to eat something. She wouldn't wallow in self-pity and waste away. She needed strength to contend with her demonic husband.

A year ago, she would have laughed at such absurdity. But a year ago, she had no notion that her closest confidant, her companion since she was a babe, was a half serpent demon. Sky. Skybright was waiting for her outside; she had come back for her. There was so much uncertainty in Zhen Ni's world now, but she should never have doubted Skybright's love for her.

Oriole followed soon after with a pot of tea and jug of rice wine, placing the tray carefully on the lacquered table. Zhen Ni nodded at the older servant in dismissal, and she slipped out of the hall on noiseless feet.

"Will you take me on, lady?" Pearl asked, her hands clutched in front of her chest. "It'd be an honor to work for the Bei manor!"

"Yes. I'll write a letter to my mother asking to keep you as part of my staff." Pearl was an annoyance but wily and skillful at sneaking and gathering gossip. She might prove useful. "Rose, take the child for a bath, and do something with her hair. Send for Ning Ning and have twelve outfits tailored. Shoes too. Choose the most expensive fabrics." She eased herself onto the carved stool and picked up a ladle to try the fragrant soup. "I've no set limit on how much to spend. Blossom will have the very best."

Rose leaned over to take the little girl's hand. Zhen Ni saw how her face softened, and her eyes lit up when Blossom curled her chubby fingers around the handmaid's. She hadn't imagined the effect the child had had on her. It was sorcery. Magic. And even though they were no longer touching, Blossom's charm on her was like some redolent perfume, suffusing her senses, lingering in her consciousness and on her skin. The small, sharp note of warning was nothing compared to the wave of love she felt from the child and for her.

"Is she hungry?" Rose breathed, her gaze never leaving the girl's face. "Should I feed her?"

If she only knew, Zhen Ni thought. It was a distant voice in her own mind.

"Take her to the kitchen first. Coax her to eat," Zhen Ni replied.

"She can have whatever her heart desires."

Rose nodded. "Of course she can." She led the girl down the steps and out into the lush courtyard.

"Sit." Zhen Ni waved a hand at Pearl, whose astonishment hadn't grown less when she had heard Zhen Ni casually tell Rose to spend as much as she pleased on the little girl. "Eat with me."

Pearl uncovered all the dishes for Zhen Ni: silk gourd with shrimp, bean curd in a black bean sauce, beef stew with carrots, and pork ribs marinated in a sweet and spicy dressing.

"Take what you'd like," Zhen Ni said. She knew the servants were treated well at her mother's manor, but to have seafood and so much meat at a meal was a rare feast. "Thank you for bringing the letter to me." They both knew Zhen Ni wasn't speaking about her mother's note.

Pearl had already taken a mouthful of food and finished chewing before she said, "Of course, lady." The girl lowered her voice—she was smarter than she acted. "Is there a message in return?"

Zhen Ni swigged a large gulp of rice wine, something she rarely indulged in. "Tell her—" She fisted her hands. "Tell her I could never forgive her for all the lies that she told. Tell her—" Zhen Ni had to stop, lest her voice wavered. "I never want to see her again."

Pearl's arched eyebrows climbed so high, it would have been comical, if Zhen Ni didn't feel so heartbroken. She knew how loyal Skybright was and what lengths she would go to save her if she realized Zhen Ni was in danger. The one way she could think of to get Skybright as far away from here as possible was to imply that she couldn't stand the thought of her presence. *She'll think that I hate her.* But Zhen Ni could live with this knowledge if she knew that Skybright would be safe.

Skybright

Pearl took forever to come back out from Bei manor.

Skybright vacillated between excitement and irritation, anxiety and fear. She wanted more than anything to change into her serpent shape, slither over the manor's tall wall, and kill all the demon guards that held Zhen Ni captive. Instead, she sat on the bench, painfully aware of the sun's gradual descent. Stone tried to distract her by making small talk—but after two millennia as an immortal, he was terrible at it.

"The birds are not singing in the trees," he said after a long silence.

Skybright flicked her senses upward. Stone was right; there were sparrows in the pomegranate trees, still and silent.

"It's because of the demons," he said.

"Hmm."

After another long lull in conversation in which she had to restrain herself from fidgeting and Stone sat motionless, he said, "They are hellhounds."

Skybright jerked to hear his voice, which had kept its resonance even after the goddess had stripped Stone of almost all his immortal powers.

"What?" she asked.

"Those statues made to look like ordinary guardian lions flanking Bei manor's entrance are really hellhounds. The hidden horns and their eyes gave them away."

She wasn't sure if she wanted to know, but she asked anyway, "What do they do?"

"They are powerful companions to demons of old." Stone steepled his fingers and stared at his hands, pausing as if considering something. "Ancient demons who had minds of their own. Not like the kind we grow and harvest for the Great Battle. You, Skybright, are from ancient demon stock." He glanced toward the statues, even as one of the magnificent outer doors of Bei manor pulled open. "I've never come across a hellhound—they were before even my time."

"What exactly are we dealing with?" she asked.

Stone tilted his head imperceptibly and grimaced before he smoothed his face. Skybright looked over his shoulder and saw Pearl flouncing her way toward them. She felt her heart leap into her throat—what did Zhen Ni say? Stone stood when Pearl arrived, more to keep a safe distance from the girl than from gallantry, Skybright suspected. The handmaid sat down beside Skybright. "Oooh, my seat is warm," Pearl said and batted her lashes at Stone.

Skybright managed not to roll her eyes, even as two bright spots of color flared on Stone's cheekbones. The Stone of old had no human physical reactions or reflexive idiosyncrasies at all, she realized, but they were appearing as if he had been in some long trance or slumber. Instead, she gripped the fool girl's wrist. "Enough flirting. What news?"

Pearl's round face lit up, and Skybright's anxiety eased. The girl must have good news. Pearl opened her mouth, then closed it again deliberately, her eyes fixed on the jeweled ornament pinned in Skybright's hair. Letting out a huff of impatience, Skybright removed the ornament and gave it to the girl. Pearl took it with a delighted smile, her fingers gliding over the shining emeralds. "Thank you, Skybright."

"Well?" Skybright asked, tapping her foot.

"I got the job as a servant in Bei manor!" Pearl said, pinning the ornament into her own hair. "You should have seen the estate, massive courtyards landscaped and planted even better than Yuan manor. And Mistress, I mean, Lady Bei was dressed like the empress herself!" The girl clutched both hands to her chest, eyes shining. "I was able to get your note to her without anyone noticing," Pearl said, dropping her voice.

Skybright leaned in. "What did she say?"

The girl scrunched her face, making an apologetic expression. "I'm afraid Lady Bei says she never wants to see you again."

Skybright reared back, and if she had been in serpent form,

would have knocked Pearl off the bench with a swipe of her coil. It felt like the girl had slapped her across the face. "What?" Skybright whispered.

"Something about all the lies that you told." Pearl had the decency to appear contrite, but Skybright didn't miss the gleam in her eyes. "She said she could never forgive you. The lady was very emphatic and—"

Stone hauled the girl up by one arm. "Thank you, Pearl, for relaying that message."

"Oh," Pearl breathed, standing now, less than a hand-width from Stone.

Stone let go of the girl. "You can leave," he said. The order was spoken in the same quiet but unyielding tone he had used to command for the last two thousand years. Even Pearl, in her swooning, heard it.

"Yes." She swayed from them, like a leaf caught in the wind. "I must pack for my new position at Bei manor. Good-bye!" She left, humming a soft tune, without another glance back, her fingers caressing her new hairpin.

Skybright doubled over when the girl was far enough that her singing couldn't be heard any longer. The rush of tears came, hot against her cold cheeks. Zhen Ni never wanted to see her again, and could she blame her? Skybright hadn't known how her previous mistress, her confidante and friend, would receive her after their time apart, but now she knew. The answer was clear and cruel in its finality.

"Skybright." Stone touched her shoulder, then stooped down so their faces were level and gently swiped her tears away with his thumb. For the first time since she'd known Stone, she truly felt his sympathy—a very human emotion. She took comfort in it. This was the young man whom his little sister, Mei Er, had adored. But Skybright didn't see him like an older brother. Not at all. A pale green handkerchief appeared in his other hand, and he offered it to her.

Grateful, she took the silk fabric and dabbed at her eyes. "How could she say such things?" Her words sounded muffled.

"Why do mortals ever say what they say to each other?"

She smiled through her tears. Stone doing what he did best, answering a query with another question. "She hates me." Skybright wiped her cheeks, her chest feeling heavy, yet hollow, as if her body was an empty carapace.

He slipped back on the bench beside her. His physical warmth reassured her in its familiarity. There was no denying it. "What do you want to do?" he asked.

Skybright almost laughed aloud at the pained expression on his face. It was clear that he had never had to utter those words before, not for a few millennia. "I can't leave her in a manor full of demons, Stone."

He opened his mouth, then clamped it shut, jaw flexing. Stone was silent for long moments, as if carefully considering his words. "I don't believe what is happening at Bei manor is a coincidence. We'll be helping Zhen Ni too if we get to the bottom of why the breach is still open. I *know* the rules of the covenant, Skybright. We both saw the breach close with our own eyes."

"I think it's connected too," she said. "And Zhen Ni is in danger."

Stone nodded, his expression grim. "We'll investigate the breach and come back to Zhen Ni as soon as we can."

CHAPTER NINE

Skybright

Skybright and Stone decided to travel through the forest, walking the hidden paths and passing beneath familiar trees, places that she'd wandered with Zhen Ni since they were girls brave enough to escape the manor to seek fun. Her heart hurt to remember it. Stone tried to distract her with small talk, awkward and halting. But the more he spoke, the more at ease his conversation became. He shared random memories that were emerging like bubbles rising to the water's surface of his life as a mortal. He remembered making mud pies with his youngest sister, Mei Er, and the delicious New Year's noodles, dumplings, and fish his mother would prepare with the limited coin they had. "I'd always spend my New Year's money buying treats or a toy for Mei Er," Stone said with a grin. The distant memory softened his features and the usual sharpness of his gaze.

Skybright might have thought he was painting himself in a generous light, but she had seen and felt his past through her own eyes and knew that he spoke truth. He had loved Mei Er especially and spoiled her as a big brother would.

After a few leading questions from Stone, Skybright slowly began reminiscing about her many misadventures with Zhen Ni—the time they got caught in a storm and returned to the Yuan manor looking like drowned cats, or the time Zhen Ni decided to rescue an abandoned "kitten," only to be told it was a juvenile red fox by Nanny Bai, but not before the animal had given Zhen Ni's older handmaid, Ripple, two scratches on her forearm that would scar for life.

They also walked often in companionable silence. She knew that Stone took as much pleasure from the wilderness as she did. Stopping by the flowing creek in the late afternoon, the sun slanted like liquid gold across the rippling water and thick foliage. They settled on a large rock alongside the creek and ate the vegetable buns they had picked up from a roadside stand in town. Skybright savored them; they were like the ones Cook used to make at Yuan manor, and it filled her with nostalgia. And try as she might to cast the thought aside, seeing this creek reminded her of Kai Sen and their time together. Being back in Chang He was more bittersweet than she'd imagined.

She hadn't realized until she returned here that her heart had let the thought of ever being with Kai Sen again go. Skybright knew she was practical to a fault, and that Kai Sen was the dreamer, the romantic, but being away from him, from Zhen Ni, from everything and everyone she had ever known, had laid her circumstances out very clearly—returning to a normal life, a human life, was something she couldn't imagine now.

How long had she been away from Yuan manor? Her life there felt like something lived by a former incarnation—by a girl who didn't know yet who she truly was. She didn't mourn her old life, the old Skybright, as much as she missed Zhen Ni and Kai Sen. But even then, she didn't dwell on the sadness because she knew she could never again be a part of their lives. Parting, loss, sorrow: these were the ways of the mortal world.

Skybright kneeled by the stream to wash her hands when a foul odor assaulted her, so discordant with the crisp earthiness of their surroundings. She snapped her head up, body tensing, ready to fight. Stone stood beside her testing his magic ability again, his shoulders tight with frustration. He had built a pyramid of rocks in front of him, moving them with his earth magic.

"Stone," she said in warning.

In an instant, he wielded a giant bronze axe, the blade gleaming with a dangerous edge. The weapon was so hefty he gripped it in both hands. It was as if he knew instinctively the saber strapped to his waist would not be enough.

Leaves rustled and stirred at the tree line, and the silhouette of a tall man emerged from the forest. Even from this distance, Skybright could see how big he was, how thick and broad. The man stalked toward them, but there was something inhuman about the way he moved, the motion of his legs and arms blurring with speed.

"I am lost," he said, his low voice as deep as a gong.

Skybright shifted, rearing high on her serpent coil so she was taller than Stone, hissing deep. Stone flung an arm out toward her in warning. Too late, she had already slithered away from him, taking a wide circle around the man who obviously was not a man. Its stench was overwhelming, even from a short distance, reeking of rancid sweat, vomit, and feces, but beneath it all, something much more sinister and menacing. The forest had gone silent around them, as if all its inhabitants held their breaths.

The thing looked enough like a man from far away, giant, a half head taller than even Stone, but as her serpentine vision scanned him for weaknesses, she saw the ways in which it was *wrong*. It wore a brown leather vest, revealing muscular arms, but it had two elbow joints, jutting out like shoulder blades. This allowed it to swing its forearms in a full circle, the joints making sick, popping noises. It had eight fingers on each hand and a face with features so scrambled, she didn't know where to focus. Its gaping mouth was where its nose should have been, and its pointed nose perched right above its squat chin. The eyes, deep set and beady, were the only feature that were in the right place, reminding Skybright of a mean pig.

"My hunger burns!" it shouted this time.

Before she had a chance to react, it had convulsed toward her at inhuman speed, closing their gap faster than she thought possible. And she was fast. This thing was as fast as Stone when he was at his most powerful. She barely escaped it throwing its trunk-like arms around her, as if it was trying to catch a stray hen. It caught the tail end of her serpent coil and held on with astonishing strength. "You would make a nice meal," it said.

She tried to twist from its grip, but the thing was too strong, and it began pulling, as if to reel her in. Stone charged at that moment, axe raised, ready to hack into the beast, when it knocked him down with one huge fist, so fast that Skybright couldn't follow the movement. In one instant, Stone was ready to attack, and in the next, he was flat on the ground, gasping.

Goddess.

But the creature had let go of its double grip on her, which was enough for Skybright to use all her strength to wrench herself away, snapping her coil to knock the demon off its feet. The thing tripped, gaping at her, surprised, but managed to stay upright. It was agile for its lumbering size. Stone had risen, scrambling back. "It's too fast," he said, sounding out of breath.

"Fast to kill." The thing leered, its thin mouth stretching wide in the middle of its face. "As my master wished." With that, it roared and was a smear of motion aimed at Stone this time, when a giant boulder flew from behind Stone, smacking the creature square in the chest.

It toppled backward.

Skybright stared, not understanding who had thrown the boulder; then she saw three more rocks floating behind Stone's shoulders. He was breathing hard, a sheen of sweat on his pale face, but it was obvious that *he* was controlling the rocks. The demon was pinned beneath the boulder, massive enough that if she wanted to sit at the top, she'd have to make an effort to climb it. But the thing clasped the boulder and tossed it as if it were a pebble.

The demon grunted, a rumbling noise, then was standing again faster than she could draw a breath. "I will eat you both." The loudness of its words rattled her teeth.

Thunk, thunk, thunk. Three more smaller boulders slammed into the creature in quick succession. The last crashed into the demon's face with a loud crunch of bone. The thing staggered, roaring. Skybright didn't hesitate; she slid toward it, taking advantage of its pain and disorientation and sank her fangs into one muscular shoulder. Her mouth filled with her own bitter venom, her senses with its putrid musk.

It lashed out, punching her in the side of the head, hitting her square in her ear, but it was too late. She slithered back, head ringing, her ear ablaze with pain. Her vision doubled, but she slid to where Stone stood, weaponless now, except for one final large rock floating behind him.

They watched in grim silence as the demon swayed, then buckled to its knees, before falling flat on its gruesome face. Its massive body twitched for a long time in its death throes before finally becoming still. A distant ringing still reverberated in her head, and Skybright suspected that if she had been in human form, she'd be knocked out cold. As it were, Stone seemed unsteady on his own feet, and she reached out to grip his arm. He glanced at her in surprise, his features tight with pain. "Sit," she said.

He didn't argue, and they went back to the water's edge. She held his arm the entire time, his frustration and pain like vinegar against her tongue. Stone manifested a large jug of rice wine and two cups on a smooth rock and poured for them. She didn't eat or drink in serpent form, so he gulped down both cups before saying, "Your venom is potent, thank the goddess, or we'd probably both be dead."

"You held your own," she rasped. "That trick with flinging the large boulders was impressive."

He snorted. "Child's play compared to my magic ability before."

"Once we fix this, close the breach,"—she slithered around him, pacing—"I'm sure you can ask for your powers back, Stone, for your role as the Immortals' liaison."

He flicked her a look, his expression glum.

"What was that thing?" she asked.

"A mistake." He poured himself another cup of wine, downed it, and the color began to return to his face. "A bungled version of those guards who passed as human protecting Bei manor."

"A failure then."

"But still impressive," he said. "None of the demons I've seen or helped to breed in the underworld for the Great Battle have looked so human. Even as scrambled as that thing's face was, it still bore the features of a human face. And it was faster and stronger than any demon I've encountered as well."

Skybright shivered, wrapping her arms around her naked torso. Before, this familiar spot had been welcoming with its rushing creek surrounded by majestic trees, full of warm memories. Now she felt exposed and the place tainted. "You mentioned ancient demons earlier …"

Stone nodded. "Thousands of years ago, they roamed this middle kingdom between the heavens and the underworld. There weren't many mortals then, so there was enough land for both to live, but whenever their paths crossed, the humans were often slaughtered by the demons."

"Did these ancient demons look human?" she asked.

"No," Stone replied. "They were part beast, like the demons you had seen from the Great Battle, but more powerful, conniving. The gods were shocked one day to discover that the human population had dwindled to almost nothing, targeted by the demons for fun and sport or wiped out by their plagues. The mortals had always prayed to the gods, but the demons had refused to. They were too selfish, too bold; they wanted to take the mortal realm for themselves and rule it."

"I think I need that drink," Skybright said. She shifted back to her human form and instantly felt the throbbing ache in her head and the weakness in her knees. Stone manifested a pale green gown and handed it to her, eyes averted. His attraction for her was something that always lingered in the air between them now.

She couldn't deny her own desire, remembered the kiss that they had shared in that ramshackle restaurant. But his attraction was something that Stone was always tamping down, trying to control. He didn't *want* to be attracted to her—that much was obvious.

She drew the gown on and tied the silk sash with trembling fingers. It was Stone who reached for her this time, his touch tingling her skin, as he guided her to sit beside him on the flat rock. He poured another cup for her and she drank, feeling the liquid burn the back of her throat, making her eyes water. She scrunched her face, and Stone let out a low laugh. "It's good wine," he said.

"I'm not used to drinking it," she replied, even as warmth slid through her, emanating from her chest, rubbing away the sharp edges of her fear and pain. "How did the tale end then, Stone?"

"The Immortals from the heavens finally realized the extent of the demons' hubris and demanded that they obey and worship the gods. The demons refused and revolted."

Skybright's eyebrows lifted. "They tried to conquer the gods?"

"The fighting was short but intense," Stone said.

She recalled the cold beauty of the Goddess of Accord and the omnipotence of her power. "The demons didn't have a chance," she said.

"No," Stone agreed. "The gods unmade them as if they never existed."

"But a few survived?" They must have, for her to exist.

Stone stared at the still corpse of the demon in the distance. "The Immortals let a few dozen demons live and cast them to the underworld, forcing them to work there eternally as punishment."

"And one of them has escaped?"

"Escaped or never captured. Maybe it's remained hidden for thousands of years, biding its time, growing in strength and honing its powers."

"Now it's pretending to be a wealthy merchant with no family to speak of," she said. "And built a compound protected by new demons who appear human. It's Master Bei, isn't it?" The wine she had swallowed felt like it was trying to rise again, sour in her mouth.

Stone nodded once. "I believe so."

"What does he want with Zhen Ni?"

"Nothing good," he replied.

"He's infiltrating the mortal realm."

"And he's bringing his demons through the breach. It's the only way," Stone said. "The ancient demons wiped out entire villages and cities before—they can do it again. Who knows how many have come through already. He's using Zhen Ni to pass as human and—" He stopped abruptly, clearing his throat.

"What?" Cold fear wound its way down her spine.

"Perhaps to spawn. I don't think it's possible but—"

All the blood drained from her face. She wanted to retch. "We *have* to go back, Stone. Now." She pounded her fist against the rock.

"I don't know if we have a fighting chance, Skybright." He wiped a hand across his face, his weariness palpable. "We might be stumbling toward our own deaths."

"I don't care," she replied. "We have to try."

Stone met her eyes and held her gaze. Even stripped of most of his powers, it still felt as if he could read her inner-most thoughts, glimpse into her soul. "I go where you go."

She felt an overwhelming sense of relief that she refused to acknowledge. Skybright would have gone back without Stone, but she was glad he chose to stay by her side, despite that this would further delay their journey. She was beginning to understand why Stone had glowed when she had glimpsed into his past and into his soul. "Good," she said. "Let's burn the body first."

It was evening when they returned to Bei manor. The crowd that had waited impatiently outside to be interviewed had long dispersed. The moon was a thin sliver in the sky, a malicious grin, casting little light. Skybright walked the perimeter of the vast outer wall, then finally turned the corner into an alleyway that ran along the west side of the estate. The narrow lane was completely dark, but Skybright was able to see with her heightened sight.

She stopped after passing a small servant's side entrance. Unfortunately, Stone's night vision wasn't as keen anymore, and he slammed into her, almost knocking her over. She bit down on a sharp yelp while Stone, still agile, threw an arm around her to keep her from falling. "Sorry," he whispered. In that one word, Skybright could hear the chagrin in his voice. "It's too risky to conjure a light," he explained, letting go.

"Can you climb this wall?" she asked.

The Bei manor wall was more than twice Stone's own height and as smooth as jade. Stone craned his neck, although she didn't believe he could actually see. "I don't think so."

She remembered Kai Sen and all those nights she'd found him perched on top of the Yuan manor wall, as easy as a cat. "I'll change into serpent form and climb up, then help you."

He nodded, his pupils wide in his brown eyes. "Use your venom on those demonic guards, Skybright. Nothing is immune to it. I'll take as many down as I can with my spade."

She gave a small laugh under her breath despite her anxiety, and Stone grinned. He was mocking himself, even when he had wielded an axe in the demon encounter. She liked the wry sense of humor that was emerging when he had been so aloof before.

She shifted in an instant, losing her clothes and her legs, shedding them like a cumbersome second skin. The air was warm against her bare flesh. "Let's find Zhen Ni." The words grated out with a hiss. Skybright used her serpent coil and propelled herself up the cool wall with ease. When she reached the top, she gripped the wide ledge with both hands. The massive estate opened below her, with multiple courtyards and a labyrinth of corridors lit sporadically by lanterns. But the underlying feeling, beyond its grandeur and beauty, was oppressive. The majority of the estate was dark, seemingly abandoned. It lacked the color and noise, the hustle and movement, the rhythmic cadences and rituals that were a part of every manor.

It made Skybright even angrier on Zhen Ni's behalf, that she had been married off not only to danger, but this lonely isolation. She reached forward with one arm, intending to swing her serpent length over the wall, when some invisible barrier flung her with brutal force away from the manor. She slammed into the opposite wall of the alleyway, so hard that she was stunned, and slid to the ground, her coil breaking her fall. Stone was immediately beside her. "Goddess, Skybright," he said, and a small travel lantern magically appeared. "To hell if anyone sees us. I'll knock them out if they do." His eyes ran over her face and torso. "Are you all right?"

Skybright pushed herself up to a sitting position with trembling arms. "I hit my head hard."

"May I?" Stone asked.

She dipped her chin in a shallow nod, and he gently touched the back of her skull. She winced.

"There's a small lump there. But it's not bleeding." He made a frustrated noise. "I cannot heal anymore." He set the lantern on the ground. "What happened?"

"I tried to climb over the wall, but something threw me back." She felt the knot with her fingers and scowled. "I'll live."

Stone cursed under his breath, something about tortoises laying rotten eggs. "The manor is under a protective spell." He manifested a cloth that smelled of Nanny Bai's medicinal room, then pressed it against her injury. The soft pad was soothingly cold, and their fingers brushed when she put her own hand there. Stone's touch seemed even warmer by contrast. "It'd take tremendous ability to cast a ward over such a massive estate. We're dealing with someone very powerful." He stood. "Someone who is more powerful than either of us."

She never needed sleep or was weary in her serpent form, but suddenly, she felt drained. Defeated. "How can we save Zhen Ni if we can't even get inside? Is the front entrance warded too?"

"The entire estate must be protected." Stone rubbed his hands together. The small travel lantern he'd conjured cast a dim halo around them, but she didn't need its light to see that his handsome face was pale from exhaustion. "We have to go to the breach—"

She laid a hand on his wrist, and he stopped abruptly. "The old breach *did* close. We saw it with our own eyes, like you said." Skybright waved an arm toward Bei manor. "There is a new breach, and it's within the estate."

"That's not possible," Stone said. "Only the gods can—"

"I can feel it, Stone," she rasped. "I sensed an unmistakable power in the daytime, but now it is even stronger, underground, deep within the manor. Why else would it be warded?"

"And what better way to bring in demons into the mortal realm than from your very own estate?" Stone cursed, the longest string of oaths she'd heard yet, something about pustules and infertility on all the farm animals, broken wheels, flooded fields, and mosquito swarms. He swiped a hand over his face when he was finally done.

"What can we do?" Skybright knew they were all in danger, but she could only think of Zhen Ni and how alone and trapped she was.

"We go to the monastery," he replied.

Although it made perfect sense, it was the last thing she expected him to say. "Can they help?"

"It depends on how many more demons Master Bei has waiting for us. At the very least, we need to warn them."

They would send the monks into battle again, send them to their deaths. And Kai Sen—was he still at the monastery?

"We can tell the Immortals," she said. "They can fix this. Kill Master Bei and—"

Stone shook his head. "I've no way to communicate with the gods. Even when I was more powerful, I could only visit The Mountain of Heavenly Peace when I was summoned. We cannot wait for the gods to intervene." He stood and straightened. "We have to do this ourselves. The next time I see the Goddess of Accord, I either live or die. I need your help, Skybright."

She shifted back to a girl, and Stone threw a tunic over her shoulders before handing her a long skirt. Stone was right. They had to warn the monks and think of a way to save Zhen Ni and close this new breach. But the odds seemed vastly against them.

Kai Sen

The abbot's funeral, along with all the other monks who had died during the attack, took place right after all the demons had been defeated. There was no time for formal ceremonies or a burial when one died by the tainted touch of a creature from the underworld. All the bodies were burned immediately, so the monastery's large square was ablaze, lit as bright as midday. Kai Sen stood at the square's edge, feeling numb, fighting off his light-headedness as he watched the flames leap. There'd been too many of these kinds of funerals this past year—hundreds of monks lost—and they had all believed they'd seen the last of the monstrosities after the breach had closed.

Ashes swirled through the night air, and the remaining few hundred monks observed in silence, too exhausted to cry out for their dead brothers and their leader. Kai Sen's own throat was raw and felt swollen shut. His eyes stung, but he never looked away. Several monks came to him after the fires had flickered out, gripping his arm or patting his shoulder. He remained for as long as he could stand, before stumbling back to Abbot Wu's quarters.

Kai Sen shot up in bed, his body damp with sweat, heart thumping hard in his ribcage. His dreams were plagued by screams and a montage of horrifying images: the rotten faces of the undead, brother monks he'd lost, eviscerated with their intestines spilling out … Disoriented, he conjured hellfire in his palm, illuminating the sparse room. He panicked for a moment, not recognizing where he was; then it hit him: Abbot Wu's old bedchamber. He had moved in the previous night, after Abbot Wu's funeral, when it was revealed among his papers that he had officially chosen Kai Sen as his successor in leading the monastery.

He swung out of the narrow, hard bed, feeling sore and bruised, tossing the ball of hellfire upward so it followed him, glowing above his head. He pushed the single door aside and walked down the dark and silent hallway toward the abbot's study. The lattice windows covering one wall of the long corridor were carved in square shapes with white panels. It was right before dawn judging by the dim grayness shadowing the hallway, which meant that Kai Sen had had four hours of fitful sleep.

Entering the study, he murmured a quick incantation below his breath and the floating sphere of hellfire vibrated, then expanded, illuminating the chamber in an eerie blue. After the abbot's body had been removed, a handful of monks remained to clear the wreckage. They propped the fallen shelves up and stacked the bound tomes carefully, took away the broken furnishings, and swept the floor of debris. But no matter how hard Kai Sen and Han tried to scrub away the dark outline embedded in the stone floor where that two-faced demon woman had died, they couldn't remove it. Kai Sen's eyes were drawn there like a compulsion.

Under the glow of the hellfire, the stain pulsed a deep red, like something alive. Shuddering, Kai Sen turned away from it to sit at the abbot's long table. Everything that hadn't broken had been returned to it, the calligraphy brushes and inkstone set at the upper edge, and his papers placed in a neat pile. But Kai Sen wasn't interested in any of those things. He reached for an oval stone as large as his palm and surprisingly heavy. Thankfully, it had not been broken during the chaos. The divining stone was carved with words and symbols he didn't recognize. In daylight, the stone was a milky gray, near translucent, but when he held it to the light, it was opaque, with a core composed of deep blue veins that seemed to swirl. Kai Sen had attributed it to a trick of the light and his own exhaustion. But now, in the dim grayness of dawn, the stone had turned a solid black in color. It appeared to have a mind of its own.

Abbot Wu had said that this could help him find the new breach, but how did it work? He had never come across a divining stone in his studies and didn't recognize it either from drawings and etchings he had seen. If the abbot was unable to get it to work after decades of study, how could he possibly? The two roosters that lived in the monastery's stockyard began to crow. Soon, the first gong would sound, and his first day as the head of the monastery would begin. He wanted to drop his head in his hands from the sheer burden he felt on his shoulders. Instead, he tried to work the stone. Concentrating on what Abbot Wu had been teaching him and his own surreptitious studies, he considered the elements of magic he could pull from: fire, earth, metal, water, and wood.

Instinctively, he drew on the earth element to call to the magic of the stone. The strands of earth magic he pulled on were different than fire, more weighted, and the more he drew, Kai Sen felt as if he could taste dust between his teeth, the solidity of it against his solar plexus. The stone began to change color, from opaque black to milky gray, revealing the indigo veins at the stone's core, which began to swirl and glimmer. His chest seized with excitement, and he continued to draw upon the earth element until a sweat broke along his hairline and dampened the back of his neck. Kai Sen tugged as much and as hard as he could, using himself as a conduit, until his vision wavered, yet the stone never grew any brighter.

The first gong sounded in the square, breaking his concentration, and the stone turned black once more. Kai Sen doubled over, wanting to retch, but instead dry heaved, his eyesight blurring. He propped himself against the desk and blinked, trying to clear his vision, attributing it to tears; his sight was obscured, like a gray veil had been dropped over him. The stone fell from his shaking hand, and to his relief, his eyesight cleared. He drew a ragged breath just as Han entered the library.

"Good, you're up," Han said.

Kai Sen cleared his throat, then swallowed. "I'm up. I have a lot to do."

Han's eyebrows drew together in concern, reading him too well, but Kai Sen lifted a hand. "You'll help me today in leading the fortification of the monastery," Kai Sen said.

"Of course, brother."

Kai Sen stood, then reached over and slipped the divining stone into a leather pouch tied at his waist. The monks were lined up in rows, dressed in white muslin tunics of mourning, ready to receive him when he stepped outside to greet them.

Zhen Ni

Zhen Ni was relieved when she finally dismissed Pearl. She tried to draw a full breath, but her chest felt restricted by the new breast binder she wore—the binder that her husband had never bothered to unravel on their wedding night as custom dictated. It was one of the many duties he had shirked—and now she knew why. Master Bei probably had no penis at all, or worse, it was something two headed and monstrous. She wanted to throw up everything she had forced herself to eat for strength. Instead, she dug her nails into her palms and swallowed hard. "Oriole," she said.

Zhen Ni hadn't even raised her voice, and the older handmaid was in the main hall within an instant. "Yes, lady?"

"Please let everyone waiting outside know I won't conduct any more interviews today," Zhen Ni said. "They may return tomorrow morning."

"Yes, lady." Oriole was dressed in a pale peach tunic and trousers with green embroidering along the collar. Silver ornaments were pinned into her hair, pulled into two tight buns. She looked every bit the handmaid of a wealthy household, but still, not as well dressed or richly adorned as Skybright had been. Without being conscious of it, Zhen Ni realized she had decided no matter how much wealthier her new husband might be, she would never elevate a handmaid to the status that Skybright had held in the Yuan household. Or the place that she had held in her heart.

Quick on her feet, Oriole had disappeared before Zhen Ni even finished her thought. Feeling exhausted and emotionally drained, Zhen Ni was tempted to put her head down on the oval table when Rose entered, clutching Blossom's hand. The little girl had been bathed, and her subtle sweet scent filled the hall, reminding Zhen Ni of honeyed cakes. Rose had combed the girl's thick hair, plaiting it into two long braids. She'd been changed out of the rice sack that Master Bei had dressed the girl in, and now wore an exquisite lavender tunic and trousers embroidered with gold chrysanthemums. The demon child was the most beautiful little girl she'd ever seen.

Not even realizing she had extended her hand until it was already outstretched, Zhen Ni said, "Darling. My petal. Come."

Blossom toddled over, wide-eyed, her cherubic face lit with a soft smile. The closer she drew, the more Zhen Ni's mood lightened, until the demon child climbed into her lap and threw one chubby arm around her neck. "Mama," she stated simply.

The little girl's touch scattered all the sorrow and fear that had crowded Zhen Ni's heart, like sunlight dispersing dreary clouds. She knew in the farthest reaches of her mind that Blossom was bewitching her, but after these past few days, why shouldn't she stop feeling anxiety and dread? Why shouldn't she allow herself to be awash in good feelings? What was the harm in it? She'd be forced to mother the demon child in the end, no matter what.

"Did she eat?" Zhen Ni asked distractedly, hugging the little girl to her.

A flicker of doubt crossed Rose's serene features. "Yes, lady. She wanted raw meat."

"Really?" Zhen Ni ran a palm down Blossom's smooth braid. "I know they take raw beef in thin slices with noodles in some of the provinces—" She stopped abruptly as Rose shook her head.

"She took the beef in large chunks, lady. And wanted organs too." The handmaid shifted on her slippered feet. "She ate a lot."

"Uncooked?"

"Yes, lady."

"What did Pei think?"

"Cook thought it was very strange, but she gave Blossom everything she wanted."

Of course she did, Zhen Ni thought. Skybright had always said that Zhen Ni didn't know how to take no for an answer, that she had always gotten everything she ever desired. But that was before Zhen Ni had fallen in love with another girl. Before she had been married off to a monster. She had a feeling that her daughter Blossom would indeed get everything she wanted in life. She could charm her victim or eat his heart out, whichever served the demon child's purpose.

Her purpose. What *was* Blossom's purpose?

Blossom squeezed Zhen Ni's shoulder with a dimpled hand, dispelling those annoying, nagging thoughts. "So hungry, Mama," she said in a sweet, lilting voice. "It's like I have a hole in my belly."

"My soft petal." Zhen Ni pressed her lips against Blossom's brow. The child smelled like honey, not of offal, blood, and raw meat. "But did you get enough to eat? Mama will have Cook slaughter a whole cow for you, if you desire."

The little girl touched Zhen Ni's face and stared into her eyes. Her perfect skin might as well have been wrought from porcelain, painted with subtle pink blooms on each cheek by a master artisan. "Thank you, Mama. I am satisfied for now."

Despite the joyful haze Zhen Ni floated in, the hairs on her arms stood on end, as if a chilling breeze had swept through the room. A visceral warning. "Rose, ask Pei to have a whole carcass butchered and ready from now on." Blossom could never go hungry. Zhen Ni would keep her satisfied with as much raw beef or pork as she desired. It was better than … the alternative.

"Yes, lady." The young handmaid bowed.

She set Blossom onto the ground. "You'll go with Rose and take an afternoon nap, petal?"

Blossom gazed up at her. Her eyes were amber—a light color Zhen Ni had never seen before—and seemed to glow. "I don't need sleep, Mama." She rubbed her stomach. "Only to eat."

"Well you go on and go play then. Rose will keep you company." Zhen Ni reached over and softly tweaked the little girl's button nose. "I'll come and see you soon, all right?"

Blossom nodded, her braids bouncing.

"But you have to be good, petal. You'll behave?"

"Yes, Mama!" She toddled over to Rose who stretched out her hand indulgently, a wide smile on the handmaid's face, and the two disappeared down the steps through the resplendent courtyard.

All the warm feelings that Blossom had brought slipped away from Zhen Ni like water from a cracked vase. It was just mid-afternoon, but Zhen Ni felt frayed by a constant sense of anxiety and terror. And she had only been a bride to Master Bei for two days—how would she survive a lifetime?

Perhaps her husband didn't plan on keeping her alive for very long.

She felt so alone again, helpless and frightened, but if she had to slam a cleaver between her husband's bulging eyes to survive, she would. Even if she died trying.

Zhen Ni almost retreated to her grand quarters to crawl into the sumptuous bed and hide beneath the silk sheet, to cower and forget the world. But instead, she took to walking through the grand manor, familiarizing herself with its layout. She wandered the covered pathways that meandered from one magnificent courtyard to another. It was an unusually hot day in early spring, and Zhen Ni finally took shelter in a grand pagoda with a green tiled roof and red columns decorated with golden lotuses. Another tribute to her from her thoughtful husband, she thought wryly. She wished for some chilled tea, but had sent Oriole away, telling the handmaid not to trail her as she normally would. The air was fragrant with the sweet perfume of wisteria which wound its way around the railing of the pagoda, a few branches curling up its columns.

Zhen Ni sat in the cool shade and surveyed the courtyard. This one was planted with crabapple trees, their deep fuchsia blooms striking against the rockwork. A large oval pond was a short distance away, and she could see golden fish with sleek bodies darting beneath the water. Never in her life would she have imagined she'd live in a manor more opulent than her own family's or be married to a husband who was as horrifying as her new home was beautiful.

"We need to speak, Wife," Master Bei said from behind her, appearing out of nowhere.

She jumped off the bench, suppressing a scream. It was as if her thoughts had summoned him like a nightmare. "Husband," she said, steadying her voice. This must be what a rabbit felt like trapped with a wolf.

He climbed the stone steps into the pagoda and sat across from her, then lifted a hand, indicating that she should sit back down. She did so, resting her hands in her lap, her palms damp against the silk fabric of her skirt.

"I wanted an obedient wife," Master Bei said in that deep voice. "But my choices were limited. Despite my wealth, I have no family name, no pedigree." He scratched his chin, thick with a black beard that had been mere shadow when she had seen him a few hours earlier. "So I had to make do with you."

Zhen Ni bristled, despite her fear. Like *he* was such a catch? "I am obedient, Husband," she said.

He barked something that might have been a laugh and turned his too large eyes to her. They glowed a deep red. Horns, lethally sharp, thick and misshapen like the roots of a tree, jutted out from his brow. "So obedient that you found my underground lair the first day as my wife, disturbing Blossom's feasting?"

The scent of smoke and fire emanated from him.

She felt the blood drain from her face.

"Yes, my hounds told me everything."

It was no use feigning innocence. "Those statues—"

"Loyal hellhounds. They serve as my eyes and ears." His large hand darted out, the motion faster than she could see, and he gripped her forearm so hard her eyes teared. Talons had emerged where his thick yellow fingernails had been. "Don't go where you're not wanted again, Wife."

He could snap her arm off by the elbow and tear her limb from its socket. She felt his strength in that grip and the power that hummed with his touch, even more frightening than brute force— ancient and unyielding. "Yes, Husband," she said through gritted teeth, then wrenched her arm away.

Master Bei let go, indulging, or else she would have twisted her shoulder, she had little doubt. "Why me?" she whispered.

"As notoriously willful as you might be, you are still from a prominent, well-respected family. My ostentatious wealth will make humans avert one eye. A pretty young wife with your pedigree will make them avert the other." The air shimmered around him, and he appeared human once again. "Play the role of good wife, and I will let you live."

"To what end?" she asked.

"So we fit in. So my name becomes an established one, a trusted one," he said. "You only need to raise Blossom as your own."

"The demon child—"

"Demonic but with a mortal's essence. Many women died in pregnancy before I was able to have Blossom."

Zhen Ni's stomach cramped, and she felt nauseated. "A woman

gave birth to Blossom?"

"Yes. She died when Blossom ate her way out of her mother's womb," he said. "It is the way of things. But she is the perfect child that will help the demon uprising."

She felt lightheaded and swallowed, her throat parched. Demons overtaking their world; this was what Master Bei was striving for. "Why a girl then?" she asked. "The men wield the power—they rule this kingdom. If you had a son, he could rise further …" The perfect boy might even become emperor, if he had enough fortune and audacity to challenge the throne.

He grinned, showing sharp yellow teeth, reminding her exactly of a wolf. "I've observed your people for centuries. Men wield the power, but it is power that other men covet. To be a man of high station in this kingdom is to be envied—a target. I needed someone to infiltrate this world and go unnoticed. Who do you think runs the daily routines of all households, of even the emperor's palace?"

Zhen Ni thought of her mother, who made sure that the Yuan manor ran smoothly, managing dozens of people and overseeing every necessary task, big and small. Then there was Nightingale, who helped Lady Yuan organize the household and the myriad of jobs, and Nanny Bai, who had served as both nurse and doctor to them for over three decades, who had helped birth Zhen Ni into this world.

"The men might rule this kingdom, Wife, but the women run it," he said. "Blossom will rise and have the emperor's ear if I desire it. She will go unchallenged because she will be underestimated."

It made twisted sense now. Beautiful women were seen as a commodity or a distraction, never a threat.

"Who can resist Blossom's powers of charm and persuasion?" Master Bei asked. "Can you?"

He was goading her, because he already knew the answer.

"Be a good mother to Blossom." He rose, towering over her. "You will help me and tell no one, otherwise you die. And everyone you love dies as well."

Zhen Ni stared down at her hands clenching her thighs; she

stayed silent.

"Let the girl feast on the human corpses. It helps her strengthen and grow."

"I will take care of her," she said, hating herself for not being able to challenge him. But she needed to stay alive if she wanted to thwart him.

"Good," he growled out. "We understand each other then."

He left without a glance back, taking the odor of smoke and fire with him.

It must be what hell smelled like.

CHAPTER TEN

Kai Sen

The morning dragged on intolerably for Kai Sen. Meditation was followed by a spare morning meal of plain steamed bread and hot soy milk, then an hour of forms. But he couldn't even practice to release his pent-up emotions, being pulled aside by various people who worked for the monastery or monks who demanded his attention or sought his sympathy and commiseration. Kai Sen was trapped with both the chef and gardener, arguing over the menu for the coming week, when he saw Han stride down the covered corridor toward them. He flashed his friend the "get me out of this" signal that they'd used since childhood, a subtle jerk of the head to the right, and Han grabbed Kai Sen's arm as he walked past them. "I need to speak with you on an urgent matter," Han said.

"Of course. Yes, we need to take care of that urgent … thing, don't we?" Kai Sen nodded to the chef and gardener. "I trust whatever you both decide." The two older men, Lao Lu and Lao Chen, who had both worked in the monastery for over three decades, barely paused in their quarreling. Although unrelated, they considered each other brothers, and a day was not right until they took time to squabble over something trivial.

"My thanks, Han," Kai Sen said under his breath as they walked away. "I saw myself ten years from now still trapped there, gray at the temples."

"Gray hairs by the time you're twenty-eight?" Han laughed.

"With the way things are going—"

Han punched him in the arm, making him wince. Kai Sen didn't wince out of practice, but his friend punched hard. "Come. I'm sad over losing Abbot Wu too, but *you* are our fearless leader now. It's a tremendous honor."

Kai Sen flicked a glance toward his friend. He loved Han like family. Abbot Wu had been a father figure to him at times, but he had never thought of him like a real father. Han, however, Han was like a real brother. Was he jealous that Kai Sen had been chosen by the abbot as his successor? "You know by this time, I'd have sneaked out of the monastery already—"

"Wandering the forest, jumping across streams, chasing after girls—"

Kai Sen snorted, then thought of Skybright, and the smile fell from his face.

"I know, Kai Sen. You'd be running wild."

"I'm trapped here now, Han." He stopped near an alcove tucked in the corner, where the covered walkways paved in limestone met. It offered an expansive view of the monastery's square, showing monks sparring in pairs. The deep green of the giant cypress trees dotting the square was a striking contrast against the pale blue sky. It was hard to believe that less than a day ago this square had been overrun by monstrosities and had been slick with the blood of their brothers. Or that by night time, thick smoke bellowed into the air as their corpses burned. "I'd give up this role to you if I could," Kai Sen said.

Han's mouth twisted. "It was the abbot's choice." He paused. "But why you?"

Kai Sen's heart grew heavier, that his friend wanted this thing he did not. "Because you are too good, Han," he replied in a low voice.

Kai Sen had always wondered why the abbot had singled him out for favor. Han might not be as fast or agile as Kai Sen, but he was every bit as strong a fighter and much more dependable. Always responsible. Truthful. Kai Sen saw now that Abbot Wu needed a successor who knew how to keep secrets and deceive, someone for whom lying came as second nature. For as long as he had known Han, he had never caught his friend in a lie. Whereas Kai Sen had lied his entire life to protect himself. He hid his clairvoyance, his ability to see the dead, his intuition that was nearly always right from everyone he knew so he could appear normal and fit in. Only the abbot was aware of his deception. And it was for the ease in which he deceived everyone, Kai Sen was convinced, that the abbot had chosen him.

"Too good?" Han said. "That doesn't make sense."

"Not much does these days, brother."

Han let out a long breath and continued walking down the covered walkway. "You'll have to take your oath soon, Kai Sen. Now that you're head of the monastery."

Kai Sen blanched. "There's enough time for that yet. We're still in mourning." An official oath would bind him forever to this life, one of celibacy and servitude. A life without Skybright. He wanted to drive his fist into the wall for his own stupidity. Skybright was long gone, beyond his reach. And the abbot had left him the impossible task of finding a new breach with a divining stone he didn't have enough power to control.

"If you despise the responsibility," Han went on, "give the role up to me then, like you said."

His friend spoke in a quiet voice, his words clear and careful. Han had thought about this and wouldn't have asked if he didn't think he'd be the better leader. In truth, Han probably would be better. Kai Sen was tempted to say yes and leave the monastery to lead a nomadic life, but he wouldn't put Han in that difficult position of upholding an ancient, twisted covenant or thwarting it. He didn't know if Han had it in him to go against established rules and traditions, much less against the gods themselves.

"I can't, Han. I'm sorry."

His friend nodded, the motion stiff.

"Will you cover for me this afternoon?" Kai Sen asked. "I have something to take care of."

It was obvious that Han didn't believe him.

"I'm serious, Han." His days of running off for fun were over. He needed to find this breach and close it somehow before the demons escaped again. They couldn't risk another infiltration like the previous day; the lives lost were devastating. One more attack like that and there would be no monks to speak of. "You know you're the only family I've ever had."

His friend scrutinized him, and after a long pause, he finally said, "Me too, Kai. I'll always help you." He tilted his chin toward the open square. "How about some sparring before the midday meal?"

Kai Sen clasped Han's shoulder for a brief moment in gratitude. "There's nothing more I'd like right now than to wallop your ass."

Han laughed, and it carried down the empty corridor. "We'll see about that."

Kai Sen wasn't able to escape the monastery until dusk. Although Han took up his role as Kai Sen's second right after the midday meal, Kai Sen couldn't take two steps without being stopped by someone who *had* to speak with him—and no one else would do. After a few hours of this, he began imagining slashing a portal right there and jumping through to escape it all. An hour after that, he wished another breach would open in the corridor and swallow the cluster of petitioners before him. Kai Sen felt a little guilty to wish it but not guilty enough to take it back.

Finally, he threw both hands up and said, "Enough!" The small group quieted instantly, gaping at him, and only then did Kai Sen realize he had conjured two giant orbs of hellfire in each hand, ready to launch them like weapons. A collective sigh shuddered through the group, and they shrank together and back at the same time, like cattle protecting themselves. He extinguished the hellfire, embarrassed that he had let his temper control his magic. "I'll speak with each and every one of you tomorrow. If it's something that can be settled with Han," Kai Sen cocked a head toward his friend, "talk to him. He's in charge while I'm gone for a few hours." And with that, he ran out of the monastery without a backward glance, slipping through the giant double doors sideways like an eel because the guards couldn't get them open fast enough.

The sun sank and the air chilled around him. He had retreated to a small cave he had found when he was fifteen and kept secret. Not even Han knew about it. Tucked behind towering pine trees, it was a precarious straight climb up the jagged rock face that had his blood pumping every time he made it into the cave's entrance, feeling triumphant, his limbs tingling with life. The cave wasn't more than a hole, deep enough for him to lie down in without his feet sticking out but not tall enough for him to stand upright. His carved figurines dotted the natural ledges inside: a rabbit, a hawk, and a crane hewn from birch sat next to each other. On a higher shelf rested a fishing boat as large as his hand hewn from walnut.

Kai Sen conjured hellfire, and it illuminated the small cavern in blue. He reached for the recessed hole in the rock wall, his fingers finding his favorite figurine, one that he had done this year. It was a carving of a woman, attired in a flowing dress with her hair pulled into two buns close to her head. He wasn't skilled enough to capture Skybright's features accurately, no matter how hard he tried. In the end, the carving could have been of any young woman.

Kai Sen tucked the figurine into his pouch. He wanted to save Skybright from Stone because it was the right thing to do—the immortal had no claim over her any longer—but it was for very selfish reasons too. He wanted to see her again, hold her again. But he was unsure if Skybright desired those same things anymore. Still, he wanted to grant her her freedom, no matter what her feelings might be for him.

But now that he was head of the monastery, making time to track Skybright might be impossible. It felt as if he were abandoning her.

Sitting cross-legged on the cave's floor, he hefted the warm divining stone into his palm again. He had been trying to work with it for hours and was suffering the consequences. He took breaks when his vision blurred from pulling on the earth magic around him and weaving it into the stone, terrified each time that his sight wouldn't return. But the stone's effects always eased the moment he stopped pouring magic into it. "Couldn't the price be paid in some other way?" he muttered to himself after a long bout of wavering vision that left him nauseated.

As if in answer, this time when he tried, a throbbing headache erupted right behind his eyes, like a giant fist was squeezing his eyeballs and his brain. He stood, almost smacking his head against the top of the small cave, and stumbled out to the narrow ledge, gasping for air. But his vision was clear, despite the excruciating headache, and he continued to gather the earth magic, infusing it into the stone.

Its spinning center began to pulse and expand, and a tugging sensation filled his entire body, as if he were a compass needle being spun in a certain direction. Excited, he tucked the stone in the pouch at his waist, gritted his teeth, and scaled down the rock face, losing his footing on small footholds three times, clinging on from sheer will lest he plunge to the jagged stones below.

By the time he reached the ground, his brow and back were damp with sweat. He swayed on his feet, his vision blacking out for a moment. Still, he retrieved the stone from his leather pouch and felt it tug him through the forest. He knew these lands around the monastery by heart, even in full dark, so he gave himself into the stone, feeding it with unseeable strands, tasting grit in his mouth from the earth magic.

Kai Sen stumbled through the forest like a drunkard, forcing himself to stay on his feet. He knew if he fell, he wouldn't be able to rise again. Something salty and warm dribbled across his lips. A nosebleed. But he didn't have the ability to lift his hand and wipe it away. He continued to lurch between the trees, his path dimly lit by the orb of hellfire floating above his head, its blue glow casting eerie shadows all around. The forest was strangely silent, devoid of life, and when Kai Sen broke through the tree line, the pungent smell of smoke and death overwhelmed him.

He knew exactly where he was: by the creek where he had met Skybright a lifetime ago, before the breach in the underworld had broken, before he had ever killed a demon. The hulking corpse he almost tripped over was charred black, but somehow still smoldering, red embers flickering inside its ribcage, behind the sockets of its skull. There was no way to tell if it had been human or beast, but instinct told him it had been demonic. The air felt unclean.

Kai Sen trembled, the pain in his head arcing through his entire body, until the divining stone jittered in his palm, then finally fell from his hand with a dull *thump*. He lost hold of the multiple magical strands he had been drawing upon, and the stone flickered out immediately. The stabbing pain thrumming in his head winked out as well. He almost collapsed onto his knees, right at the burnt husk's feet, his relief was so intense.

But then a familiar twinge in his chest made him stiffen.

Skybright.

He extinguished the hellfire that would have given him away and waited. The twinge in his chest grew into something solid, definite. A knowing that was irrefutable whenever Skybright was near. It took all his will not to run to her, to shout at the top of his lungs. But instinct held him back. A tiny golden light flickered in the distance, across from him on the far side of the tree line. It grew brighter, and he heard the soft murmur of two people talking, their footsteps more pronounced in the silent forest. Was she with Stone?

Two figures emerged from the darkness, and Kai Sen recognized her even from afar. The small travel lantern cast a warm glow about her, as if she were an actress on stage. She was dressed resplendently in pale green, head tilted toward her companion, speaking in soft tones. His heart felt as if it'd hammer right out of his chest at the sight of her. He was like a beast restrained by an invisible tether. *Not yet.* If it was Stone, the element of surprise would work in Kai Sen's favor. She and the man walked closely together, their strides, despite the height difference, in sync. Skybright was comfortable, at ease. So she couldn't possibly be with Stone.

The man beside her was dressed modestly, in a tan tunic and trousers. He held the travel lantern at waist level and toward Skybright, so his own features were shadowed. But the closer they drew to Kai Sen, the more the back of his neck prickled in warning. He recognized that long stride, the confident way Stone always carried himself, by virtue of the power he wielded.

Kai Sen touched his throat, where his birthmark had been, the one Stone had erased from his skin right before he had stolen Skybright. Seething anger surged through him mingled with shame—that he had had to pretend to be someone else all his life, someone *normal.* He had been self-conscious about his birthmark, thinking that was what tied him to his clairvoyance. He was wrong; his ability had been innate. Even so, the marking wasn't something that he wanted removed against his will, least of all by Stone. Kai Sen knew he could never best the immortal in magical power, but that didn't mean he couldn't take Stone unawares, perhaps stun him enough so Skybright could escape. He would likely die trying, but he didn't care.

What energy had been sapped from using the divining stone was replaced by raw emotion: fury, disappointment, and hurt. Kai Sen yanked on strands of fire magic around him with so much ferocity that the embers in the still smoldering corpse snuffed out. Hellfire might not hurt Stone, but it could blind him momentarily. Skybright and Stone both paused, frozen. On alert.

Within striking distance.

He wrenched so hard on the element, pulling as much as he

could into himself, that it felt as if he were burning from the inside out. Like he could breathe fire through his mouth. He let go the moment he couldn't hold any more magic and hurtled a ball of blue flame as big as himself at Stone. But—

Would hellfire hurt *Skybright*? Was *she* of the underworld?

"Sky!" Kai Sen roared, bounding toward her.

The hellfire enveloped Stone, crackling and ablaze. But Stone had pushed Skybright out of the way a breath before, and she rolled from him, letting out a cry of shock and pain. Before Kai Sen could reach her, a fist-sized rock slammed him in the ribs, hard enough to knock the air from him. Another large stone hurtled toward his head, and he ducked just in time, feeling it glance too close to his ear. Quickly surveying where the rocks were flying from, Kai Sen saw several floating behind Stone, his figure illuminated in hellfire, so bright he couldn't look straight at the immortal for more than a moment.

Kai Sen cursed under his breath and retreated, making sure that Skybright appeared all right. She was rising to her feet, unhurt but shaken. Another rock flew at his head, and he dodged again in time, beginning to call on wood magic. Wood was the element that controlled the air, the winds, and he drew these strands to himself, feeling light on his feet, as if boosted by a zephyr itself. When the next large stone sped toward him, it hit the wall of air he had woven, and Kai Sen then flung it away from himself at Stone. Stone's figure shimmered. He twisted out of the way but was lifted off his feet, swept helplessly backward by the powerful gale until he was plunged into the creek with a loud *splash*.

Kai Sen felt smug despite his weariness. Stone did not seem so invincible now, and he was more than happy to take advantage of it. "Skybright!" He threw out his hand. "Run! I'll hold him for as long as I can."

Inexplicably, Skybright didn't move.

Kai Sen summoned another orb of hellfire over his head, this one the size of a large gourd. The moon was slender this evening and dim. "Sky, it's me," he said, his voice hoarse.

"Kai," she whispered, her eyes wide and dark in her pale face. Skybright stared at him with something bordering on horror. As if he were a ghost or a stranger. He didn't know which was worse. Then, her gaze wrenched away to the bedraggled figure climbing out of the creek. She took a step toward Stone. *She must be under his spell*, Kai Sen thought, *enchanted somehow.*

Panicked, Kai Sen grabbed onto strands of water magic. His ability in this element was weaker, and he'd had little practice. Still, he was able to create a small waist-high wave that knocked Stone back into the flowing water. He disappeared for a long moment, then emerged above the creek's surface, sputtering.

"Please, Sky!" Kai Sen tried again, hoping to snap her out of whatever spell Stone held over her. "Run!" He gathered the last of his strength, for he was exhausted, and the water began to rise again around Stone as he struggled to keep his head above water.

"No!" Skybright said. "Stop!"

He was stunned.

But Kai Sen didn't listen. He used the last of his reserves to yank harder on the strands of water magic until the black water undulated, rising like a sea serpent, engulfing Stone beneath.

Skybright

Skybright had left the Bei manor with reluctance, unable to shake a sense of foreboding. She felt as if she were abandoning Zhen Ni, although she knew there was nothing they could do for her right now. Still, she whispered a mantra of protection under her breath and wished it upon the wind, that it'd carry to her friend.

She and Stone took the same path through the forest that they had earlier on their way to the monastery. It provided cover, and they were both more comfortable among the trees. They were discussing their alternatives on how they might infiltrate Bei manor when they broke through the forest and emerged near the creek. She lifted her chin, as she thought she caught whiff of a familiar scent. But when she concentrated, all she could smell was the burned demon they had killed earlier, its corpse still flickering with embers in the distance, the pungent odor turning her stomach. Her head throbbed where she had slammed it earlier, and she was having trouble concentrating. In truth, she wanted to shift into her serpent form and rid herself of these mortal inconveniences, the hunger and the aches. But could it ease the anxiety she felt? Her sorrow and fear?

They were midstride, Stone's travel lantern casting a small aura around them, when the burned corpse's red embers extinguished at once, as if doused by water. Stone stiffened beside her, and she stopped as well. There was a dark figure standing behind the dead demon that she hadn't noticed before, and all her serpentine senses leaped toward it.

Another demon? She latched on to the figure's scent—a scent that had been so familiar to her in the past.

It couldn't be.

In the next instant, a gigantic blue ball of fire flew toward them at breakneck speed, and before she could react, Stone had shoved her away from him. Taken by complete surprise, she fell to the dirt, crying out when her shoulder hit hard against the ground. The blazing blue fire enveloped Stone, but he stood in the center of it, seemingly unhurt. It crackled, shooting blue sparks outward. One lashed her bare shin, where her skirt had rumpled up, burning her so painfully that she screamed, rolling away from Stone.

"Sky!" Even through her haze of pain, she knew that voice.

"Keep back!" Stone said, although it was too bright to see his features. "It'll burn out. It can't hurt me."

Tears obscured her vision as she crawled away from Stone, her breathing coming in short gasps, before she struggled to her feet. The strange blue fire was so incandescent she could barely make out the outline of Stone's figure within it. Her shin throbbed, each twinge reverberating through her entire body like some strange poison, and she wondered if she were dying. Kai Sen was attacking Stone but did he mean to hurt her too? Had Abbot Wu finally convinced him to finish the job?

A gust of wind swept past her, and the blazing brightness of the blue fire disappeared. Where was Stone?

"Skybright," Kai Sen shouted again. "Run! I'll hold him for as long as I can."

Confused and reeling from pain, she turned to him. She felt her pulse in her throat, could hear her heartbeat pounding in her ears. "Kai," she whispered. She didn't know what to think, what to feel, what to believe.

The young man she had made love to, whom she had found so familiar, had changed. This Kai Sen appeared taller, broader, and his shoulder-length hair had been cut short, cropped close to his ears. The most unrecognizable part was his face, leaner now, so his jawline and cheekbones were more defined. Any remnant of boyishness had disappeared entirely since the last time she had seen him at hell's breach. His eyes were haunted. Dried blood was smeared across one cheek and over his chin like he had been feasting on raw meat. But even as the gruesome thought crossed her mind, a droplet of blood fell from Kai Sen's nose; he didn't seem to notice.

Could she trust Kai Sen? Skybright didn't know. Loud splashing drew her attention to the rushing creek, where Stone was struggling to climb out of the water. She felt an overwhelming sense of relief to see that he was all right. She took a step toward Stone.

"Please, Sky!" Kai Sen shouted behind her. "Run!"

The dark waters in the creek began to swirl like a whirlpool, gathering behind Stone, when a wave struck him straight on, thrusting him back into the creek. He disappeared underneath, then popped to the surface a long moment later, sputtering. Skybright knew from playing in this same creek that it ran deep at its center, and as she watched Stone's upturned face, she suddenly understood that he didn't know how to swim.

When he was more powerful, he didn't need to know, and if

he had known as a young man, he'd certainly forgotten how a few thousand years later. The dark waters began to rise again around Stone, like magic.

Magic.

"No!" she shouted. "Stop!"

She whipped toward Kai Sen, who stood with fists clenched, staring at the turbulent waters with glazed eyes. The wall of water continued to rise, before slamming down on Stone, swallowing him into its depths. She shifted. The excruciating pain quieted to a twinge in her serpentine body, and Skybright dove headfirst into the creek. She had never learned to swim as a girl but instinctively could in her serpent form. The currents churned, roused by Kai Sen's magic.

Despite her heightened vision, she could see nothing in the black waters. Instead, she used her serpentine senses to locate Stone, who was struggling beneath the surface, in a deep chasm where his feet couldn't touch the riverbed. She lunged for him, wrapping her arms around his torso, and hauled him upward, using her powerful serpent coil to propel them. He stiffened in fear for a moment, then realizing it was her, relaxed and let himself be dragged to the surface. He would have been much too heavy for her had she been in mortal form, but as half serpent with her demonic strength, she easily pulled him on to the muddy bank.

He crouched on his hands and knees, coughing violently, looking as pathetic as a sodden dog. She let him be, tasting in the air his wounded pride more than any serious injury. Stone didn't want her to linger, she knew; he needed to gather what dignity was left for him to muster.

Kai Sen stood, a lone figure in the distance, the single fireball still hovering over his head, illuminating him in cold, blue light. But as she observed him longer, he began to take on a faint glow, lit from within. Confused, she blinked, trying to clear her vision. But the glow didn't fade, and she realized what she was seeing: Kai Sen's *goodness*. She had almost forgotten about her own magic in gauging the souls of mortals. And all those times in the past, when she had seen Kai Sen from afar, and he appeared to be limned in faint light—that was her power manifesting before she was aware of it.

Slowly she slithered to him, his dark gaze never leaving her face. She stopped less than an arm's length away and lifted her hand toward him. He flinched, forced himself from jerking backward. She knew how in control he always was, how spare his movements; he had to be to be a good fighter, to be a good monk. Still, he was afraid of her in her serpentine form. Why shouldn't he be? It was instinctual and visceral, crucial to his survival. This would *never* change between them. No matter what he said. No matter how much he was willing to try. Her demonic side would always be monstrous to him.

Her heart ached to know it.

She swept her fingertips across his bloodied cheek. Her hand was wet, and it smeared the dried blood, wiping away some of it. The planes of his face, more defined now, cutting, were unfamiliar to her. He felt more like a stranger than a lover. "You've had a nosebleed," she said, her voice coarse as gravel.

He caught her wrist, and it was her turn not to wrench back. She wasn't used to another's touch while in serpentine form, and definitely not from Kai Sen. Even his scent had altered, sandalwood mixed with ash, determination with grief. Mortals could change so dramatically in the span of a few months. *How different would Zhen Ni be now?* she wondered. But she liked his touch—her skin against his skin—remembered how well their bodies had fit together.

"Why?" he asked, softly so only she could hear it.

But she didn't know what he was asking. So much had happened since she last saw him, since she agreed to give up her mortal life to save his and Zhen Ni's. It was as if they were speaking to each other in different languages.

"I wanted to save you," he said, when she didn't answer him.

"But I don't need to be saved," she replied.

Kai Sen blinked, searching her face, appearing completely lost. Then he laughed, that full, unrestrained laugh she remembered, shaking his head. "Skybright," he said. "Never mincing words." He still held her arm and tenderly rubbed his thumb across her inner wrist, igniting her senses. His touch almost familiar.

He never stopped glowing with that inner light, and she felt herself pulled into him, unable to control her power in glimpsing his past and his secrets. She twisted her arm free, not wanting to intrude with her magic. Kai Sen jolted; she had pulled away with more force than she had intended.

The light around his figure dimmed. "I see," he said, his jaw flexing.

No. He didn't. She wanted to explain.

Stone gave a short laugh behind them. He had changed into dry clothes, but his hair was still wet. "That is a true understatement," Stone said with a sarcastic curve of his mouth. "Skybright doesn't need to be saved."

Kai Sen's eyes narrowed at the other man, his fingers curling, and she could smell the magic emanating from him like the air before a storm. Skybright said, "I'm all right. Stone has no hold over me any longer."

"Then why are you still with him?" Kai Sen asked.

There was too much to say, and she had so many questions. Instead her head felt muddled and her tongue too thick to speak properly. "We're trying to close the new breach," she finally managed.

"So am I." Kai Sen leaned down and picked up a large oval rock. The moment he touched it, its core lit with pale blue light.

"A divining stone," Stone said from behind her shoulder. "A powerful one."

Kai Sen clutched it closer, glaring at the other man with suspicion. "It was a task given to me before Abbot Wu died."

"Abbot Wu ..." she said.

"The monastery was attacked," Kai Sen said. He swiped an arm over his face, smearing blood. "We have wards set, but they broke through somehow."

"So you are the chosen successor," Stone said.

Kai Sen stiffened but didn't respond, although his expression was answer enough.

"Abbot Wu would never have shared that divining stone with anyone but his chosen. And no other would be taught to wield elemental magic," Stone went on.

"Is it true?" she asked. This news was as shocking as learning that Zhen Ni had wedded without her even knowing she had been betrothed.

"I was declared his successor, yes," Kai Sen said, staring at the ground. "But I haven't taken my oaths yet."

"A formality," Stone said.

"You seem to know everything," Kai Sen replied, and the wind whipped up once more around them, the air chill against her damp skin. "Yet you don't know how to swim." Kai Sen thrust his arms forward, palms out, and a strong gust forced Stone three steps back. "Here's what *I* know," Kai Sen said as another gale pushed Stone backward. "For as much as you talk, you're not as powerful as you once were." He stalked forward, shoving his palms out again, and Stone staggered further toward the creek.

"Kai Sen, no," she said.

Frustrated, he paused, and the gravel stirred against the ground. "Why do you protect him? After all that he's done?"

"Exactly for everything that he knows," she said. "We *need* him to close the new breach."

"No," Kai Sen said, eyes flicking back toward Stone. "We don't." He raised his arms to use his magic, and without recourse, she whipped her serpent coil out. Being agile, he jumped, and she missed, but she was still faster. When he landed on his feet, she snapped her coil again and knocked him over. He landed backward on his hands like a crab, then jumped up, but the winds he had conjured died.

"Please, Kai," she said. "We *have* to work together. These demons that we've seen, they're unlike anything else that has crawled from the underworld."

Kai Sen crossed his arms, his stance rigid and unyielding. But she sensed him softening, even if mingled with the scent of reluctance. "I've seen them myself," he said. "Appearing almost human. Speaking words."

Skybright nodded. "With you, we would have a better chance in fixing this."

He unfolded his arms and ran a hand through his short hair, a gesture that was so familiar to her, like something rising out of a dream; bittersweet.

"I *have* to save Zhen Ni," she said, her desperation clear despite her coarse voice. "She's trapped in Bei manor where we believe the new breach has opened."

"All right," Kai Sen said, "but I don't trust you." He directed his words to Stone. "Or like you."

"Fair enough," Stone said.

His expression had never altered during his exchange with Kai Sen. But Skybright knew him too well now, could read the cues of his physical stance, shoulders rigid, chin slightly lifted. Even more telling was his scent: frustration mingled with shame. Ire exuded most strongly from him in waves, acrid as smoke. Yet his features gave nothing away.

A large *thud* startled her, and Kai Sen whipped around, vibrating with magical power. It was a large boulder, the same one that Stone had flung at the demon they had killed. Stone had lifted it again with his own magic, ready to cast it at Kai Sen from behind if necessary.

The way things were going, Skybright thought, Stone and Kai Sen would kill each other before they ever made it back to Bei manor.

CHAPTER ELEVEN

Skybright

Kai Sen joining Skybright and Stone completely changed the dynamics of everything. The ease she had felt with Stone disappeared; his defenses went up, as surely as if he had built an actual wall around himself. Things with Kai Sen were even worse—painfully awkward. They needed to speak alone, but there was neither time nor opportunity. She remained in her demonic form, preferring her serpentine speed and power. It allowed her to stay aloof in a way, separate from them. She didn't want to be encumbered by her human body—or all the aches and overwhelming emotions that came with it.

They stood in an awkward triangle, Stone keeping further away at its pinnacle. It was an uneasy truce between him and Kai Sen, and she wished she didn't feel as if she were caught in the middle, playing both arbitrator and peacekeeper. Skybright didn't miss the irony that this was the place where she and Kai Sen had shared so many moments and good memories, where they had been able to talk to each other freely. Now the rushing waters of the creek were a threat, menacing, and the expansive forest behind them dark and secretive. The comfortable familiarity of this place had been replaced by violence and conflict, marred by the charred remains of the demon they had slain.

"We were headed to the monastery to warn the abbot," she said in her coarse voice. Before, she would have felt embarrassed, ashamed to sound so monstrous. She didn't feel that way any longer, Skybright realized; this was simply another side of her, another part that made her whole.

"Abbot Wu warned me something was off balance as he lay dying," Kai Sen replied. "Now I know the divining stone was pulling me toward Bei manor—"

She felt Stone tense, even from a short distance away. An owl hooted in the thickets as if in warning. "What?" he asked. "The abbot knew?"

"Abbot Wu had sensed a new breach opened into our world, a strong source of malevolent power," Kai Sen said in a tight voice. "He told me the divining stone could lead me to it, if I had enough magic to make it work. I did."

"But not without consequence," Stone said.

Kai Sen flicked his eyes toward Stone, his distrust of the other man tasting sour against Skybright's tongue.

"It takes tremendous power to wield such a strong talisman," Stone went on.

Kai Sen ignored Stone's comment, instead saying, "That's why I couldn't open a portal into Bei manor when I wanted to see Zhen Ni."

Stone nodded. "It's warded by strong magic."

"You can create portals?" Skybright asked.

"I taught myself," Kai Sen replied. "And once I learned, I had no issues going anywhere except within Bei manor."

"There's but one way to confirm our suspicions," Stone said. "We see where the divining stone takes us."

Kai Sen stared down at the black stone, letting out a long silent breath, his shoulders heaving once. He was exhausted—Skybright didn't need her heightened senses to know. Dark shadows stood out beneath his eyes; compounded with the dried blood smeared across his face, he looked like a drunken madman, barely stable on his feet. She wanted to reach out for his arm in sympathy, to steady him, as easily as she and Stone had done earlier, but she didn't. She didn't know how Kai Sen would react.

Clenching the stone, he stood silent for a long while, black brows drawn together. Finally, he said in a hoarse voice, "I don't think I can. Not now." The way his mouth twisted, it was a hard admission.

"It uses the earth element?" Stone asked, but it sounded more like a statement than a question.

Kai Sen nodded.

"Let me help you," Stone said. "I can add my magic to yours."

Kai Sen clutched the stone closer to him.

"It is the one elemental magic left to me," Stone said. "Let me make some use of myself in this." He had abased himself on purpose, because Skybright knew Stone was as prideful as Kai Sen could be rash. But Stone was perceptive now in a very human way and shrewd enough to do whatever necessary to close this breach so that he could live.

Kai Sen scrutinized the other man, and said, "No tricks, or I'll kill you the next chance I get." He then opened his palm.

Stone nodded. "No tricks. Let me weave my magic with yours."

They stood silent for a long time, eyes on the divining stone, but their sight turned inward, not really seeing. The tension she had felt like a caustic net around them disappeared while Kai Sen and Stone worked to combine their magic. The stone's color turned milk white, then revealed the swirling blue at its core. The corners of Kai Sen's mouth lifted in a faint smile, and Stone looked triumphant.

"It's pulling me," Kai Sen said.

He didn't need to explain. They followed him through the forest, the stone glowing brightly in his hand, his fireball illuminating the path for them. Its light had grown weaker, however, as Kai Sen directed his energy into the talisman. But Skybright needed no light. Rustling with life, the earthy tang of the forest filled her senses, and she took pleasure in feeling her serpent body slither along the soft dirt laden with pine needles. It was well past the thieving hour. Anyone who might see her in town would likely be drunk or could attribute the sight of her to a bad dream or illusion. The pain from the blue spark hitting her shin had receded to a distant twinge.

Stone walked beside her in silence, his pain in working the talisman radiated from him in waves. His face had gone white, and sweat beaded at his brow. She watched Kai's straight back, the dim fire trailing above his head like some ghostly spirit. He suffered too, barely walking in a straight line. But although weakened, she still felt his magical power. His ability after half a year of study was impressive. She always knew Kai Sen was special and was unsurprised that he would take to magic with such ease, given his natural gift of clairvoyance.

The divining stone was indeed leading them back toward Chang He. They passed the Yuan manor, and she remembered all those dark nights she had sneaked out to learn more about her serpentine side. Shifting and the sensations of searing heat and her lower body breaking and melding had felt so frightening and strange. Now it was the opposite: familiar and so often a relief when she turned. The shadowed streets made the town appear foreboding and unfamiliar, dark silhouettes looming at every corner.

Kai Sen kept guiding them, though his steps faltered a few times, and Skybright could hear Stone's labored breathing. Both men had begun bleeding from their noses. The talisman was exacting a severe price to divulge its secrets, and she was almost glad when the magnificent Bei manor appeared. Kai Sen slipped through the dark alleyway where she and Stone had tried to climb into the manor, then turned the corner until they were at the very back of the estate. Bei manor was not a long walk from Yuan manor but also bordered the forest's edge.

The divining stone flew from Kai Sen's hand and struck the base of the manor wall, the blue light within so bright it appeared white. Kai Sen bent over, his entire body convulsing. The scent of fresh blood was strong, tasting sharp and metallic. Stone conjured a handkerchief for himself and handed one to Kai Sen.

"That was the worst pain," Stone whispered, sagging against the manor wall. It was shocking to see his bloodied face. She had seen Kai Sen injured before during the Great Battle, but Stone had always appeared untouchable, above mortality. His hand shook as he wiped away the blood. "I'm impressed you got as far as you did working the stone by yourself," he said.

Kai Sen leaned against the wall too, the whites of his eyes standing out in his face, stark against the blood. He used the handkerchief Stone gave him, then closed his eyes and tilted his head back. "I would be glad never to handle it again," he said in a harsh tone. "But we have our confirmation. The new breach is within Bei manor, and we have no way of getting inside."

Skybright slithered to the divining stone and tried to pick it up, but it might as well have been part of the manor wall. "You are still wielding magic?"

"It is glowing of its own accord," Kai Sen replied.

The stone was so bright, it encompassed them all in its shifting white light tinged with blue. "The entire estate is protected, Stone?" she asked.

"There is no way through the entrances or over the manor walls," Stone replied.

"But what if from beneath?" she asked. "Look at how the divining stone slammed to the ground, not just the manor's wall. The breach is underground. I knew I felt it there."

Stone stooped and touched the glowing rock but could not budge it either. "It would make sense; the one at the base of Tian Kuan Mountain was too."

"So is it as simple as digging under the wall to get in?" Kai Sen asked.

Stone said something under his breath, and the talisman's brightness faded, then winked out. "We dig and see what happens." He handed the stone back to Kai Sen, proffering it with both palms open in obvious reverence. Kai Sen took it and slipped the talisman into a leather pouch at his waist.

"We'll need shovels," Kai Sen said.

"I can conjure shovels easily enough," Stone replied. "But digging this packed earth would take a long time, and it's hard labor. We'd still be here when the sun rises."

Skybright slithered along the smooth wall, trailing her fingertips against it. "This outer wall extends at least two hand widths below ground."

"You can know that?" Kai Sen asked, amazed.

"Because I can sense life," she replied, looking him square in the eyes. "And no living creatures dwell until three hand widths beneath the entire expanse of this wall."

"There's another way," Stone said.

She and Kai Sen turned to him. Kai Sen was still guarded with the other man, but he was more open to listening, his posture not completely closed. *He and Stone had bled together after all*, she thought, *to make the divining stone work.*

"What is dirt but earth?" Stone grabbed a loose handful from the ground and let it trickle through his fingers. "We can make a tunnel by shifting the earth itself."

"Manipulating the ground beneath and using magic on what we can't even see?" Kai Sen let out a soft laugh that ebbed with the night's breeze. "Now the possibilities seem endless."

"This is only earth magic," Stone replied. "With your powers in all five elements? The possibilities *are* endless."

Kai Sen

Kai Sen wished that Skybright would change back to a girl. It almost seemed like she had chosen this form on purpose because she could sense his unease when she manifested her demonic shape. He couldn't control it. No matter how smooth he made his face, her proximity in her serpent form, with the glimpse of those sharp fangs tucked beneath her upper lip and her forked tongue darting out, made him either want to run or unsheathe his saber. He would never admit this to her though, because it was an ugly truth. The angry, raised scar that slashed from the corner of her eye down her left cheek was a painful reminder that he had almost killed Skybright—had tried to decapitate her like all the other demons he had been fighting night after night. Demons that he and his brother monks were still fighting.

But he still trusted Skybright. She hadn't chosen to be half-demon just as he hadn't chosen to be clairvoyant. He wished they could spend some time alone, to talk without Stone skulking nearby like some jealous rival. Although she and Stone kept their distance now, there was no mistaking the ease and closeness they had with each other before he had intruded. Kai Sen hated that somehow *he* had been made to feel like the interloper in this strange scenario.

He trusted Stone as much as he would trust a starving vulture. But he was willing to work alongside him to close the breach and save Zhen Ni. He realized with reluctance that he needed Stone's magic and knowledge to finish the task as much as Stone needed him. Even with their combined powers and Skybright's abilities in serpent form, the odds were against them.

Skybright was slithering a short distance away. Her hair was wound up in two buns as she always wore them, but it meant her upper body was unclothed, her chest bare ... her shoulders and her arms. There was too much smooth skin exposed for him not to stare, remembering that his mouth and hands had touched her there. Her red serpent scales rose above her midriff, stopping short of her full breasts. Skybright caught him staring, and he looked away, embarrassed. The sight of her was both erotic and terrifying. He felt lightheaded for a long moment, black circles flitting across his vision.

"Ready?" Stone asked, cutting through the thick fog of exhaustion that had descended upon him.

"What?"

"We still have some time before dawn," Stone said. "Follow my lead."

Kai Sen nodded. "I'm not sure how much I can help." He hated to admit how weak he felt. But there was no point in lying. When he had been working the talisman with Stone, they could feel each other's magical powers as they wove the earth element they were pulling together. Stone would be able to sense exactly how much he was contributing.

"Give what you can," Stone said.

Stone began gathering earth magic, tugging so hard that the air tightened around them. As much as he disliked Stone, the man knew how to use the earth element. He manipulated it in ways Kai Sen had never imagined, had never read about in the books from Abbot Wu's library that he had secretly studied. Kai Sen didn't believe Stone was actually stronger than him in his magic ability anymore. Kai Sen could work all five elements of magic from nature, and the other man was limited to earth. Yet what Stone could do with that one element was impressive. Kai Sen supposed Stone had a few thousand years to practice. Still, he felt a grudging respect for him, especially as Stone was not shy in sharing his knowledge.

Kai Sen began drawing the earth element to himself as well and wove it into Stone's strands. The man had pulled the invisible threads into a sharp pointed tip, like the tapered end of a calligraphy brush and sent it beneath the earth along the wall. Kai Sen's own strands were thin, weaker, as that was all he could manage, but he could feel Stone's magic, could sense exactly how he was using it.

While Stone forced the element beneath the ground like some kind of worm, he simultaneously thrust the strands outward, hollowing a tunnel. The earth shifted for him, as if answering to his bidding, moving below the thick outer wall. Stone tried to go under the wall's foundation and into the estate, but their magic bounced back hard, making Kai Sen's teeth clack in shock.

They had struck the ward.

Kai Sen cursed, and Stone shook his arms, looking angry, his face ghostly pale, tinged blue by Kai Sen's globe of hellfire. The kickback from the ward would have hit him much harder than it had Kai Sen, as Stone was wielding the majority of the magic. Skybright hadn't moved from where she was a short distance away, her gleaming eyes missing nothing. Her hands were clenched in fists at her side. The moon was hidden behind clouds, so she lurked mostly in shadow, but even the hint of that monstrous serpentine body made Kai Sen's skin crawl with fear.

Taking a deep breath, Stone continued, undeterred. Plowing even lower into the ground along the outer wall's edge. The earth churned, vibrating, a distant groan beneath them. Inspiration struck, and Kai Sen began twisting his strands hard, so the sharp point rotated as it burrowed, forcing a wider path. Stone, immediately recognizing what Kai Sen was doing, began imitating him, twisting his strands as well to increase their momentum. Plunging more than the height of two men beneath ground, they wove their magic together, in perfect sync, and then veered, furrowing straight into the estate.

The ward did not extend that low.

Stone grinned in triumph and nodded at Kai Sen, and he almost smiled back. In the next instant, their magical threads met no resistance at all, and Stone let the strands unravel into the darkness below. "We're in!" Stone said in a low voice, edged with excitement. "The tunnel we've made goes below the manor into some type of vault or cellar." He drew a sleeve across his forehead, and Kai Sen didn't miss the trembling in his fingers.

Kai Sen wasn't feeling steady on his feet himself. He went to the opening as Skybright slithered to them, and they both leaned over it.

"There is a small stirring of air from below," she said. "But it smells rank."

Kai Sen could not smell anything.

"Demons," Stone said.

"Corpses," Skybright added, then turned to them. "I'll go in first," she said in that coarse voice.

"No," Kai Sen said. "It's too dangerous. I can go first."

She gave him a leveled look that made him want to fall to his knees and eat his words, beg for mercy. Instead, he somehow managed to stare back defiantly, even if his legs felt weak.

"It is easier for me to navigate the tunnel," she replied. "My senses will warn me if there's danger ahead."

"She's right," Stone said. "And her venom can slay anything."

Considering how drained he was feeling, he'd as likely tumble head first down the hole and break his neck. "I'll be right behind you then." Kai Sen gave Stone a challenging glare.

"Fair enough," the other man said, steady as ever.

It was almost admirable, but Kai Sen still wanted to punch him in the face.

Skybright slithered into the hole he and Stone had made; it took a while for the last of her long serpentine body to disappear into the tunnel. Kai Sen followed immediately after, on his elbows and knees, the globe of hellfire lighting the way. Narrow and low, the dark tunnel was cool, smelling of damp earth. He glimpsed the red scales of Skybright's tail ahead, and he scooted inelegantly downward, his head scraping the top of the tight passage.

His chest seized with anxiety; he hated small spaces, had always had an irrational fear of being smothered and suffocating to death. "It is not for much longer," Skybright's rough voice, lowered to a whisper, drifted up to him. *How did she know?* And yet, her reassurance helped, and he let out a long breath, concentrating on crawling ahead. He could hear Stone doing the same behind him.

But as if the God of Luck was mocking him, Kai Sen felt a deep rumbling over his head, as a portion of the tunnel collapsed on top of him, burying his head and upper body in musty dirt. He tried to scream, but earth filled his mouth. No.

No!

"Kai!" He heard Skybright's muffled, panicked shout.

He felt the packed dirt loosen around him, shifting, being manipulated by magical strands. Stone was working the earth element to free him. He tried to help, to pull on his own magic and weave it to Stone's, but his mind had gone empty from terror. He was exhausted, unable to draw a breath. Dirt filled his nose, his mouth, his vision. He would die like this, buried, too feeble to summon his magic.

Then his head was free, and he spat out, gasping, tears squeezing from his eyes. Skybright, unable to turn around in the tight space, was using her serpentine tail to sweep earth away, even as Stone continued to use his magic, forcing the dirt back from Kai Sen.

His heart pounded hard against his ribcage, fear thrumming through his whole body. He tried to summon a burst of air to sweep the dirt from his hair and clothes, but he couldn't focus enough to grasp onto the wood magic.

"Keep crawling, Kai," Skybright said. "We're almost there."

He forced himself to edge forward on his elbows, dust falling into his eyes. But he could breathe again, however musty the air. Still, he didn't have enough wherewithal to thank them for saving him. He wanted to get out of that tunnel.

After what felt like a lifetime, Skybright stopped. "We've reached the opening," she said. "It's a steep drop, but the wall beneath is filled with footholds and ledges." She slipped out and seemed to disappear into thin air. Kai Sen's heart almost stopped as he scrambled toward the opening. But her face popped back into view; she was somehow dangling against the wall. "It is not a long climb," she said in a whisper. "I can help you down."

He drew a deep breath of air, stale, but still welcome after being trapped beneath a mound of earth. Skybright's face was tilted upward, watching him, awaiting his answer. She had changed since they had last seen each other at the breach. The girl he had known had been loyal, practical, and brave. But she had felt doubt, often seemed to struggle with conflicted feelings he didn't fully grasp until he learned that she was half-demonic. She had truly grown into her own since they'd been apart, was assured and confident now, comfortable in her demon shape. Her thick hair had come loose during the long crawl and floated in wisps across her bare shoulders, unfurling like snakes over her breasts. There was a feral element and an etherealness that distanced her from him. He desperately wanted to reach her, the girl he had known, and bridge that gap. But he didn't know how.

"Are you all right?" she asked.

"I'll climb," he said, his voice hoarse. He felt steadier but at the heart of it was too prideful to ask for more help. And even harder to admit, Kai Sen couldn't reconcile the thought of touching her serpentine body. He wasn't ready for that yet.

She nodded, eyes unblinking, and shifted aside for him. "Be careful," she said.

Kai Sen flipped onto his back and wriggled out so he didn't plunge forward headfirst. He managed and found a wide ledge in the wall for his feet as he searched with one hand for another hold. They were in some sort of dark, unlit corridor, his ghostly blue hellfire providing the only light. It appeared to be empty. He took his time climbing down, making sure each foot and hand hold was secure before he took the next step. Dirt fell from his clothes and body, clattering against the rocks like grains of rice. He was halfway to the ground when he heard Stone say above him, "Could you help me down?"

Kai Sen's head snapped up, and he saw Stone wrap his arms around Skybright's coil. She had shifted so he could climb onto her like a steed. She clung to the rockwork with her hands, but the wall offered enough ledges providing easy traction for her serpentine length. She lowered her tail and Stone let go, jumping the rest of the way. "Thank you, Skybright," he said.

Kai Sen almost snorted out loud.

That shameless bastard.

Skybright

Skybright watched Stone wrap his arms around her serpentine body and felt her cheeks burn. She was so rarely touched in her demonic form because it had made both Zhen Ni and Kai Sen nervous and afraid. And for the longest time, she did not know if she could trust herself around them as a serpent—would she be overcome by the compulsion to hurt those she loved?

But Stone had never been afraid of her, had always accepted her for who she was. Even after most of his power had been stripped and the Goddess of Accord had divulged that Skybright was free to kill him with her venom if she desired it, he had never once feared her. She knew he had the advantage of spending a few thousand years as a powerful intermediary to the gods, but he had trusted her long before she was able to trust herself.

It was an unexpected gift from an unlikely person. She would never tell him this though.

Instead, Skybright undulated her coil and lowered him gently as he clung to her. It was an oddly intimate moment to share, and she was glad when he let go, landing on both feet below.

A spike of jealousy that burst from Kai Sen was so strong, he might as well have shouted his feelings in words. He jumped down a moment later, his hairline damp with sweat. He hadn't wanted to touch her. It wasn't distrust, but a complicated mixture of feelings wound tight and held close. But she knew now that he wanted to keep her, at least in serpent form, at a distance. It saddened her, but his reaction seemed inevitable. *There were no love stories between monks and serpent demons*, she had told him so long ago in the forest.

She had been right.

Stone had conjured the giant axe again and nodded at them.

She slithered to the front without a word. The wide corridor was more like a cavern with natural gray rock composing its sides. It reminded her of the other cavern she had been in at hell's breach.

Kai Sen's fireball didn't cast light far, but her sight allowed her to see almost as clearly, as if it were broad daylight. No creatures stirred here, no insect or rodent. The smell of rotting flesh hung in the air, growing stronger as they walked.

"Undead?" Kai Sen asked, hefting his saber.

"No," she replied. "These bodies have stayed dead … so far. I don't sense any living thing down here." She swallowed a deep hiss that threatened to rise. "But I can sense everyone above us. I can feel Zhen Ni."

Zhen Ni was still alive, thank the goddess.

"Good," Stone said. "How many demons?"

"Ten now. But I cannot say if one of them is Master Bei."

They continued downward in the steep corridor, their movements almost silent, until the foul odor of rotting flesh became overwhelming. She resisted the urge to press a hand over her nose and mouth. A slight stir of air, and the corridor opened into a large cavern. Human corpses were strewn on the floor like rag dolls, most with their flesh stripped as if eaten, some picked more clean than others.

Kai Sen murmured something, and after a pause, a dozen globes of blue fire darted over her head, flying into the cavern. They couldn't see what she saw in the dark, but Kai Sen's magic illuminated the grisly sight.

"Goddess," Kai Sen choked out.

"It seems Master Bei has been feeding something that enjoys the taste of dead human flesh," Stone said.

She slithered between the corpses, eyes averted, yet her heightened senses forgave her nothing. The eyes had been gouged out from every skull; the tongues ripped from gaping mouths. Lips had been gnawed off like delicacies. If she had been in human form, she would have doubled over to retch. "There is an exit across the way," she said. Kai Sen followed, his eagerness to leave this place as great as her own. Stone trailed behind them both, taking the whole scene in, his eyes sweeping over each corpse, as if one of them would divulge the answer to some great mystery.

The massive door was set into the wall, following the natural curve and rough rockwork of the cavern. The only indication that it led to another chamber was the rectangle lines marking the door. The faintest red glow seeped from its tight seams. "I can barely see an indication of a door this near, much less from afar," Kai Sen said, sounding impressed.

"The red glow was what drew my attention." She ran her fingertips along the door's seam.

"I see no red glow," Kai Sen said.

Skybright looked toward Stone, and he shook his head. She then pushed against the door's rough stone surface. It didn't budge.

"Is that the best idea?" Kai Sen asked.

Stone slanted his head. "You sense no life beyond?"

"Nothing." She pressed her palm against the jagged rock. "But I can feel tremendous heat—like at the other breach."

"Let's see what we're dealing with," Stone said. His eyes took on that glazed look when he began working his magic. He would use the earth element to open the door.

"Show me," Kai Sen interrupted.

Stone's dark eyes focused again, his pupils constricting to pinpoints. He nodded once. "Link your magic to mine."

Kai Sen thrust his chin up, but his shoulders relaxed as they began working together.

She had always sensed enchantment in nature, in the colors of the flowers and the leaves, even the speckled rocks that lay in the riverbed, and with the exhilarating renewal of each spring. She felt its powers in every sunrise and sunset, in the ever-changing faces of the moon. But it wasn't until she manifested her serpentine side did she realize the extent of the magic around them. She couldn't feel these elements that Stone and Kai Sen spoke of to wield their elemental power, but she was not surprised they existed. She had seen a goddess with her own eyes, after all, witnessed a flying dragon whelp shake the water from its beard.

Both Kai Sen and Stone were already tired, but each was as stubborn as the other. She smiled a small smile. At least in this instance, it was a benefit. The door gave a low groan and pushed back a few hands width. A fiery glow filled the doorway, spilling into the dark cavern.

"Yes!" Kai Sen was grinning, although he appeared ready to sway on his feet.

She touched his shoulder, then gripped it, steadying him. He jumped. "Well done," she said.

He blushed, looking for the first time entirely like the boyish Kai Sen she had known, then smiled wider. "Thanks, Sky."

A burst of hot air swept over them from the chamber beyond. Both men gripped their weapons tighter as she slid past, easing through the wide crack between the enormous door and cavern wall. Although her senses told her nothing alive or moving lay beyond, she was still cautious, ready to strike with her fangs or serpentine coil. The chamber was empty and much smaller than the one they had walked through; a corridor opened on the far end, emanating an intense red glow. The sickening stench of corpses had been replaced by that of fire and sulfur. "It's empty," she said. Kai Sen entered first with Stone bringing up the rear, both their eyes swept the chamber, their weapons at the ready.

She slanted her head toward the corridor.

"You still sense nothing?" Stone asked.

"No life," she said, then slithered across the small cavern into the corridor. "But I can feel tremendous power and perhaps magic. Nothing I've come across before or can recognize."

The air was hotter here, oppressive. But at least there was space enough, not like the tunnel they had made to crawl through. The passage veered steeply downward, and it felt as if they were walking into the depths of hell itself. For the first time, Skybright wondered if they would make it out of this alive. She'd do everything in her power to free Zhen Ni from the clutches of Master Bei and whatever insidious plans he had concocted for her. This transgression, to prey on her lifelong friend, angered Skybright as much as it frightened her.

Stone and Kai Sen trailed behind, alert but not speaking

a word. The air grew so hot that sweat gathered at her hairline, then slid down her back. She swiped a hand behind her neck. The rockwork began taking on an ominous red glow around them, and the corridor narrowed as they went deeper. That combined with the rising heat made it feel like the walls were closing in, ready to swallow them whole. She couldn't shake the notion that they were caught in a trap, and the net was tightening around them.

Finally, they emerged into another cavern. This one had a ceiling which arched overhead, so high she could barely see it. A deep, circular pit pulsed in its center, like a living thing. The air sweltered here, worse than the hottest, breezeless day. Bubbling magma swirling in the pit illuminated the vast chamber, their jagged walls glowing a deep red. Stone bounded to the nearest wall.

"No," he said. "It can't be." Stone touched his fingertips against the rock, and the red glow from within wavered before the wall turned translucent. A pale form was curled within the rock, and though it had coarse features and sharp talons for nails, it looked human enough.

Skybright's stomach clenched. She remembered now what this place reminded her of: the caverns that bred the demons in the underworld for the next Great Battle. The one that was overseen by the talking demon Ye Guai, who had reeked of hatred for Stone. Stone was running down the length of the wall now, which curved around the pit. The cavern walls became transparent where his hand touched but spread beyond, like a network of fissures until the entire cavern revealed what it hid behind its misshapen depths.

Human-like demons.

Hundreds of them.

"There's more," Kai Sen said.

She whipped toward him in horror. He pointed to four more tunnels glowing a sinister red, leading to other caverns growing more of these things. The glare from the hell pit could not disguise the pallor of his face.

"Are we in the underworld?" she asked.

Stone gave a humorless laugh. "Far from it. But Master Bei has managed to make his own hell. And if these more human demons are anything like the ones we've encountered, they'll be able to talk and are smarter, stronger, and faster than those from the Great Battle."

"Those were bad enough." Kai Sen cursed. "I fought a talking demon made to look like a woman, though the results were monstrous. She almost killed me."

Skybright shivered despite the raging heat around them. Kai Sen was one of the best fighters she had seen on the battlefield, one of the most agile. This gave a clear indication of what they were up against. The monks would lose, and every mortal slaughtered like cattle, if Master Bei wished it.

"He needs no breach to hell then," she said. "He's growing his own army right beneath the manor."

Stone walked to the edge of the fiery pit in the middle of the cavern. "There is a breach. Right here."

"But it's filled with lava," she said.

Stone replied, "The breach only needs to be a physical connection to the underworld: a deep crevasse or a magma pit. Both would serve that purpose."

She slithered to Stone, who was gazing into the molten lava. Her eyes burned, and she blinked, looking away. "Why?" she asked.

Stone clasped her arm, then drew her away from the pit. For once, his touch felt cool against her skin. Kai Sen stood with his back to them, peering inside the translucent stone at the demons growing within. His saber was raised, and his feet staggered, as if ready for battle.

"Growing demons is a complex process," Stone said. "You need hell's essence, which can only be gathered in the underworld. I'm certain Master Bei has an ally there."

They drew up to Kai Sen, who was staring at a woman with long black hair nestled within the rock. Her lithe legs were tucked beneath her chin, and her features were delicate, with a sensuous full mouth. A beautiful face. But a thick horn jutted from the top of each shoulder like a ram's, tapering to lethal points. "What is the point of closing the breach," Kai Sen said in a quiet voice, "if the monsters are already here?"

"I cannot sense them," Skybright said. "They are not yet truly alive."

Stone nodded. "They are still incubating. But many are close to taking on life; then they will emerge from the rockwork. It is best to strike when they are trapped in their wombs. They are vulnerable here."

"How?" Skybright asked.

"We use earth magic and bring the walls down," Stone said, and locked his dark gaze with Kai Sen's. "It is the only way."

Kai Sen's jaw flexed. "Are we strong enough?"

"We'll have to be," Stone replied.

Kai Sen nodded, his expression grim. Skybright smelled his determination as if a large flame had been struck, acrid and intense.

"How much time do we have?" she asked.

"Some demons are already beginning to stir." Stone pointed at a muscular demon with his thick arms wrapped around his knees. It was easy to miss in a glance, but the defined muscles of his biceps and calves were twitching. "They will not all emerge at once. But enough are on the brink. The sooner, the better."

"I can raid Bei manor while you work these caverns below." She wished she could help Stone and Kai Sen bring the caverns down. It seemed like a tremendous and impossible task for two people, no matter how powerful their magic. But she needed to find Zhen Ni.

"Yes. Lead the attack above ground, Skybright. And don't underestimate yourself," Stone said, as if he had looked into her mind. "Your venom is quite possibly the one thing that can kill Master Bei."

Kai Sen made a low noise in the back of his throat, and Stone swung his heavy axe, planting it in the dirt ground beside him. "Even with our magic combined, we are nothing against Bei. He can counter whatever we might cast at him."

"But he can kill Skybright before she gets close enough to strike," Kai Sen said, his dark brows pulled together. He looked furious, yet she smelled fear. Fear for her well-being.

Stone didn't refute him, but turned to her with one corner of his mouth tilted upward. "You will get close enough."

Sometimes, life offered no choices. *We do what we must,* Lady Yuan used to say. "I attack above, and you destroy below." She drew a long intake of breath that turned into a hiss. "Tonight?"

"I can't," Kai Sen said. "I have little magic left."

"We all need rest," Stone replied. "We have no chance if we try to do this as exhausted as we are."

"Let's go back to the monastery first then. I will choose monks to return with us to fight above ground." Kai Sen turned to her. "It will give you better odds, Sky."

She was eager to save Zhen Ni but accepted that they needed time to regroup, as well as eat and sleep. "There has to be an entrance from below directly into Bei manor," she said. "We can bring the monks in through the tunnel we made and infiltrate the estate from underground—catch them by surprise."

Stone lifted his axe again. "Let's find that entrance first."

They all three nodded together, as if agreeing to a pact.

One of life and death.

They discovered the entrance into Bei manor easily enough, in the opposite direction of the steep corridor they had emerged from. A long rope ladder dangled from the dark trapdoor set above. Skybright thought she smelled Zhen Ni's lingering scent on the rungs but didn't know if it was her desperate imagination.

Standing beneath the tunnel exit they had excavated, Stone sealed the entrance aboveground, creating an illusion that made it appear that nothing had been disturbed.

Kai Sen watched him with interest. After Stone was finished,

Kai Sen said, "That wasn't elemental magic."

"No," Stone replied. "My conjuring is an ability that the Goddess of Accord gave me."

Kai Sen then slashed a portal to take them back to the monastery. Skybright felt that familiar tingling sensation when the scene split in front of them, but it fizzled, then snapped closed. Kai Sen cursed under his breath and tried again. The rent opening into the large square was even smaller the second time and disappeared within a heartbeat.

"Is it the ward?" she asked.

"The spell protecting Bei manor allows for portals *out*," Kai Sen replied in a frustrated tone. "It's not working because I'm empty." He cast a sheepish glance her way. "We'll have to crawl back out and walk."

It wasn't a far distance from the town of Chang He to the monastery, but this evening, it seemed to take twice as long. Both Stone and Kai Sen were spent from working the divining stone, then using their magic to make the tunnel. She could sense that they put one foot in front of the next from sheer determination. They stumbled more than once, and she was always ready to break a fall with her serpent coil but gleaned that they'd prefer the pretense of being all right than her help. In truth, Kai Sen and Stone were likely to fall asleep standing soon if they didn't get some rest. Skybright remained in serpent form, alert for any threats, feeling protective of the men in their weakened state.

The skies were still dark, and the night wind chill against her skin, welcomed after the insufferable heat and stale air in the caverns below Bei manor. The forest hummed, enveloping her senses with pine and earth, life and decay. Finally, they reached the monastery and were let in by a gaping gatekeeper, who stared at his feet after a word of reprimand from Kai Sen. She recognized the large square from when she had climbed up a cypress tree upon Zhen Ni's urging and had glimpsed Kai Sen for the first time. He had said it felt like their fates were intertwined from the start, but she'd venture he never guessed in this way—fighting to the death against an ancient demon lord.

The square was empty, although she knew that the monks began their days soon after dawn. Slithering behind one of the massive cypress trees dotting the edge of the enormous square, Skybright shifted, out of respect for the monks. She was no longer shy about her naked form but did not want to elicit strange reactions from either Kai Sen or Stone. The more she became comfortable with her bare body, the more they seemed to be disconcerted by it. Stone kindly handed her a pale pink tunic and skirt from the other side of the cypress trunk, and she murmured her thanks.

Exhaustion, thirst, and hunger almost brought her to her knees. She pulled the clothes on with trembling arms, then leaned against the tree, her vision swimming. The terrible pain from where Kai Sen's blue fire had eaten into her shin had lessened, feeling like a day-old burn. She hitched her skirt up and stared at the injury—an angry welt as thick and long as her thumb marked her shin. She touched it gently with a fingertip and winced.

"I am always hurting you," Kai Sen said.

She had sensed him before he appeared in front of her, as exhausted as she felt, swirling with a mixture of conflicting emotions. Straightening, she said, "You were trained your entire life to hurt my kind, Kai."

"Don't say that." He drew closer and reached for her hand, interlacing their fingers. With his other hand, he lifted her chin so their eyes met. "You are not one of them."

She smiled, but inexplicably her eyes filled with tears. She had suppressed so much for so long in her demon form. "You're right," she replied and squeezed his hand. "I am my own self."

It had taken this time apart, stripped of everything she had ever known or found comfort in, to accept herself, to truly appreciate her duality. And in doing so, she had lost Kai Sen along the way, perhaps Zhen Ni too.

He leaned down and brushed his lips against hers, briefly, and she took comfort in the love that she felt from him, underscored now by the hard edges of unknowing and *fear*. She reached up and cupped his face, and he drank her in with his eyes aglow from the small blue flame he had conjured, flickering beside them like a glimmering fairy.

"It will heal," she said.

"I didn't think when I cast the hellfire—"

"This blue light ..." She jerked away from it, realizing that even this small cool flame could cause tremendous pain.

"It only hurts those of the underworld," he said.

She gave a rueful smile. "There is the confirmation none of us needed then. Even if I were born in these forests, I am still *of* the underworld."

He traced the scar on her face with his fingertips, barely grazing her skin, causing the flesh of her arms to pimple. "I'm sorry, Skybright."

"Don't be. I regret nothing."

"Ah," Kai Sen said in a thick voice. "Is it over then?"

She took a step away from him, so she could really see him. This familiar stranger he'd become, a grown man with haunted eyes. She wished she could wind back the days like silken thread on a spool, reel them back to a more innocent time, when they were just discovering each other, when they were able to make each other forget their fears and loneliness, even if for a short while.

"Oh, Kai," she said. "You are the head of the monastery now. And I ... I cannot refute my serpent side. It is a part of me as surely as the stars make the night sky."

"I know. I can accept that—"

"I cannot accept your fear of me."

Stricken, he glanced away. "It is something I need to grow used to."

She took his hand and kissed his knuckles. "No, Kai Sen. It isn't. Your reaction is natural, key to your training and survival. I don't fault you—"

"No, Sky." His eyes gleamed. "Don't say these things."

"What will you have me do then?" she asked. "Shall I move into the monastery, be your bedmate in your quarters?"

He looked down at their entwined hands.

"Will you leave the monastery? Abandon your role as its new leader?"

"I don't want to be the new abbot," he said, his brow furrowed in frustration. "But that corrupt covenant must end. Enough innocent lives have been lost; enough monks slaughtered. I see no other way to thwart it but to take this role." He ran a thumb over her open palm. "Still, we could see each other, be together—"

"You would take the oath—one of celibacy—and break it, Kai?"

He wrenched free of her grasp and ran a hand through his short hair so it stood on end.

"I know you," she said. "As rebellious as you might like to be, when you take an oath, you keep it."

"Your practicality will ruin it for all future lovers, Sky."

She let out a surprised laugh.

Kai Sen slipped a hand behind her neck, drawing her to him, so close she could feel the beating of his heart. They clung together, and it felt as if they were bearing each other up. "Neither of us knows what the future might hold," he whispered in her ear, his lips brushing her lobe. Her entire body reacted. Her skin remembered those lips, that touch, and she wound her arms tightly around him, drawing her hands down his muscular back, tilting her face up. "I regret nothing, either," he said and bent down to kiss her.

It was no chaste kiss like before, because deep down, they both knew this would likely be their last. They took their time, hungry for each other, saying with their lips and their tongues, with their teeth and their hands everything that words could not convey. He was tasting her neck, alternately biting and sucking on the tender flesh there when someone cleared his throat loudly behind them.

It barely registered the first time from where they hid behind the giant cypress, and the interloper had to do it again, even more loudly the second time.

"Kai Sen," the man said, and it resounded as loud as a whip cracking in the empty square.

They jumped apart from each other, both out of breath.

"Han," Kai Sen said, blinking.

She smoothed her dress, retying the belt, trying to gather herself.

"I interrupted," Han replied, "because the man standing alone in the square said that we are going to battle within the day."

Stone.

"He explained as I was about to attack him, for he appeared out of nowhere," Han went on. "Care to explain, brother?" He lifted his dark eyebrows, his brown eyes flicking to Skybright for a breath. He recognized her but didn't acknowledge her.

Kai Sen cleared his throat too before speaking. "It's true. We've discovered another breach and a breeding ground for hundreds of new demons."

Han's tanned face went pale, and he shook his head.

Kai Sen clasped his friend's shoulder. "Let's regroup in Abbot— my study. I'll fill you in."

"So the man spoke truth," Han said. "I almost killed him."

"Stone?" Kai Sen replied. "He is not so easily killed."

They walked together from the edge into the center of the square, where Stone stood like a lone statue. But not before Kai Sen looked back, and his eyes met Skybright's. His mouth quirked in a faint, sad smile. "Come," he said to everyone. "We'll discuss strategy, then eat and rest before we attack."

After going over the details of their plan together, Han left to gather weapons and prepare the monks for battle. Skybright, Kai Sen, and Stone shared a simple vegetarian meal of hot rice porridge, lotus root, tender bamboo shoots, and spicy bean curd together. Weary, they ate in silence. Kai Sen then led Skybright into a spare chamber with a narrow bed and told her he'd be sleeping in the study. She slid the wooden door closed as Kai Sen and Stone were unrolling thin pallets on the floor. Stone glanced up then and caught her eye, nodding once before the door clacked shut. He had kept his distance ever since they arrived at the monastery, and she didn't know where his thoughts lay. But during their discussions on how to infiltrate Bei manor, she could feel his focus and determination, despite his tiredness. Stone's life depended on their success, just as much as Zhen Ni's. She leaned her brow against the rough wood for a moment before lying down on the hard bed and instantly falling into a deep slumber.

CHAPTER TWELVE

Skybright

A light touch against her shoulder woke Skybright, and she shot up, crying out. Stone clasped her arm, his fingers warm through her sleeve. "It's me," he said. "We leave at the next sound of the gong. Kai Sen is speaking to the monks."

She nodded, her heartbeat thundering in her ears.

He looked better than she felt, his dark eyes clear, the color having returned to his face. "Skybright—"

The tone of his voice caught her attention.

"I wish I could be there with you when you go after Master Bei," he said.

It surprised her because it sounded almost sentimental. "I'll do all I can to move close enough for striking distance, Stone," she replied. "Even if I have to do a song and dance."

His smile was fleeting enough that she wondered if she'd imagined it.

"I'll be all right." She bunched the coarse blanket between her fingers. "I hope Zhen Ni is still safe."

They left the monastery at nightfall, a silent group. Kai Sen and Han had hand selected thirty monks to bring to Bei manor. Han stayed behind. The two had exchanged heated words before they left, but Kai Sen had forbade his friend to come with them, designating Han as the head of the monastery while he was gone. Kai Sen led the group, illuminating their way with a singular globe of blue fire. She and Stone brought up the rear.

She was first to go down the tunnel a second time. Shifting, she felt the monks' fear swell behind her, and a collective tension reverberated through the group. But she did this in their defense as she was able to sense if anything had changed in the dark caverns below and be swift enough to react to it in serpent form. She heard whispers of "demonic" and "temptress" scatter among the men.

"How is she to be trusted?" a monk said in a too loud whisper. "She is one of *them*."

Blinding blue light flared above the head of the foolish man who had spoken out of turn, and he cowered in surprise and fright. "I am the head of the monastery now," Kai Sen said in a commanding voice. "You obey me. And you trust Skybright because *I* trust her. Any more dissent and you can return to the monastery and scrub pots until your skin peels off." Kai Sen's dark eyes swept over his men. "Are we clear?"

The monks nodded together, shocked and silent.

Skybright had not had a chance to speak with Kai Sen alone since waking. She wanted to show her gratitude, with a smile or brief touch, but those private moments between them were gone. She was glad to see him appear more steady and rested, clearheaded enough to steer his men. Without a word, she headed into the tunnel. Stone crawled behind her this time and climbed down the wall by himself. He manifested a small lantern and cocked his head to one side, then gave her a questioning look.

"No one has been down here since we left," she rasped.

"Good," Stone said. "Master Bei has set everything in motion and is simply biding his time. A direct attack will be the last thing he expects."

She slithered back up the wall and whistled twice, signaling to

Kai Sen to begin bringing the monks through the tunnel. Dropping back to the cavern floor, she slid up the corridor, toward where the rope ladder dangled from the trap door above. "No one is directly above us," she said to Stone. "But I can sense Zhen Ni."

"And Master Bei?" he asked.

If the ancient demon wasn't within the manor, their chance at catching him would be lost. "There are ten demons above ground, but how can I tell if one is Bei?"

"You'll know," Stone replied. "He will smell different—more powerful than any other demon you've encountered."

She cast her senses above ground, touching upon all the individual demons. The fourth presence reminded her of Ye Guai, ancient and formidable, pulsing with a suppressed energy that she would have missed if Stone hadn't asked her to search for it. "He's here, above ground in the manor; he feels very much like Ye Guai."

Stone grabbed her wrist, surprising her. "How so?"

"The energy coming from him is exactly like Ye Guai's, but I can sense his strength and magic, more potent than what any of us wield, Stone." She glanced at him, trying to tamp down the fear rising within her.

"I would bet my life it *is* Ye Guai," Stone said. "That traitor. He was biding his time, plotting and hiding his true power from me." He slipped his hand from her wrist to clasp her fingers, squeezing it. "But your venom can still kill him, Skybright. Use the element of surprise to your advantage."

She felt the first monk drop to the dirt floor farther down the long corridor. She changed back into her mortal form. "I want you to conjure something resplendent for me, Stone, fit for an empress."

"As you wish." He spoke an incantation and a dress of jade green pooled into his outstretched hand, the fabric shining even under the dim lantern light.

Skybright swept her palm over the silk fabric. The dress was embroidered with chrysanthemums in deep and pale pinks, accented with gold thread. A pair of gold slippers, embroidered as magnificently, appeared on top of the dress. This would be her armor. Stone's eyes were downcast, but there was that recognizable scent of desire exuding from him, even as he tried not to look at her, to pretend she was not fully naked less than an arm's length away. She took the dress and slippers from his hand, murmuring thanks, and he turned his back to her, a knot of annoyance and frustration directed toward himself.

She slipped the dress on, tying the intricate belt around her waist when Stone turned, holding a gold hairpin encrusted with jade and rubies, and a pair of large emerald earrings. She tucked the hairpin into her braided bun, saying, "You'd make an impressive handmaid."

He gave a small laugh as she put in her earrings, their weight heavy against her lobes. "You cannot meet him unadorned," Stone said. "He obviously takes pleasure in beautiful things, believes he can have a place again in this earthly realm and pretend he isn't a demon at his core." He touched an emerald that hung from her ear, his fingers grazing one cheek. She stopped the shiver in time but couldn't quell her attraction to him. "It is foolish to deny your true self, to pose as something you are not. I believe he'll meet his match in you, Skybright."

She steadied herself before saying, "Should I carry a dagger?"

"No," Stone said. "He would sense the weapon, but he won't be able to sense your magic. Use this against him."

He stepped back as Kai Sen came through the corridor, followed by twelve monks. "The rest are on their way," Kai Sen said and stopped midstride when he saw Skybright. "Ah," he said. "You look beautiful."

She smiled at him, though it was not one of mirth. "I'm ready to fight."

Without hesitation, he drew her into his arms, embracing her for a moment before letting go. His men, wisely, kept silent. She breathed in his familiar sandalwood scent, underscored by steel. Kai Sen untied a leather pouch from his waist and handed it to her. She had seen him slip the divining stone into it earlier. "Keep this safe for me."

She nodded and tied it to her sash but didn't like the gesture; it seemed one of finality. On impulse, she reached out and caressed his cheek, not caring what the monks might think. They stirred behind their leader, as uneasy as a flock of hens near a wolf. But Kai Sen smiled at her, eyes aglow, before saying, "You follow Skybright now. Do as she commands." Kai Sen unsheathed his saber, although where he and Stone were headed, there was no need for such weapons. She tasted his courage, brash and bright.

They waited until the other monks joined them; then Kai Sen used his metal magic to manipulate the lock set in the wooden trap door above. It popped open a moment later. Skybright began climbing up the rungs, the rope ladder swaying as she did so, and she was grateful for the grip her slippers provided. Halfway up, she glanced down and saw both Kai Sen and Stone's faces turned up to her, their grim expressions a mirror image. But there was determination too, so strong it was like something tangible rising from beneath, buffeting her upward.

When she finally reached the top, she pushed the trap door, and it opened with ease. Skybright knew there was no one within these quarters and pulled herself through. The chamber was dark, except for the wan light from a lantern outside casting an eerie yellow glow. She ran her hands down her dress and touched her hair, making certain everything was in place, then waited as the monks each climbed up to join her.

They were swift and moved noiselessly, yet she was still eager to leave this place—to confront Master Bei and find Zhen Ni. But as the last monk closed the trap door beneath him, Skybright sensed one of the demon guards veering their way, swift as an animal. She lifted her hand. Thirty pairs of dark eyes followed the motion, and the monks all snapped to attention, poised, reminding her of cats about to leap. She raised one finger and motioned to the courtyard beyond the quarter, then at the door leading into the empty study. Using hand signals, she sent four monks out to meet the demon guard. She couldn't shift and kill the guard herself, wanting to keep her demonic side secret until her encounter with Master Bei.

The remaining monks were so silent that she was convinced they had turned into ghosts. But a moment later, they could all hear the scrape of the main door from the courtyard sliding open. Then nothing, until a guttural shout erupted from the other chamber to theirs. A monk began to chant in a low voice, and she felt the ones in the room with her lean forward, as if ready to surge into the other room.

"No," she said, loud enough that she knew they heard her. The sounds of fighting came fast and intense from the main chamber, and the floorboards actually shook beneath them like someone wielding a giant hatchet was slamming it into the ground over and over. Other than the one monk's low chanting of a magical mantra, no other monks made a sound—not a grunt, a shout, or cry. But the demon roared, in rage and in pain, loud enough to warn the other guards and Master Bei.

Finally a loud *thud* resounded through the floor and walls. The door between the main hall and the study slid open; all the men with her tensed. One of the monks stuck his head in, his face splattered with black blood. "It's dead," he said in a grim voice. "Kai Sen was not exaggerating when he said your tracking ability is keen, lady."

"I can sense all around me," she said in a clear voice as the other three monks rejoined them. Two were bloodied and one was limping, but they were all still able to fight. "Well done." She nodded to them. "We have little time. The estate is large, but four more guards are already headed this way. You can separate and intercept them." Quickly, she gave the location of all the demon guards at the moment, sketching a rough map on the wooden floor with a piece of charcoal a monk passed her. "Master Bei is in the southwest corner. Leave him to me. You cannot win against him, even if all thirty of you attacked at once."

"And you can, lady?" asked one of the bolder monks hidden in the shadows toward the back.

"Yes," she said. If she could not kill Master Bei, she'd injure him enough so Zhen Ni could escape. There were no alternatives.

The monks filed out of the empty chamber, taking the raw scent of fear and excitement with them, each gripping a steel blade. The powerful stench of death from the giant demon guard assaulted her. Skybright averted her eyes and followed the monks outside into the courtyard.

The men, dressed in black, disappeared into the shadows like wraiths. She doubted now that the gods listened to their prayers, but she whispered a protective mantra for them anyway, and another for Kai Sen and Stone, facing their own impossible task below. She moved as quietly as the monks did on her slippered feet, avoiding the covered corridors that were brightly lit with lanterns, her serpentine senses alert, even in human form.

She could feel where Zhen Ni was, near Master Bei, but not within the same chamber—probably in an adjacent quarter. It took all her willpower not to run there first, to see her friend and make certain she was well. No. In order for Zhen Ni to be safe, for all of them to survive, she must find Bei. Stone had said once that the serpent demon had the best tracking ability among all the demons, and by the way she could sense every living being within the estate and their movements, she knew he was right. She would use this to her best advantage.

A silent foreboding enveloped the estate. It was hard to believe that thirty monks were within the manor, hunting down eight demon guards. The lush landscape that must have looked beautiful in the daylight seemed ominous now—gnarled and jagged branches of trees appeared like threatening fingers ready to grab passersby, the tall rockery around the small fish ponds like looming monsters. She shook these images from her mind and concentrated on one thing: finding Master Bei. He had remained in the same area where she had sensed him, and despite the expansive size of the estate, she was able to hone in on him.

Too soon, she stood facing an elaborate door carved with ferocious beasts. Upon closer inspection, these animals all bared sharp fangs and talons, and horns jutted from their heads. Master Bei was within these quarters, his presence so heavy and powerful it weighed against her chest like stone. She slid the door open, noiselessly, and stepped inside.

The reception hall was sparsely furnished, with two simple curved backed chairs, an oval table, and a few stools. A lantern burned low in the far corner of the rectangular chamber, casting a dim red glow that reminded her of the breach to the underworld. The air was pungent with the smell of smoke and fire, though none burned within the chamber. Master Bei was nowhere to be seen, but his presence dominated the entire room.

Sweat dampened the back of her neck as she cast her eyes about, searching every dark and hidden corner. Finding nothing, she turned her attention to another door, slightly ajar, opening into a different chamber. Sliding the panel open, she stepped through to what should be Master Bei's bedchamber. It was empty except for a small platform bed set against the farthest wall. Rich brocaded curtains in lavender and silver draped the four corners of the bed, and it was lit by three purple lanterns strung above, softly illuminating the bed as if it were a stage.

A child lay in the bed, her hands folded across her stomach. Skybright hadn't been able to sense the girl, and this frightened her. Perhaps she was masked by Master Bei's presence in the chamber—but then, where was he? Could he be disguised as this child? Slowly, she walked to the bed, her senses so alert her entire being felt as if it was thrumming.

The little girl of perhaps three years was the most beautiful Skybright had ever seen, with long curling lashes sweeping rounded cheeks touched with a blush of pink. She wore a white night dress with lavender plum blossoms embroidered along its collar and sleeve edges and looked like a perfect doll. Standing near, Skybright could smell the girl's sweet scent, reminding her of the honeyed cakes Cook used to make and Zhen Ni would have her steal by the dozen from the kitchen.

The girl's eyes snapped open.

Skybright's hands jerked in surprise, but she managed to keep her expression smooth.

The child's eyes were a deep amber and seemed to glow. "Hello," she said, watching Skybright with interest.

Not knowing what to say, Skybright replied, "I didn't mean to wake you."

"Oh, I was not asleep." She spoke like an educated adult, enunciating the words perfectly in a little girl's voice. "But Mama insisted that I rest like everyone else. And she said to pretend to sleep means that I must close my eyes."

Mama. Could it be Zhen Ni?

"Is Mama here, little girl?"

She reached for the girl with her senses and realized she couldn't gauge her emotions at all. Nothing radiated from her. Disturbed and propelled by a strange urgency, Skybright tried to glimpse within the child's soul, but it was like leaping into a void. There was nothing there. No darkness, no light. Her scalp tingled, and she had to force herself not to take a step back. To show fear, Skybright intuitively knew, was to pique this creature's interest—to reveal oneself as prey.

"My name is Blossom," she said in that sweet voice. "But Mama calls me *petal*. She sleeps alone. I would love to be in her bedchamber instead, but Baba insists I stay in his."

"Is your baba near, Blossom?" she asked, her voice hitching higher.

The girl stared at her with those bright, unblinking eyes. "Baba is always near."

Blood drained from her face when Skybright felt the air gather behind her, thicken with the oppressive stench of smoke and fire. "What is this?" said a deep voice. Skybright was unable to quell her fear when she heard it, the words stretching out like thick tendrils assailing her. "Turn," the demon said, and she obeyed.

Master Bei was a brute, with a misshapen head that barely appeared human. "With the monks crawling all over the estate, I expected their leader here, not some girl." His glowing red eyes roved over her body, then lingered on her face. "I know you."

Those three words gripped her heart in a vise. This close, there was no disguising Ye Guai's scent. It was one that she could never forget—but unrestrained power and magic exuded from the demon lord now.

"I'm Skybright," she said, curling her fists against the cool silk of her elegant dress. She took a slow step toward Ye Guai. Then three more. He simply watched her with those eyes. Ye Guai wasn't afraid of her—why should he be? "And if we have met before, I'd remember."

Ye Guai said nothing to correct her, although the closer she drew, the more she wondered how anyone could mistake his coarse features as human. The lumps on "Master Bei's" brow appeared ready to sprout lethal horns.

"You have a soul, but you are not fully human," he said, thrusting his head to one side, as if trying to unravel a puzzle. "I sense ancient demon blood in you. Has the monastery fallen so low to be led by demons?" He grimaced, his mouth pulling wide over sharp teeth. She realized he was smiling. "I was hoping to be rid of them once and for all by raiding the monastery. But they fought harder than I expected."

Her steps were slow and careful, as if she were gliding on water, her dress barely rippling around her legs, her heavy emerald earrings not swaying.

"Why would you be on *their* side?" he asked. Then he revealed his true self. Thick horns sprouted from his forehead, deathly sharp, and his fingernails stretched into knife-like talons. His nose became even broader, muzzle-like, and he thrust it in the air, sniffing as a wild beast would. Ye Guai stretched taller, his legs elongating and thickening, and his strange ugly feet cleaved into hooves.

An ancient demon lord.

"I grow weary of my human skin," he growled. "But we both know what it means to reveal our true selves to mortals." He sneered, and thick saliva dripped from his protruding fangs.

She had drawn to two arm's length away, close enough to kill any mortal and most demons. But she knew now that Ye Guai was not like most demons. He lifted a hand, talons raking the air, as if to say she'd moved close enough. When she tried to take another small step, she found that her legs had locked in place. The ancient demon had immobilized her without so much an incantation, as Abbot Wu had done months back. Her stomach cramped from that horrifying feeling of powerlessness and not being in full control of her own body.

"Show yourself true," the demon said.

The three characters that the abbot had carved into the inside of her arm, the scars that she always tried to hide under a long sleeve, seared through her, as if someone held an actual flame to her skin. It didn't burn as cruelly as the blue fire that Kai Sen had cast but still her eyes teared. But none of this was as awful as the twisting that was stirring deep within her, a responding hiss from her very soul. He was making her turn against her will.

Skybright fought him, teeth clenched, trying hard to control her demonic side. She was stronger now than when she had met Abbot Wu, more in control. Ye Guai's blood-red eyes widened a fraction. He unfurled his talons, as if beckoning her, and spoke archaic words in a harsh tone; the tugging within her grew ten-fold.

Her body shook so violently that she knew if it weren't for his magic holding her immobile, she would have collapsed to the ground.

"Baba," Blossom's sweet voice shot through the air like a bright butterfly. "You aren't hurting the pretty lady, are you?"

"I do not trust her," the demon said. "So I must kill her. You can feast after."

"Oh, I am ever so hungry." The little girl let out a long sigh. "But I like her—she reminds me of Mama."

The conversation barely registered for Skybright as she fought not to turn, but in the end, the urge was too overpowering. Within a breath, she was in her serpent form, hissing low. She lunged at Ye Guai, because although she was still rooted to the spot, her long serpent length provided more range. He jumped back and let out a loud bark of surprise.

Blossom clapped behind them. "What a lovely trick! She has such pretty scales!"

"A serpent demon!" Master Bei said with genuine pleasure. "I haven't seen one in over a thousand years. Beyond the foolish mortal folklore, I had thought your kind had ceased to exist." His hooves clacked against the stone floor. "Such a shame I have to kill you."

With that, a surge of wind lifted her into the air, and invisible fingers closed around her throat, squeezing her windpipe shut. She thrashed and clawed at her neck but was helpless against Master Bei's magic. Her heart felt as if it would burst from her chest, and even as she fought for breath, the world was beginning to fade around her, graying along the edges. Before she lost consciousness, she heard Blossom say, "Mama."

A furious, shrill scream rang through the entire chamber. *Zhen Ni.* The demon grunted, staggering forward, and in an instant, the invisible hands released Skybright. She crashed to the ground, choking, even as the blood rushed into her head and her vision returned. Zhen Ni stood behind Master Bei, Nanny Bai's dagger plunged deep into his thick neck. The demon seemed more annoyed than hurt, and even as Zhen Ni struggled to free the dagger so she could strike again, he swatted his giant fist and knocked her aside. Zhen Ni struck the hard floor with a sick *thwack*, boneless and silent.

"Mama!" Blossom screamed.

But Zhen Ni's sacrifice had given Skybright the opportunity she needed. Furious and stricken to see her friend hurt, she launched herself at Ye Guai, who twisted, giant fist raised, talons out. But it was too late—she was within striking distance. Even as his hand tore her shoulder, ripping through muscle and bone, Skybright sank her fangs into his muscular forearm.

He threw her aside, and she fell, bleeding out, her arm slack.

But it was done.

Ye Guai stared at the puncture marks. Twin drops of black blood erupted from the wound, and his strange face was so incredulous, mouth gaping and eyes bulging, that she laughed. Triumphant through her pain. His ember eyes locked with hers, but the flames within were already dimming, and he swayed on his hooves.

"Mama?" Blossom was bent over Zhen Ni, gently touching her cheek. "You hurt her!"

"Blossom," the demon said, deep voice trembling. "Come. You can save Baba."

Skybright lifted her head, dread washing over her, more powerful than the throbbing pain in her ripped shoulder. "No," she whispered.

The child gazed at the demon with unblinking eyes. It was then that Skybright fully realized Blossom was both demon and mortal, like herself. "Why?" the girl demanded.

"Baba is hurt." Ye Guai plunged to his knees. "Come give me a kiss."

"You have never asked for a kiss before," Blossom said, observing him with bright eyes.

Skybright's skin crawled. He was taking much longer to die, but there was no doubt in her mind that he was indeed dying. And though she didn't know how Blossom could save him, Skybright believed the girl could. And if that happened, all was lost.

Blossom took a single step toward Ye Guai when Zhen Ni's arm shot out, gripping the girl by the wrist. "No, petal," she said in a soft voice. "Stay here by Mama."

"You witch!" the demon spat, but his words were slurred. He tried to lunge toward Zhen Ni and Blossom, but the little girl pulled Zhen Ni beyond his reach, so fast it was a blur. "Turning … my own … against me," Ye Guai managed.

"How would you have her save you, *Husband*?" Zhen Ni asked, pushing herself up by her hands. "By drinking her blood? Stealing her soul?"

"I made her!" He writhed now like a worm toward Zhen Ni and the little girl. "I *gave* her her human and demonic essences."

Skybright thrust herself up with her good arm and slithered forward. The demon's face was turning purple, his red eyes containing the barest flicker, yet he still dragged himself forward.

"Baba's hurt," Blossom said, looking toward Zhen Ni.

"I know, my heart," Zhen Ni replied. "But he would hurt you to save himself. Do you believe Mama?" The demon child turned her thoughtful, unblinking gaze from Ye Guai to Zhen Ni. "You know Mama loves you?"

Blossom nodded. "I feel it. Just like I love Mama."

"No," Ye Guai said, the one word deep and resonant, like it was erupting from the very heart of the underworld. "You obey me, Daughter."

The little girl began walking toward Ye Guai, one plump hand extended. But then she glanced up and paused. Skybright had stopped over the demon's crawling figure. She slipped the hairpin Stone had given her from her locks and stabbed Ye Guai through the base of his skull, holding it there as he bucked. She was dizzy from blood loss, her sight blurring, but she didn't let go until he stilled. Only after the monstrous body had been motionless for a while did she straighten, trembling, the demon's black blood smeared across her hand.

She felt his life leaving him, like smoke rising from a flame.

Kai Sen

After Kai Sen had made sure that each monk had climbed into Bei manor and the trap door closed again above them, he nodded to Stone, and they backtracked, going down the long steep corridor into the caverns below. Kai Sen lit the way with a single globe of hellfire, and Stone held his lantern in one hand. The stench of the decomposing corpses hit them much sooner this time, and he gagged, swallowing hard. They walked past the bodies quickly, Stone leading the way. He didn't seem bothered by the ravaged corpses surrounding them.

They had not spoken the entire way, until Stone said, "I've known countless abbots as the chosen before you. You are the most magically adept among all of them."

Kai Sen felt pleased by the compliment, and this both surprised and irritated him. He still did not like nor trust Stone, but he did respect him, and had no doubts about Stone's capability as a cohort in this grim task. Warily, he cast a glance at the other man and said nothing.

"You have a natural intuition that helps you wield the elements to their fullest potential," Stone went on, his stride never faltering as he picked a path between the decomposing bodies. "This can make you one of the most powerful abbots that the monastery has ever seen."

"Why are you telling me this?" Kai Sen asked. He couldn't help but be suspicious.

"Because I was arrogant and cruel when we met at the first breach. Because I think you should know," Stone replied with a directness that Kai Sen envied. "You are one of the most magically inclined mortals I've ever come across. This will give us better odds at bringing the whole place down."

"I'll drink to that," Kai Sen said, feigning a lightness in his tone to mask his fear.

When they reached the large stone door set into the cavern wall, they used their earth magic in silence. They worked well together, their strands weaving with ease, their magic strengthened exponentially by the other. The door grated open, and Stone slipped in first.

When they entered the vast chamber, the air seemed even hotter and more oppressive than last time. The walls pulsed blood red in a rhythm that mimicked a heartbeat. Although the majority of demons within the walls remained suspended and frozen, Kai Sen saw movement among some in the rockwork, a curling of the fist here, a twitch of the leg there. More were beginning to stir.

"If we had discovered this any later," Stone said. "It would have been too late."

"How do we do this?"

"Have you worked two elements of magic at once before?"

"Yes," Kai Sen said. "But never to full potential."

Stone strode to the crater at the center of the cavern, bubbling with magma. "You'll have to use your full potential today. And more." He met Kai Sen's gaze. "I need you to create a protective shield over us, then add to my earth magic to bring these walls down."

"Are we going to survive this?" Kai Sen asked.

"Not likely," Stone replied. "But the demons in their current state are as vulnerable as we are. And this breach to the underworld will be buried under rubble—inaccessible to anyone. If we succeed."

Their success would also mean their deaths. For how long could Kai Sen weave a shield to protect them? Long enough to do what needed to be done, he hoped. Without saying another word, he began pulling wood magic to himself, which controlled the air and wind. He drew from the deep roots all around them, from the trees planted above ground in the estate, from the walls and doors of the manor itself. Wood magic was both brittle and yielding, ancient as the oldest trees and as young and pliant as a new shoot in the earth. He deftly wove a dome over himself, then around Stone, and the other man began weaving the earth element.

Stone gathered strands of magic from the rocks and dirt surrounding them, then cast the multiple strands back into the cavern walls. Kai Sen felt the impact, a jarring of his senses connected to the elements. Stone tugged hard again until he was at the heart of hundreds of strands—Kai Sen couldn't count them all—and thrust them back once more against the rock. The ground shuddered beneath their feet.

Reaching for the earth element himself, he tied his strands to Stone's and realized that the man had extended his magic much farther than he knew, delving down the tunnels to the caverns below. In his mind, Kai Sen pictured Stone like some hideous insect with a thousand legs sprouting from him. Stone hurled the strands again, slamming them into the rock, and jarring Kai Sen's teeth. This time, a shower of rubble rained down, rattling against their shields. "We can retreat backward as we work," Kai Sen shouted. "I can move the shield with us."

Stone gave him a dark look, as if he were a fool. "I won't be able to strike as hard from the cavern's entrance. But you move back, and I'll follow." Kai Sen could tell that the other man was indulging him.

Kai Sen slowly retreated toward the cavern's tunnel entrance, shifting the shield with him. Stone stood his ground near the pit at the center of the chamber. Kai Sen could feel the brute strength in which Stone worked the strands. His face shone with sweat, pale against the red glow of the cavern walls. Kai Sen added his own strands, as much as he could give while still keeping a tight hold on the magic for their shields.

Stone flung the earth strands again and again until boulders began to crash down to the cavern floor. Kai Sen worked in unison, sweat sliding down his back and dripping into his eyes. He didn't bother to wipe the sting away, he was concentrating so hard on weaving his magic to Stone's. On the eighth strike, the strands broke through the cavern walls themselves, tunneling like giant worms. Kai Sen sensed the hundreds of strands as they shot through, splitting the earth and rock, creating fissures. This time, the ground shifted beneath their feet.

"Pull back!" Kai Sen shouted above the angry roar of the shaking walls around them. A giant boulder bounced off Stone's shielding, and Kai Sen grunted, as he had barely been able to hold the strands together to protect Stone.

"One more time," Stone shouted.

Frustrated, Kai Sen worked to strengthen his hold on the shield as Stone sent his strands outward again. Kai Sen twined his magic with Stone's, giving so much that he began to shake, then fell to his knees; the impact shocking his entire being. This time, the strands punched through again, expanding all the existing fissures until everything began to crack like an eggshell. The ceiling groaned overhead, and a large portion of it collapsed onto Stone and the path between them.

Instinctively, Kai Sen had thrown his own shield toward Stone's, strengthening it and leaving himself exposed. Rubble rained down, but Kai Sen dodged the largest of them, although a sharp rock glanced against his brow, and blood dribbled into his eye. He cursed. Incredibly, the shield over Stone had held but barely, and Kai Sen had to focus all of his remaining power to hold it in place. Stone was nowhere to be seen, completely buried under the rubble.

Unshielded, he leaped over the boulders, using his instincts to dodge the rocks crashing down on him. Kai Sen spared a fraction of his power to shift a few large rocks around Stone but lost control of his hold on some of the strands. A massive boulder thunked down where the shield had been, and Kai Sen's heart dropped to his stomach. No man could survive that. "Stone!" he shouted, though it sounded small above the groaning of the walls all around them. Kai Sen glimpsed Stone crouched against the ground, head bowed, accepting his fate. The boulder had fallen right next to him, grazing his side, but not crushing him.

Goddess have mercy.

Stone glanced up through the small opening, staring at Kai Sen with unreadable eyes. "You fool," he said. "Go."

"I didn't come back for you to play the martyr," Kai Sen said. "Come on!" He dodged more rocks, and Stone crawled out of the small opening. When he was clear, Kai Sen released the strands of his shield. The heavy rocks collapsed to the ground in a thunderous roar, sending up plumes of dust around them. Kai Sen shifted the shield above them like a canopy. But Stone was clumsy on his feet, falling a few times before rising again. He could tell that Stone had used his magic to the point of exhaustion, and Kai Sen was nearly there himself.

But curse the hell lord if he died here, buried with dead demons. "Follow me!" Kai Sen said. His clairvoyance and agility allowed him to pick the best path toward the cavern's exit into the small corridor. Their shield was waning above them as Kai Sen weakened from the exertion of trying to run to safety while working the magical strands at the same time. He glanced back. Stone was stumbling far behind, unprotected by the shield, his face and tunic stained with blood. The lurid red glow continued to pulse, like some erratic heartbeat, and Kai Sen was certain they were in the core of hell itself. He didn't have enough power to extend the shield farther, so he paused, giving the other man time to catch up.

The entire cavern was rumbling now, shaking like there was a massive earthquake. Demon bodies had toppled out of their cavities; most were crushed and still, but some creatures mewled piteously, flailing against the rocks which pinned them down. Searing heat blasted from the walls and lava pit, overflowing as more large chunks of rubble plunged into the hole, splattering magma. Stone finally reached where Kai Sen stood. The man's eyes had become sunken holes, standing out coal black against his white face. But his cheekbones were flushed bright red, as if he were suffering a fever. He buckled to his knees, and Kai Sen hauled him up by the elbow. Stone had paid a high price for bringing the walls down around them. "Go ahead of me," Kai Sen shouted above the roar and pushed the man forward.

Stone lurched toward the exit, but as he was about to reach it, Kai Sen saw immense boulders plummet from above. Without thinking, he used his remaining magic to thrust Stone forward, so hard that the man flew through the opening right before the giant rocks smashed to the ground, barely missing him.

Kai Sen's arms fell heavily to his sides. The last burst of power he had used on Stone had drained him completely. He limped toward the exit, blocked now by the massive rocks which would have crushed Stone. Feeling boneless and lightheaded, he ran his hands over them, searching for a crevice, a crack, some way to climb out or wedge himself through an opening. But he did so half-heartedly, because he already knew by intuition—the one exit out of these caverns was completely blocked.

He was trapped inside.

Even as he came to terms with this, the ground heaved, knocking him off his feet, and the cavern walls fell inward as the ceiling crashed down on top of him.

CHAPTER THIRTEEN

Skybright

Skybright stared down at Ye Guai's corpse, unable to believe she had actually killed the powerful demon lord. The rubies and emeralds from her hairpin glinted at the base of his skull, winking at her. She swayed on her serpent coil.

"Sky!" Zhen Ni shouted and ran to her, grasping Skybright by her uninjured arm. "You're hurt! Blossom, please bring the sheet from your bed."

The little girl stooped down near Ye Guai's corpse and touched the sharp horn protruding from his head. "Is Baba dead?"

"Yes, petal," Zhen Ni said. Her fingers tremored against Skybright's skin.

"Can I eat him?" Blossom asked as innocently as if she were asking for a sweet.

"No," Zhen Ni almost shouted. "No more corpses, remember? Now be good and help Mama because Auntie Skybright is hurt."

"Yes, Mama." Blossom ran to her bed, her legs blurring with motion, and returned with an embroidered sheet within two breaths. "But I am hungry."

"We'll eat when we're safe, love." Zhen Ni winced but found Nanny Bai's bloodied dagger on the ground and used it to cut the sheet in strips, tying it securely around Skybright's wounded shoulder.

Skybright watched her old mistress under the wan lantern light. Zhen Ni was the same girl she knew, that she had grown up with, but her face was harder now, and there was a knowing in her eyes that had never been there before. If there had been stubbornness and determination in her bones before, they had strengthened to steel beneath. Tears streamed down Zhen Ni's face as she worked to tie the strips firmly, and Blossom observed with interest, like a curious sparrow.

"Why does water flow from your eyes, Mama?" she asked.

Zhen Ni let out a small laugh. "Mama is sad. I'm worried for Skybright."

"Not for Baba?"

"No." Zhen Ni's expression hardened. "Not for Baba."

Skybright wanted to hug her friend to her—there was so much to say and explain. But she felt awkward and shy, and Blossom's strange questions acutely reminded Skybright of her own demonic side. But if she shifted back to her girl form, she'd likely faint. "Thank you," she said in her rough voice.

"Thank *you*, Sky." Her friend wiped her eyes, then touched Skybright's face. "I had sent that message with Pearl so you would leave me. I wanted to keep you safe. But I should have known that you'd never abandon me if you could help it. I'm sorry I ever doubted you."

Skybright grabbed Zhen Ni's hand in gratitude, her heart aching but feeling full, when the earth groaned loudly beneath them. Their eyes met, and Skybright knew Zhen Ni had the same thought, this all felt terribly familiar—when the breach had closed the first time at the base of Tian Kuan Mountain.

"Stone and Kai Sen are working to collapse the caverns below ground," Skybright said. "We have to go!"

Blossom ran ahead of them out into the courtyard, and Zhen Ni tried to put an arm under Skybright to support her. "No," she said. "Go on, I'm all right."

Zhen Ni nodded, following Blossom as the ground heaved beneath them, rumbling, still grasping Nanny Bai's dagger. Skybright slithered right behind, then saw Kai Sen's leather pouch on the ground where it had fallen after she shifted and grabbed it, clutching it to her. She was still woozy but strong enough to keep up. "Where do we go?" Zhen Ni asked over her shoulder.

"We have to leave the estate."

Zhen Ni led them, but Blossom had run ahead, disappearing behind a large pavilion. "Blossom!" Zhen Ni shouted, following the demon child. She truly loved the girl, and Skybright couldn't understand why. Even as the thought crossed her mind, Zhen Ni tripped in front of her. Skybright smelled the corpse before she saw it. Blossom was crouched over a monk and had gouged out his eyes, clutching one eyeball in a small fist, with the other shoved in her mouth. She was making contented noises, savoring the meal. Skybright remembered the rotten corpses below ground, most gnawed to the bone.

Blossom had eaten them.

Zhen Ni slapped Blossom's arm, then grabbed her wrist, pulling the eyeball from the girl's bow-shaped mouth. "Drop it," she said, her voice harder than Skybright had ever heard it. "No."

The girl let go, unblinking amber eyes turned upward, and Skybright would have shivered if she had been in mortal form. She had no doubt that Blossom could kill Zhen Ni if she wanted to. But shockingly, the little girl loved Zhen Ni back; Skybright could sense their love for each other, a warmth that emanated between them. The ground shook harder now beneath their feet, and Zhen Ni held on to Blossom's hand. "Stay with Mama."

The girl obeyed, and they ran on. An ear-splitting crack filled the night sky, sending shock waves through the air. Skybright looked back and saw a dark crevice opening in the ground, zigzagging its way toward them at lightning speed. Kai Sen and Stone had succeeded—but had they survived? There was no time to cast her senses downward for them as she followed Zhen Ni and Blossom, trying to make it out alive.

Zhen Ni knew where she was going, winding her way through the courtyards and covered corridors without slowing, her hand clasped with Blossom's. The demonic child kept up, likely holding back, her chubby legs a blur of motion. The yawning crack that chased them had diverted in a different direction, but the ground didn't stop shuddering. Sounds of screaming and fighting drifted to them from within the massive estate, yet they never encountered it firsthand. Although Skybright could see no flames, the pungent odor of smoke and fire penetrated the night air. Her wound throbbed, but since emerging into the cool outdoors, she'd become focused, her senses even more keen, so intent was she on their survival.

"We're almost there," Zhen Ni shouted over her shoulder.

She had barely spoken when a giant roar reverberated across the rockwork in the courtyard they were in, and Zhen Ni skidded to a sudden stop in front of Skybright. Skybright slithered forward so she was beside her friend. Two massive demon hounds paced in front of them, blocking their way. She recognized them as the statues she had seen guarding the main entrance of the manor. Their ruby eyes glowed red flames now, and wisps of smoke curled from their mouths. Squat and muscular, they were as tall as large stallions, with golden claws that cut deep grooves in the dirt. One lifted its powerful head, lips pulled back to expose sharp teeth and fangs. Fire shot from its mouth.

Pouncing, one of the hounds leaped at Zhen Ni, its lethal claws extended. Skybright pushed Zhen Ni behind her and lashed her serpentine body out, thwacking the beast in the face. She stunned it, but the hound was too large and powerful for her to wrap her coil around, so she grabbed Zhen Ni and they crumpled to the ground, Skybright covering Zhen Ni with her own body.

Within a breath, the hellhound was on top of them, exhaling smoke so hot that it singed the skin on her bare back. She bit her lip so she wouldn't scream in Zhen Ni's ear. The beast had planted both giant paws on either side of them; the talons were curved and as long as her palm. When the beast chose to swipe, Skybright knew she'd be eviscerated—if it didn't rip her head off with its powerful jaws or burn her to a crisp first. She was ready to launch herself at the hellhound's front leg and sink her fangs in, hoping she'd be fast enough before the giant beast reacted and killed them.

But a girlish voice cut through the thunderous rumbling of the ground beneath them and the low growl in the hellhounds' throats. "No," Blossom said. "Leave them be." The snarl she heard from the hound above them stopped, and Skybright saw the other hound sit down on its haunches, also quiet.

"*I* am your master now," Blossom said matter-of-factly. "Baba is dead."

Skybright could feel Zhen Ni shaking beneath her. The demon child's chubby legs approached them. "Get off Mama and my new auntie," Blossom commanded. "If you hurt them, I will kill you."

The hound crouching over them whined, so sharp it hurt her ears, and carefully shuffled backward until they were free. Skybright pushed herself up and was going to help Zhen Ni, but Blossom already had her small hand extended. "Well done, petal," Zhen Ni said, smiling at the demon child through her tears. Again, Skybright felt the strong bond between her friend and the girl, a genuine warmth and connection. Blossom was eloquent and as beautiful as a doll, but Zhen Ni had never been taken with small children. It perplexed Skybright.

Blossom spoke again to the hounds, imperiously, "You shall protect us."

The ground tilted beneath their feet and hot acrid air rushed at them. They ran together, with the giant hellhounds bounding beside them. Skybright spared one glance back and saw that the chasm had caught up, had likely spread through the foundation of the entire Bei manor. She slithered right behind Zhen Ni and Blossom, and they all crashed through a side entrance of the estate. The two hellhounds rammed against the small exit, until the stone broke and the beasts burst through, panting. They heeled near Blossom, as they all tried to catch their breath.

But before they could recover, a deafening *boom* filled the skies and the walls of Bei manor folded inward, collapsing before them. Zhen Ni pulled Blossom back, and the hounds bounded away, retreating from the manor's perimeters. Skybright watched as the entire estate was swallowed by a yawning gap in the earth, devouring tall trees, tiled roofs, and rock gardens alike, until her vision was filled with dust clouds and the thick stench of smoke.

She threw her senses downward, but there was too much disturbance within the earth for her to pinpoint any life below. The ground shuddered again, and she had to force herself back from the estate's edge while the manor continued to collapse inward.

How could Kai Sen or Stone have survived this?

Shouts of fear and excitement filled the night air. It was well past the thieving hour, but Bei manor's fate had not gone unnoticed. Servants and handmaids began trickling out of the various rich estates bordering the manor, intent on collecting news and gossip for their ladies and masters. Skybright slithered away to the back of the manor near the forest. She didn't want to be seen, but neither did she want to shift back to her mortal form. As a girl, she'd feel exposed, in more ways than one. Zhen Ni followed with Blossom clutching her hand and the two hellhounds closing the rear like demonic guards, which they were to the little girl now, Skybright realized.

The grounds of Bei manor were so expansive that no one was near the back where they had entered through the tunnel. The tall wall above the tunnel still stood for a few lengths, likely because it was on the outer most perimeter of the estate, far from the center of the manor. But no one was there. She felt her heart plummet, and she cast her senses as far below as she could.

Stone.

Without saying a word, she dove headfirst into the narrow hole, ignoring the panic that was rising in her chest. She found him collapsed midway through the tunnel, unconscious. "Stone," she said and touched his cheek. He stirred a little, groaning. "Stone!"

He lifted his head. "Skybright?"

She knew he couldn't see her in the darkness. "Give me your hands. I'll pull you up."

He struggled to lift his arms overhead in the cramped space, and when he finally managed and she clasped both his hands in hers, she was flooded with such relief that her face burned. She pulled him, using her powerful serpent coil to shift back and up the steep tunnel. Her torn shoulder screamed in pain, but she ignored it, gritting her teeth. Stone, obviously weak, worked with her, pushing with his feet. The earth shook around them, the manor's collapse still sending shock waves. Dirt and rubble rained down, and she was terrified that the tunnel could crash in on them at any moment.

Finally, after what seemed like an eternity, she felt the cool air on her scales, and she was free with Zhen Ni beside the entrance, waiting anxiously. Stone crawled through, coughing, covered in dust, his face blackened with soot, and dirt, and dried blood. "Thank you," he gulped another breath, "Skybright."

"Kai Sen?" she asked, deep down already knowing Stone's response.

Stone gave a weak shake of his head. "He gave his life saving me."

She wanted to fall to the ground and howl from grief, to cry until she was hoarse and could not shed another tear. But she could not cry in serpent form and instead held still as a statue. "You saw him die."

"No," Stone said. "He was trapped within the cavern."

Zhen Ni reached for her arm, gripping it, trying to offer comfort and strength.

"He could still be alive then," Skybright said and cast her senses again, going deeper to where the demon spawn had dwelled. Some demons still lived far below; she could feel them, their lives like flickering flames. But they were all near death. Then a glimmer of recognition, so fleeting it was like trying to capture mist in her hands. "I sense him!" She lunged toward the tunnel entrance but amazingly, Stone moved fast enough to block her way.

"No."

She jerked her good arm back to knock him aside. He lowered his chin, ready for the blow, but stood his ground.

"I can save him," she rasped.

"Skybright," Stone said in a thick voice. "Kai Sen is gone. The entire estate crashed down on us. *I* barely made it out alive." He lifted his head, and his face was wet from tears. "To go back in is suicide."

The sight of Stone crying was so shocking she dropped her arm and snapped her coil, sliding away from him. His display of emotion unsettled her—something she never thought she'd see from Stone, who had always been stoic and impassive. "I can try." Her throat felt closed, raw.

"Sky." Zhen Ni was beside her again, wrapping her arms around her. "Please. Stone is right. I-I can't lose you again."

Zhen Ni laid her head on Skybright's good shoulder, and she felt as if her chest had crumpled, been crushed as terribly and fast as Bei manor had been. Her friend kissed her softly on the cheek, as she used to do when they were little girls and Skybright had scraped an elbow or knee or had had a nightmare and needed comforting. Skybright's throat filled with the salt of tears, but they didn't reach her eyes.

"We have to go," Zhen Ni said. "It isn't safe here."

"I have to do one thing," Stone said. "Do you have the divining stone, Skybright?"

For a moment, she didn't know what Stone was referring to. Then she remembered the leather pouch Kai Sen had handed her before he hugged her farewell for the very last time. She still gripped it in one hand, through the hellhound attack and escaping the estate's destruction, as if her life depended on it. She opened the pouch and pulled out the heavy divining stone and gave it to him.

But she felt something else in the bag and retrieved it. It was a wooden figurine of a woman, and Kai Sen's scent lingered on the piece, as if he had held it often in his hand. She examined it, and although the face was too rough to be recognizable, the woman wore a bun pulled to each side of her head, as Skybright often did. *I enjoy carving too*, Kai Sen had said when they were first getting to know each other. She had never seen his work, but somehow she knew that his hands had made this, and it was meant to be a figurine of her.

She ran her fingers over the delicate carving, her chest feeling hollow, when Stone broke her reverie and said, "The breach is closed. The divining stone is not responding at all. It's done." Stone's shoulders dropped, his relief as palpable as his exhaustion. They had closed the breach in time—he would live.

But Kai Sen ... She threw her senses downward again, searching, searching for that ephemeral essence that had touched her mind for a heartbeat, that she *knew* had to be him.

Nothing.

Skybright nodded slowly. "It is done," she repeated and let Zhen Ni take her hand. Blossom slipped up to them, and her friend clasped her other hand with the child's. They returned to the forest, followed by Stone and trailed by two demon hounds. Stone gave them suspicious looks, keeping clear of the demonic beasts as best as he could.

But even as she slid into the forest, she kept casting her senses back to Bei manor and the deep caverns beneath it for that familiar glimmer—a wisp in the darkness.

Kai Sen.

Kai Sen.

Kai Sen.

No one spoke during the long trek through the thickets. Entering its depths usually lightened Skybright's heart, but this time, she barely took note of her surroundings. She slithered in a daze, as if she dwelled in a waking dream, her senses cast behind them toward the destroyed estate, even as her hold grew more tenuous the further they traveled. Her mind filled with images of Kai Sen: running, leaping, slaying demons. Then she recalled their last passionate, lingering kiss and how Kai Sen looked at her with desire and tenderness but also with a wistful regret.

She had said things she knew would hurt him, but they needed to be said. Kai Sen was always the impractical dreamer, but he was even more so a loyal and fierce fighter, and he had given up his life to save Stone … to save them all. Skybright ran her thumb over the figurine and concentrated on the strange scent of the hellhounds, snuffling and snorting behind Blossom, who was tireless, keeping up with all of them on her chubby legs. She still couldn't sense the girl, other than as a void, something she'd miss unless she knew to look for it.

"You should return to Yuan manor, Zhen Ni." Skybright stopped when they passed near the path that led to their old home. What had always been comforting to her, these trees, the night noises, and the well-worn way back to Yuan manor, seemed distorted now. It was hard to speak, but she forced her mouth to form the words. "Your mother will hear about Bei manor's destruction, and she'll be worried for you."

"With these hellhounds in tow?" Zhen Ni asked. "We can't release them into the forest."

"They are able to change their appearance," Stone said. "At least, that is the lore." He stood apart from them, his features masked in shadows. But as worn down as he was, Skybright could feel the tension in his stance, his readiness to fight if the hellhounds turned.

Blossom stood in front of the giant beasts. They towered over her, smoke curling from their mouths, eyes glowing like they offered a glimpse into the underworld. The demon child didn't reach halfway to their powerful front legs that ended in paws larger than her head. "Change," Blossom commanded.

The demonic beasts let out a low whine that shivered through the leaves, silencing the forest. But then they obeyed, each morphing before their eyes, turning into large mastiffs. Still huge but not even a quarter the size of their demonic selves. The horns and sharp claws receded, along with their glowing eyes. By all appearances, they were just giant dogs. Blossom reached up, and the beasts lowered their heads so she could rub them between their ears.

Zhen Ni touched Skybright's hand. "You'll be all right?"

"Yes." She squeezed her old mistress's fingers.

"Come to Yuan manor after you are done with your tasks," Zhen Ni said. "You're always welcome."

Skybright gave her a small smile. "I'll visit as soon as I can." She hugged Zhen Ni. "Keep safe."

Zhen Ni nodded and turned toward the familiar path back to Yuan manor, holding Blossom's hand, the mastiffs flanking them.

Skybright watched until they disappeared into the darkness, even as she followed their footsteps with her senses. Stone began walking toward the monastery, as they needed to give Han news of what happened.

He wanted to speak with her, but she felt him holding back, respecting her need for silence. The forest and creatures of night welcomed them, rustling the branches above and turning the dirt beneath. But Skybright was incapable of enjoying the life and wonder surrounding her, weighed down by Kai Sen's death. Something, she realized, that she had never allowed herself to truly fathom, despite how many times Kai Sen had met danger head-on wielding only a saber. She didn't notice they had reached the monastery until Stone stopped before the grand double doors.

"Will you shift, Skybright?" Stone asked her in a soft voice.

She stared back at him, not speaking.

"You cannot go in like that."

"I'm not shifting," she rasped. To face Kai Sen's death was hard enough in serpent form, when she felt removed, emotionally aloof.

How could she survive her grief in her human form?

"You should speak to Han. You ... knew Kai Sen the best."

She swallowed and tasted the trace of bitter venom in her mouth from sinking her fangs into Ye Guai. "Then I will speak to Han like this."

Stone appeared as if he would say something else, but then nodded and knocked on one of the massive double doors. It swung open immediately, as if they were waiting for them. Han stood at the opening himself, and his eyes widened a fraction when he saw her, but he never let the surprise reach his smooth face. He signaled with a hand to someone they couldn't see behind the door and stepped out. The giant door slammed shut behind him. Han was obviously taking no risks.

"What news?" The words were burdened by what Han didn't ask. But as it had been for Skybright, she was certain he already knew.

Stone seemed to be waiting for her to speak, but since she remained motionless and silent, he said finally, "The attack was a success. We've closed the breach and destroyed the demon nests."

"And my brother monks?" Han asked.

"Likely dead," Stone replied. He dropped his chin and drew a shaking breath. "The entire manor is destroyed, sunken into the ground. I'm sorry."

"Kai Sen too?" The blood had drained from Han's face, and his eyes shone like obsidian in the faint moonlight.

"Trapped in the caverns," Stone said. "He gave his life so I would live."

Han spun around and punched the giant door with his fist. Then he did it again and again, until Skybright could taste the tang of his blood in the air. He whipped toward her and snarled, "Are you satisfied, temptress? Now that he's dead?"

It felt as if he'd slapped her, and she almost reared back on her coil. But she recognized his grief and anger and pain, tasting as harsh as the draughts Nanny Bai used to brew. An exact reflection of everything she felt herself. Tears streamed from his eyes. "He would want you to take his place, Han," she said in her rough voice. "You are the leader of the monastery now."

The young man winced, like she had been the one to inflict physical pain. "Kai Sen knew I wanted to lead," he choked out. "But not like this. Never like this."

"He always spoke well of you, Han," she said. "You know he thought of you as a brother."

The young man was sobbing now, his grief heavy in the night air, pressing against her own sadness. Stone met her eyes in the dim moonlight, and she gave a slight shake of her head. Never one to betray his thoughts, she still knew exactly what was on his mind: the covenant. Han was the chosen one now. Who would tell him about the agreement between the mortals and the gods, to uphold the next Great Battle?

No one, Skybright thought. Kai Sen had called it a twisted agreement, costing innocent mortal lives. He was right. Zhen Ni would have died as the chosen sacrifice if Skybright had not given herself as a captive to take her place. But Kai Sen was gone now. So it would end with her.

"The successor is usually trained by the abbot in more powerful magic," she said. "Under the circumstances, I think you'll find Stone to be a great mentor."

Han lifted his head and assessed Stone with sharp eyes. Even if he was not as magically inclined as Kai Sen had been, she knew he would be a good leader for the monastery.

Skybright had sensed Stone's surprise by her suggestion, but he hid it. "I am willing to help, Han."

Han's features hardened, even though his cheeks were still wet from tears. "I have to give the news to my fellow brothers," he said in a low voice. "I'll take into consideration all that you've said, but I have no reason to trust you." He rapped on the door in a short series of knocks, and it swung open. "Kai Sen did, and look where it got him." Han slipped through the opening without a glance back.

Skybright gripped the wooden figurine in her hand so hard it bit into her palm. Suddenly, she felt lightheaded and swayed on her serpentine coil, her torn shoulder throbbing.

Stone clasped her by both arms, keeping her steady. "Your binding is soaked with blood," he said from what seemed like a long distance. "You need to rest."

Her body was not hers to command any longer, and she felt herself growing limp. Just then, her skin tingled, and her hair lifted from her head. A portal opened before them, offering a glimpse of a lush garden and a velvet sky spangled with stars. "I will speak to you both," a voice said, from without, but also within their own minds.

Skybright recognized that voice.

The Goddess of Accord.

"Yes, goddess," Stone said. He was holding her up now. She rested her head against his shoulder, breathing in his earthen scent, and heard nothing more.

CHAPTER FOURTEEN

Skybright

Skybright's senses were suffused by the perfume of tuberose, delicate and fragrant. Her cheek was pressed against something gloriously soft, and she was reluctant to open her eyes. The sharp pain in her shoulder had disappeared and so had her exhaustion. Surely it was a delirious dream, and she must not wake, because waking meant aching and loss, suffering and grief.

Then she felt someone stroke her arm, and a melodious voice said, "She is fine, Stone. But tired ... and grieving."

It could only be the goddess, as hearing her words lifted Skybright's heart, as if letting sunshine and spring air in. "You need rest too," the goddess said. It sounded like a command.

"I will, lady," Stone replied. "After I take my leave."

The goddess eased Skybright up, and she unwillingly opened her eyes. She had been resting in the goddess's lap, her face pressed against the soft fabric of her dress, which shone in the dark, its colors flowing and shifting like liquid. "Rise, Skybright. Stone is worried for you."

He was pacing a short distance from them, still dirty and

disheveled, to the point where he was almost unrecognizable, because she was so used to seeing him meticulously dressed and presented. "You're awake." He broke into a relieved smile, looking no older than the eighteen years he had spent as a mortal thousands of years ago. She was still in serpent form and rose on her coil, slithering away from the goddess, feeling frightened but also hesitant. It was hard to put from her mind what she had witnessed last she had been with the Goddess of Accord, how easily she had stripped Stone of his powers, as if plucking a petal from a flower.

There was no doubt in Skybright's mind that they had been summoned back to where the Immortals dwelled. She was overwhelmed by potent scents that made the mortal realm pale and wanting by comparison. The half-moon was radiant on the horizon, and Skybright had never seen so many stars, silver and white, blue and red. They glowed liked jewels in the sky. Vibrant flowers surrounded them, and she glimpsed orchids and peonies glimmering in the darkness. In the distance, there were peach trees laden with fruit, their sweet ripeness carrying over on a soft breeze.

The goddess was draped on a stone step leading into a magnificent pagoda, as nonchalant as any maiden, but her omnipotence exuded from her, impossible to ignore. Skybright bowed to the regal woman. "Thank you, goddess, for healing me."

"It was a terrible wound," the goddess said. "You would not have died from it, being half-demonic, but you would have suffered." The goddess floated to her feet and expanded, stretching to twice any mortal's height; she towered over Skybright and Stone. "I am pleased that you closed the breach." Her voice reverberated through the quiet garden. "You have kept your promise, Stone, and done well."

Stone bowed this time, graceful and measured, despite his unkempt appearance. "Thank you, goddess."

The lady lifted one hand, slender fingers pointed toward the infinite sky. "I will grant you your immortality back, Stone, lift you to your previous status." She turned her wrist elegantly, and Skybright trembled at the vitality that radiated from her, that coalesced in the air around her. The goddess made the magic that Kai Sen and Stone wielded appear like child's play.

"No," Stone said.

Pausing mid-motion, the goddess's perfect mouth curled into a mysterious smile. She appeared as a statue hewn by the masters, glowing like a star herself. "No?" The force of that one word swept over Skybright and Stone, and they both staggered back.

Stone dropped to his knees and bowed his head. "No, goddess. I have decided not to reclaim my former role as intermediary between the realms."

"You believe you have a choice?" the goddess asked.

Stone pressed his brow against the ground, not replying.

Shocked, Skybright stared at his still form. What was Stone thinking, to reject the far-reaching powers he used to have, to reject *immortality*?

"Apologies, my lady. I am presumptuous and overstep my bounds," Stone murmured, "But if I were given a choice—"

"Why?" The goddess's all-encompassing voice spiraled into the air, but its resonance did not force them back this time.

Stone remained silent for a long moment, long enough that Skybright's chest tightened with anxiety.

"Because I have not felt in so long, goddess," he finally said. "Because I had not truly *cared* for too many years. At my most powerful, I was above it all, the pain, the jealousy, the hate, all the human foibles—" He paused. "But I was also set apart from the joy and wonder and love. Nothing ever truly touched my heart. My magic and status made me arrogant and careless." Stone lifted his head, and his eyes shone. "Now I know what it is to feel again."

The goddess's hand dropped, a lithe motion that was both beautiful and terrifying. Skybright knew she could grant wondrous gifts and unimaginable punishments with a flick of her fingertips. "A touching speech, Stone." She glided in front of them, back and forth, her dress aglow and shifting in a myriad of colors. "What say you, little one?"

Skybright blinked, never expecting the attention to turn to her.

"Stone fought well and bravely." She did not go so far as to tell the goddess what she should do.

"And you? Did you fight well?" The goddess paused and turned her full gaze on Skybright. A hint of a smile curved the corners of her perfect mouth. Her black eyes were fathomless.

"Yes, lady." Skybright dipped her chin in reverence to the goddess. "I did."

The Goddess of Accord constricted in size until she was the same height as a mortal woman and cupped Skybright's cheek for a moment, her touch as ephemeral as morning dew. "Your mother would be proud."

"My … my mother?" It was the last thing she anticipated the goddess would say, and she almost slithered away from her. But she felt a spike of agitation from Stone, enough warning that Skybright held still. "You knew my mother?"

The goddess's beautiful features began blurring, like an image underwater, until she took on another face. It was like looking into a mirror; Skybright was an exact likeness of her mother. "Your mother was a solitary creature," the goddess said. "She had never associated with the gods, keeping to herself, though she did help during the Great Battles, working with Stone." Crisp chirping began to fill the gardens, and the skies above were taking on a golden pink hue. "But Opal beseeched the gods one day, and I answered her call."

Stone had risen and moved to stand behind Skybright. She wanted to reach out and grab his hand because she suddenly felt very frightened and alone, face-to-face with the image of her dead mother. Stone, as if sensing her unease, drew even closer. It helped.

"I summoned her here to The Mountain of Heavenly Peace, and she told me that she had grown weary. She had lived for more than a thousand years in the mortal realm and was able to see into the hearts of men and glimpse their sins. Opal exacted revenge and killed these men when she thought fitting, but she was … tired." The goddess gazed into Skybright's eyes with Opal's face, and it felt as if her own mother was reading her very soul, extracting each secret, shame, and desire. "She had been alone for so long. She asked me, 'Could you give me a child? Could I have a daughter?'"

A knot rose to Skybright's throat, as the goddess's compelling voice had changed when she spoke those questions—and she knew that she was hearing Opal's own voice, dulcet and lilting. She must have sung so beautifully.

"Demons are not made to bear offspring, I told her. I can bestow upon you a daughter," the goddess paused, "but it would cost you your life."

Skybright gasped, and she felt Stone's hand clasp her shoulder.

"I am willing," Opal said. "But grant me one wish. Let my daughter see the *good* in people. Let her see the light too and not only the sins."

The goddess's face blurred again, changing back to features as remote and perfect as a statue's. "I gave Opal her wish."

Skybright pressed her face in her hands, but no tears came. Stone's touch was a comfort, but she could also feel his bewilderment and shock at the goddess's revelation.

"I made you in the exact image of Opal, but half-mortal, so you could live within and understand both worlds, Skybright," the goddess said. "You have a soul that your mother lacked. You are a child of both realms, the mortal and the divine."

She felt the blood roaring in her ears and her heartbeat racing. Opal had given up her own life so Skybright could have hers, for reasons she might never fully understand. "Let me take Stone's place," she said. "Let me be the new intermediary."

Stone's hand tightened on her shoulder, and she slid away from him, distancing herself. Would he betray her? Say that she was wrong for the role, that she intended to thwart the covenant? The skies were awash in the brilliant colors of dawn, but more vivid and sublime, as they would be where the gods dwelled. Skybright felt the garden erupt into life with the rising sun, small creatures scurrying from their burrows, the butterflies taking flight, and all the birds beginning their morning in lively song and animated conversations. It seemed that her fate hung by a delicate cobweb.

The Goddess of Accord arched one raven brow. "You wish to be fully immortal?"

"No," Skybright replied. "If you grant me the power to travel between the underworld and the mortal, it would be enough."

"Why do you want this, little one?" the goddess asked.

Skybright swallowed, steadying herself, before saying, "For exactly all the things you said. I am of both worlds and would make an ideal intermediary." She was grateful for her demonic, inflectionless voice. It gave nothing away.

The goddess was silent for some time, shimmering and aloof, scrutinizing Skybright with her piercing gaze. Skybright tried to shield everything that was in her heart, but feared that in any moment, she would fall to the ground, blathering all her secret intentions.

"Very well," the Goddess of Accord replied. "You can help oversee the covenant between the mortals and gods." She turned to Stone. "I will allow you to keep the small magic that you have, and you can accompany Skybright ..."

Stone bowed his head, and Skybright followed, relieved beyond measure.

"If she desires it," the goddess finished. "You have the ability to travel where you wish now, Skybright, and create portals as Stone was able to." Her image began to dissipate, whorling like mist. "We are done here," she said and was gone.

The goddess's sudden exit left a void. It felt as if the magnificent dawn had dimmed and the morning blooms retracted in her absence. Skybright and Stone stood in silence for some time, both trying to comprehend the consequences of what had taken place.

"So," Stone finally said in a hoarse voice. "Do you truly want the role?"

"I do," she replied.

She believed Stone knew her motives—he was smart enough to guess—but his questions were left unspoken. Relieved, she slithered to him. She couldn't be certain if he would keep her secret after thousands of years of ensuring that each Great Battle took place as was agreed upon by the covenant. Skybright had feared that Stone might argue against her taking the role or told the goddess what he suspected.

Weariness seeped from Stone. Skybright felt as refreshed as if she had slept for days, yet he had not received the goddess's attention or care. She touched his wrist, then gripped it when his exhaustion washed over her. "Thank you, Stone."

They were eye level, and he studied her as she breathed in his familiar scent: tilled earth mingled with the sharp tang of lemon. It was such a comfort to her now, and she couldn't say why. Instead, she wrapped her arms around him and buried her face in the hollow of his neck. He stiffened, but their embrace seemed to steady him. Skybright wanted to cry, but she closed her eyes and took refuge in feeling his arms around her.

"I'm sorry, Skybright," he said.

She had never told Kai Sen that she loved him, had always held back, and then ended things because she was half-demonic, knowing he could never fully accept her as she was. Still, if she searched deep down, if she allowed herself to unlock all the boxes she'd hidden away in those dark recesses, the truth would be blindingly obvious. She *had* loved Kai Sen, even when she knew it was foolish, even when she knew that it would never last. She had loved him, and she never told him. And now, it was too late.

Skybright swiped her eyes against Stone's dusty tunic, even though no tears came. She pushed on her serpentine coil, drawing closer, when she felt Stone's growing excitement pressing against her. Then she was aware that she was completely naked, her bare breasts pushed to Stone's chest, his tunic the only thing keeping them from feeling skin against skin. Desire came with this sudden awareness, slow burning, but insistent. Blood surged through her entire body, and she reared back from him, breathless.

He stood there, dirt smudged and red-faced. "Skybright, I—" he faltered.

She had never seen him so flustered. "You want me," she said. It sounded like an accusation. She was clutching him again by his wrist, and their desire for each other ricocheted between them, a living, needful thing.

"I can't help but react, Skybright. I'm tired—"

"Not that tired," she said pointedly.

He laughed and twisted his wrist from her grasp, rubbing his eyes. "I apologize."

"You don't *want* to want me."

He stilled, holding her gaze until she looked away. "Because I always knew your heart was elsewhere."

She let out a low breath, her chest aching, but her attraction to Stone was still strumming through her.

"You're grieving, Skybright," he said. "I can be a friend to you but not a distraction to be thrown aside."

She slid away from him, furious that he was so calm, spoke with so much *sense*. She had always been the practical one, but it felt as if she were unraveling. "You were the one who agreed with me once that it was 'only a kiss.'"

"Well," he replied in a low voice, "it wouldn't be just that for me anymore." His cheeks grew redder. "I *feel* everything now."

There were words he left unsaid, but she wasn't in the mindset to hear them, to try and untangle all the thoughts and emotions wound up within her. "Please show me how I can travel with magic."

"All right," Stone said. "But how long will you stay in serpent form?"

She did not answer him.

Stone taught her the simple incantation to transport herself anywhere within the mortal realm and the more challenging task of creating a portal until she was able to with his guidance, taking Stone with her back to Tian Kuan Mountain.

There, they parted ways.

For four months she stayed in serpent form, traveling alone, her sole possession Kai Sen's carved figurine which she wore on a leather cord around her neck. She used her magic to roam from one province to another, exploring different forests, sliding across unfamiliar peaks—some barren, others lush with life—and vast deserts. She didn't give a thought to those she had left behind because she had always been able to count them on one hand, and that number, she realized, could dwindle in an instant. Mortal lives were lost within a breath, yet she would remain, outliving all of them.

She wanted to sing in these vast, empty spaces, but she couldn't bear to sing in her rough, demonic voice. So instead, she neither spoke nor sang for all those days she was alone.

In the beginning of the eighth moon, when the Ghost Festival had come and gone, she thought about Zhen Ni and missed her and wondered how she was doing. Was she still caring for that strange demon child who ate corpses? And to be truthful, she also wondered about Stone. Where was he now?

She used her magic to return to Chang He, near the Yuan manor, but her keen senses told her that Zhen Ni no longer lived there. It was late at night, and she stayed in serpent form, avoiding stragglers who were wandering through the small town, and followed her senses to find her friend.

The journey took her through more narrow streets, not the grand roads that the Yuan and Bei manors were built on. She finally stopped at a modest home, a fraction of the size of Bei manor but well constructed. The double wooden doors were painted a deep blue, and two bronze handles with bats holding a ring pull were set in each door. Feeling feral and completely lacking in decorum, Skybright simply slithered over the tall wall into a square courtyard. It was not grand in size but beautifully planted. Water pattering from a fountain made a pleasant, peaceful sound. But before she could glide to one of the quarters, where she sensed Zhen Ni sleeping, she heard a deep growl from behind a plum tree, echoed by another.

Two giant mastiffs stalked out from the shadows. Skybright recognized them as the massive hellhounds in disguise. The two beasts bared their fangs, not quite as long as their demonic ones, but long enough. They both poised to spring, and she gathered her own coil, hissing deep, demonic beast against demonic beast.

"Fluffy!" a childish voice said from some dark corner. "Cuddles! Heel!"

Blossom emerged from the darkness, attired in a pink sleep dress. She wore two long braids and her round face was like a cherub's. Skybright still could not detect her presence.

"It is only Auntie Skybright," Blossom said. "Mama will be so pleased. She has been so worried over you."

"She is in bed with someone else," Skybright said, her voice even more coarse from months of silence. When she had found Zhen Ni with her senses, it briefly touched on another person, and without thinking more, she had assumed it had been Blossom. Now she was reminded that Blossom was hidden to her serpentine magic.

The little girl approached her, fearless, her amber eyes wide with curiosity. The two mastiffs trailed beyond the small child, protective and loyal. Blossom reached out a hand and stroked Skybright's serpent coil, marveling at her scales. "Mama is asleep with Auntie Sun. She lives here with An An—it helps Mama feel less lonely."

"An An?" Skybright asked.

"Auntie Sun's son. He is six and a troublemaker," Blossom replied matter-of-factly. "But he does not bother me."

Skybright laughed; it sounded low and unnatural. She hadn't laughed in so long and hadn't expected the strange demon child to elicit laughter from her. Skybright was certain that little An An left Blossom alone indeed, guarded as she was by two fierce mastiffs and her own powerful magic. She lowered herself on her coil so she was eye level with the child. The girl had grown a little taller since she last saw her, and prettier, if that was possible.

"Your scales are lovely to touch, Auntie," Blossom said admiringly. "So smooth and glittery."

Skybright smiled, revealing her long fangs, but the girl wasn't afraid. "Thank you, petal," she said, remembering Zhen Ni's pet name for her. "Could you wake Mama and ask for her to meet me in the courtyard? Alone."

Blossom nodded and toddled off, the mastiffs padding after her. The child obviously had the beasts as well trained as puppets pulled on strings.

She slithered to an alcove near the pond beside a stone bench nestled between plum trees. The lotus flowers were blooming on the water, adrift among full lush leaves. A rustle sounded, and Zhen Ni emerged from behind an ornamental pine. "Skybright!" she said, and flung her arms around her neck.

For the first time in months, Skybright felt at *home*, her heart at ease. She hugged her friend back, feeling the pressure of tears that could not be shed.

"Are you all right? Where have you been? I've been so worried for you. And Stone, he has been visiting every few days. Finally, I had to tell him to stop coming because it appeared so improper, my being a grieving widow," Zhen Ni paused for breath. "I said I'd tell him as soon as I received news of you. But I still see him lurking around town—I think he's as worried for you as I was."

Or he's keeping an eye on Blossom, Skybright thought, *and those hellhounds.*

Zhen Ni gripped her shoulders and shook her. "Never do that to me again, Sky!"

Skybright smiled and let herself be reprimanded. "I'm sorry, Zhen Ni. I really needed to be away—to think and be alone."

Her friend dropped her hands and wrapped her green silk robe more closely to herself. "I know, Sky." She reached over and touched her cheek.

"This is your manor?" Skybright asked.

Zhen Ni's expressive eyes swept the courtyard. "It is. It was chaos after Bei manor collapsed. The entire town banded together to clean up the rubble. My large chest of gold and silver coins was recovered, along with a few other very valuable items. I was able to buy this small manor for myself so I can properly take care of Blossom."

"She's dangerous, Zhen Ni."

"More dangerous than you?" her friend countered in a sharp tone.

"It's impossible to know," Skybright paused. "She eats corpses."

Zhen Ni let out a sigh. "She did. That's what Master Bei wanted. I realized that it made her magically more powerful, if she consumed dead human flesh. It also helped her to grow very quickly, many months in just one day." She lifted her chin, a prideful movement that Skybright had missed. "But I've found a way to suppress her power and growth—she simply eats raw animal flesh and organs. It is enough for her."

Her friend said it so casually that Skybright knew it had all become normal for Zhen Ni, raising a beautiful demon child who preferred raw liver to dumplings and steamed buns.

"She is obedient?"

"She is a perfect child," Zhen Ni replied. "I couldn't ask for a better daughter."

"Blossom's love for you is the one thing I can sense from her when you are together," Skybright said. "Nothing else."

"Her charm does not work on you then."

"The girl has charmed you to love her?"

Zhen Ni smiled. "Yes. But I believe I have charmed her back. She loves me truly. Something she never felt for Master Bei, who was incapable of love."

"And this Auntie Sun who shares your bed?" Skybright arched an eyebrow.

Her friend gave a low laugh and blushed. "Li Jing, another young widow I met. We are both prime examples of virtuous wives who refuse to ever marry again after losing our husbands. The entire town is quite taken with our sacrifice and speak highly of us. They like that we are able to take … comfort from each other." Zhen Ni's mouth quirked with mischievous amusement.

"I see." Skybright couldn't help but smile back at Zhen Ni, seeing her eyes shine with joy.

"Oh, she is wonderful, Sky. I can't wait for you to meet her."

"I cannot wait either." She couldn't be happier for her friend, that she'd found love and made a home for herself.

"Remember when Madame Lo said that I would have two children? Between Li Jing's son An An and my Blossom, that is two." Her friend reached for both Skybright's hands and held them. "And she said that you were *strong*, Sky. She was right. I've never known anyone stronger than you." Zhen Ni stared at their interlocked hands. "I'm sorry that I ever doubted you in my mind. But Kai Sen never did. Not even when—" She paused. "Not even when we saw you murder a man."

Skybright pulled away from her friend. "You witnessed that? Stone forced me—he threatened to kill some innocent bystander if I didn't obey him."

"That brute!" Zhen Ni said with vehemence. "If I had known, I'd have shut the door in his face for all those times he came to ask after you."

Skybright thought about Stone when he was immortal, truthful, but so out of touch with feelings and what it meant to be human. The Stone she had left behind was still honest but struggling with learning about his mortal past and dealing with all the emotions that came with refusing immortality. In the end, he had chosen to *feel*, to be able to empathize. "He was used to being obeyed," she said. "But he believed he was helping me learn about my demonic side. That man you saw me with lived."

"He did?" Zhen Ni let out a small breath.

Skybright was touched that her friend was willing to accept her wholly but knew that Zhen Ni was relieved she had not murdered someone after all. "Yes, and I refused to ever try again," she replied.

"Stone respected my wishes."

Zhen Ni nodded.

"But how did you find me in that alley?"

"Kai Sen," Zhen Ni replied. "He used his magic to search for you in all the provinces. I told him he was mad, but he was determined."

Kai Sen had never mentioned what he saw to her. And no matter how uncomfortable he had been with her demonic side, he had never lost faith in her, had never doubted her *goodness*. Skybright drew a hand across her face, feeling wrung out.

Sensing her sadness, Zhen Ni grabbed her hand again and squeezed her fingers. "Sky, know that you will always have a place in my home. Just as you always have a place in my heart."

"As you are in mine." Skybright lifted their joined hands to touch her own heart for a moment, then rose on her coil. "Thank you. I'll return again soon."

Zhen Ni stood and hugged her once more. "Be well, Sky."

Skybright left Zhen Ni's manor, sliding over the wall in the same way she had entered. A single growl erupted from behind her but was quickly silenced, no doubt by its young, demonic mistress.

Not knowing where to go, Skybright slithered toward Bei manor, compelled to see the site one more time. The persimmon trees and carved stone benches still lined where the entrance of the grand manor had been, but the estate was leveled and cleaned out. The town folk had worked hard to remove the rubble and fallen trees, but it was still in ruins, roped off to warn people from straying too near and falling into its gaping foundation.

She slid to the back, so she was more hidden from prying eyes, casting her senses deep below the grounds.

Nothing.

But she didn't give up, sending her keen serpentine magic deep, where the second breach had been and where Kai Sen was lost, lingering there.

A flare of familiarity, bursting bright then gone, like a luminous flame snuffed.

Skybright tried over and over to grasp it again, but everything below was dead now. Silent.

Then her senses did touch on someone alive and near.

Stone.

She almost spun around to avoid him, but she couldn't bring herself to leave. Not after feeling his cautious hope and his concern for her. He stood, a lone figure in the back of the former estate, near the tunnel he and Kai Sen had made together.

"You've returned to us," he said, his smooth face not belying all the emotions he hid beneath the surface.

She stopped an arm's length from him. He looked well, handsome, and immaculately dressed in a dark blue tunic and trousers, his black hair pulled into a topknot. His earthen scent had not changed, and he smelled like *home* to her too, as much as Zhen Ni had. "How did you know?" she rasped.

"Blossom told me," he said. "She sent a bat, like I taught her to do."

Skybright laughed for the second time that night, the notion was so ludicrous. "A messenger bat? And the demon child as your spy?"

Stone smiled and shrugged. "She's very smart and does not sleep."

"But how did you know to find me here?"

He followed her gaze to the fallen estate, and his expression grew serious. "A hunch. I've returned to this site many times. Some of the monks survived, more than we had hoped, and I helped to pull a few men out myself. Zhen Ni's three servants managed to escape in time, too."

"But Kai Sen?"

Stone shook his head. "They plan on filling this hole soon and building a park over it. The caverns are buried too deep below, they're impossible to reach. It's safer that way."

It had been a futile, hopeless wish.

They stayed silent for some time, and an owl hooted in the distance, plaintive and lonely.

Finally, Stone said, "It wasn't just for the pleasant weather that I had transported us into the future."

For a moment, Skybright had no notion what he was referring to, then remembered when they had stepped from an oppressive summer into the crisp spring of Qing Chun, that quaint southern town filled with canals.

"I believed six months was long enough for those who loved you to forget," Stone went on, an ironic smile touching the corners of his mouth. "Human lives are so short, their memories faulty and their emotions fickle. I couldn't go too much into the future but thought for certain half a year was enough time for them to have moved on, to have given up, to have cast the memory of you aside." He gave a soft laugh. "How foolish I was to underestimate love."

"But it did work in a way, Stone," she replied in her coarse voice. "It only took a few weeks away from everything I'd ever known to truly accept this." She swept her arm down toward her long serpentine body. "To come to terms with the fact that I could never return to my former life as a simple handmaid."

"You began that journey long before, Skybright," Stone said. "And did that realization make you love those you cared for any less?"

She paused and studied his face, hidden in shadows, but not from her keen serpentine sight. He kept his features impassive, reminding her of the aloof man she had met so long ago in the forest. But she wasn't fooled, sensing the tangle of emotions Stone tried to tamp down. His relief in seeing her again was like a bright lantern lit above him. Skybright shook her head. "I loved them the same. I only missed them more."

He closed the small distance between them, standing close

enough that she felt the warmth that emanated from him still. "Don't you think it's time?"

Stone gave a smooth flourish of his wrist, and a sky blue dress manifested in his hand. "You cannot deny your human side any more than you can suppress your demonic one," he said.

Stone, always logical. Always right.

She shifted and felt the weight of the world on her shoulders, the weight of grief and sadness against her heart. Tears, hot and endless, streamed down her face. Stone said nothing as she slipped into her dress, her vision blurred, feeling everything all at once. She twisted her thick hair into two buns and pinned them against her head with silver clips he gave her. Their fingers brushed. He grasped her hand for a heartbeat, his touch was a solace. Steady. Beneath the overwhelming loss, she felt a sense of hope, of anticipation for what lay ahead. Felt Stone's admiration of her and his respect, as strongly as she had felt Zhen Ni's love and loyalty.

Finally, she straightened and met Stone's dark eyes, holding his gaze. "There is work to be done," she said.

"Centuries worth," he replied.

Skybright smiled through her tears, a genuine smile with sharp edges. "I am ready."

ACKNOWLEDGEMENTS

As ever, many thanks to my agent Bill Contardi—our partnership has outlasted most Hollywood marriages! You have been there with me from the start (2008), and I'm grateful! To my publisher Georgia McBride, who has done everything to support me as an author and my titles. I'm so happy that Skybright found a home with Month9Books and that we have been able to take this journey together. It has been amazing. Thank you!

Thank you to my editor Cameron Yeager for your careful reading, thoughtful comments, and taking this novel to the next level. But most of all, thank you for giving *Sacrifice* the perfect title it has!

To my amazing critique group: Kirsten, John, Amy, and Mark; my books would not be half as good if not for your valuable feedback throughout the years. Your encouragement and friendship, I value even more!

To Holly, Delia, and Sarah for taking the time to talk through this novel with me in Mexico. Holly: I'm sorry I didn't include a sex scene as you had directed. I shall endeavor to make up for this in future writings. Delia: You suggested that it'd be best if someone died. Well. Sarah: Blossom is our love child! Baby demons 4ever! And much gratitude to Cassie for having me! *Sacrifice* got its start in San Miguel de Allende with all of you.

Fuzzy hugs to Malinda Lo for taking the time to beta read and offer insightful feedback.

This novel is inspired by the incredible women writers in my life, who make me laugh, encourage me, and lift me up. They show me what it means to be brave, and take risks in our art, each and every day. Thank you always. Never stop being amazing and being exactly who you are.

In memory of Taru Rivera, fellow Chinese brush artist and troublemaker who loved all the fantastically weird stories that I write. This one's for you, Taru. We miss you.

And last but never least, for my m, sweet pea, and munchkin. I love you!

San Diego
June 29, 2016

CINDY PON

Cindy Pon is the author of *Silver Phoenix* (Greenwillow, 2009), which was named one of the Top Ten Fantasy and Science Fiction Books for Youth by the American Library Association's Booklist, and one of 2009's best Fantasy, Science Fiction and Horror by VOYA. Her most recent novel, *Serpentine* (Month9Books, 2015), is a Junior Library Guild Selection and received starred reviews from School Library Journal and VOYA. The sequel, *Sacrifice*, releases this September. *Want,* a near-future thriller set in Taipei, will be published by Simon Pulse in summer 2017. She is the co-founder of Diversity in YA with Malinda Lo and on the advisory board of We Need Diverse Books. Cindy is also a Chinese brush painting student of over a decade. Learn more about her books and art at http://cindypon.com.

OTHER MONTH9BOOKS TITLES YOU MIGHT LIKE

SERPENTINE
NAMELESS
CLANLESS
EMERGE
IN THE SHADOW OF THE DRAGON KING
THE REQUIEM RED

Find more books like this at www.Month9Books.com

Connect with Month9Books online:
Facebook: www.Facebook.com/Month9Books
Twitter: https://twitter.com/Month9Books
You Tube: www.youtube.com/user/Month9Books
Tumblr: http://month9books.tumblr.com/
Instagram: https://instagram.com/month9books

SERPENTINE

"Unique and surprising, with a beautifully-drawn fantasy world that sucked me right in!" — **Kristin Cashore**, *New York Times* bestselling author of **BITTERBLUE**

A JUNIOR LIBRARY GUILD SELECTION

CINDY PON

NAMELESS

JENNIFER JENKINS

"Jenkins brings edge-of-your-seat adventure to this intriguing new world. I can't wait to read more!
- Jessica Day George
New York Times bestselling author of
SILVER IN THE BLOOD

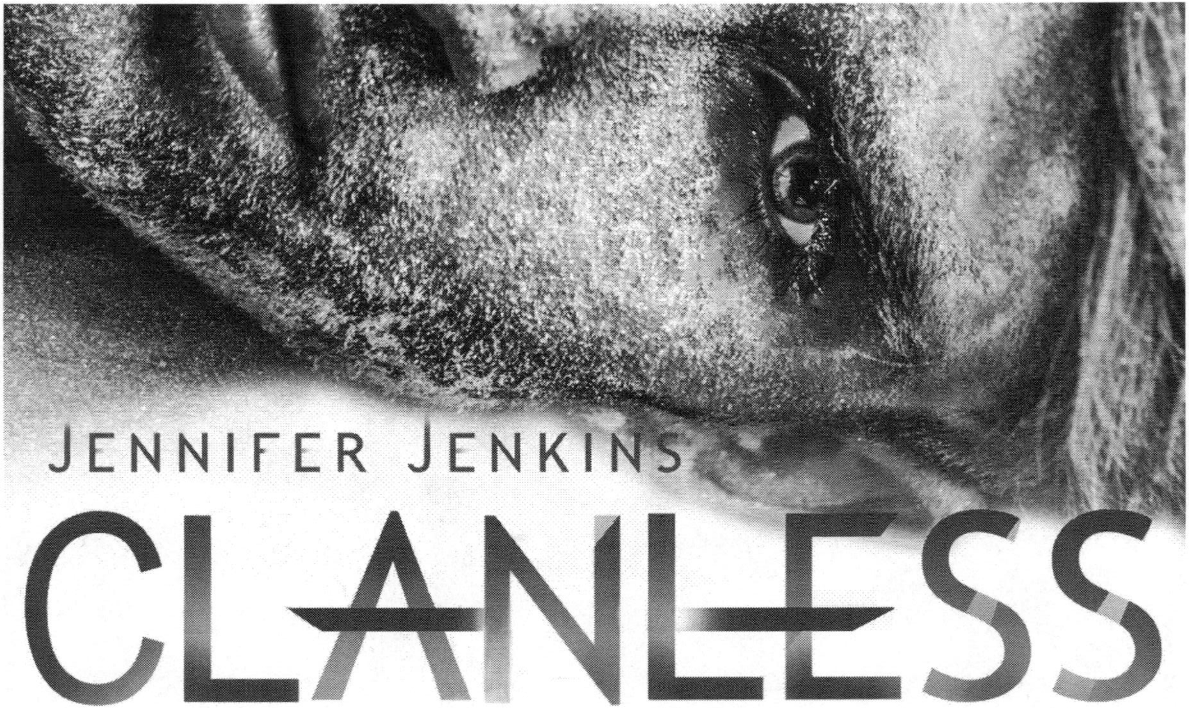
JENNIFER JENKINS
CLANLESS

MER CHRONICLES
BOOK 1

She will risk
everything to stop him
from falling in love with
the wrong girl.

Emerge

TOBIE EASTON

"The most fun I've had reading in a long time!" —Wendy Higgins,
New York Times bestselling author of the *Sweet Evil* series

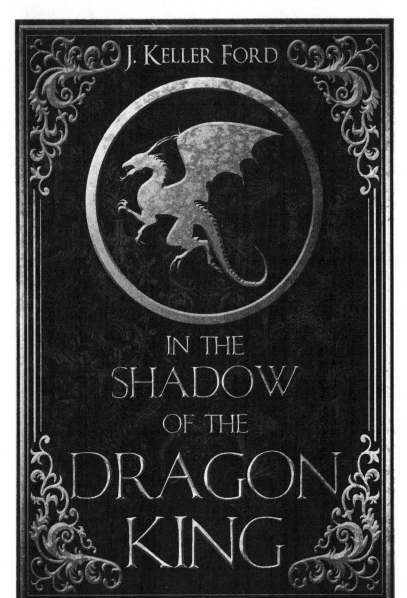

J. KELLER FORD

IN THE
SHADOW
OF THE
DRAGON
KING

BRYNN CHAPMAN

'Exquisitely written! This book will remain forever in my heart!'
- *New York Times* Bestselling Author Darynda Jones

THE
REQUIEM RED